TAKE MY BREATH AWAY

SILVER FOXES MM ROMANCE SERIES

ALI RYECART

SYNOPSIS

Rescuing a beautiful boy wasn't supposed to be on my Friday night To Do list...

James

Perry's my oldest friend's young, sweet as sugar, totally adorable Executive Assistant, so when I find him slumped over a table, blind drunk and alone in the corner of a bar, *not* rescuing him isn't an option. I can give him everything he needs to help him become the man he wants to be. But there's one thing I can't give him, and they're the promises I always break.

Perry

James came to my rescue when I needed him most, but any secret fantasy the sexy silver fox with the come to bed eyes could be my Knight in Shining Armour is only good for fairy tales. James lives his life free of ties and commitments, whereas all I want is to commit to being entangled.

♥♥♥Take My Breath Away is a slow burn, sweet with heat age gap MM romance. Expect forced proximity, a touch of angst, a secret crush, plenty of snark - and adventures with a farting dog.♥♥♥

To find out more about the author visit:
www.ryecart.com

Disclaimer

This book is a work of fiction. No part may be reproduced, by any
means, without the written permission of the author. Names and
characters, businesses, organisations, products or services and places
and events are either the product of the author's imagination or are used
fictitiously. Any resemblance to actual persons, living or dead, is
entirely coincidental.
Contains material of an adult nature.

DEDICATION &
ACKNOWLEDGEMENTS

Mark, thank you for your unstinting support and encouragement.

With thanks to Angela, Barbara, and Iola — I appreciate your help so much.

CHAPTER ONE

JAMES

The music's turned up another notch, and the rhythm's got harder. Already dim, the lights dip lower. The bar's packed and it'll only get worse.

It's Friday night in Soho, and anything is possible.

Leaning back on my bar seat, I look out over the small dance floor, packed with bodies grinding to the beat beneath the pulsing strobe lights. It's a familiar scene, and I could be in any gay bar in London, Manchester, Brighton, New York, San Francisco... I've been to enough in all these places, and beyond.

Blue's one of my regular haunts, and I recognise a lot of the men in the bar.

Many are about the same age as I am and we look like what we are: middle-aged and affluent, with plenty of spare cash to flash on anybody who takes our fancy, and that attracts a lot of younger guys, hoping some of that cash will be spent on them. I don't mind buying a few very pricey drinks if it's going to whet the appetite. There are plenty of good looking guys around and I can have my pick of any of them. Several have looked my way, their gazes lingering, but that's as far as it's got and is likely going to get. Because tonight, just as on so many other nights over the last few months, I'm just not feeling it. So, I let my gaze move on, not holding eye contact, not giving out that silent signal, that silent beckon.

I'm about to throw back the rest of my drink, ready to call it a night, when a hand slides up my thigh. I must be losing my touch, as I've not noticed the young guy pitch up next to me.

I don't mind his hand on my leg too much; it's subtle, as far as places like this go. He's smiling, in that pouty, practiced kind of way, and even under the low lights I can see the carefully applied gloss and the sultry look in his eyes. He's cute and blond, although I don't think it's a blond that's ever been classified in the natural world. I should be interested, but here and now, this whole charade's about as appealing as week-old fish.

"I've been watching you. You're very aloof. I find that attractive in a man."

He edges in closer and looks up at me through his lashes. His hand on my thigh's getting hot, and becoming somewhat uncomfortable, rather than the turn on it's supposed to be. I smother a sigh. His come-on, whilst not crude, needs some practice and a little refinement. I do my best not to laugh. Refinement? Since when has a come-on ever meant to be refined?

"I'm just here having a drink."

He answers with a simpering giggle.

"Nobody comes to Blue just to have a drink."

He's right, of course, no man comes to Blue *just to have a drink*. They come for other things. They come for men like him. Men like *me* come from men like *him*. Yet tonight, I don't want him or any of the cute young things milling around. I've no appetite for it, whereas months or even weeks ago, I'd have gorged. It's time to give him a polite brush off, and go, and I'm about to remove his hand from my thigh when he leans in even closer, and whispers in my ear.

"Maybe Daddy's been waiting for the right boy to come along."

His voice is breathy, and his hand creeps up another couple of inches. If he gets any closer he'll be sitting in my lap with his hand on my dick. I wrap a palm around his wrist, bringing a halt to his progress.

Daddy... *Really?*

It seems like the greyer my hair becomes, the more I get this. I mentioned it to my friend Elliot, but he just looked at me with horror in his eyes and said that maybe I should consider dyeing it. My response, let's say, was colourful.

Easing his hand away, I shift my position. It forces him to move back; it's either that or fall face forward. He looks put out, and well he might.

I'm all for saying what you want upfront, but the whole Daddy thing feels calculated as well as downright cheesy.

Not tonight, sweet cheeks.

"Whilst I'm very flattered by your attention, I should inform you it's misplaced tonight."

All traces of his former simpering vanish, replaced by a confused frown.

"I'm sorry, but it's not what I'm here for tonight," I say gently. "Let me buy you a drink. Blue's cocktails are legendary." They are, if you enjoy something lurid with straws and pieces of fruit. I prefer a good G&T but I imagine the cocktails are more to my uninvited companion's taste. But he doesn't accept my offer of a very pricey drink.

"What do you mean, it's not what you're here for? If you're not, then what's the point? It's what everybody's here for. To hook up. Look," he says, edging closer, the smile creeping back on his face. "I think you're seriously hot. You can fuck me, if you want, or I can go down—"

"No."

I really don't want to hear what I can do for him, or what he can do for me in the toilets, or outside in one of Soho's many small, dark, twisting back alleys. I know more about what two men can do with, and to, each other, than he'll ever know, because I've been doing it since before he was even born. That thought in itself should be a shot of cold water, but it's not — it's what he said before: what's the point?

I don't have an answer.

The guy's already turning away. He's lost interest, thank God, and a second later he disappears into the crowd, in search of somebody who'll be a lot more amenable to fulfilling his fantasies for the night. I don't even bother finishing my drink. Seconds later, I'm pushing my way out onto the street, his words still ringing in my ears.

It's almost ten-thirty, but that's early for an area like this, and many of the clubs and late night bars are only just beginning to fill up. There are literally dozens of places I could go, but I don't want to, even though I'm feeling restless and edgy. Perhaps it's the guy's question, the one I couldn't answer.

I huff and jiggle my shoulders in an attempt to dislodge the amorphous dissatisfaction creeping up my spine. I should go home and put this evening behind me, but returning to the empty silence of my huge Highgate house that was built for a sprawling Victorian family and its servants, but which is now home to just me, fills me with gloom.

What the bloody hell's the matter with me tonight?

It's another question I can't answer.

Soho's streets are teeming, packed with revellers marking the start of the weekend. I've no interest in joining them, as I head towards the tube to make the journey home. Turning into a small street, a neon light burns bright. It's the distraction I need, and seconds later I'm pushing open the door to the café-bar that's a Soho institution.

Café Alberto, or Bert's as it's commonly known to those of us who have been coming there on and off for years, is a long, narrow, austere-looking place. Its walls are covered in black and white photos of either long dead or currently decrepit Italian-American film stars. The seats towards the back have always sat in the perpetual gloom of low wattage wall lights, and tonight is no different.

There are only a few customers dotted around. Much

of the café's business will done later, when Soho's clubs and bars finally disgorge the drunk and the drugged, the mad, bad, and possibly dangerous to know. For now, those who are here are mostly intent on their phones.

An Americano with an extra shot is my caffeine of choice and, heaped up with three sugars, it's the fuel that keeps me on the go for much of my working day and beyond.

My greedy eyes examine the contents of the display case, packed full of sugary delights. They're like crack cocaine for my sweet tooth. Since hitting fifty, three years ago, even the odd pound or two of excess weight seems harder to shift. Not that anybody would know that. It's not vanity, it's just a fact. I dither, but decide on just the coffee. There's a vacant table situated by the window, as I may as well watch the free cabaret that's taking place on the streets outside, when movement at one of the tucked away, up against the wall tables towards the back of the café catches my eye. It could be anybody, but something makes me take a closer look.

"Perry?"

The shadowy figure, already slumped, slumps further. I take a step closer. Yes, it's Perry, Elliot's young Executive Assistant, the man I tease and flirt with unmercifully every time I call into Elliot's office.

Perry, always smart looking, pristine, buttoned up, the man I refer to as sugar on legs, just to make Elliot squirm. He's not those things now because he looks like he's been dragged through a hedge backwards. I sniff, and wrinkle my nose. He's pissed.

I put my coffee down on the table, and pull out the chair opposite him.

"James," he slurs. Blinking his big brown eyes at me from his gloomy corner, he makes me think of an owl. "Join me for a drink." He tries to push himself upright, but clumsy and uncoordinated, he gives up and slumps back. "But you'll have to pay, 'cause I don't have any money left. It's all gone." He goes to pick up the bottled beer in front of him, but his hands are unsteady and I grab it before he can send it flying across the table. "S'my beer." He tries to take it back off me, but I'm holding it out of reach. Losing what little balance he has, he falls face first on the table. "Ooh, fuck," he mumbles.

"I think you might have had a few too many." A few? He's completely trashed.

"Not enough. Buy me a drink and I'll give you a kiss. Reckon you'd like that." He pulls himself upright, and grins, and blinks his owlish, and very glazed, eyes.

Perry reckons correctly. At any other time, I would like a kiss — but not now, especially not when he's drunk off his arse. He sways in his seat, trying to sit upright, before he gives up the fight and crumples against the wall.

"Yes, I'll buy you a drink. A very strong coffee."

Perry frowns, and belches. "Rather have a beer."

I ignore him and nip to the counter, keeping an eye on him, although it's not as if he's going to be able to make a run for it — I doubt he can even stand up on his own. Moments later I'm armed with a large Americano that's so strong I swear it's got muscles.

"Listen to me. You're going to drink this, and then I'm going to get you home."

He glares at me, doing his best to look stroppy, but I glare back at him and he drops his gaze and complies, picking up the mug in shaking hands. Not too much of it slops over the side and onto the table, but still, I jump up and drag my chair around so I'm next to him. Placing my hands over his, I guide the mug to his lips to stop him from spilling it down his front. This close, the alcohol fumes are stronger, not just beer but spirits, too.

Perry takes a sip. "Don't want any more." He turns his head away, the way babies do when they've had enough of whatever slop the parent's trying to get them to eat.

"Too bad, you're drinking it. You need to sober up." It'll take a lot more than a mug of coffee to achieve that, but it's a start.

"Don't tell me what to do. I'm fed up with everybody telling me what to do."

"I'm not everybody, I'm James. Which means you're going to do as you're told. *Exactly* as you're told."

His head jerks around, and he stares at me with unfocused, saucer eyes. This close, it's impossible to miss the honeycomb-gold flecking the deep brown, or how thick and dark and long his lashes are, or how pillowy and plump his lips, which are parted and forming an *O* of surprise. Pretty Perry, so, so pretty, and so young looking — younger than I know him to be — but he's plastered and stinking of booze, which means this isn't the time or place to be noticing.

Yet I have noticed him, ever since he started working for Elliot, three or so years ago. Pretty Perry. Teasing him, watching the flush creep up his face, and sometimes even coaxing a shy smile, I've enjoyed every minute of it, and I think he has too.

The boy is utterly gorgeous, from the top of his head to the tips of his toes, and maybe that's why I've never done more than tease. Yet, he's not a boy, he's a man. Twenty-five, twenty-six, maybe, but he's so fresh faced, it's easy to forget.

It'd have been so easy, during the time I've known Perry, to launch a full scale seduction, but I've always stayed on the right side of the line, confining myself to flirting. It's all because there's a *but,* and it's called Elliot. He wouldn't think too much of me making a full-on move on his assistant, and he'd let me know it in no uncertain terms because he knows the sort of man I am. *I* know the sort of man I am. I don't give a damn what most people may think of me, but Elliot's my oldest, most valued friend, which doesn't make him most people.

I've got some scruples, even if they are hidden somewhere deep and dark.

He burps and I'm enveloped in a beery cloud.

"James. James, James, James," he says, slurring, his lips curving up into a sly smile. "Bet you like telling people what to do. I mean really, really, *really* like. Always flirting with me when you come into the office. Don't think I don't notice. 'Cause I do."

"And there was me, thinking I was being subtle. Here, drink some more."

Perry does as he's told, his former resistance forgotten.

He nods his head slowly, and his brow puckers as though he's thinking hard, and trying to gather his thoughts.

"I've given it a lot of consid—consid—thought. Yes, thought. You're hot. For an old man," he adds.

"Very kind of you to say so." Perhaps I should take the opportunity to tell him I still have all my own teeth and hair.

"You're very welcome." He takes another sip, this time

managing to hold the mug himself. He's still drunk, but the strong coffee seems to be taking the edge off his intoxication. "Can't drink anymore. Sorry." He puts the mug down with a clatter on the metal-topped table. Three quarters of it's gone, and that's good enough. Now, it's a case of getting him up, out, and home.

"We going clubbing?" he says, when I pull him to his feet. He's managing to keep upright, but he's unsteady, swaying like a reed in the breeze.

"Not tonight. You need to get home and go to bed."

And look forward to the monster hangover you're going to have in the morning.

"Go to bed with you. I could show you what I can do with my—" He lurches forward, slinging his arms around me.

His surprise attack catches me off guard, causing me to stumble back a step or two.

"We can do all kinds of stuff. Kinky stuff. Do you like kinky stuff? You look like you like kinky stuff. Yeah, bet you're a kinky old fucker." He tries to kiss me, but I manage to duck and his lips slide across my ear, but I can't duck his leg, which he manages to hook around mine as he starts to dry hump me.

"Stop. At once." I slap him hard on the arse and he yelps; he drops his leg and blinks at me, making me think of an ill-treated puppy.

"That hurt. Don't like spanking. Grant likes it, but I don't. Bet you do. Knew you were kinky. I'm not kinky. And I told Grant that, I did. I said, I'm not wearing — certain things. And you know what he called me? Mr Whippy. Mr fucking Whippy. Didn't get it, not at first. But then I did. Cold, bland, and vanilla. You don't think I'm a Mr Whippy, do you?"

"No, Perry, I don't. Not at all. Don't you take any notice of Grant."

I have no idea who Grant is, but I can guess. So this is the reason for Perry's intoxication: boyfriend troubles.

Draped around me, he's tightened his hold. His arms are coiled around my neck and his head falls forward onto my shoulder as I manhandle him out of the café. The burly Italian-looking guy behind the counter gives us a nod and a raise of his brows. He's seen this and a whole lot more before.

"I'm taking you home. Perry? Where do you live? Do you live with Grant?" Grant who likes to spank Perry… I push the thought away. "Perry? Come on, tell me where you live." Wherever it is, I'm going with him, because he's too vulnerable to be left alone in the middle of Soho.

"In the basement." He starts to laugh as though he's said something hilarious, but I can't see the joke.

I hail a cab, and the driver's smile falls away when he sees the state of Perry.

"If he throws up—"

"He won't," I snap. Or at least I hope not. "Do you want this fare, or not?"

I don't give him the chance to argue as I bundle Perry into the back.

"Where do you live?" I hope it's not some godforsaken suburb miles and miles away.

"Told you. In the basement. At work." He flops back into the corner and looks at me as though what he says makes perfect sense. "Don't have a real home. Not anymore." He frowns, something getting through his drink-soaked brain that he might need to explain a little.

"Gents—"

"Just wait."

The cabbie mutters something I doubt is complementary but I don't give a damn.

"Perry, have or have you not got a home, a proper home, to go to tonight?" I keep my voice low, and gentle. Huddled in the corner, his suit rumpled and his tie hanging loose and partially undone, he looks tired, dejected and unspeakably sad as his eyes fill with glittery tears.

"No." He shakes his head and turns to face the window, as though ashamed to be seen as he fights a losing battle against the tears streaming down his face.

There's only one decision to be made. I give the driver my address, because tonight, Perry's coming home with me.

CHAPTER TWO

PERRY

"Oh God. Oh God, oh God, *oh God.*"

My head feels like somebody's taken an axe to it and as I try to push myself up to sitting, the room spins and all I can do is collapse back down and clamp my eyes shut.

If I lie here, just for a minute... It's warm, and comfortable, the sheets are silky soft and the duvet as light and fluffy as marshmallow. I prise open my eyes, and look around but it hurts. My eyeballs are too big for the sockets, every movement a colossal effort. The chink of light coming through a gap in the curtains is enough to confirm the creeping suspicion that I'm not where I expect to be.

The huge bed, the high ceiling, the plain painted walls. The blond wood freestanding wardrobe. The open door by the big window, showing a glimpse of a claw footed bath. There are no stacked boxes of musty files, no blanket and flat pillow bundled up behind them. This isn't the basement of the office block where I work, stuffed full of crap nobody goes to investigate from one year's end to another. No, this is—

"No! Oh, Jesus Christ!" I slap my palms over my face, and wince as a shot of pain sears through my shattered head. It all comes back, every horrible, excruciating moment of it.

Half a bottle of rum. Beer. Tequila.

James.

Oh, bloody, sodding, frigging hell.

James, pushing me into a cab, pulling me out of a cab. Me, raging and crying, and raging again. And flirting with him. And trying to kiss him. Was that before or after I threw up? Because I'm sure I threw up. The taste like a decomposing rat in my mouth tells me I threw up.

There's an odd whimpering sound, and it's coming from me. It's not a sound to be proud of, but pride's the last thing I'm feeling. I'm in his spare room. He's put me to bed — and I freeze. The sheets are beautifully soft against my bare skin.

Oh, no, please don't say he undressed me…

Pulling my hands away from my face, which is throbbing with cringing embarrassment, I pick up the duvet, peek underneath — and let out a relieved breath. I'm wearing my underwear, so I'm not totally naked which is one good thing. The other is that I'm *not* wearing the ones covered with cartoon fluffy sheep, which my friend Alfie sent me for my last birthday. Pulling the duvet up and over my head, I have to work out how on earth I'm going to face James.

A soft knock, and a slight creak as the door opens tells

me I'm going to have to face him a lot sooner than I thought.

"Come on, Sleeping Beauty, I know you're awake."

James' voice, a low and growly purr like a classic car, is edged with amusement. I'm glad somebody's laughing because it sure isn't me.

If I just stay very still and pretend…

The duvet's tugged away from my head and I gasp as I stare up into James' face. A crooked smile's pulling at his lips and one brow's raised. He doesn't look angry, which is something I suppose.

"Errrggg…" What's meant to be the start of an abject apology is nothing more than a strangled, incomprehensible moan.

"Feeling that good, eh?" James' arched brow moves up another notch, towards his short, steely hair. "There's a glass of water and a couple of aspirin on the side, here. I've also brought you some clothes to wear. They won't fit but they'll have to do. Your own are a — little mucky. Everything's been washed, but they're not dry. Once you've had a shower, come downstairs. I think we need to have a talk."

Before I can even think what to say, he's gone.

I stare up at the ceiling, my head hammering and my heart matching it thump for thump. Oh, God. A talk. It's the last thing I want to do but somehow I don't think James is going to give me any choice in the matter.

Swallowing the tablets, I stand up, but have to plonk down on the bed again as the room tilts. A minute, I'll make my way to the shower in a minute. The minute up, I stagger and lurch to the en-suite and into a shower I reckon is bigger than the whole bathroom where I live.

Correction. Where I *used* to live.

Turning the lever, the hot water falls in a torrent. I lean against the tiled wall and slip down into a heap on the floor, wondering how the hell I'm going to explain.

I'm half way down the stairs when the salty, savoury aroma of bacon hits me. My stomach's been churning, in protest at the booze from last night and how I'm going to be able to face James with at least a scrap of dignity (big clue about that one: I won't be able to), but the smell of fry up is an instant comfort blanket. My nose twitches and my mouth waters at the same time my stomach rumbles. It's Saturday morning and I haven't eaten a thing since Thursday night. I've existed on coffee, alcohol and self-pity.

Like a dog, I follow my nose, which leads me to the kitchen at the back of the house.

"Hello," I mumble, as I poke my head around the kitchen door.

James swings around from the large stove where he's frying enough bacon to feed an army. The skin at the outer corners of his eyes crinkles as he smiles, and his dark green eyes sweep over me.

"How are you feeling? What's the score on the Crap-O-Meter?"

"If it's out of ten, then I'm at a solid eleven."

James laughs, the sound rich and assured and filling every corner of the huge, sunny kitchen. I've a vague, unformed memory of being led in here last night, and can only hope and pray that this wasn't where I chucked up.

James peers at me, and I shift from foot to foot, acutely conscious that I'm wearing his clothes.

The tracksuit bottoms, T-shirt, and hoodie are too big for me, just as he said they'd be, and I feel small and puny in them. It doesn't help that I've lost weight recently, which I can ill-afford to do. James is taller than me, not by a huge amount, but he's got more muscle on him. But, I'm glad of them, because my own clothes…

"Thank you. For the lend of the clothes. I'm so sorry, I—"

"Sit down before you fall down." He slices across my words, stopping dead the start of what is sure to be my stumbling apology. "Breakfast first, and then you can say sorry as much as you like, but to be frank I'd rather an explanation as to why I found you on your own in the middle of Soho and blind drunk — and why you claim to be living in the basement of Elliot's office block."

CHAPTER THREE

PERRY

"Better?"

James scrutinises me over the rim of his coffee cup. I've avoided eye contact as much as possible, and I do it again by looking down at my empty plate, every scrap of breakfast gone. The restorative power of a fry up, along with pain killers and a couple of pints of water on the morning after the night before, is nothing to be scoffed at. I've also finished my coffee, and I could do with another. As though James knows exactly what I'm thinking, he pours a steady, nutty stream from the cafetière.

"Much, thank you. And thanks, too, for helping me out last night — I was in a state, and I owe you one — and for the lend." I wave to the borrowed clothes I'm drowning in, and am about to say I can take them home to wash them, before I stop myself.

James shrugs. "No problem. They're just some old sweats." He doesn't say anything more, just sips his coffee.

Old sweats, the last thing I could ever imagine James wearing.

I've never seen him in anything but sharp-as-a-knife tailoring, classic Savile Row, and shined-to-within-an-inch-of-their-life shoes. Suited and booted, the words were invented to describe James Campion. But not today.

Tailored suit trousers have been replaced by narrow legged dark jeans. A plain light blue shirt hugs his toned upper body. The top couple of buttons are undone, displaying the crisp white crew neck of the T-shirt beneath. Folded back shirt sleeves reveal forearms with a light scattering of dark hair and — a glimpse of a tattoo. *Tattoo?* *James* and *tattoo* go together about as well as vegan and pork pie do. This isn't the James I've come to know from his frequent visits to the office, and as for the ink...

A low, rumbly chuckle fills the air and my gaze snaps up, locking onto his. That crooked smile is there on his lips once again, and the questioning lift of a brow as though he's daring me to ask. Heat flares in my cheeks. I've been gawping, and caught in the act.

He pushes his sleeve further up his arm, to reveal more.

"The result of forty-eight hours leave spent drinking too much beer in Hamburg," he says. "I was in the army. It's my regimental badge, but that was years ago."

James, in his army uniform, as fit as they come. It's a mouthwatering thought but one I don't want to dwell on, not when he's sitting opposite me, not with that cocky smile on his face.

A place to stay, clean clothes, and breakfast. It's not just thanks I owe him, but a massive apology for his Friday night I managed to royally screw up.

"I'm so sorry for ruining your evening. Sorting out a drunk wasn't top of your To Do list, I reckon."

James shrugs. "There was no evening to ruin. I'd gone out from habit rather than any real desire to do so."

There's a tinge of what sounds like resignation colouring his words — which is a surprise, from somebody as assured as James — but my hungover brain's sluggish and clumsy, and incapable of close scrutiny of anything other than the coffee in my cup.

We fall into silence for a few moments, before he asks the question I know is coming.

"So, are you going to tell me?"

I groan. "Do I have to?" I peek up at him through my lashes.

He tilts his head to the side and studies me, and it takes all I have not to fidget and squirm under his moss green gaze.

"I can't make you, so perhaps I should ask Elliot? I'm sure there are employment laws against having members of staff living in the basements of their places of work."

"What?" My whole body jerks and I snap my head up so hard my neck cricks. "Oh, God. No. Please. Don't say anything to Elliot." The idea of my boss knowing... It's mortifying.

"Then you tell me."

I hesitate for a second, trying to think of a way to explain my shit storm of a life.

"I, erm, lost my home recently."

"Lost your home? You were repossessed?"

I shake my head, and force myself to hold his gaze.

"No. I was living, until a few days ago, with my boyfriend. Grant. He—he threw me out."

I just want the earth to open up and swallow me whole. It's humiliating to admit to, but it's only the tip of the iceberg.

"We had an argument. Again. I went to work, and when I got back to the flat he'd changed the locks. I went to a hotel, to get a room just for the night, to let Grant calm down, but when I tried to pay both my debit and credit cards were declined. We…"

It's no good, I can't hold James' gaze any longer. I let my eyes fall as I stumble through my sorry tale.

"We had joint accounts — not long after I moved in with him, he said it'd make things easier with paying bills. That was about six months ago. Like a fool, I agreed."

I swallow hard, unable for a moment to talk. What the hell must James think of me? Whatever it is, it can't be less than I think of myself.

"He cleared them out?"

I nod. "Closed them, too. They were with internet banks, and only one authorisation was needed."

"So, you have no place to live and no money. Correct?"

"Well, sort of yes and no."

"That doesn't make a lot of sense, Perry."

His voice is softer, coaxing almost, and I force myself to meet his eyes. I have to salvage something from this pathetic tale.

"I don't have anywhere to live, but I'm going to line up some rooms to go and see. The basement, nobody ever goes down there, and I needed something quick. And free.

Grant cleared out the ready cash, and I don't have anything until I get paid. What I had on me, I drank it last night." I wince, at the thought of how he found me as much as the lingering hangover I've got. "But, I've got other money. The problem is, it's tied up in special accounts which take time to unlock."

Inheritance money, deposited at a private bank. It's not the kind of account where I can take out a few quid at a hole in the wall machine. I have to apply for access, and wait for it to be granted. God alone knows why Granddad attached so many stipulations to it. It's a sizeable sum of money, and no doubt he thought it was in my best interests, but my best interests, right now, would be for me to be able to get my hands on it quickly and easily.

"Wasn't there somebody who could have helped you out with some money and a place to stay?"

I shrug. "Not really. My parents live in Spain, where they own a bar. They'd have sent me some money, but they'd have also asked a lot of questions I didn't want to answer. As for friends, none are really in a position to let me stay. Except for Alfie—"

"Alfie?"

I nod. "He's an old friend. He'd let me stay, no question. Only problem is, he's not in London at the moment and I'm not sure when he'll be back. Could be days, weeks, or months. So, it means I need to get myself sorted, and fast, on a temporary basis at least."

"By sleeping in the basement of an office block?" He quirks a brow, and his lips twist into an incredulous smile, as though it's the most ridiculous thing he's heard. He's right, it is, but it's the position I'm in and a flash of anger sparks through me.

"Yes. I didn't have too many choices when I found myself confronted with a key that no longer fitted the lock, radio silence from Grant, and cards that were no more than useless bits of plastic. I think I showed initiative."

"Indeed you did. But I know when I'm being told off, and rightly so. I'm sorry."

"And I shouldn't have snapped, not when you've been so good to me. Anyway, I thought if I bunked down at work for a few nights, until I could get sorted... But there are a couple of security guards who do the rounds, and Elliot, he gets in early. Then I hit on the brainwave of the basement. Nobody goes down there."

There's an intensity in James' moss green, feline eyes that's almost dazzling. His face is set and serious, more I think than I've ever seen before.

"So, would it be fair to say you're up shit creek with only a very small paddle?"

"A small paddle's enough to get me moving."

James laughs, lights sparking in his eyes.

"However," he says, jumping up and gathering the plates, "you can't stay in Elliot's basement. You're not a bloody troglodyte. Have you any idea when this friend of yours is likely to be back?" He leans over as he stacks the dishwasher, his jeans stretching across his muscled arse. I look away, not wanting to be caught staring again.

"Alfie? Not sure, to be honest. Last time I spoke to him was a few weeks back. Sometimes he likes to go off grid."

"Off grid?" James looks at me over his shoulder. "He's not one of those grungy sorts who lives on bits of twig and a few berries and believes a good steak, or just a simple sausage, is a crime against Mother Earth, is he?"

James looks so horrified it's impossible not to laugh but I wince as my alcohol-pickled brain protests.

"He'd certainly qualify as grungy, but not the rest of it."

"So were is he, being all off-grid?" James asks, coming back to the table.

"He's somewhere in Scotland, or he was the last time I spoke to him. On a mountain and living in a yurt. He's a shepherd." James' eyes widen. I've surprised him and I can't help smiling. "When he's not being an urban street poet, that is."

"An urban street poet? Give me strength. How do you even know somebody like this?"

"We met a uni. He studied accountancy, so when he's not—"

"Being a rap goatherd?"

"Shepherd urban poet. There is a difference, you know." James snorts, and rolls his lovely eyes, but they're filled with good humour. "He earns money by contracting, then he takes off again. He says the city's too confining. But he's smart, and bought his own place as an investment, when we were still students. When he's in London he's got a kind of open door policy. The last time he was here, he had a mime artist, a circus skills instructor and an, er, exotic dancer and her snake staying."

James chuckles. "Sounds rather intriguing. Anyway, your clothes should be dry now." He gets up and disappears through a side door near the French windows into what must be a utility room, and returns with my stuff. My heart sinks like a stone. It's time to get dressed and go.

"Thank you. I'll change then make a move. Leave you

to your weekend. But thanks, again, and I'm sorry for, well, everything." *For crass flirting, and being sick…*

For a moment I wonder if he's going to try and stop me, but he doesn't. Why should he? Despite what he says, I screwed up his night out and now he'll be glad to see the back of me. I push myself up without enthusiasm. I'll while away a few hours away in parks and galleries before I bed down for the night again in the musty, dusty basement.

"When you're dressed, we'll go and pick up your stuff."

I'm in mid-turn, but I stop. What's he talking about? I don't have any stuff in the basement, beyond a blanket and towel and some toiletries — there's a shower at work, thank God — and a change of shirt and underwear I've been forced to buy. But why would I be picking them up?

James is looking at me as though he's waiting for something to click. When it doesn't, he tuts.

"Don't you want to get your things? From the flat?"

"Yes, but I can't get in. Grant won't answer my calls or texts, so I don't know—"

"Don't worry about that. We can still get your belongings."

If there's some way of getting my stuff…

I don't have much there, but what I have I could easily store in boxes in the basement until Alfie's back from the wilds. But how the hell does James expect to be able to help me get my things back from a flat that looks like a poster for Fort Knox?

"…back here, somewhere stable whilst you sort yourself out."

James is staring at me, one brow arched as he waits for me to answer.

"Err…"

James sighs. "You really haven't been listening to me, have you? We'll collect your things, locked door or not, and you'll come back here to stay. You can't live in an office block basement, you've got nobody you can stay with, and not a lot of ready money. To get back on your feet, you need a helping hand. Or a fairy godfather. I can be both."

"Oh, no, I can't—"

"Why not?"

I open my mouth, snap it shut, and open it again. *Why not?* I don't have an answer.

James slaps a palm on the blond wood table, hard and decisive, the decision made, before he stands.

"Good, that's sorted. Get dressed, I want to be on the road in ten minutes."

It doesn't even occur to me to argue as I rush from the kitchen.

CHAPTER FOUR

JAMES

Perry's been quiet for the whole of the journey. He's embarrassed by his predicament, ashamed even. He's been foolish, of that there's no question.

I throw him a quick glance. Huddled in his seat, he looks small, defenceless, and fragile. Touch him too hard, and he'll shatter. It's a sharp reminder again of how much younger than me he is. I wonder about this Grant character. The guy sounds like a piece of work which makes me glad — very glad — that I've got Perry's back.

"It's the second turning on the left. See where the bakery is, on the corner?"

It's a street of mainly small Victorian terraced houses, but there are some new flats too. We pass a newsagent, dry cleaners, and a minimart. In the depths of south London, the street is as suburban as you could get.

"Just here."

I park outside a low-rise block and switch the engine off, plunging us into silence.

"Will he be there, do you think?" I nod towards the flats.

"I don't know."

Perry looks down at his phone. He's been trying to get in touch with his turd of an ex on and off since we left, but has been met with a wall of silence. Not that it matters to me whether he's there or not.

"He started going out on Friday nights and not turning up again until late on Sunday. It's what caused the rows, or some of them. He wouldn't say what he was doing, but it didn't take being a rocket scientist to guess." His words are edged with a bitterness that's so at odds with his sweet nature.

"It's irrelevant whether he's home or not. We're just here to collect your things. We'll do it quickly and without fuss, and then get out." I take his hand, and squeeze lightly to give him reassurance.

He gives me a shaky, worry-filled smile that makes me want to hug him close and tell him everything will be all right. I don't, because I can't promise it will be, but I'm determined to make this as pain-free as possible for him.

"I still don't understand how you think we can get in? Not unless you're going to try and kick the door down." His eyes widen and I have to bite my tongue to not laugh.

"Nothing so crude. Do you trust me?"

"Sorry?"

"I said, do you trust me?"

"Yes, I suppose."

I huff. "You *suppose*. That'll have to be good enough, I

suppose. Come on, I don't want to hang around any longer than we need to."

I click to lock the Range Rover, giving the small group of smoking teenagers who are nodding towards the car a steady stare. *Don't even think of touching my car...* They get the silent message, and lope off.

Perry keys in a code and with a click the entrance door unlocks.

"It's on the top floor." Worry threads through his words, and I follow him up.

Moments later we're standing outside a green-painted door with a new and heavy looking Yale lock. It might present a barrier to Perry, but not to me. I bang on the door. If this Grant piece of shit is here, it'll save entry by alternate means.

My heavy hammering's met with silence.

"How—? Oh…"

Perry stares open-mouthed at the small box of picks I pull from my pocket.

"You didn't honestly expect me to kick down the door, did you? Really, give me some credit for a modicum of finesse."

"But that's breaking in. It's illegal. Isn't it?" he says, the words rushing from him as he watches, wide-eyed, as I insert the thin metal pin into the lock.

So's being fleeced of your money... Except, Perry's willingly if stupidly sunk his pay into a well that his scum bag ex has been drawing very deeply from. There's probably little if anything Perry can do to get any money back, and he no doubt knows that. I don't say anything because there's no point in making him feel worse than he already does. This is a damage limitation exercise. We get in, get his stuff, and go. And then he comes home with me.

"Where did you learn—?"

"Later." Now's not the time for me to explain my somewhat irregular skill set.

It takes just seconds for the tumblers to click and the door to swing open. Perry goes to walk in, but I stop him with a hand to his chest and shake my head. He looks at me, a questioning frown on his brow. I'm listening hard for any sign of life, but there's nothing.

"Let's get this done as quickly as we can."

"I'll get some bin bags, from the kitchen."

Damn. Of course. We haven't brought anything to carry his stuff away in.

I follow him into the small kitchen. My nose twitches. The yeasty aroma of toast hangs in the air. Perry grabs the bags from under the sink and dashes out. I lay a hand on the kettle. It's warm. Wherever Grant is now, he's not long been gone.

Cupboard doors slam followed by Perry's howl of distress, and I rush to find him.

He's standing in the bedroom, in front of an open, and empty, narrow wardrobe.

"Everything's gone. My suits for work. My shirts. My shoes. There's nothing left." He gasps, his eyes so wide they all but swallow him whole. "Oh no, he can't have—" He pushes past me and I'm on his heels, as he runs to the living room and to a small bookcase in the corner. He's pulling books out, left and right, throwing them to the floor. "They're gone, they're fucking gone."

On his knees, he stares up at me, desolation dulling his deep brown eyes.

"They were my granddad's, and they came to me when he died. He had them as a kid. Adventure stories for boys. He used to read them to me."

The tears he doesn't try to stop stream down his face. He's deathly white and without thinking I pull him up and into my arms.

Every part of him is trembling. It's shock, and anger too, I suspect, at how his life has spiralled out of control, and treasured possessions discarded, as it finally hits him that he's been eradicated from the life he had in a place he'd called home.

"I don't understand. Why's he done this? Why? My clothes, but—but Granddad's books? He knew how much they meant to me."

The tears are flowing freely and I tighten my arms around him, letting him know I'm here and that he can lean on me.

His sobbing quietens, and he looks up at me. He's a mess, no doubt about it. His eyes are red and puffy, his face wet and mottled and snot smears his upper lip, but all I want to do is to hold him tight.

"I'm sorry," he whispers. "I didn't mean to… Oh, look, I've made a mess of your shirt. Sorry."

There's a gunky wet patch on my chest, and he tries to wipe it away but only makes it worse. I still his hand.

"There's nothing to be sorry about." My voice is gruffer than I'd like, and I clear my throat. He's staring up at me, blinking his tear glittered eyes. I pull a paper tissue from my pocket. "Here, blow your nose," I say through the dry gravel that's lodged in my throat.

Perry nods. Taking the tissue, he steps back, taking the warmth of his small body with him.

"Is any of your stuff here?"

"A bit. Not much. I didn't have a lot, but—" He stops and gasps, and I've no need to ask why. He's not the only one who's heard the flat's front door open and slam closed, and footsteps coming down the short hallway.

"What are you doing here — and who the fuck are you?"

I turn around to face the bulky, dark-haired man standing in the living room doorway. I grin, and it feels like my skin's about to tear apart.

"Hello Grant."

CHAPTER FIVE

PERRY

"What have you done with my books? The ones from my granddad? I don't care about the money, but where are my books?" I'm shouting, and shaking with shock and rising anger, at the smirk on Grant's face. I do care about the money he's stolen from me, but it's nothing compared to the loss of granddad's books.

"Sold 'em on eBay. There was a little matter of unpaid rent."

"Unpaid rent?" He's fleeced me of money, locked me out of my home and forced me to live in the basement of the office where I work, and he talks about me *owing rent?*

Fury bursts from me, and I go to fly at Grant. He's big and burly, he could swat me away like a fly, but I don't get anywhere close as I'm pulled back with a hard tug.

"I've come with Perry to collect his belongings. Which

don't appear to be here. It's been a tedious journey across London, and for that reason alone we're not leaving empty handed."

I look up at James, his bored drawl shocking me out of my rage.

"What the fuck are you on about? Whoever you are, get out of my flat."

Grant squares his shoulders and juts out his chin as he glares at James. A shiver of apprehension runs through me.

Grant's heavy set. I've had more than a few pushes and shoves from him in recent weeks, and I've felt the force of them. There's nothing here for me. My books have gone, my clothes too, whether in the bin or a charity shop I don't know. All I want now is to get away, as far away from this dingy flat, this vicious and vile man, and the shit storm my life's turned into. But what I also want is for James not to get involved and risk getting hurt, not for me.

"Come on," I mumble to James. "There's no point being here." I tug at his arm, to pull him away, but he doesn't budge an inch. He's as immovable as a mountain.

"Compensation is in order, wouldn't you agree?" James says, ignoring me. He's looking around and when his eyes alight on the guitar standing in the corner, he smiles — and I shiver.

There's something dark and dangerous in the way his smile widens to a grin, and in the glint in his eyes. He's stock still but looks ready to pounce, like a cat watching its prey. James, little more than average height if that, and compact, he'd be easy to dismiss up against Grant's brawn, but the tingle lighting up my nerves and prickling at the back of my neck whispers that it'd be a very, very unwise assumption.

Grant makes that assumption.

"You think you're going to take my guitar, that you're even going to touch it? Just fuck off, the pair of you."

"It's a Gibson. Very expensive. Good condition, too. Would have set you back a good five thousand. I assume you used Perry's money rather than your own?" He takes the couple of steps to the guitar, not taking any heed of Grant.

James' voice is light, almost conversational, but his grin is stretching, growing wider, displaying bared teeth that are ready to bite. But Grant, his face angry and mottled, doesn't see it, doesn't see it at all, doesn't realise the wrong and dangerous choice he's making as he lunges for James.

I stumble back as James' arm shoots out, his hand bunched into a fist which lands square in the middle of Grant's face. There's a crunch, and blood splatters over Grant's T-shirt. James doesn't make a sound, but Grant's anger, pain, and shocked bellow fills the room, bouncing off the walls as he falls with a heavy thump onto his arse, his hands clamped to his face.

"Wh...?" It's as far as I get. My head snaps from Grant, wailing and groaning on the floor, rocking back and forwards, to James, cool and self-possessed as he gazes down at Grant, his nose wrinkling as though he's smelling something bad.

"Is there anything left here that's yours?"

"I—I don't... No..." I try to think, but my thoughts are slow and dense.

My eyes land on the books I've thrown around. Two or three of them are mine, either missed by Grant or not bothered about. But they're mine, and I'm taking them with me. I dart over and grab them up.

"Right, then let's take the guitar and leave."

I shake my head. "No, I don't want it." I could sell it, I could eBay it, the way Grant has my treasured adventure stories. But I don't want it, I don't want to be like Grant. I've got damn all else, but I have some pride left.

"I'm sure you don't," James says quietly, and it's as though he's reading my mind. His cold, steely smile has turned into something warm and his eyes have lost their hard glint as they lock onto mine. "But I'm sure this will fulfil some teenager's dream of being the next guitar hero," he says, picking it up.

A rage-filled bellow's demanding blood. I swing around, my heart hammering hard. Grant's staggered up to his feet, a broken down prize fighter who's taken a pounding, now out for revenge.

James sighs, long and loud, as if it's all too much of a bore.

"Take your hands off that, you fucker," Grant shouts, but his words are soggy with blood.

He's lumbering towards James, who's no longer smiling but peering at Grant with narrowed eyes.

"James, please, I don't want it. Let's just go." I don't want the guitar, I don't want anything other than to get out and leave all this mess behind me. James takes no notice.

"James!" I shout as Grant launches himself forward, sudden, fast, unexpected, arms raised to grab the guitar from James' hold. He's furious, humiliated — and heavy. If he lands on James—

I gasp and throw myself forward to try and do something to push Grant off course, but I'm too late and too uncoordinated as I trip and stumble to the side, hit the edge of the sofa and tumble backwards to the floor with a heavy thud.

Grant's momentum is relentless and sickness rises up in me as James brings the guitar up over his head, leaving himself exposed to take the full force of Grant's attack. Grant's moving fast, but James is quicker. The arc's smooth and comes down hard, connecting with a crunch to Grant's elbow.

The howl's terrifying, as Grant collapses in a shuddering, wailing heap.

"You've broken my arm. You're a fucking head case."

"More likely a fracture, but you'll be in plaster for a few weeks. Such a shame about the guitar." James examines the dent in the back. "It'll be costly to repair, but worth it. It's time Perry and I were leaving but before we do I want you to listen to me."

Still holding the guitar, James leans over Grant and my heart jumps — if Grant grabs him, takes one last throw of the dice — but he cringes back. He's still for a moment, before he nods. The fight's gone out of him. He's a spent force, he's been beaten in more ways than one, and he knows it.

"You are of course at liberty to call the police. Why wouldn't you? But what will you tell them? How will you explain what's happened? Hmm? You're in a tricky situation here, Grant, and I think you have just enough sense to realise that. So here's what's going to happen. Perry's coming with me. If you try and get in touch with him, try to make any kind of contact, wait for him outside his place of work, or attempt any nasty little stunt to get back at him, you'll have me to deal with. Take what's happened here today as just a taste of what to expect if you wake up tomorrow, or next month, or next year feeling brave. Do you understand?"

Grant answers with rapid nods.

"Good, I'm so glad we have an understanding. Now, I'd suggest you call an ambulance because you really don't want complications arising due to your injuries not being tended to, do you?"

James smiles down at Grant, who nods, shakes his head, then nods again.

James turns away, the movement dismissive as though Grant's not worth another moment of his time. And he's not. James fixes me with his green eyes.

"If there's anything more here you want get it now, because you're not coming back here. Ever."

"No, no there's nothing else," I croak.

"Then let's go."

He strides ahead, leaving me to hurry after him and slam the door on my former life.

CHAPTER SIX

PERRY

We dump the guitar, propped up on a pile of bricks, in a skip. Bright red and shiny, it's a dented beacon.

James asks me again if I'd want it, but I don't. Stupid, maybe. No, definitely stupid, but my life with Grant and all that went with it, is behind me and I don't want any reminder. I try to tell myself it's about pride, but I don't feel very proud. James doesn't try to persuade me otherwise, and I'm sure there's a hint of approval in his dark green eyes. As we drive away, a quick backwards glance shows the guitar's already been claimed.

I've fallen asleep on the way back, jerked awake as the motion ceases and the engine turns off. We're back at James', just a couple of hours after leaving. The enormity of what's happened, of the deep pit I've fallen into and the mountain I have to climb to reach any kind of semblance of a normal life crashes down on me. I begin to shake.

"Let's get you inside." James' voice is calm and in control, as he climbs out of the car. He comes around to my side and opens the passenger door for me, but all I can do is sit here.

"Perry?" He leans in, his eyes clear and assessing. "Come on, you've had a shock. Let's just get you inside, eh?"

I nod. Fast, and over and over, but I still don't move.

James' lips form a crooked smile. "I could throw you over my shoulder, it's one way of getting you to come inside with me, but I think it'd be easier for us both if you make your own way. You can, can't you?" His brow wrinkles in concern.

"Yes," I whisper.

He could carry me, I've no doubt of that from what I've seen today, and I know he'd do it without a second thought, but… I push myself out of the car, and it feels like the hardest, most exhausting thing I've ever done.

With one arm slung around my shoulders to keep me steady, the other cradling the books I've rescued — the ones Grant's missed, and not sold on eBay — James guides me the few steps to his door. I lean into him, glad of his strength and the solidity of his presence. It would be easy to get used to, but I mustn't let myself. For the second time in less than twenty-four hours, he's come to my rescue.

He takes me into the kitchen, drenched with summer sunshine, but I can't stop shivering.

"Sit down." James eases me into a seat at the table. I do as I'm bid, too numb and tired to protest. It's easy to do as he says, to just go with that unfussy command, and I let myself give in.

A couple of minutes later, a mug of steaming tea's placed in front of me.

"Here, drink this." James' voice is gentle but it's impossible to miss the thinly veiled order. I do as he says, take a sip and grimace. It's thick with sugar and I push away. "Sweet tea's good for shock, and that's exactly what you're feeling now." He pushes the mug back to me.

I shake my head hard. "No. What I feel is stupid, so fucking stupid." Add in pathetic, lame and useless, but they're not nearly enough.

"Yes, I expect you do."

If his words are meant to startle me, they work, and I jerk my head up to meet his steady green-eyed gaze. Everything about him is calm, controlled, self-possessed and totally unruffled, as if rescuing a homeless drunk, breaking noses, fracturing elbows, and using an expensive guitar as an offensive weapon is an everyday occurrence.

"Thanks for the vote of confidence," I mutter, as I pick up the tea I don't want. It's disgusting and syrupy and it makes me want to throw up, but I force it down under James' unflinching gaze.

"I've got every confidence in you."

He doesn't elaborate. I consider asking him why, when I've got so little confidence in myself.

The kitchen's warm and quiet and it'd be so easy to lay my head down on the table, or even better, crawl off to the comfy bedroom and bury myself under the light and puffy duvet, but the ring of church bells drifts in on the still air, tolling the hour. It's two o'clock, and time to go. I push myself up on unsteady legs.

"There's a toilet down here. Through the utility room." James jerks his head over his shoulder. I shake my head.

"Thank you, but it's time I went. I've caused you enough trouble already. You've been very kind."

James snorts and all but rolls his eyes. "Do you really think I'm going to let you slink back into that basement you've been camping out in? For goodness sake, just sit down before you collapse, and think." I do as he says without question, because it's easier. As for thinking, I'm so tired I hardly know my own name.

"Look," he says, lowering his voice. It's that classic car purr, the voice that says everything's being looked after, everything's in hand, and I give into it

"You've nowhere to go. You said so yourself."

"Not yet, not until Alfie gets back." Alfie will let me crash with him, no questions asked. Well, I'm not so sure about the no questions. But he has a sofa... A sofa that's lumpy and a bit smelly...

"And in the meantime, you'll carry on living in a musty basement, hmm?"

"I'm going to view some rooms, as soon as I get paid. Once I realised what had happened, and what a mug I'd been, I got my pay switched over to an account that's only got a few quid in it, just to keep it open. At least I made one smart move."

"But that's not now, this moment, is it? You can stay here. Give yourself some breathing space and time to get back on your feet."

My eyes prickle, and I look down, blinking hard. Yes, I need those things and James is holding them out to me, but I also need to push myself and get my life moving. This is a beautiful and comfortable house, and it would be easy to get settled here. His generosity is overwhelming, but I've crash landed in his life and I'm realistic enough to know it won't take long before he finds having me hanging around awkward and irritating. But the thought of the basement…

"Thank you. You don't know how much I appreciate you offering to help me — again." He answers with a shrug and a hint of his lopsided smile. "If I can stay here short term, it'll give me time to sort myself out with somewhere, and that doesn't include the basement, I promise."

"Good, then that's settled," he says, voice crisp and clipped. "For now, you need to sleep. I'm guessing you've not slept well in weeks?"

I shake my head, and he jumps up and rummages under the sink, emerging with a first aid box which he clicks open.

"Here, this'll help. It's a mild sedative, that's all, nothing you can't get over the counter. Go on, you need to get your head down. You know where the bedroom is."

It's only mid-afternoon, but I'm tired, more tired than I can ever remember being, so I do as I'm told because it's easier than arguing, which I haven't got the strength for at the moment.

"Thank you. For… Well, you know."

He doesn't say anything, just gives me a light smile as I get up and stagger out of the kitchen, too numb and too weary to even try and think.

Back in the comfortable bedroom, I pull the curtains closed to block out the bright sunlight. Moments later I'm burrowing under the duvet, drawing it up over my head as I let myself sink into the dark warmth where everything's quiet and safe.

Just a few nights… maybe a week or two…that's all…

CHAPTER SEVEN

JAMES

Saturday night, and instead of being at a bar, club or party, I'm sitting in front of the TV with a curry I've had delivered, and a Cobra beer. It's an almost unique situation, because I can't remember the last time I was at home like this.

Upstairs, Perry's asleep, and he has been for hours. I looked in on him a couple of times, just put my head around the door. He won't stir until morning, but it's got less to do with the mild sedative I gave him than his own mental and emotional exhaustion.

I've no qualms about what I did to that bastard Grant. I'm not a violent man by nature, but I know how to be violent, in a controlled and measured way. How much to inflict, how far to go, how to damage without endangering life. An army career, followed by the police, taught me certain skills that have come in useful, from time to time, and they came in useful today.

I think I hear a noise from above, and I mute the TV. Has Perry woken up? I strain my ears to listen, but hear nothing more. Instead of turning the sound on the TV back on, I leave it. Dumping my plate on the coffee table I slump back into the sofa and let my thoughts roam.

Thank God I found Perry in Bert's. He needed rescuing. It's as simple as that, or it is to me. My stomach clenches and the heavy curry I've eaten feels like lead in my guts, and I push down the anger that's surging up in me. He's such a sweetheart, so how he got himself mixed up with a shit like Grant... I unclench the fists my hands have balled into. He can stay here for as long as he wants, but there's no denying it does bring with it some complications due to the nature of my private life.

Elliot, rather sniffily I've always thought, describes my bed as being akin to a revolving door: as one man gets out, another gets in. There's been a lot of truth in that, but not so much lately.

Bringing home random men has lost some of its savour, in just the same way the bars and clubs that have been a second home to me over the years have lost their allure, and more often than not I leave early and alone. The nameless pick-ups might have fallen by the wayside, but there is Aiden, whom I see on a semi-regular basis.

It's a loose arrangement, and it suits us both. I like him. He's smart, with a sharp mind hidden behind the gym bunny body and we've even been known to have proper, adult conversations, but there's no illusion we're in any kind of relationship beyond the physical. There's no attachment, and that's the understanding. He's stayed over on a few occasions, but only because we've both all but passed out with exhaustion, yet even so he's been up and out the door early the next day. There's certainly been no long or leisurely breakfast or talk of brunch. That's not the deal, and we both know it. Now, though, Perry's here, and that makes a difference.

I gather up the crockery and after I stack it in the dishwasher I go back to surfing the TV, when my phone buzzes. Talk of the devil.

I read Aiden's message. To the point, it's almost terse.

Where are you?

At home, I thumb in.

I can come round.

I stare at the message. Any other Saturday night or indeed any night I was home I'd be keying in yes and looking forward to some of the hottest sex I've ever had.

I glance up at the ceiling. But not tonight.

No. I've got somebody staying.

A guy?

Yes. A friend.

He can join in. Three's fun.

I'm frowning. The suggestion feels wrong and disturbing in a way I can't quite define. My stomach turns over, but it's got nothing to do with the heavy food I've just eaten. I take a deep breath, because Aiden's not to know, he's just reacting to what he knows of me.

You there?

I've been staring at the screen for several seconds, so I thumb in the reply.

No threesomes. He's staying with me for a while.

He's hampering your style. You can come to mine.

We'll sort something out but not just yet.

Aiden doesn't reply and I guess he's taken the hint that the conversation for now is at an end. I power down my phone and set it aside.

Switching off the TV, I leap up from the sofa. I'm feeling restless, suddenly, and for a moment I wonder if I should change and go for a run. It's what I do, day or night, when I've got an excess of nervous energy, and for some reason I'm overflowing with it now. I dismiss it for the bad idea it is, as the curry's siting like a stone in my stomach, but the real reason for not pounding the nighttime streets is because of the exhausted, defeated young man sleeping upstairs.

Back in the kitchen, I pull out another beer. Popping the cap, I drink deeply as Aiden's words spin around in my head.

Will Perry cramp my style, as he puts it? I suppose he will, for the time he's here. When he leaves, normal service will be resumed. I suppose. Maybe he wouldn't bat an eyelid at a stream of anonymous men appearing at the house but I don't want to give him the chance for any batting, especially not with his impossibly long lashes.

My gaze falls to the books Perry brought back with him, perching on the edge of the table. I hadn't taken any notice of them earlier, too intent on looking after Perry. They're big, thick hardbacks and their titles surprise me.

Advanced Sugarcraft Techniques, and *Professional Sugarcraft.*

I put down my beer, and flick through. Glossy photographs of cakes covered in intricate and complex icing, they're works of art. Celebration cakes of all descriptions, this isn't cake decorating for the faint of heart. With their arty photography, these could almost be coffee table books but the pages of detailed instructions and diagrams put that idea to rest.

Many of the recipes have hand-written notes jotted down next to them, and some parts have been highlighted in bright yellow. Splatters and greasy finger prints are evidence the books are well used. It's a side to Perry I never knew existed, and despite being full, my mouth waters. I've a sweet tooth, and even though I try my best to resist a slice or three of cake, I don't always succeed.

The events that have brought him to my home have brought change with them, at least for now. I'm more than okay with that because Perry needs my help and I'm willing to give him exactly that. I'll help him to get himself sorted out and then maybe he'll meet a nice boy who'll appreciate all that shy sweetness. A nice boy just like him. As for me, I'll resume what Elliot always describes as my *slutty ways*.

I quickly finish off the beer and make my way upstairs to bed with that thought ringing in my ears. Yes, normal, predictable service will be resumed. It leaves me stone cold.

CHAPTER EIGHT

PERRY

It's early, barely light, but I creep downstairs to the kitchen as quietly as I can. I've had more sleep in the last day than I've had in weeks, but I've been awake for almost an hour and I'm desperate for a cup of coffee. The most basic instant will do, although I'm sure a man like James wouldn't have any of that in the house.

I wonder if he'll mind me helping myself like this. In fact, I wonder if he'll regret his actions. Bringing me back here and assuming some kind of responsibility — although I'm not his responsibility at all — is a huge gesture. I'm glad of it, more glad than he could know, but I can't rely on it for too long, and I'm determined to get myself sorted out as soon as possible. Because I can sort out my own life, and take responsibility for myself. I did it pre-Grant and I can do it post-Grant. If I make it my mantra, recite it like a prayer morning, noon, and night, I might even come to believe it.

There is instant coffee, it's a small jar of something good, but there's also an all-singing, all-dancing coffee machine and I know exactly how to work it because there's the same model at work. I hadn't noticed it yesterday, but I wasn't in a fit enough state to notice very much at all.

It doesn't take me long to get the thing going and I throw nervous glances towards the open kitchen door. I'm sure James wouldn't mind, but it does feel a little strange to be tip toeing around his kitchen and making myself at home.

Pouring myself a cup, I stand by the doors leading out to the long back garden. The sun's only just coming up, and a light mist hangs in the air, softening the summer sunrise.

It's a lovely garden, mature and secluded, and although we're in the middle of busy Highgate, no houses intrude on its privacy. It's a world away from the flat I shared with Grant… I press my head against the cool window and my breath leaves a little circle of mist. I've got so much to do and think about, and honestly, it feels overwhelming.

"Oh God," I whisper.

"Almost, but not quite. But I'm working towards it."

I swing around, almost dropping my coffee. James is standing in the doorway.

He's in running gear, the Lycra moulding itself to his flat stomach and strong thighs, and outlining the impressive bulge between his legs. His face is a little flushed, and his ash grey hair's sweat soaked and plastered to his head. He's fit and strong, and even hot and sweaty, he looks incredible. But it's not so much his physical presence that makes my mouth water, it's his confidence. It's so well honed, it borders on arrogance. Maybe it comes with age and experience, or maybe it's just because he's James. Whatever it is, the whole silver fox thing's as sexy as fuck.

My breath hitches, my mouth goes dry and my heart almost crashes through my ribcage as he strides towards me, full of purpose. He stops at the sink where he fills up a pint glass and glugs it back as I gaze, transfixed, at his Adam's apple moving like a piston.

"That's better." He wipes the back of his hand across his mouth before he narrows his eyes and gives me his lopsided smile.

"I'm sorry, I hope you don't mind?" I croak as I hold up my mug. "I just thought—"

"Of course not, I want you to make yourself at home. Did you sleep well?" he asks, as he leans against the edge of the sink.

I nod. "Whatever it was you gave me, I had the best night's sleep in a long time."

"Good. I stink to high heaven so I'm going to jump in the shower. You get the breakfast on, and I'll be down in about twenty minutes."

James doesn't give me time to answer as he swings round on his heel and heads out of the kitchen. I stare after him for a moment, before I open the fridge and get to work.

"That was great, thank you." James mops up the last of his egg before flopping back into his chair with a satisfied smile on his face.

A small thrill runs through me. He's been doing everything for me since Friday night and if I can repay him, even if it's just with cooking breakfast, then I'm happy for it.

"No problem, it's the least I can do." I clear my throat, ready for what I need to say next. "I've been thinking."

That's stretching it a little bit but one thing I do know, in all this mess, is that I need to at least try and present myself as being proactive and not the pathetic specimen he picked up in the café.

"It'll take time to get myself sorted out, I know that, so that means I'm going to start looking for somewhere to live, from today. A room in a shared house will probably be the best, because I wouldn't be tied into any long rental agreements."

A room in a shared house, where you have a bit of shelf space in the fridge, and somebody steals your milk… God, I thought I'd left that behind when I stopped being a student. But being somewhere I can give short notice, somewhere cheap, or cheapish, not having ties to anything or anybody, is going to be important if the secret dream I've always harboured has any chance of becoming a reality. The ideal would be to crash with Alfie, but the truth is I have no idea when he'll be back.

"Even a house share will mean putting down a hefty deposit," James says, his voice measured. "Also, you need to buy yourself a whole new set of clothes. Very lovely though your suit is, I really do think you need a few more items in your wardrobe, and I don't think my old sweats are fit for much beyond these four walls."

I stare down at the hoodie and trackie bottoms I've put back on. They swamp me, and the cuffs are turned back.

Clothes. How could I have forgotten? I need at least one more good suit, which will set me back. As for the rest it'll have to be from somewhere cheap and cheerful. Fighting through the Primark hoards for the best in nylon doesn't fill me with joy.

"I get paid in a couple of days time, so I can get a few things then. At least Grant won't be able to get his hands on any of my salary this time."

"Don't you want to stay here?" James asks, as a tiny frown furrows between his eyes. His gaze is steady upon me, serious and almost a little disappointed, although I'm sure I'm imagining that bit.

I lick my lips. They're suddenly dry and this is turning out to be harder than I thought it would be. I was expecting to see relief in his eyes, despite what he's said about me staying. Because it's what people do. They say things they don't mean as they try to be nice. I've just smashed into his life, so why would he want me hanging around?

"No, it's not that, it really isn't. You've made me very welcome, but…" I struggle to find the words.

"But?"

James is still looking at me, his head tilted slightly to the side. There's a stillness about him as though he's waiting for me to make the next move. He's giving me no choice but to make it.

"I'm in your house, which means I'm in your way. I don't want to be that, not after everything you've done for me. I don't want to be an inconvenience."

"In my way? It's a big house if you haven't already noticed. You're hardly going to be *in my way*. And besides you're going to be at work all day, and so am I. Also, I'm quite often out late into the evening. In fact, I'm not here very much at all." The corner of his mouth twitches in the smallest of smiles, barely noticeable. And something passes behind his eyes, giving me the feeling there's more to what he's just said than the bare words.

"But I still don't understand why you would want me here?"

The words are out of my mouth before I can stop them.

He leans forward, his gaze cool and steady and never leaving mine. It's irresistible, like a magnet, and I can't pull mine away even if I want to.

"Because at the moment you need all the help you can get, and I'm more than willing and able to give it to you." His voice is low, almost a purr. His feline eyes, moss green and unreadable, fix on mine.

Seductive.

The word's a gun shot in my head. I try to swallow, but my throat muscles have seized up.

His eyes narrow as a smile plays on his lips.

"Of course, I can't force you to stay here, though I hope you will. Just think about it for a moment. You need somewhere safe and settled and that's what I'm offering for as long as you need it. Don't tie yourself up in knots about being in the way or cramping my style."

Cramping his style? I can almost see the quotes around the words.

"You'll be doing nothing of the sort. But it's up to you. All I would say is think about it carefully before you make a decision, because rash decisions have a way of coming back to bite. Promise me you'll do that?"

Rash decisions coming back to bite... I'd moved in with Grant just weeks after meeting him, and I'd not only got bitten, I'd got chewed up and spat out.

James is looking at me, waiting for my answer. Not pressing me, just waiting for the one and only answer I can, and want, to give.

"I… Yes. Thank you. But just for now, until I sort myself out."

"Just for now," he says, quoting my words back at me. "You want your independence back. I understand, I really do, but for now it's settled?" He raises a brow and I nod. "Good." He says the word with a hard finality, letting me know that for now the conversation's over.

I set about making some more coffee as James fills the dishwasher.

"Your books, I put them out the way. I didn't want them to get any more food splattered than they have already." He nods to some shelves on the other side of the kitchen. My sugarcraft books, the ones I rescued from Grant's. "They look very complicated. I had a look through them. I hope you don't mind?"

"Yes, they are and, erm, no I don't."

I can feel the heat burning up my face. They're a clue to that secret ambition of mine, but for now I don't want to say anything. It feels too fragile and ill-formed and if I expose it to the light of day, and James' assessing gaze, it might just dissolve to nothing.

James smiles, small and almost secretive, which makes me feel like he's reading my mind. And perhaps he is, because he doesn't ask why I have two very big, and very well used, books on advanced sugarcrafting.

CHAPTER NINE

JAMES

Perry's a determined little bugger, I'll give him that.

He's been staying with me for exactly one week, and he's already got places lined up to look at. He feels he has to assert his independence, and be proactive. I understand that, and admire him for it. But I wish he wouldn't, at least not yet. What he *needs* is to take time and not make any rash decisions, but it seems he's going to have to discover that for himself.

When I insisted I'd come with him, telling him an impartial opinion could only help, he at least didn't give me any pushback. I've got opinions, all right. On a late Friday afternoon, I can think of better things to do than traipse around grim ramshackle shared houses that smell of damp and mould.

We're on the third viewing. The place is disgusting, yet it's the best of a desperate bunch.

"… and this would be your room. It's nice and cosy," the would-be landlord says.

I peer into the bedroom and wrinkle my nose.

"Room? Don't you think that's something of an over-statement? It's little more than a cupboard." I cast a glance at Perry, but he's a polite boy and keeps his neutral smile in place.

"It's cosy, like I say. The former tenant had no complaints."

The middle-aged guy giving us the tour of the tatty pair of semi-detached houses which have been knocked into one scowls at me, at the same time he scratches at an impressive patch of acne on his sparsely stubbled chin. A flake of dry skin floats down and lands on his T-shirt, stained with what looks like the ghosts of many a meal. Or at least that's what I hope it's stained with.

"It's a little smaller than I was lead to believe from the details." Perry steps into the room, and I follow. "And, erm, very — red."

I snort, and Perry throws me a pained glance. Oh, yes, it's very red all right. Red walls, red ceiling, red curtains, red threadbare carpet. It looks like there's been a massacre. A very bloody massacre.

"Animal pens have more room in them. I'm sure this must be illegal."

There's barely room to move. The bed, which sinks in the middle, is wedged up against the wall, with about a foot of space at the bottom. The open shelving is just a small built-in cupboard that's had the door wrenched off.

"Where's the wardrobe?" I swing around and almost knock Perry off his feet.

Acne Man, who hasn't come in because if he did we'd have to be shoehorned out, jerks his head to a battered cupboard on the other side of the hallway.

"Perry, this is ridiculous. You can't be considering living in this dump?"

"I don't need much space because I won't be bringing a lot with me…" He looks around at the nasty little room, his polite smile slipping.

Irritation wells up in me. Why in God's name are we here, looking at this bloody hell hole, when he can stay with me for as long as he wants? I know why. It's because he's proud, he wants to prove to himself he can 'move on'. But to *this?*

I ball my hands into fists, fighting the urge to drag him out and back home. He needs to come to his senses, and if the journey entails looking at dumps like this, then so be it.

"I can show you the kitchen." Acne Man's fingers are scratching again, this time terrifyingly near to his crotch. I make a note not to shake his hand on the way out. "You have your own space in the fridge, and you've got a locker. You supply your own padlock, and—"

The door to the next room crashes open. A huge bald man waddles out, zipping up his jeans. Perry and I gag as a noxious cloud of poisonous gas fills the air.

"Toilet's blocked again. That's the third time this week. It's not going down at all." He throws a disinterested glance our way, and thumps down the stairs.

"That's wet wipes," Acne Man says, his face contorting into a scowl. "I put a sign up: No Wet Wipes." He glares at me and Perry as though we're responsible for the lavatorial crisis. He makes his way downstairs and we follow.

"I do like the look of your new housemates. Charming and civilised, I think you'll be very at home here."

Perry looks at me over his shoulder. "It's not ideal, but it's cheap," he whispers.

His shoulders sag, and I bite back. He needs to do this, needs to demonstrate to himself that he's not reliant on anybody. I grind my teeth. There's no way on earth I'm going to let him come to a place like this, but he has to see that for himself.

"This is yours." Acne Man nods to a locker bolted to the wall. It's got scorch marks on it, and a broken hasp for a padlock. "And you get a shelf in the fridge." He opens one of two fridges that were all the rage, in 1972, and a stench that makes the stink from the toilet smell like angels' breath wafts out.

Perry covers his mouth with his hand, and I swear he's gone green.

"I think something might have gone off—"

"Gone off?" I say, coughing hard. "Something's more than gone off, something's died in that thing."

Acne Man has the grace to look embarrassed, but he doesn't offer an explanation.

"Anything else you want to see?"

"Oh, I think we've seen everything we need to — don't you agree, Perry?"

Perry nods. He looks like he's ready to throw up.

"I'll think about it," he says, switching his attention from me to Acne Man, who's now scratching at the back of his ear, like a mangy dog. He looks at his nails, and digs something out from under them.

"Don't think about it too long, there's demand for rooms around here. This area's on the up."

"On the up from where? The sewer?"

"James," Perry hisses at me, but I don't care.

I've had enough of looking at shitty rooms in even shittier houses inhabited by the sorts of people you cross the road to avoid.

"Thank you for showing us around. I, erm... It's not quite what I'm looking for—"

"Yes, we really are sorry, but blocked toilets, box rooms which look like the walls have been painted in blood, and dead rats in the fridge really aren't on my friend's list of desirables in a new home."

I smile at Acne Man but it just seems to confuse him.

"So you don't want the room? You'd be lucky to get anything for the price around here."

"The only thing you'll get here is a case of diphtheria, cholera and possibly the Black Death."

Perry groans, and gives me his pained look again.

"Thank you but no, it's not really for me."

"It really isn't for anybody who doesn't want to get a nasty rash on their—"

"Goodbye and thank you," Perry blurts as he shoves me towards the kitchen door.

A moment later we're out, on the cracked and broken path.

"God, that smell..." He's gone a deeper shade of green, I'm sure of it.

"There isn't anywhere else to see, is there?" I ask, as we head along the litter-strewn street. With graffiti-covered, closed-up shops, the place is like a war zone.

"No, that's it. I didn't realise they'd be so—

"Filthy, stinking, nasty, a threat to human health?"

Perry sighs, and shakes his head. "I suppose I've been lucky in where I've lived. But there must be something better out there?" He looks at me with downcast eyes, and I want to shout *yes, there is, you're bloody well there now...* But I don't say anything, not yet. He had to do this, to see what the alternative is.

"I feel like I need to have a good scrub and soak in the bath for a few hours." He pushes his fingers through his hair, and pulls them out sharp. "God, you don't think I've picked up anything from there do you?" His eyes are wide, and horrified.

I shrug. "Fleas, probably. Maybe even lice." *And a large dose of reality.*

"Oh, God..." He shudders, and I can't help smiling.

"I'll have to start looking again tomorrow. Maybe be a bit more specific."

My smile disappears.

"Let's forget about that for now. We'll go home and you can have that scrub in the bath whilst I order a take-away. Pizza from Angelo's okay?"

The thinnest, crispiest pizza from the excellent little Italian just five minutes from the house. It puts a smile on his face, and brings mine back. It's the first thing we've had to smile about in the last three hours as we'd trudged from one slum to the next. But I'm going to make sure I put an even bigger smile on his face when we're home, because I'm going to make him an offer I'm determined he won't refuse.

CHAPTER TEN

PERRY

"All the fleas washed away, I hope?" James asks, as he dishes out the pizza and pours a couple of large glasses of wine.

"Think so, but I'm not so sure of the lice." I rub at my hair, still damp from the soak in the bath. I smile but there's a sting in our words.

The houses we saw earlier were disgusting and from what I've looked at online, it's depressingly clear I'm just going to find more of the same crappy, slummy rooms.

"Thanks," I mumble as I take a seat at the kitchen table.

It's only early evening, but the sky outside is dark with heavy rain clouds. It's a dank, chilly, English summer evening, and the perfect match for my mood. At least here in the kitchen it's warm and the air's laced with oil, garlic and herbs. In the background, bluesy jazz is playing. It's not what I'd normally listen to but I like it.

Taking a sip of the chilled wine, I sigh, and sink back into my chair.

It's lovely here, in this beautiful kitchen in this amazing house. But it's not just the bricks and mortar, it's James. The sexy silver fox with the come to bed eyes has been so good to me when he really has no reason to. The man who every time he turned up to visit Elliot would flirt outrageously with me... I know he was having a bit of harmless fun at my expense, but it didn't stop the tingle dancing down my spine, or the flutter deep in my belly, but I suppose that's what happens when you have a crush.

Crush. Jesus, I'm twenty-five, not fifteen. I'm not supposed to have a *crush*. Or at least I don't think I am. It's my little secret and I'm going to have to keep it tucked away and out of sight from a certain pair of moss green eyes, because if he guesses...

Oh, God, talk about embarrassing...

But, however lovely the house is, and however good James is to me, I have to remember it's nothing more than a stop gap. At some point soon I'll be moving on and this little breathing space, us sharing a meal at the blond wood table, will be over. And for what? Blocked toilets, a space in a fridge that stank like it had a corpse thawing out in it, and the dubious company of a guy with a flaking skin complaint.

Fuck. Fuck, fuck, *fuck*.

"Stop looking at the pizza and get your chops around it. I could say it'll make you feel better, but I think it'd take a lot more than one of Angelo's finest."

"They were so, so awful," I blurt out, taking no notice of the food on my plate.

James throws back his head and laughs, filling the kitchen with its rich rumble.

"Awful? Well I must say, that's a very polite way of putting it. Perry, my dear, I've shat in better — and cleaner — places than any of those hovels we looked at earlier."

I glare at him across the table. Even though I don't doubt that at all, I don't want to be told.

"Yes, they're nasty but those hovels are within my price range. And I don't like being laughed at because of it. I'm sorry they're not Highgate, that they're grotty terraces and badly converted semis, but they're all I can stretch to at the moment."

He stops laughing and stares at me, his expression unreadable. I've snapped, and bitched, and been bad tempered when all he's done is lend me a hand and pointed out the truth. I'm ashamed of myself, and he deserves an apology.

"James, I—"

"You don't have to move anywhere like those places. I've told you."

"For a little while, yes, and I'm grateful I really am but—"

"Will you just stop being grateful? Stop bloody apologising."

His words take me aback, not so much by what he says but by the steely edge to them which matches the edge I see in his eyes.

"Look," he says, leaning forward, all his focus on me. "You can trawl the internet, look at rooms for rent signs in shop windows and local papers until you're blue in the face, but you'll find the same thing over and over: substandard accommodation I wouldn't house my pet rat in. If I had a pet rat, which I don't. But you get the idea. To get anywhere reasonable, let alone good, you have to pay out a lot in this wonderful but undeniably overpriced city of ours. I have no doubt Elliot pays you well, but it'd still be more than you could afford on your own. I'm sorry, Perry, it's a plain, hard fact," he adds, his voice softening.

He's right, I know he is, but it doesn't mean I shouldn't try... The basement's looking more and more appealing.

"But I've got a proposition for you. One that if we can agree to the arrangements will work for us both. Rent a room from me. For as long as you need to. If you're determined to shell out on rent, you can pay it to me."

I blink at him, as I try to make sense of his words. Letting me stay for a while is one thing, but proposing he becomes my landlord...

"But you weren't looking for a lodger. Were you?"

"No, I wasn't."

"Then why turn your life upside down? I don't get it."

From staying a few days, a couple of weeks maybe, to something longer term, something more settled... I can't push down the rise of excitement in my stomach... This lovely house, the comfortable room upstairs overlooking the secluded garden... This fabulous kitchen... And, well, James himself... It's tempting beyond belief, but he hasn't answered my question.

"Why, James?"

He tilts his head and studies me. He's got beautiful cat-like eyes, and they're just as hard to read, but he's assessing me, weighing me up, and for a second I wonder what it is he sees.

"Those places we saw earlier, living somewhere like that, they'd grind you down. They'd crush your spirit."

"I think that's over-egging it…"

"Is it?"

I don't answer because what he says sounds too much like the truth.

"Perry, I'm not offering you charity — I wouldn't dare to because I know you'd refuse — I'm offering you a place to live. Without fleas, and dead things under the floor-boards, if the stench in that last place was anything to go by. But just listen to me, to what I have to say, and then make your mind up properly now that you've seen what's out there. I know you'll refuse to be a kind of long term guest, so become that lodger I didn't think I was looking for."

He's smiling at me, and I can't help but smile back.

"Pay me rent each month…" He names a figure that's just under half of the rental on the rooms and I open my mouth to protest, but he holds up his hand and his face is so stern, my protest dies on my lips. "But in addition, you take care of the cooking. I can rustle up a fry up or throw a steak on the grill, but not a lot else, and I'm getting tired of restaurant food and takeaways — sorry Angelo," he says, as he takes a bite from his pizza. "We'll both put in a set sum into the pot each week, as well, to cover essential food items. Like biscuits. And chocolate."

"Biscuits? And chocolate? Any particular kind?" I ask, as laughter bubbles up inside me.

"I'm not fussy. Or not about chocolate. Just as long as it's sweet, so none of that dark stuff for me."

His face is deadpan but it's impossible to miss the

laughter in his eyes. There's no way I'm going to say no, and I know there's no way he'll let me.

"Can you guarantee a lice-free environment, and a lack of blocked toilets?"

"That's open for negotiation. So, are you saying yes?"

I nod. "I am. I don't know what to say—"

"Then don't say anything."

Across the table, James turns all his attention to the food. The conversation's over, the decision's been made. The invisible weight that's been pressing down on my shoulders lifts, and in the first time since what feels like forever, I'm calm.

CHAPTER ELEVEN

JAMES

It's been almost two weeks since I found Perry in Bert's but we've not seen very much of each other at the house, as most nights I've been out until very late, all of it down to work.

Meetings with government ministers, senior police officers, and sometimes representatives from MI5. I'm officially a civil servant, but my speciality is in matters pertaining to the defence of the realm. It sounds glamorous, but it's less James Bond and more dull and interminably long meetings, trying to broker agreement between factions with competing interests. It often keeps me tied up until late into the night. I could say it's not always like this, but it'd be a lie. Whereas I'd almost always hit a bar afterwards, to wind down and find a way to relieve some of the tension, now I get home as fast as I can. In just days, my house feels like a home rather than the beautiful but empty place I've always done little more than rattle around in.

Each night, as I've walked through the door, I've sensed the changes that are happening in my life. Coming home, eager for the warmth of another's presence, it's a surprise, I'd even go as far to say it's a shock. For so long I've lived my life in a way that's kept anything hinting at cosy domesticity at arm's length. That life's for others, not me, yet when I close the door on the world those hard lines and certainties no longer feel quite so sure and clear cut.

Mostly, by the time I've got home Perry's gone to bed, leaving only a note to say there's some bolognese, or chilli, or something equally as delicious in the fridge, or in a pot on the hob, along with a freshly baked cake. His notes are almost apologetic in tone, which is madness. He's a wonderful cook and he's taken to that part of the deal we've struck with enthusiasm. Tucking in to something which I suspect has been made for me rather than being mere left overs, feels good even if I am eating alone in the small hours.

Thursday evening, and I'm trundling home on the tube. It's almost the end of a long and gruelling week and for once it's a reasonable hour and that means I can spend some time with Perry. I don't think about which bar to go to, and about how the night might pan out even though they always pan out the same. There's no savour to the thought, no sizzle of expectation, and I'm more than happy about that. Perhaps I can treat Perry to a takeaway, as a thank you for all the lovely meals he's made. We could watch a film together on Netflix... The thought's as warming and delicious as the food Perry cooks.

It's a few minutes walk from the underground station to home, and as soon as I'm through the door my senses are captured by a rich and warm aroma. Garlic, oil, and herbs combine to make my mouth water and my stomach rumble. Setting my briefcase down, I make my way through to the kitchen.

Leaning on the doorjamb I watch Perry, half-humming, half-singing to himself as he moves between the sizzling pan on the stove and the chopping board piled high with vegetables. I spot a flash of earphone leads. He's lost in a private world, happy and relaxed, and oblivious to my presence.

Perry's been forced to restock his wardrobe — whatever that shit Grant did with his clothes, they're long gone — and Perry's restocking includes the tight jeans hugging his pert little arse and legs that seem to go on forever. I can't help admiring, and smirking. Sugar on legs is how I've always thought of him, especially when red-faced and flustering, and as I drink him in now I've no reason to change my assessment.

The light blue T-shirt he's wearing, as tight as the jeans, has ridden up a little at the back, revealing a strip of tantalising, creamy skin. Small and on the thin side, a little too thin perhaps, a puff of wind would surely blow him away.

He looks young, not much more than nineteen or twenty, and even though I know he's older, a disquieting knot tightens in my stomach. I'm old enough to be his father, and it's a sobering thought. Elliot and Freddie may have a similar age gap, but theirs is a different situation entirely. Perry's here because he needed rescuing, which puts him in my care and under my protection, to a degree. It's something I have to remember, but as I watch him, unaware of my presence, I know without any doubt that's going to be a whole lot harder than it sounds.

I push my fingers through my hair, my hands not as steady as I'd like. He swings around and all but screams in shock as he wrenches the earbuds from his ears and stares wide-eyed at me.

"I didn't know you were here." The words rush from him. "I'm cooking dinner," he blurts out.

"And very good it smells, too." My mouth's gone dry and I have to force the words out and paste a smile on my face as I walk into the kitchen. "You don't need to cook every night." Disappointment shadows his face, and I could kick myself. "It's a lot to do, from scratch, after being at work all day," I say, hoping it takes out the sting my comment's inflicted.

"I enjoy cooking, and I'm more than happy to do it. It's pork." A frown wrinkles his brow. "I've not given you pork before. Do you like pork? I just assumed—"

"Oh, yes, I'm very fond of pork."

Very fond indeed.

A smile lights up his face, all apprehension vanishing.

"I love pork, too, always have," he says, brightly. "It's so versatile. There are lots of things you can do with it. I used to have a book, which I found in a charity shop when I first started at uni. *One Hundred Things To Do with Pork,* it was called."

One hundred and one, if you eat it... It's on the tip of my tongue, but I bite it back.

"It's going to be casserole. To make sure the pork's nice and juicy, and not dried out, it'll have to cook slowly in the oven for about an hour. Hope that's okay?" Perry's smile is wide and sunny.

Juicy pork... I clear my throat. "Yes, that's fine. I mean, nobody wants their pork to be dried up, do they?"

"Oh, no. It's got to be juicy and tasty or it's not worth having."

"No…"

He turns his attention back to the cooking.

I love pork... juicy pork... He's not the only one, and I'm thankful I'm still wearing my raincoat which is hiding my pork talk inspired semi.

"I'm going to jump in the shower." A hot shower, and a soaped-up hand…

"There's also chocolate fondant. For afters."

"Chocolate fondant?"

"Yes, because who doesn't like chocolate? It's almost as good as pork," he says, laughing lightly.

That's a matter of debate... Instead, I say, "I think you should stop working for Elliot and stay here as my full-time live-in housekeeper and cook. What do you reckon?"

His eyes open wide, almost as though he's considering it, before he throws back his head, and laughs. I could always coax laughter out of him whenever I breezed into Elliot's office. It was all part of the fun, making him smile, making him blush, making him laugh. It's a light, almost sing-song sound, and it weaves its way around me, and I know without any doubt that I want to hear it over and over again.

≈

The food's delicious and even though I'm not much of a cook I recognise his skill. It's every bit as good as food I've eaten in high-class restaurants.

"Where did you learn to cook?"

Perry smiles, but there's a tinge of sadness. "My granddad got me interested."

"The one who used to read to you?"

He nods. "He was a chef before he retired, in a big London hotel. He believed being able to cook well was an essential life skill — like knowing how to swim, or drive. Or the Heimlich Manoeuvre, just in case anybody choked on a poorly filleted piece of fish, as he always put it. His speciality was cake making, more specifically cake decorating. He made quite a name for himself, and even after he retired he used to undertake commissions, for weddings and such like."

The books on sugarcraft suddenly make sense. I open my mouth to ask him about them, but there's a faraway look in his eyes, as his much loved grandfather fills his thoughts. I snap my jaw closed.

"Anyway," he says, coming back to the present, "the cooking gene bypassed my mum, who's terrible, and from a young age I cooked most of the family meals. Granddad gave me the basic training, which I added to by reading cookbooks and watching all the cookery shows on the telly, but when I was eighteen I took an intensive course to really up my skills. I wanted to work the ski season when I took a gap year before university, so if I was going to cater for a chalet in one of the top resorts, I had to have the credentials."

"Where did you work?"

"Verbier. In Switzerland."

Verbier… I've been going there for just about every season for years. We may have walked past each other on the street, stood in the same queue for the ski lift, drunk in the same bars. Our paths could so easily have crossed but I know they never did, because I'd have remembered.

With a thought that's so hard it's a thump in the chest, I can only thank God we didn't because I know exactly what I'd have done: sweet talked him with the sole purpose of getting him into bed, before walking away without a second thought, the way I have with just about every other man in my life. A bitter taste coats the back of my throat, my tongue, my teeth, my lips, and I drag my hand across my mouth as though to wipe it away.

"…a friend of my parents own an upmarket travel agency. It was her who got me the job."

He's looking at me, waiting for a response, and I scramble to catch up.

"Did you enjoy it? Being a chalet hand's hard work."

Perry's face flushes an alarming shade of red.

Oh, I see.

A teenage Perry, away from home for probably the first time. Young, innocent, clueless and fresh faced, and very, very pretty. It's easy to see where this story's going.

"It was hard work, but, erm, warding off the drink induced advances of the guests was the really tough part. Chalet hands are often seen as one of the perks, as I soon found out."

I'm just about winning the fight not to cringe. It could be me he's talking about, and something that feels very much like shame fizzes in the pit of my stomach.

"Anyway," he says quickly, "when the season was over, I transferred to a small cruise ship and spent the next few months working in the kitchens assisting the pastry chefs. Again courtesy of the family friend. There wasn't a guest under the age of seventy, I reckon, so I wasn't having to fight off wandering hands."

"So much easier if those hands are gnarled and arthritic."

Perry's eyes widen for the briefest of moments before he bursts out laughing.

"Yeah, plus at least they couldn't chase me around the kitchen — not easy with a Zimmer frame." He goes red again.

Chased around the kitchen, brandishing a wooden spoon to protect his honour…

"Why didn't you go to catering college? Becoming a professional chef would seem the natural step."

He shakes his head. "I love cooking, and baking in particular, but working in a restaurant or hotel kitchen as a career isn't what I wanted, and still don't. Cake making and sugarcrafting is my thing, just like it was for granddad."

He hesitates for a moment, running his top teeth along his full lower lip as though he's considering what to say next. From one side to the other, all I can do is follow the movement of teeth scraping across lip, completely transfixed.

"What I ultimately want is to have my own business specialising in high-end patisserie and specialist celebration cake making and decoration. The luxury end of the market."

It explains the books on advanced sugarcraft, the love of cooking, the influence of his much loved grandfather. His admission doesn't come as a surprise.

"Aiming high, and why not."

"Exactly. I've taken specialist courses, as it's where my interest and skills converge. It's something I've been thinking about for quite some time, but the recent changes in my situation," he says with a grimace, "have kind of sharpened up the idea, brought it into some kind of focus. If there's a time to try and make the dream a reality, it's now. I've got photos of some of the cakes I've made. Would you like to see them?"

Hesitancy threads through his words, as though unsure whether or not I'd be interested. Of course I am.

"Yes, I would."

His smile's big and bright as he pulls his phone from his pocket and scrolls through. Without a word he hands it over. To be honest, I'm not sure what I'm expecting, but it's not this.

"Perry, these are incredible." And it's no more than the truth.

I take my time going through the photos. Traditional wedding cakes festooned with sugarpaste flowers, through to a child's birthday cake with fairies and unicorns and mermaids. There's even a rainbow PRIDE cake, edged with hearts. He's got a talent that deserves to be unleashed on the world. I hand him back his phone, which he takes with a self-conscious smile.

"I'll need to speak to my parents, as they've always said they'd help me out when the time comes — they've always run their own businesses, so they'll be supportive. Don't get me wrong," he says, concern creasing his brow, "I enjoy my job and Elliot's great to work for, but it's not what I want to be doing in five years' time."

I give him a conspiratorial wink. "Don't worry, your

secret's safe with me, but you really mustn't keep it too much of a secret because—"

My phone rings, cutting me off. I don't want to take any work calls, because I've no doubt that's what it is. I want to hear all about Perry and his ambitions. It crosses my mind to ignore it, but I'm not in the kind of job where that's possible.

"Sorry, but I'd better." I fish out my phone and hold it up. Perry nods as he pushes himself to standing and gathers up the used crockery and cutlery.

"Campion," I bark.

There have been some issues at work in the last few days and I'm half-expecting to receive calls. Weekday evenings, weekends, Christmas Day, Easter Day, the Queen's bloody birthday, I'm on call 24/7. Official or not, it's the way it is.

"That sounds very butch and in command. Are you wearing one of your fuck off suits with maybe the tie a little loose?"

I swallow a sigh. Aiden. He'd got a thing about me being suited and booted, all buttoned up, as he puts it. The guy's got a serious suit fetish and I seem to feed him until he's full. I throw a quick glance to where Perry's stacking the dish washer, because I really don't want him to hear me talking to Aiden. Getting up, I make my way to the living room, and close the door.

"I know you're there because you're breathing hard. Have I caught you doing something you shouldn't be? Maybe we should switch to a video call." Aiden laughs and I hear the intake of breath as he draws on a cigarette.

"I'm busy. My friend, remember? I told you about him.

He's still staying with me and we're finishing up dinner."
In other words, you're disturbing us.

"Still with you? Ah well, I was hoping we could meet up to have a little fun. The offer's still open for him to join in."

"I really don't think that's his kind of thing." There's a hard snap to my voice. No way is that going to happen, not a hope in hell. Silence stretches out between us.

"So, we're putting our arrangement on ice for a while?"

There's a tentative edge to Aiden's words. It's a valid question because this is the second time within less than three weeks I've given him the brush off. I don't have an answer for him.

"O-*kay*, but let's not leave it too long. Although we'll have a lot of catching up to do when you've finished being the perfect host," Aiden says as he laughs. "Anyway, thought you might like to know that Harry's having a party at his place tomorrow. Interested? If you can manage to tear yourself away from your friend for a few hours, that is."

Party. It's a euphemism, a handy piece of shorthand. Yes, it'll be a party all right, with sex and drugs and rock 'n' roll. Except for the rock 'n' roll. It certainly won't be pricey nibble food from Waitrose and polite chat over glasses of white wine. Ordinarily, would I have gone? There's no doubt about that, but now the thought leaves me feeling vaguely queasy. A home-cooked meal and Perry smiling shyly as we sit huddled in the kitchen…

"James? Are you still there?"

"Yes, yes I am. And no, I won't be going."

"Because of your friend?"

"Yes, as a matter of fact." My words are brusque, and there's another silence.

"Right, I think I'm sensing something here. If you're trying to find an excuse to step back—"

I close my eyes, telling myself I'm not hearing the faint edge of disappointment in his voice.

"That's not what I'm doing." I'm not sure if that's true. "Look, it's just that circumstances have cropped up that I've had to respond to. I'll be in touch." The words feel hollow in my chest.

A moment's silence, before he answers.

"Okay, sure. Maybe speak in a few days' time?"

"Yes, let's do that."

We end the call and I let go of a long breath. I like Aiden and we have, or had, I'm not really sure which it is as I slump against the wall, an arrangement that works for both of us. But the whole tone felt off, in a way I can't quite put my finger on.

I switch my phone off and shove it in my pocket. I don't want any more calls. Work can bugger off too; if they really need me, there are other ways of getting hold of me. I make my way back to the kitchen where I find Perry pouring coffee and opening a box of chocolate mints.

"I thought, to round off the meal…"

"Perfect." That's exactly what it is, and all thought of Aiden disappears like a puff of smoke. "And I've got a very good brandy we can have after as a nightcap. Feet up and a film?"

Perry answers me with a wide smile which makes me forget about everything that exists outside the walls of my home as, with a tug deep in my chest, I know that there's nowhere else in the world I'd rather be.

CHAPTER TWELVE

PERRY

By six o'clock everybody's left not just for the day, but for the weekend. It's been a busy week, more so than normal, and I'm wondering what to cook for dinner. James and I haven't shared many meals together, mostly because of his work commitments, but when his eyes light up and he gives me an appreciative smile, I can't help the warmth that uncoils in my stomach.

Like last night.

Chatting in the kitchen, James back early for once, it felt homely, domestic, and settled. It's a side of James I didn't know before. It's a lot more serious and caring, so different to the flirty and coolly arrogant man who visited Elliot. I liked that man, I liked him *very* much, but I like this version of James more.

I lean back in my chair, turning it from side to side as I look out over the empty outer office.

I'd surprised myself that I told him something about my idea for the patisserie and cake business, which I'm only just sorting out in my own head. It still feels like such a fragile idea, but James is so easy to talk to that telling him seemed to be the natural thing to do. He makes me feel safe and secure but then he would, I suppose, because after all he rescued me. I huff and shake my head. Twenty-five year old men really shouldn't need saving.

Safe and secure are the last things I should be getting used to. Leaving my good job with Elliot to set up a business is a risky venture. But, it's not just a business I'm planning, but a whole change of life, because I want to do all this down in Brighton on the South coast.

I didn't tell him that last part, and I'm not exactly sure why.

"Perry? Are you all right?" Elliot's standing in the doorway to his office, a slight frown on his face as he peers at me.

"Erm, yes, I'm fine. Just thinking about things I need to do this weekend."

"Then you should go off and do them. There's nothing pressing that needs you to be here at this time on a Friday," Elliot says, shrugging into his coat.

He's smiling at me yet I recognise an order when I hear one. Elliot's orders are always cloaked in soft velvet.

"Nothing urgent, like you say." I switch off my computer and stand up. A ringing phone cuts through the silent office and I look to see where it's coming from, so I can dash to answer, but Elliot's already pulling his mobile from his pocket, a big smile on his face. I know who it is.

"Hello, sweetheart."

Elliot throws a quick glance at me. He's gone a little red and his mouth curls up in a sheepish smile, as he turns aside and talks to Freddie, his fiancé. Elliot's voice is low, but I can't help but catch the talk about drinks and dinner out somewhere as I get ready to leave. A date night. Drinks and dinner, Elliot and Freddie wrapped up in each other. It's lovely, I'm happy for these two good and decent people, but Elliot's voice, soft as he speaks to Freddie, leaves me feeling emptier than I have in a long, long time.

Ending his call, Elliot's bidding me good night, and he's gone, leaving me alone in the office. I'm about to leave when the phone on my desk rings, and I pick it up without thinking.

"Elliot Hendrick's office," I say, as my hand automatically reaches out to restart my computer.

"I was right, you are still at work." The voice, the deep purr of a classic car, sends shivers across my skin. Down the telephone line, James chuckles. "If Elliot's going to have you working at gone six on a Friday, you need to put in for a pay rise."

"He told me to go, so I'm just leaving."

"Good, because that means you can meet me at The Breaker's Yard. There'll be a glass of something chilled and white waiting for you in five minutes."

The empty place in my chest begins to fill. My day has just got a whole lot better.

I spot James as soon as I push open the door to the pub. God, but he looks good. Suited and booted, sharp and clean cut, a silver fox fantasy in classic Saville Row. Is it any wonder I've harboured a crush on him since the first day I set eyes on him? There's no denying James is very… crushable.

In truth it makes me feel a bit silly, because crushes are only for teenagers. Allegedly. Perhaps I should call it an infatuation instead. Hmm, no, perhaps not, because that makes me sound like some kind of stalker.

Lounging back in his seat, I'm struck once again by his ease and self-assurance. It's magnetic, and I'm not the only one who recognises that, because the guy James is talking to is focused completely, one hundred percent on him. The guy's so tall and muscular, he could've stepped out of a fitness magazine. He's smiling as he runs his fingers through his hair, flirting for all he's worth, and James is smiling up at him and something cold and heavy settles in the pit of my stomach. Jealousy, as hard and unmissable as a punch in the face.

But what's the point of jealousy? A man like James won't look at a man like me…not seriously… we've become friends, but that's all…

James says something to the man and they both turn to look at me. My heart lurches. I've been standing here gawping because I didn't think they'd seen me, that I'd been as invisible as I always am.

Mr. Muscles doesn't look happy, but James' smile is wide and bright but also softer. Even across the busy pub, it's impossible not to know that he's looking at me and only me, as though there's not a soul around. A bump and a muttered apology shakes me out of my trance. The hubbub rushes in and breaks the spell. Mr. Muscles has gone, leaving James alone at the table where he's waiting for me.

"New Zealand sauvignon blanc." He edges the glass across as I sit down opposite him. "That's right, isn't it?"

"Yes, it is. Thank you." I take a sip, swallowing down the wine as I swallow down the urge to ask who the guy was.

"How was work? I hope Elliot's not been giving you a hard time and keeping you chained to your desk?" He smiles at me over the rim of his glass, mischief shining in his eyes. I shake my head, and laugh.

"No, that's not his style. I mean that's not to say he doesn't expect me to work hard because he does, but I enjoy working for him."

"I've not seen him for a while, I really must get in touch."

"He's gone to meet Freddie this evening. A date night, by the sound of it." Despondency creeps into my voice.

"Oh?" James quirks his brows in response, looking at me as though he's waiting for me to elaborate. I swallow the groan. Elliot's my boss, but he's also James' best friend. I'm wondering what to say, when James throws me a lifeline.

"Was Elliot getting all moony? And by that, of course, I don't mean was he showing you his naked arse."

Thank God I've not got a mouthful of wine, because I'd be spraying it all over James.

"No," I splutter. "They were just having that couply kind of conversation." I sip my drink and look out over the busy pub. Couply conversations. Date nights. What to do together over the weekend. Deciding on trips away… All the things people do in happy, settled relationships.

"Ah, the couply thing. I think if awards were handed out for coupledom, they'd be getting one with a big pink bow tied to it. It's the road they've taken and I know their journey will be smooth and strewn with rose petals, but for me it was scattered with rocks, pot holes and more than a few landmines."

I start. I'm not totally surprised by what he's said, but more the fact that he's said it, and to me. It's the first piece of truly personal information he's given me.

"It didn't really work for me, either." The car crash that was Grant, but he wasn't the first, not really. Boyfriends who made it clear they weren't interested in much after the first few fucks.

"Not yet, but I'm sure it will. I think being settled and living in a nice house with a white picket fence will suit you. No doubt you'll have a dog, too, that wears one of those tartan coats."

"You're taking the piss," I grumble, but I rather like the picture he's painted.

James laughs. "Just a little. Some are cut out for that kind of life. For those who aren't, try though they might, they're ultimately doomed to failure."

His brow creases and he takes a slug from his glass. He looks over the rim at me, meeting my eyes and seeing no doubt the million questions I've got about what's put him on the rock-strewn path. James sighs and puts down his glass.

"There's no reason not to tell you, because it's no big secret."

"You don't have to tell me anything." *But I hope you will…*

"I know, but I want to. But first, we'll have another drink." He jumps up and weaves his way to the bar, leaving me hanging on the cliff edge.

The place is getting busy, and it takes him a little while to get served. I watch him as he laughs and chats with other customers, drawing long, admiring looks. He could have any man he wants in this place.

But it'll never be me…

Fuck it. I really need to stop thinking like this. I'm tired, it's been a long week, I've got a lot on my mind. That's all it is and, anyway, he's just as good as said he steers clear of *coupledom.*

As soon as he's back in his seat, James doesn't waste any time.

"I was with somebody for four years. I was in my mid-thirties, so I don't have the excuse of having been too young to have tried the whole settling down thing. We lived together. Alex was — is — his name. He was lovely. Kind, gentle, thoughtful. It was impossible not to love him—"

"And did you?" I burst out, unable to stop the words flying out of my mouth. Mortification grabs me by the throat. "I am so sorry, that was…"

James gives a half shrug. "Yes, I did. The problem was I didn't love him enough. That's what he said, when we finally split up, and he was right. Everything was great, at first, being the loving and committed couple but the novelty wore off. For me."

Oh. I know what's coming and James' lips twist in a small, humourless smile.

"Other men. Temptation, lots of temptation I didn't try very hard to resist. We tried to mend what had been damaged, what I'd damaged, because the fault was all mine. We even went for couple's counselling."

He barks out a hard laugh, and takes a slug of his

drink.

"It was a waste of time, because I knew what the issue was. It was as though I was condemning myself to eating the same meal at the same time every single day, when all I really wanted was the never ending choice of a constantly changing smorgasbord. Which is just another way of saying that I didn't want to tie myself down to one man. Who in their right mind would put up with that? Not Alex, not in the end. When we split up, I made my share of the house we'd bought together over to him. It felt like the right thing to do. I walked away with nothing."

James' lips set in a straight line, his eyes darker somehow, and guarded. It's as though he's pulled on a mask. It's impossible to know what he's thinking, but those last words... They resonate with something that sounds like sadness.

He smiles, that crooked smile that's so typically James, bringing the life back to his features.

"It's not an untypical story, I don't think. Two people who want different things from life. I like to claim it's hereditary. My grandfather had a whole separate family. My parents, before they died, remained married but both had always been serial adulterers, and my brother makes no secret of his numerous affairs and the resultant offspring. At least that isn't an issue for me." He tilts his head and gazes at me, one brow cocked. "Do you think I'm a complete and utter bastard, or just a common and garden, plain and simple one?"

"You're truthful at least, which is something. You're clear about what you do and what you don't want. I suppose anybody you got involved with would know where they stood."

He huffs, or kind of, which I take to be confirmation. He's right about it being a common enough story, but something heavy and dull seems to settle in my stomach.

"What happened to him? To Alex?" The need to know what became of the man James didn't love enough claws at me.

"Oh, he found the life and the happiness he'd never have got from me. He's been married for a few years, now, and the last I heard he and his husband were living in a French farmhouse growing grapes and raising chickens. Or goats. Well, some species of smelly animal."

It's a nice image, but I keep that to myself. I open my mouth to say something, but whatever it is it's knocked out of me as I gasp and lunge forward over the table, spilling most of my drink. Twisting around, there's a beefy guy standing behind me. Clutching a pint, he's swaying and slopping most of it over the side. He's plastered.

"Watch what you're doing, you idiot." James' voice, which is more of a growl, is hard and menacing, and my attention darts back to him. His eyes are narrowed slits. Cold and dangerous, they're fixed on the guy who's staggered into me.

"It was an accident, s'all. No need to get narky." The guy's slurring slightly. His eyes slide to me, and he grins. "Sorry gorgeous." He slaps his hand hard on my shoulder, almost pushing me face down on the table.

"Get off—" I try to shake him off, but his meaty paw's heavy.

"Take your hand off him. Now."

James' voice, clear, clipped, each word so sharp it could draw blood.

The drunk's hand jerks off my shoulder, and he stumbles back a step.

James is sitting up ramrod straight, not a muscle moving. Tense and coiled, he's ready to spring into action in a heartbeat.

My heart thunders in my chest, and I look from James, still and icy calm, then back to the drunk.

The guy's in danger, and he knows it even though he's pissed. Something's pierced the beer haze and he's wondering what to do and how to save face. The small group of men he's with stop talking and they're looking between us, at this quiet little stand-off. The drunk grins but it's more like a grimace, as he takes another step back and holds up the hand not clutching what's left of his pint.

"Sorry. An accident, okay?"

James smiles, as warm as an iceberg, and the guy mumbles another *sorry* as he turns round to his mates. As one, they move away a few paces.

"Are you okay?" James asks, turning his attention back to me, his eyes full of concern.

"Yes, I'm fine. And thank you." I resist the urge to rub my shoulder. The guy had squeezed hard.

For a second James doesn't say anything as he keeps his gaze fixed on me, before he nods and carries on drinking. I'm thankful the situation didn't escalate. James closed the guy down with a few clipped words, icy enough to freeze over the Sahara.

"Bloody hell," he mutters as his phone rings. "Sorry, I have to take this then I'll close the damn thing down."

As James gets caught up in his call, I cast surreptitious glances his way. The pub's noisy and he's speaking low and fast. I can't hear him but it's not his conversation I'm thinking about, but the fact that he's rescued me again. I shift around in my seat and finish what's left of my drink, doing my best to ignore that James' controlled display of top dog was totally alpha, and kind of hot.

Fuck. I really, really, *really* can't start thinking along those lines, and especially not after what he's told me.

"Earth to Perry."

"What? Sorry?"

James is giving me his narrow-eyed, crooked smile, the one that always makes me think he has a secret.

"I said, shall we get out of here? Maybe head somewhere a bit quieter?"

The bar's got busier and making our way out is like wading through treacle. James is behind me, and I'm convinced my gasp can be heard over the din when his breath wafts against my ear.

"I've not eaten much today and I'm starving." He places a hand on the small of my back, guiding me through the crush. A shiver runs through me but this isn't a touch I want to ease out of. He's not the only one who's starving. I am too, but it's not for food.

Oh, God... Everything he's told me, it should be a clanging, deafening alarm, but just the feel of his hand through my jacket and shirt, is enough to set my pulse racing.

"There's a really good Indian place just off one of the smaller side streets. The curries are light and fragrant, with not an oily vindaloo in sight. What do you reckon?" he says, just as we emerge onto the street. He's smiling and there's a kind of anticipation in his eyes, like he's hoping I'll say yes.

Of course I do.

"That'd be great." My stomach rumbles its assent. "But

this is my treat, okay?"

"But you cooked yesterday. Most days, actually."

"That's not the point." And it isn't. James is charging me a token rent, and we both know it, so if I can pay for dinner then I will. I hold James' gaze, determined not to back down.

James' smile turns deliciously wolfish.

"Are you offering to buy me dinner, Mr Buckland? I don't put out that easily, you know."

It's the second time this evening he's made me gasp.

"No, that's not why…"

James' answering deep chuckle tumbles down my spine.

"I was only teasing. You should know that's what I do. And as for putting out, it takes a side dish of aloo gobi and a naan for that to happen."

He strides off and I dart after him.

Aloo gobi and naan… Maybe I should add them to the shopping list…

CHAPTER THIRTEEN

JAMES

When the bill arrives I go to pick it up, completely forgetting Perry's insisted on paying. I don't want him to pay and I have to tamp down my natural inclination to take the lead.

"Thank you," I say. He looks pleased, and I smile, because that pleases *me*.

As he deals with the bill and chit chats with the waiter, I think back to the incident in the bar

What happened was an accident, I know it was, yet my reaction was extreme. Seeing the guy's hand on Perry and the leer in his eyes when they raked over him, every button and switch had been pressed and flicked. And that's not me, it's not who I am. Not when it comes to men.

Or not until now.

I throw back the rest of my beer, and scrub my fingers through my hair.

When was the last time I reacted like that? Over Alex, maybe? If I did, I don't remember. But when that guy touched Perry...

"James?"

Perry's already standing, ready to leave.

"Sorry, I was miles away. Come on, let's go." I get up and head out first. I don't want to meet his eye, not yet, scared he'll read the thoughts that are swimming too damn near to the surface.

Outside, the streets are more crowded than ever. Even though it's summer there's a hint of chill in the air, yet it's not enough to stop drinkers from spilling out of the pubs and clogging up the pavement. Friday night, and people are fuelling up before they head off to late-night bars and clubs and everything those places promise. Any other Friday night I'd be doing the same.

"Would you like to go for a drink somewhere, or get a coffee?"

Perry shakes his head. "I think I'd rather just go back if you don't mind?"

And I don't mind, I don't mind at all. I go to hail a cab but he pulls my arm down.

"There is such a thing called the underground you know. And Leicester Square tube station's just up the road. It's only a handful of stops to Highgate."

"Do you really expect me to travel on the underground?" I glare at him in mock outrage. But he's right, and I've got a pass which I might as well use. We grin at each other and we head off to the tube.

Everybody's travelling into the centre of the city rather

than out of it, and the pair of us board a near empty carriage. Sitting side by side, our thighs bump each other's. I could shift my legs but I don't really want to. We start to chat but the trundling of the train is noisy and defeats attempts at conversation. On the seat next to him, Perry picks up a discarded copy of the Metro, the free London newspaper, and flicks through it, as we sit in companionable silence.

Glancing around I catch our reflections in the window opposite us, against the dark background of the tunnel. Our bodies are angled towards each other; the train jolts, jolting us with it. When I look again we've shifted positions, and I wonder if my imagination has played a trick, making me see what's not really there.

It doesn't take long for the train to pull into Highgate station, and a ten minute stroll later we're back at the house. I let us both in, gladder than I've been in a long time to close the door on the world.

"I can make the coffee, if you like?" Perry says.

"Sure, but why don't we get comfortable first? I don't know about you but I'm sick and tired of having been trussed up in a suit all day."

At the top of the stairs, he goes one way and I go another. I peel off my suit and hang it up, imagining Perry doing the same, behind his closed door.

Stripped off, I disappear into the en-suite and step into the shower, turning the tap to full. Throwing back my head and letting the hard jet of hot water drench me, my mind wanders.

In what feels like little more than the blink of an eye, my life has been turned upside down. I've had no thought about bars and pubs, other than tonight with Perry. Clubs and parties haven't crossed my mind. My hook up apps have been turned off, and I've cancelled my membership of the exclusive escort agency I've used from time to time. Aiden hasn't called back, and I wonder if he will. I like the guy, not just for the wild sex we've indulged in over the last couple or so years, but for the man he is — or for the man he's chosen to reveal to me. Yet, if I were never to hear from him again, would I be sorry? I already know the answer.

Now, all I can think about is getting home as soon as I can. It doesn't matter that Perry's mostly been in bed and fast asleep by the time I've got home, what's important is knowing he's here.

Elliot would be proud of me. I huff, sniff up a noseful of water, and sneeze.

My body's slippery with shower gel. Soaping around my balls, my cock stiffens.

"Ah, shit."

They're heavy, and my cock's standing to full attention.

Running my hand down my full length, I lave my thumb pad over the nervy slit. My breath hitches and escapes in a shaky exhale. This isn't a pleasure, this is a need. It's about achieving release and emptying my balls, and it doesn't take more than a few frantic tugs on my dick to have me spraying over the tiled walls of the shower cubicle, Perry's name stuttering from my tongue. The splattered cum's washed away almost immediately and I press my brow to the wall and breathe out hard and deep.

Christ, but Perry doesn't need this. He doesn't need this now and he doesn't need it from me, fantasising over him as I jack off in the shower like some randy, out of control teenager. He's come out of a bad relationship, and needs to get himself together. I've offered him a place of safety, a sanctuary where he can do just that. I've offered him, for want of a better word, my protection, and I'm not going betray that promise.

I *can't* betray it, even though my *slutty ways* as Elliot describes them, are hammering at me to do just that.

Running my hands down my face, I step out of the shower and dry off before pulling on some loose tracksuit bottoms and a T-shirt. Closing the door on my bedroom, I make my way downstairs. Perry's beaten me to the kitchen, where the rich scent of coffee hangs in the air.

He's already pouring, and he nods towards a packet of biscuits on the counter.

"I bought those a couple of days ago."

Chocolate Hobnobs. Sweet, crunchy, and delicious.

"I'll put out for these, every single time," I say, picking up the packet and grinning, but Perry only answers with a tut and an eye roll.

With coffee and biscuits in hand, we head to the living room where we huddle on the sofa.

There's not a lot on TV, so I stream a film.

"Oh, this is really good," he says, getting comfortable before munching down on a biscuit.

He's next to me but not close enough to touch and as the drama unfolds he's as still as a statue, engrossed in the film. I slide a glance his way. He's not engrossed, but asleep, and he's listing towards me. A moment later he slumps against my shoulder, out for the count. He doesn't wake up as small breaths and a gentle snore pouts his lips.

Slipping an arm lightly around his shoulders, I anchor him to me. I'd be happy to sit here all night like this, but I know that can't be. Gently, I disengage myself from him and get up.

"Hey." I give him a soft shake. "Maybe it's time you went to bed."

Perry's eyes flicker open, and for a moment he stares up at me as if he's not sure who or where he is, or who I am.

"I'm sorry, I must be more tired than I thought." He pushes himself up to standing, but he's still more asleep than awake and he stumbles.

I catch him in my arms and hold him lightly, telling myself it's just to stop him from falling. He blinks up at me but doesn't move, and I force myself to take a step back.

"Are you okay to make your way to bed?"

He nods. "Yes, I'll be fine." He hesitates for a moment and I'm sure he's going to say more, but he doesn't. Giving me a sleepy smile, he staggers off and I listen as he makes his way up the stairs.

I switch off the drama on the TV that's no match for the drama in my heart. Pouring myself a brandy, I settle back into the sofa. It still bears his presence, the warmth of where he's been, along with the sweet vanilla scent of his shampoo as I ask myself, just what the hell's happening?

CHAPTER FOURTEEN

PERRY

On a Saturday afternoon the café on Old Compton Street, in the heart of Soho, is packed.

I'd suggested Barista Boys, a great little place tucked away in a side street. I was surprised James knew it, but he probably knows every café, restaurant, club, pub and bar in the epicentre of gay London. Barista's was rammed, and with a queue snaking along the small street, we had no choice other than to find somewhere else — which, thank God, isn't Café Alberto, or Bert's as James calls it, where he found me, pissed as a newt and making a fool of myself with clumsy flirting and clumsier kisses. The hazy memory makes me want to crawl into a deep, dark hole.

Somehow, we've managed to snag a table. James has left me in charge of the shopping bags, filled with new shirts and a couple of pairs of shoes he's bought for work. When he'd made the tentative suggestion earlier today that I go with him, I'd jumped at the chance.

It's been a long process — I've never known anybody to be so particular and fastidious. Everything needed to be just right. Not nearly, not almost, no compromise.

We've spent hours going from one high end and very high spend shop to the next, and the spend has been *very* high. The assistants all seemed to know him, and I swear I saw a look of trepidation on all their faces. In one place, I think one of them fled the shop floor. Maybe they were going on their break, but more likely to still their nerves with a sneaky cig out the back. However, I can't be too critical of James' exacting approach to shopping, it's that attention to detail and knowing exactly what works that goes towards the eye-catching and mouth-watering package that he is.

My gaze rests on James, waiting at the counter, and my stomach knots. He's dressed casually, but there's nothing remotely sloppy about him. He's as sharp as a razor.

Black jeans and a fitted shirt that's an exact match for his green eyes. He's had his hair cut recently; it's short to the point of severity, and it reminds me he told me he'd been in the army and then the police force. James, in uniform… My dick stirs, which I really don't want, not in a busy café.

I look away quickly, hoping the replacement sight of a wizened old man gumming his way through a sticky bun will dampen things down. My dick goes back to sleep, but I can't help my eyes from sliding back to James.

Just as he always seems to, he's got talking to a guy in

the queue. They're too far away, so I can't hear them, but they're both smiling and holding eye contact. Flirting, because it's what James does.

They're standing close, and it would only take a small shift from either for their bodies to brush against each other's. The café's crowded, that could be all it is, but as James says something, the guy laughs and taps James on the shoulder, and leans forward, just a little, as though he's got something to say for James' ears only. And perhaps he has. Perhaps they're making arrangements to meet up, swapping numbers. Because James isn't pulling away, isn't stepping back. And why should he? He likes to play the field, he likes variety, he told me all that just days ago. It's not my business, but I can't help the tightening muscles in my stomach, and I force myself to drag my gaze away.

I pull out my phone, and scroll through the endless pointless posts on social media, anything to divert my attention from James and the random guy he's flirting with, maybe making arrangements with…

It's not my business.

A burst of laughter from the counter has me snapping my head up. James is at the head of the queue.

The guy he was talking to a moment ago is gone, replaced by a smiling, blond, and very good looking barista, who looks like he's been hired for skills that haven't got much to do with coffee making. It's a bitchy thought, and no doubt unwarranted, but I can't help it, not when the barista has a very dirty smile spread across his face.

The barista leans across the counter and says something, his eyes narrowing, and James' own smile deepens.

A moment later, James turns away and threads his way back to the table, leaving the barista staring after him with a smirk on his face.

"They'll bring the drinks over with our food," James says as he sits down. "You okay?" He cocks his head and scrutinises me. "You look, how can I put it? Pissed off."

"What? No, why should I be?" My faces throbs with heat under his stare. I'm not pissed off. Or not really. I'm...

Jealous.

The word whispers in my ear, and crawls over my skin.

"I don't know. Perhaps you can tell me?"

"I'm not... but maybe looking pissed off is my natural expression?" It's the only thing I can think of to say.

James chuckles. "No, Perry. You're the least pissed off person I know. What's this?" he says as he pulls his phone from the inside pocket of his jacket, just as I put mine away. "It's Cosmo, my cousin," he explains as he reads the text. "What's he after now..." James mutters, but he's smiling as he says it.

He plugs in a quick reply before shoving his phone away.

"Cosmo and Freddie used to be housemates, before Freddie and Elliot got together. He wants me to run a check on a prospective replacement to ensure they're neither a closet straight nor a Manchester United supporter." He chuckles as he shakes his head. "Highly irregular, of course, but I'll see what I can do. He's an annoying little sod, but I really couldn't risk him sharing with somebody who follows Man U. Chelsea would be acceptable or even, God forbid, Spurs." He smiles and gives me a wink.

"How do you mean, check them out? I don't follow."

He doesn't say anything for a moment as he gazes at me, and I wonder if he's even going to acknowledge the question. He leans forward slightly.

"My work allows me to run background checks on people."

Background checks. Somehow I don't think he's talking about credit worthiness. He was in the army, then the police, and is now some kind of civil servant, which is pretty vague. I've not asked him about his work because I've not wanted to appear nosey, but now I can't not ask.

"What is it you do?"

"I'm a humble civil servant."

"Humble? There's nothing humble about you."

James' answering laugh is rich and rumbly. "Perhaps not." His laughter dies and the scrutiny's back in his eyes. "My role is primarily advisory. I work closely with the police, security agencies and various government departments and their idiot ministers. I've signed the Official Secrets Act, so if I told you anything more, I'd have to kill you."

"You sound like James Bond rather than James Campion." *A gay James Bond...* I shift in my seat.

"Nothing so glamorous. Much of my time is taken up with very long, very dull meetings. And before you ask, no I haven't."

"No you haven't what?" I don't know what he's talking about.

"I haven't run a background check on you."

"What?" I start.

"Isn't that what you're wondering? It never crossed my

mind because I know all I need to about you. And I never will, that's a promise."

"Even if you did, you wouldn't find—"

The rest of my words are cut off with the arrival of our food and drinks.

The waiter's as blond and handsome as the barista, in fact he's a clone. It's another mean thought, especially as the guy's smile is friendly rather than flirty. He's only doing his job.

I'll leave a decent tip.

As soon as he's gone, I bite into my sandwich and sigh. Opposite me, James laughs.

"Better?" he asks, his voice low and deep, edged with the classic car purr, and I nod, my mouth too full to answer. "You've got dressing smeared on your lips."

I swallow, grab a napkin, and wipe my mouth, not wanting to look like a kid who can't feed himself without causing a mess.

James shakes his head. "You've made it worse, not better. Here." He leans over the small table, and sweeps his thumb over my lower lip, wiping up the tangy, slightly salty dressing.

"Oh," I croak, staring at the creamy blob on his thumb. I peer up at him through my lashes. I'm not the only one staring.

James' cheeks have gone red. He's unsure what to do, when this man is never unsure. He looks up and his eyes meet mine. They're glazed and dark, the pupils distended. But it's for a moment only, as he snaps back into himself and cleans away the mess on his own napkin.

"That's better. Don't want to look like you've gone

head first into a bucket of mayo," he says, his voice clipped and louder than before.

Don't want to look like you've just wiped your cum off my face, either...

Oh, God...

"Err, no," I just about manage to say, stirring my coffee and finding fascination in the little frothy bubbles.

When I summon the nerve to look up, James has finished his sandwich and is studying the menu again, his brow wrinkling in concentration. He looks up and his eyes lock with mine. They're bright and clear, with no sign of the dark intensity of a couple or so minutes ago. For a second it makes me question what I saw, but a light flush still colours his cheekbones, giving me my answer.

"They've a good choice of cakes and pastries." He grins and there's something conspiratorial about the lift of his lips. James, and his sweet tooth.

"If you have cake, you won't be able to fit into your new shirts." James' silk, torso-hugging shirts. "Is it worth the risk?" My voice is raspier than I'd like.

"So, you're saying you don't want one?" His brows raise, almost imperceptibly. There's challenge in his eyes, and I intend to accept it.

"I'm saying, surprise me."

I hold his gaze, and his eyes narrow before his lips curl up in a slow smile that has more than a hint of smirk.

"You've not the faintest clue how I might surprise you," he says as he pushes himself up and strides to the counter.

Oh, but I think I do have a clue, and it's not faint.

My dick obviously shares the same opinion as it pulses and pushes up against the fly of my jeans.

I tug my hoodie down and drag my chair in closer to the table. I look for the toothless old guy again, the sight of him and his gummy munching a surefire way to deflate a very inconvenient erection, but he's gone. Instead there's a middle aged couple.

The guy's grinning broadly at whatever's being said to him and offering up a fine display of perfect white teeth marred by flecks of what looks like mashed up spinach. My dick decides to return to sleep mode, and just in time as James arrives back at the table with two plates, each with a large slice of cheesecake. The sandwich filled me up, but the sight of the sweet treat makes my mouth water. This is one surprise I can handle.

"They're going to bring over another couple of coffees, too." James places one of the plates in front of me and sits down. "Cheesecake and another coffee, it's the least I can do for dragging you into every shop in the West End, and—"

"James? I thought it was you."

James' words are sliced off as his head whips around to a guy standing a couple of feet away from our table, holding a takeaway coffee and a small brown paper bag. The shock that flares in James' face is gone in a flash, replaced with a smile which is both friendly and guarded at the same time.

"Hello, Aiden."

The guy called Aiden is smiling at James. It's a dark smile, speaking of secrets and knowledge, and it slithers over my skin. I lower the hand holding the fork with a knob of cheesecake balanced on it, the clatter of metal against china louder, way, way louder than it should be in the café that's fallen inexplicably silent.

I drink in Aiden, every part of him, and I can do it without fear because he's not looking at me, he hasn't even noticed me, as all his concentration, and his dark and secretive smile, is on James.

Strikingly good looking, and in his late-thirties I reckon. He'd turn heads anywhere with his close cropped dark blond hair, longer on top and flopping forward over his brow. Tight clothes mold to his muscular frame, making no attempt to disguise what lies underneath. His eyes are hooded as he stares at James, twinkling with amusement, the tip of his tongue sweeping across the edge of his top front teeth. He oozes sex and I can't help but stare at him, at this man who radiates gloriously dirty, filthy sex and who's looking at James with both knowledge and desire in his hooded eyes. My mouth's a desert, and my throat rough gravel.

"Haven't seen you in a while," Aiden says, amusement threading through his words.

"Life's been busy. Work, amongst other things."

I tear my attention away from Aiden to James. His smile, still friendly, still guarded, remains stuck to his face, but it's his voice that causes my pulse to pick up the pace. There's an undertone, a warning, and it's edged with danger.

If Aiden's noticed, it doesn't show as his smile widens.

"Other things. Yes, I remember you saying. But we shouldn't let all those *other things* get in the way. We really should make arrangements to meet up again, and soon."

James, still smiling, still guarded, gives a barely there shrug.

"Let me introduce Perry."

Aiden turns his attention to me, his smile still in place. Even though it's broad and bright, and I'm exposed to the full sunshine of it, there's a subtle change. It's the hard, bright sun of winter.

"James' friend."

I can't decide whether or not he lays a slight emphasis on the word *friend* but I've no time to consider it as he carries on. "James said, last time we spoke, he had somebody staying with him. You're in a bit of a fix, apparently."

Aiden, tall, muscular and gorgeous, stares down at me. His smile's dropped away a little, and he's waiting for me to stumble out a response, tripping up as I go.

Fuck you.

I return his smile, lounging back in the seat with an easy, relaxed confidence I'm not exactly feeling.

"I was, but James has been brilliant. I'm living with him."

Shock widens Aiden's eyes, just for a moment. He covers it well, but a bitchy little thrill sparks in my blood.

Perry One, Aiden Nil.

Aiden considers me for a moment longer before he turns back to James.

Their gazes lock, all their focus on each other, leaving me forgotten and nothing more than a spectator relegated to the sidelines. Something unsaid passes between them, so strong and tangible I can almost touch it, taste it, smell it. I force myself to look away.

"I should be going. Nice to have met you Perry. I'm sure we'll meet again. James, what do you reckon?"

Aiden's voice, like his lips, barely holds back a smirk. I throw a glance at James. His expression's neutral, but it doesn't hide the stiffness in his jaw or the chill in his eyes.

"Unlikely." James may as well have said *not in this lifetime* for all the promise in his tone, but if Aiden notices he doesn't care as he gives a low chuckle.

Without another word Aiden turns and leaves, and both James and I follow him with our eyes. The door closes behind him, and I sag forward onto the table, almost knocking over the fresh coffee I didn't see the waiter bring over and set down.

"Perry?" James' voice is soft, all the hard edge of the last few seconds, minutes, hours or however long it's been, gone. "Are you okay?"

"Yes, why shouldn't I be?"

"I feel I should explain—"

"There's nothing to explain."

"There is. Aiden's somebody I've known for a long—"

"So he's a former boyfriend." *Oh, Christ.* I don't want to know, even though I already know… That's complete crap, because I want James to tell me exactly who and what Aiden is.

James stares at me before he shakes his head hard. "No. Not my boyfriend. He's not, and never has been, my boyfriend. We had what you might call an arrangement. It was mutually beneficial."

A mutually beneficial arrangement.

Of course…

Begins with Fuck and ends with Buddy. It's not difficult to figure, because James has made it clear he doesn't have boyfriends and relationships.

"It's over," he says, quietly.

I don't know what to say, so I just nod and pick up my coffee. It's tepid.

Not my business, nothing to do with me... But, I can't help the shiver that runs through me because whatever James says, I'm not so sure Aiden's got that particular memo.

CHAPTER FIFTEEN

JAMES

Since Aiden's sudden appearance, on Saturday, I've been edgy. There's no other way to describe it. I'm not an edgy person, never have been, but I am now.

I don't like surprises, being left unprepared and caught on the hop, or situations and events slipping their leash; but that's exactly what happened when Aiden walked into the café.

It was like two completely separate parts of my life collided, each alien to the other. I'd seen the way Aiden's eyes had raked over Perry, and I'd known exactly what he'd been thinking. Like with the guy in the bar, it'd taken every part of me not to bare my teeth, growl and bite like a damn guard dog. There was no reason why he wouldn't have looked at Perry and thought about how to include him in the games we've played so many times. Aiden knows me, or thinks he does, yet for the first time ever I'm wondering whether I really know myself.

I take a deep breath before I sip my drink and look out over The Breaker's Yard, watching out for Elliot's arrival, but my mind soon drifts as it goes over, yet again, what happened in the café.

"Whatever it is you're thinking about, stop it now because it's making you look as miserable as sin."

Elliot drops into the seat in front of me. He's looking well, better than I've seen him in God alone knows how long. Well, and content, and happy. Elliot's another who craves the always and forever life. He's got that with Freddie, his soon-to-be husband. They've even got a dog, even if the stinky, farty thing was Elliot's first. Elliot peers at me, a frown carving itself into his brow.

"Are you all right? Do you have wind? I've some Rennies in my briefcase if you want some?" I glare in response, but Elliot only grins. "You're lucky I'm free this evening. Monday is normally our intermediate salsa class night but this week—"

I sit up straight. "Excuse me? Salsa? You're learning to *salsa?*" Even in the flickering lamps lighting up The Yard, it's easy to see Elliot's gone red. "What's Tuesday? Couple's Crochet? Gay Gardening?"

"We've been going to class for a while, because we want to do more than stumble around for our first dance," Elliot says, as he looks around for somebody to take our order, deftly avoiding my eye.

His and Freddie's first dance as married men, at their summer wedding next year. Elliot's still tomato red, and still avoiding my eye, and out of nowhere an overwhelming tide of love and affection for this man rushes through me.

"You and Freddie will be spectacular together." And they will be too, but it's not the dance I'm thinking of. I clear my throat of the emotion that's making it rough and dry.

"James, are you all right?" Elliot finally gives up pretending to beckon a member of staff, and turns his attention to me.

"I'm fine." I catch the eye of a young waiter, who bustles over. I know what Elliot wants without asking, and I order us two large G&Ts, before I turn my attention back to him. He's giving me a critical, questioning look.

"What?"

"Are you sure you're okay? No recent bang on the head? Or a sudden loss of appetite?"

Elliot's doing his best to keep his face straight but he's having a hard time of it.

"What are you talking about?"

"You completely ignored the waiter. Blond, pretty, nice arse, etcetera etcetera, and you didn't even glance at him. Something must be up. Or not." Elliot snorts at his own joke, just as the waiter returns.

This time I do look. The waiter's exactly what Elliot says he is. He smiles at me, the come-on shining bright in his eyes. Any other time, I'd have already arranged to meet him for some quick and dirty fun, but his blue eyes aren't chocolate brown, and his blond hair isn't the colour of autumn leaves. I nod my thanks for the drinks and turn away.

"Well, that's a first," Elliot mumbles, as he raises his glass to his lips.

Sipping his drink, his eyes never leave mine. He's waiting for me to speak, to reveal why I sent him a text just an hour ago asking him to meet me.

I want to tell him about me and Perry. Except, of course, there is no *me and Perry,* not in the way most would understand that.

"Look, I suppose I should have told you before, but Perry—"

"You mean *sugar on legs.*" Elliot snorts again, the second time in less than ten minutes. "That's how you described my Executive Assistant to me, one time. Do you remember? It took me a good couple of days to look him in the eye. Anyway, what about him?" Before the words are out of his mouth, his eyes widen. He puts down his glass with a clunk. "Oh no, don't tell me he's finally succumbed to your cheesy flirting?"

"I'll ignore that remark. And my flirting isn't cheesy. Look, Perry's staying with me, just for now. He's renting a room in my house because he needed to find somewhere else to live, and fast. I don't want to make a thing about it, but I thought you should know. In case you call round, and, erm, find him there. At my house."

"Whatever it was I was expecting, that wasn't it." Tilting his head to the side, Elliot studies me.

I'm not a man who's easily intimidated, and I certainly don't cringe, but I'm having a hard time meeting Elliot's steady, level gaze. He's a master of the silent stare, just as I am, but right now, in this very moment, cringe is exactly what I want to do.

"Well, I thought at least one of you would have told me, although technically it's not my business." He sounds put out, even a little hurt, because by *one of you,* he really means me. "So why is he staying with you?"

I explain as succinctly as I can the broad facts, but leave out Perry's stint at basement living. I also tell him Perry's considering a change of career, as part of his life reassessment post the shit of a boyfriend. I've no doubt overstepped the mark on that front, but it's too late to backtrack.

"The change in career doesn't surprise me."

"Oh." I'm taken aback by Elliot's calm acceptance.

He smiles. "I've seen what he can do. My chief accountant got married a few months ago, and Perry made and decorated her wedding cake. It was amazing, a work of art. He's exceptionally talented and he should put those talents to good use."

"He showed me some photos," I say, nodding. "Like you say, works of art. Yet you seem extremely relaxed knowing the best Executive Assistant you've ever had is going to be leaving you in the lurch. Aren't you concerned about that?"

I wish I could bite back my words, which feel mean spirited, because I couldn't imagine anybody less likely than Perry to do something like that.

"He won't leave me in the lurch, as you put it." Elliot's words echo my thoughts. "Perry's not like that. I don't expect him to stay my assistant for ever, but I'll miss him when he does decide to move on — which should probably be sooner rather than later so he capitalises on the impetus created by the sudden change in his circumstances. Catastrophes often create opportunities, and this sounds like it might be his. The boyfriend, or should I say ex-boyfriend, sounds like a piece of work.

Perry's well rid. I should be grateful it was you who found him and came to his rescue. So, how long has he been with you?"

"Just a few weeks, not long."

"Weeks? Not days?" Elliot narrows his eyes, as a sly smile lifts his lips.

"Perry moving in, does it explain your complete and total disinterest in the waiter? His interest was flashing like a Belisha beacon, and you didn't even notice. That's not the James I know, love, and completely despair of."

"No, of course it doesn't."

My interest in other men has taken a nosedive since I brought Perry home. I can tell myself that having him stay has cramped my style, but it'd be a steaming heap of bull. If I want a man, I can have a man, anytime and anywhere I want. The simple fact is, I don't want. I've no interest, and it's the first time I haven't been interested in men pretty much since I was hanging off my mother's tit. I think of Aiden, temptation oozing from every pore. Deliciously dirty Aiden, who's as hot as they come, who now, and just as he did in the café a couple of days back, leaves me stone cold.

The loud, theatrical cough grabs my attention. Elliot's looking at me still, an amused smile tugging at his lips.

"You were miles away, which is also not like you. Are you sure you're not James' long lost twin?" I give him my best glare but all he does is raise a brow as he sips his drink. "Perry's very young," he adds.

"I could remind you you're on the point of marrying a man half your age, the same age more or less as Perry."

"Touché," he mutters. "I know he's not a kid, but in many ways it's how I've always thought of him, because he looks so much younger than he is. A scarily efficient kid, but a kid all the same. Just be careful with him."

"What do you mean by that?"

Elliot sighs, but he meets my gaze and his doesn't waver.

"He's fantastic at his job, he doesn't take BS from anybody and that includes me, but for all that I think he's quite a sensitive soul and easily hurt."

"And you think I'm going to hurt him?" I snap. "I told you, he's just lodging with me."

"Why are you being so defensive?"

"I'm not." So much for not being caught on the hop, or the back foot. Any pretence that I'm running things here is unraveling like a ball of string.

Elliot doesn't speak for a few seconds, but when he does his voice is measured, his words chosen with care.

"If he's just been through a break up, he'll be vulnerable even if he doesn't think he is. No matter how good a front he puts on, something inside will be fractured. Maybe even broken. He'll need time to mend, and the right person to help him." Elliot leans back, closing in on himself, shoulders hunching.

Oh, Jesus... If anybody knows about break ups, it's Elliot. I take his hands in mine, and squeeze tight, just for a moment, before I let go. He's talking about himself as much, if not more so, than Perry. Elliot's been damaged too, left broken by betrayal, but he's been mended and made stronger by having Freddie in his life. For a blinding, devastating second, it's intoxicating to think that I could be the one to heal Perry, but Elliot's next words are ice cold sobriety.

"Don't give him false hope."

"What do you mean?" My words are glass shards in my throat.

"James, I've got eyes in my head. All the flirting when you've visited the office, it's always been… What's the word I'm looking for?" Frowning, he drums his fingers on the table. "Intense, I suppose. More so than with the likes of…" He gestures towards the bar, to the waiter, to the barman, to every man Elliot's seen me tease. "Don't do anything to make him believe that you're giving him anything more than a helping hand when he needs it."

"Or a promise I'm incapable of keeping, you mean?" I can't keep the sneer out of my voice. Elliot continues to hold me with his cool blue gaze.

"That's exactly what I mean. He's not a toy to be picked up, played with, and thrown aside. That's what you do, James, you always have. I'm not judging you—"

"It damn well feels like it. I wanted to tell you the situation because I thought you had some kind of right to know, as my friend and Perry's employer, but maybe I should have kept my mouth shut."

"Stop throwing your fucking toys out the pram."

It's not the hard edge in Elliot's voice that jerks me backwards, it's that he's sworn. Elliot rarely swears, or gives in to shows of temper. I feel chastised, as I'm sure I'm meant to.

"James, I'm not judging you. Really, I'm not," he says, his voice softer. "But involvement, for want of a better word, doesn't sit well with you. It never has. I don't pretend to know anything of Perry outside of the work environment, but I think I'm a good enough judge of character to think he may be on a different page to the one you've spent your life writing on. Give him all the practical support and help he needs — and I'll see about sorting out some kind of bonus. He works hard enough so it's not like it's not deserved. But for his sake, if nothing else, leave it at a friendly helping hand."

Elliot swigs back the last of his drink. "I've got to go. There's shepherds pie waiting for me."

"Life on the edge, eh?"

"No, but it's life exactly how I want it."

Seconds later he's gone, his words echoing around my head.

CHAPTER SIXTEEN

PERRY

It's been a handful of days since the encounter with Aiden in the café. I keep telling myself it's not my business because it isn't. I know that, I really do know that, but... when I'm not busy, when my mind's free to roam, I can't help thinking of them. Together. Which is both hot and kind of gut wrenching because in those vivid imaginings, Aiden somewhere along the line turns into me.

Although I can't ever imagine a man like James wanting me over somebody like Aiden.

There was something hard edged and mocking about Aiden, but there's no way I can't pretend he's not gorgeous. Tall and muscular, over short — or shortish — and puny. James is the kind of man who can have anybody he wants, and I've no illusion that what he wants has very much to do with me.

That crush I've got is destined to go the way of all crushes — unspoken and unrequited, which is probably just as well. I've had enough complication in my life recently, and I'm not sure I really like them very much. One thing I am sure about, and that's my sexual frustration.

I've always had a lively sex life — it was what happened after, when I thought there was an after, as in maybe something more long term and stable — that was the crap part. But now? Nothing. Not a sausage. I'd smile at my own joke, if the situation were funny. The shower's been a good refuge, where it's been me and my soaped-up hand, but something more, something intimate, something filling as well as fulfilling is what I want, need and crave.

Crave.

My groan seems to fill every space in the house.

My cock's certainly craving. The denim across the front of my jeans is stretched tight and I press my hand down over my shaft, rubbing along the hard ridge, and this time it's a shuddering sigh that forces its way through my lips as my hips cant upwards to meet the pressure of my palm.

Maybe I should buy some sex toys. Maybe James has some sex toys. Maybe we could play with some sex toys together—

No. No, no, no.

Even meaningless, no strings fun is dangerous for me, because meaningless and no strings never seems to stay that way. It's exactly how I find myself landing face first in the shit, every single time. James doesn't do anything but meaningless and no strings; he made that as clear as day. Even when he was with his boyfriend Alex, it's what he did. He's said so, spelled it out, and I've got the memo in triplicate. And the T-shirt.

No use thinking about that. James likes his life as it is, keeping it casual with men like Aiden, as hot as they come Aiden. I try my best to reheat the agonising fantasy, but my cock's gone off the idea, and I let my hand slip away from my deflating, softening dick.

But sexual frustration's not my only concern at the moment.

In front of me on the kitchen table is my spare work laptop, open on yet another commercial estate agent's site. None of the agents are in London, but in Brighton, down on the South coast.

My plan doesn't only involve setting up a business, it's also about me moving away and completely starting again. Yet even the briefest, most cursory look online makes me feel like my dream's melting away in front of my eyes like fondant icing in too warm a room. It's not that there's a shortage of properties in Brighton, but few if any are suitable. Wrong location. Too small. Too big. Wrong usage classification. And all of them eyewateringly expensive. Add into that the set-up costs, as well as finding somewhere to live that's not a South coast replica of those disgusting rooms we looked at...

I can't stay here with James indefinitely. If nothing else, it's not good for my physical and mental health because the sight of him, especially in the suits that fit him like a second skin, send my blood pressure sky high and my heart thumping and jumping out of control.

He likes me being here, he doesn't disguise it, and I like being here, too. It'd be very, very easy to get way too comfortable and it's exactly what's happening. The one thing I dread happening is him getting in first, suggesting it's time for me to move out, and that means me getting my skates on before that happens. Because it will. He'll soon get tired of the restrictions my presence has placed on him, and I've got my dignity, even it did take a knock over the whole Grant situation.

My eyes fall to the last place I looked at online. The kitchen is no more than a cupboard but still the cost is astronomical. Not like this kitchen, this huge and beautiful room that's at the heart of the house. But there's no point in dreaming when what I really need is to get the wheels rolling on Operation Perry. Or it would be if I could find something, anything, in Brighton that looked like it didn't cost an arm, leg and kidney and wasn't next to a tyre fitters or a broken down charity shop.

The front door slams, signalling James is home from work. It also coincides with the timer on the oven bleeping, which I get up and turn off. Taking the casserole out, I lift the lid and take a peek. It's bubbling away, too hot to eat, and besides it'll taste all the better for resting and cooling down.

"Is that chicken and mushroom casserole?" James asks as he wanders into the kitchen.

"It is. I'm going to do garlic and butter mash, if that's okay?" It's more than okay, because I know this particular combo is one of his favourites. His face lights up with a big grin, and my heart does a little happy dance.

"Perfect. I've only had a very substandard sandwich today, and coffee that tasted like the boiled up scraping from the bottom of a budgie's cage." He grimaces.

Tugging his tie loose, he undoes the top two buttons of his shirt before he shrugs off his jacket. He's wearing a waistcoat, because it's always a three-piece suit for James. As he runs the fingers of both hands through his steely grey hair, I have to look away.

James absolutely rocks the slightly dishevelled silver fox businessman look, and I have a vivid and startling picture of him locking the door to his office and inviting his executive assistant who kind of looks a bit — a lot — like me to come and take down more than a letter. I rummage around on the veg rack, almost knocking the whole thing over, ostensibly looking for potatoes to mash, anything other than the delicious agony of watching him, seeing the slow lift of his lips and the narrowing of his eyes as his gaze meets mine, eyes that always seem to see right through me.

"What's this?"

I walk over and stand beside him. He's looking at the list of commercial properties on my laptop. His focus shifts from the screen to me. There's a stiffness to his jawline, and his eyes are unreadable. I feel sort of caught out, which is silly, because he knows I want to make a change to my life and move on.

"Brighton." The word falls dull and heavy from his lips. "You're considering setting up in *Brighton?* That's bloody miles away."

"Well, yes. If I can find the right place—"

"It's the first I've heard of it."

His words are hard his face closed off. The ground beneath my feet feels like shifting sand.

"I'm trying to get a good idea of the kind of premises available, and their price range." I gabble, as I rush to explain myself. "Although to be honest there doesn't seem to be very much. But I need to start getting the wheels turning. I've made a list of commercial estate agents and I'm going to get in touch with them in order to go through properly what my requirements are. Then I'll get a better idea of what's doable, and that means I can talk to my parents. Also I think it's about time I started to think about getting out from under your feet." *So I stop cramping your style, so you can get back to Aiden, so you can—*

"You're not under my feet. I told you, you can stay here for as long as you want."

"I know you did, and you can't even imagine how much I appreciate what you've done for me. But this," I say nodding towards the laptop, "I've always thought of striking out on my own, doing what I really want to. What better time than now, when I don't have any ties to anyone, or any place?"

The muscles in his jaw twitch, hardly noticeable, but standing so close to him, feeling the heat of his body and the in, out of his breathing, I notice. Panic presses down on me. I need to explain myself, and the words rush out of me.

"What happened with Grant and him kicking me out, it's given me a kind of freedom, a blank slate if you like, to start writing out my life." I'm trying to explain but I feel like I'm making a hash of it.

"Brighton," he says. "I've got very fond memories of Brighton." He smiles suddenly but it's a hard smile. "But it hasn't got anything to do with cakes. I've been there for a few Prides. It's also called London-on-Sea, which explains the prices. Did you know that?"

"Yes, I did, but the property prices are even higher than I was expecting if I'm honest. But it seems like the right sort of place to think about setting up. A busy town, but by the sea."

I look at the photograph on the screen. It's a place just off of The Lanes, that little network of tiny streets full of artisanal shops. It'd be a perfect location but the figure quoted for the rent alone makes me want to weep. An overwhelming, all engulfing wave of gloom comes over me. Maybe it's all a pipe dream, and as unattainable as a day trip to Mars, but if you don't have dreams what do you have?

Not a fucking shop in The Lanes, that's for sure.

James must feel my spirit sag, because when he speaks his voice is softer.

"Do you know anybody who's doing this work full-time, and making a living from it?"

"Yes, a couple I met on one of the courses. They've got a patisserie and a very high-end bespoke cake making business, but not in London. It can be done. I know it'll take time to get established, I'm not that green, but part of that is being in the right location."

"And you think Brighton's it?"

I feel myself bristle. "Yes, I think it could be." Or I would if I could find somewhere for the right price, in the right place.

"How many commissions have you actually—?"

"Plenty. You've seen what I can do — I showed you the photos, remember? It's not like I've just made a few cup cakes and a Victoria sponge for Sunday tea," I snap. It's an attack because I'm cornered and I don't like it. But I'm not going to let him think this is some pie — or cake — in the sky, idea. "Weddings, christenings, birthdays, plus some special orders for a couple of boutique hotels. Corporate work, too."

My shoulders want to slump at the lost opportunity that was. But I won't let them. "I did that with somebody I got to know on a residential course. We even got referral work, and we began discussing going into business together — getting premises with a small high-end patisserie attached to it."

"Then why didn't you?" James' voice is softer, losing the hard abrasiveness from earlier.

"Maddy's circumstances changed, out of the blue and dramatically. Family issues. She had to go back to Canada."

"So your plans came to a standstill?"

I nod. "As far as getting our own place, yes. When we were working together, we did it out of somebody else's premises."

James' eyes are full of questions, and somehow I feel he deserves all the answers.

"Where I used to live, before Grant, there was a small café around the corner. An older couple owned it. They did the best sandwiches and I used to pick one up each day, on the way to work. Dead cheap, too."

It's impossible not to smile when I talk about Joyce and Ian.

"I got friendly with them and I asked if me and Maddy could rent some kitchen time and space from them. I explained why, and they were really enthusiastic. You need room to do this kind of work, and proper storage facilities. Most domestic kitchens don't cut it. Anyway, it worked out really well, and I think they were happy to get some cash in hand. When Maddy went home, it was just me. The orders were still coming in, but working a full-time day job, it was getting difficult to keep up. I didn't let down any clients, but it was a near thing. But then it all came to a sudden stop."

James' brow crinkles. "How do you mean?"

"Joyce died suddenly, and Ian sold up. It all happened so quickly. The area was going through a lot of gentrification, and the café, and the other shops along that stretch of road, are all flats now. Shortly after, I moved in with Grant, and I couldn't work from there because his kitchen wasn't much more than a cupboard. So it all ground to halt."

Plus, Grant didn't like me monopolising his excuse of a kitchen to make *fucking fairy cakes*, as he always put it. I keep that nugget of humiliation under my belt.

With a final glance at the laptop, James wanders over to the fridge and pulls out a couple of beers. He flips the tops and hands me one. It feels like a peace offering and I'm more than happy to take it. The whole issue of Brighton has shocked him. I'm not sure why. It won't make any difference to him where I go when I finally leave. The thought's a heavy weight in my stomach, but it's nothing more than the truth.

He takes a long glug from his bottle before he rests his feline gaze on me.

"I've a friend," he says. "I might have mentioned him, I'm not sure. His name's Jack. He and his husband have a very successful bakery, but they also do a lot of private commission work. I think you should talk to them. They know what they're doing and they've made a great success of it. Contacts, Perry, they're what make the wheels turn." Chucking his empty bottle into the recycling, he heads for the door. "I'll send him a text and get something sorted out," he throws over his shoulder, as he wanders out of the kitchen.

~

JAMES

Escaping to my bedroom, I close my eyes as I slump against the door, taking in deep, steady breaths. I've had a shock, it's the only way to put it. It's the first I've heard of Perry wanting to set up on the South coast, and it's come as a complete bombshell.

He's got plans and ambitions and dreams and desires, and I admire him for it, just like I admire the way he wants to get his life back on track after the disaster of Grant. And what he says about having no ties in London, to people or places, is true in a blunt, stark way. There's nothing to hold him, he's as free as a bird, but knowing he wants to take to the air and fly far, far away is a hard and heavy punch to the gut. Not that Brighton's that far, just an hour or so on the train, but it's far enough to loosen the bonds we've formed. If he leaves the city, those bonds will unravel and fall away.

I've got used to him being here, with me. No, more than used to it, because that sounds like it's something to be put up with, and Perry will never be that. He's become an integral part of my home just like he's become an integral part of my life, and I can't imagine either without him.

For the first time in years, I look forward to coming home and closing the door on the day. The after work siren call of bars and clubs, full of heat and the smell of sex, has gone silent, and it's all down to Perry.

Sinking down on the bed, I send Jack a message with a very brief explanation. If I can help Perry achieve what he wants, I will, even if I resent it, knowing it means he'll go.

Jack and his husband Rory will be honest about what it means to set up and run a business of the type Perry wants on a full-time basis. It'll be a useful reality check, just like looking at those disgusting rooms was. The phone vibrates in my hand, and I read Jack's reply. Just as I expect he and Rory are more than happy to help, and I make arrangements for the four of us to meet later in the week because I sure as hell am going, too.

I throw my mobile aside and flop back on the bed, staring up at the ceiling. I'll help Perry, but it doesn't mean I have to like it.

After a quick shower, I make my way back downstairs, to the kitchen filled with the warm and delicious aroma of the meal Perry's cooked for us. My heart drops, knowing that times like this are numbered.

"I've made arrangements with Jack for us to meet later in the week, after work if that's okay?" Perry's dishing up the dinner. He looks at me, a grin breaking out over his face.

"That's great, thank you."

I nod but don't say anything as I sit down.

Maybe running his own business single handedly from his own premises will turn out to be too much to take on; maybe he could do it part-time; maybe he'll stay working for Elliot; maybe he'll stay here and not talk about leaving. But they're selfish thoughts, and all about what I want because that's all my life has always been: what and who I want, on my terms.

But not this time. For the first time ever I'm thinking about what somebody else wants, about their dreams and ambitions, and I hate it.

Perry's chatting away, about this and that, and I tell him as much as I can about my day, anything to not have to think about why it is I don't want him to go.

CHAPTER SEVENTEEN

JAMES

At his desk, Perry's concentrating hard on his computer, his fingers flying over the keyboard. Standing next to him, Elliot leans forward slightly, nodding as he reads whatever it is Perry's typing out. Neither of them has seen me. It's been a while since I visited Elliot at his office and it seems a little strange seeing Perry here working in his other life. I'm also very aware, almost viscerally aware, of my and Elliot's talk in The Breaker's Yard.

Elliot says something and, straightening, spots me standing in the doorway to the outer office. Perry looks up too, and smiles, his cheeks reddening.

"I'm taking Perry to meet a couple of friends of mine who run a bakery. We're going to be spending the evening talking about buttercream icing and sponge cake, and the awful drudge it is to run a cake shop. Isn't that so, Perry?"

"If you mean you're introducing me to contacts in the hospitality industry, specifically within artisanal bakery, then yes, you're correct."

Perry's voice is even and professional although he's still blushing as red as the cherry on top of a Bakewell.

"You're not yet," Elliot says, frowning at me. "This acquisition correspondence needs to be sent out." Elliot looks down at Perry. "If you could just get those emails out with the attachments, I think that's all we can do for today." He looks up and fixes me with a hard stare. "And no, nobody's going to make you a coffee whilst you wait, if that's what you're thinking. You can do it yourself if you want it, or you can come into the office so you don't disturb Perry."

"Oh, he's so butch sometimes. How can you stand it?" I mutter to Perry as Elliot strides towards his office, leaving the door open for me. "Make sure you're ready to go at the dot of five. Rory and Jack keep disgustingly early hours now that they have the baby taking up every spare minute they're not in the bakery." I give him a quick squeeze on the shoulder before I follow Elliot to his office.

Closing the door, I flop into the chair opposite Elliot's desk.

"You really shouldn't be encouraging my Executive Assistant to leave."

"You've changed your tune, because that's not what you said to me in the bar."

Elliot snorts. "Perhaps I've changed my mind. He's been invaluable over this latest acquisition."

"Then I hope you recognise that in the appropriate manner."

Elliot glares at me. "It's bonus and pay review time,

soon. It'll be sorted then." He taps hard at this keyboard, all his concentration on whatever it is on his screen. "It'll be hellish when he goes, but I meant what I said the other night. Leaving will be the best thing for him, in the long run."

The muscles in my shoulders tighten. Best for Perry that he's away from me, is what he's really getting at. We've already had this conversation, but I can't help biting.

"Best for him to get as far away as possible from me, before I can no longer restrain myself and fuck him into tomorrow before throwing him on the scrap heap, you mean? Give me some credit for self control, Elliot. Perry's become a friend, a good friend, and I know about lines you don't cross."

Elliot takes his time to close down his laptop, allowing my burst of anger to fade. Fade, but not disappear. He leans back in his chair, and looks at me across his desk.

"That is *not* what I meant. He has an ambition, and he should do his best to chase it. Whatever you read into my words is for you to dissect."

I don't say anything for a moment. I feel like I've been told off, which I probably deserve.

"It's good you're helping him, if this is what he truly wants."

There's a softness to Elliot's voice, and I meet his eyes across the desk. I let out a long sigh as I let go of my residual anger.

"I do want to help him realise his ambition, I just don't want to help him realise it in Brighton. I only found that out a day or two ago. Brighton, for God's sake." I shake my head. It's only sixty-odd miles, but at the moment if feels like the dark side of the moon. "He seems to have his heart set on going there, and he's been looking at suitable properties online."

"Expensive location. I hope he's got the funds to back it up."

"He said his parents are willing to lend a hand, but he'll have to get a mortgage as well, I imagine. And business loans." Long hours hunched over vats of buttercream, and loans heaped on loans...

Maybe he'll reconsider; maybe he'll think twice; maybe he won't go to bloody Brighton...

I'm wishing failure on him, and it makes me sick to the stomach. I'm a better man than that.

Am I?

"If you've become friendly and are essentially just giving him a hand, as you claim, then why does it matter to you so much where he goes?"

Because his smile warms me down to my marrow. Because all I want to do is rush home at the end of the day to a house that now feels like a true home. Because I want to wrap my arms around him, hold him close and keep him safe. Because no other man has ever made me feel that way, and it thrills me as much as it scares me. Because when it comes to more than light and shallow, I fuck up. And when he's gone, all that warmth will go with him, and my life will revert to what it was before.

Elliot's steady, questioning gaze is resting on me as he waits for the answer I'm not ready to give, but I'm saved from offering up a limp response by Elliot's desk phone ripping through the silence.

"Excellent, thank you Perry. It's all we can do for now so you might as well finish for the day."

I'm more than happy to escape the spotlight of Elliot's keen gaze. Telling him I'll see him soon, my back muscles twitch with the weight of his stare following me out as I leave.

"It's hard work. It's harder than you ever imagine it would be. It becomes your life. If you're not there doing the baking, you're spending time thinking about new recipes and new offers, experimenting with new flavours which more often don't work than do. And then there are the customers. Most are lovely but some are a pain in the arse. Nothing's ever quite right, and they moan — very loudly — about what they think is wrong, then they come back and do it all again the next day. Honestly, we had to ban one man, he was so rude to the staff and other customers. And talking of staff — we've been lucky, touch wood — but last Christmas we had to hire a couple of temps and I walked into the store room and found one of them with a ring donut hanging off his, well, you know what. Fortunately Mabel, who's our senior assistant, was on duty and she threw him out. She's very brave, and feisty. We took all the ring donuts off sale, and it was a good few weeks before I could even think about reintroducing them. On top of that, there's all the order-ing, the invoicing, and the balancing the books stuff which is vital but really, really boring. Owning and running a bakery-café is a nightmare except when it's a dream and then all the late nights and all the early starts are totally worth it."

Rory, who's barely taken a breath, at last runs out of

steam. He flops back into his seat with a wide smile, and Jack joins in.

It's been a long time since I've seen my friends, mainly because their lives have changed so much and that life is the antithesis of mine. They're now a family, and for the next couple of hours or so their baby girl Bella is in the care of the nanny. The bakery-café is a piece of cake to being parents, they always say, and although the two of them look tired, the happiness and contentment with their lives shines stronger than the sun.

"So, the focus is commission work, with a small café attached? That's right, isn't it?" Jack asks.

"Yes. As far as the café side's concerned, I want to go high-end as my thinking is that it'll also serve as a kind of advert for, and supplement, the commissioned work."

"Hmm, that's one option I suppose. Where are you looking to set up?"

"Brighton. I've had a few changes in my life recently, and it's the right time to move away and make a new start somewhere fresh, away from London. Brighton seems a good place to do it, and being by the sea is a huge bonus as I love the coast."

Move away… A fresh start…. He says it with such conviction my stomach drops. Pretty much the only time I ever leave the city is when I'm getting on a plane to go somewhere hot and sunny or cold and snowy. If I'm honest very little exists for me outside of the M25. It's another mark of how fundamentally different Perry and I are, I suppose.

"Good choice." Rory nods. "Busy town with the right demographic for your offer. And commissioned, or bespoke, or made to order celebration cakes — call it what you want — is big business. It really is booming, and there's lots of work out there, because people are increasingly looking for something different.

"But," Rory says, leaning forward, "if you really want to have a small café attached to it, to attract those with plenty of disposable income you'd have to offer not only the high-end products but also gluten free, veggie and vegan choices. We're selling more and more *free from* goods in the shop. It's an expanding market. If you don't, you run the risk of filling your seats with pensioners looking for cups of tea and toasted teacakes. No offence to senior citizens, of course, but they can make a cuppa and a slice of cake last for ages. That's a hell of a lot of baking in addition to the commissioned work — and that means employing good, reliable staff. They're harder to find than you'd think. If you get the staffing wrong, it can be a nightmare." Rory shudders.

Ring donuts as dick decorations, anybody?

All of this is what Perry needs to hear, this is absolutely what he needs to know, although I'm not so sure about Rory's agreement that Brighton's the right place to do it all in.

"Rory's right, it's incredibly hard work and having a small team of solid gold staff is crucial," Jack chimes in. "It was a big help that Rory used to work as a pastry chef, but a lot of this stuff we picked up as we went along and we're more than happy to share what we've learned — about what's worked as well as what hasn't."

"It's the commissioned work that really interests me, I want that to be the focus. Maybe having a café side business would be too much."

"To be honest, I think it would. Have you accepted any

special orders? From strangers, I mean? Don't take this the wrong way," Rory says, a flush filling his face, "but making a birthday cake for friends or family is a lot different to charging mega bucks for somebody's wedding cake."

Perry smiles. "Yes, I have, quite a few times, and I'm not just talking about a Victoria sponge. I've made…"

He rattles off what he's already told me. Perry's enthusiasm is infectious, and I can't help but feel proud of him. Both Rory and Jack's eyes widen when he tells them about the specialist courses he's taken, but their eyeballs all but burst from their sockets and roll around on the floor when he shows them his portfolio of photographs, the ones he showed me weeks ago, and tells them about the hotels he's supplied and the corporate work he's carried out.

"Wow, that's really impressive," Rory says. "And your sugarcraft, it's amazing — so you already know how time consuming this type of work is, and how clients want everything yesterday."

Perry laughs. "You can say that again, but I was fitting it in around a full-time job. I think that's one of the things that made it so difficult. But going forward, the big stumbling block I'm coming across is finding the right premises, in the right location. I've scoured the internet, but the commercial premises available are so expensive, even ones that would involve a lot of compromise…" Perry shakes his head, his eager smile fading.

"What's your opinion, James?" Rory asks. "You've been very quiet on the subject. What do you think Perry should do?"

Stop thinking about going off to Brighton or anywhere else by the sea, and stay here.

"You only get one shot at life." I try to sound more light-hearted than I feel. "Yet, there are always practical considerations and many businesses fall at the first hurdle." *Ouch.* Perhaps that's not what I should have said as three pairs of eyes laser into me.

Jack nods. "You're right. It's a sad fact that many businesses opened by people with more enthusiasm than cold, hard business sense collapse within their first year of trading. But that doesn't mean you don't try if that's what you want to do. As Rory said, we do a lot of commissions and it's a growing and very lucrative market. For us, though, it runs alongside the bakery-café which is our core business and main love. You don't have to have a physical presence on the high street, not for commissioned work. But you already know that, as you were renting kitchen space, not running a café — that's what you said, wasn't it?"

Perry nods. "But I think I just got lucky with the old couple who had the café."

"Maybe," Jack says, "but the point is, you should ditch the idea of a café if that's not your focus — and it isn't by your own admission. Which means there are other ways to approach this, which in turn widens your options."

Perry leans forward. "How do you mean?"

He's looking intent and focused and even in the pub's low lights I can see his eyes are sparkling.

"You can set up an at home business, backed up by a killer website, which you'd need in any case. Obviously there are hoops to jump through with the council as you'd be making products to sell to the public from your home." Jack's brow's wrinkling hard, as he thinks it through on the hoof. "You already know you'd need a large kitchen, with loads of storage and separate bakery business facilities to your own private domestic kitchen. But if it's bespoke bakery that you're really interested in pursuing, being home based automatically increases your options."

Perry mashes down on his lip as he thinks hard about what Jack's said. His excitement is almost palpable.

"It could be the answer," Rory adds. "You could always expand into shop premises later, if things go well. Just don't start out that way."

"I hadn't thought of it from that angle before." Perry's voice is quiet; it's almost as though he's talking to himself. "It's certainly worth considering. More than worth it."

"It is," Rory says. "We know quite a few bakers who run home based businesses, and it's working well for them all. Why not for you? Especially with the experience you've already had, and you've shown you can already attract prestigious clients. If I were in your shoes, I'd consider getting somewhere that is, first and foremost, a home, especially as you're looking to relocate, and extend the kitchen if needs be. And, you'd stand a better chance of not ending up as a failed business statistic which sounds harsh, I know, but not something you can afford to ignore."

"I think there's a lot of sense in what Rory's just said." Jack places his hand over Rory's and gives it a squeeze as he smiles at his husband. "Brighton's a good choice, but it's expensive. It's not called London-on-Sea for nothing."

"That's what I said," I chip in.

"How desperate are you to live down there?" Rory asks.

Perry doesn't answer for a second or two, and I swear my heart stops beating.

"Desperate?" he says slowly, "no I wouldn't go so far as to say desperate, but it's certainly somewhere I like and the idea of living and working by the sea holds a hell of a lot of appeal. I love London's vibrancy but I think now's the time to make a change before I sort of get too settled again."

He picks up his drink and takes a sip. He's not looking at me, not even glancing my way. His focus is on the road ahead and the future that's opening up for him, a future I know I have no part in. I turn my glass around in my hand; the gin's warm and the tonic's gone flat.

"So what's the dream ticket?" Rory asks. "Somewhere vibrant with the right client base for your offer. Somewhere bursting with affluent people who are willing to spend their disposable income. Somewhere with a community that supports independent artisanal craftsmen and women. Somewhere that's a home first of all, but which has the right kitchen in place or potential to rejig, or expand." Rory is counting off the points one by one on his fingers.

"That's it, in a nutshell."

"I know the coast, and Brighton in particular, is the ideal, but is setting up and staying in London a complete and utter no-no? Because this is where the really big market is," Jack says.

"No, but to be honest I'm not sure I could afford it in London, not somewhere with the space I'd need, even with help from my parents. In fact I know I can't. But this is as much about a change in lifestyle as it is a change of profession."

"So a lot to think about," Rory says. "In my view, you need to get the location squared off first." His expression's serious but his eyes begin to widen at the same time a smile lifts his lips. "But you're in exactly the right place. You do realise that, don't you?"

"I don't understand what you mean?"

But I know what Rory means. I know exactly what he's saying as he glances at me and his sunny smile widens even further.

"You're in exactly the right place where you are. Highgate. There's more money sloshing around in that area than just about anywhere in London. If you operated from there you'd make a mint. James' kitchen, it's huge. It would make the perfect location." Rory's really laughing now at the joke he thinks he's made, and Jack's joining in.

"Ever fancy going into the cake making business, James?"

CHAPTER EIGHTEEN

PERRY

When Rory and Jack say they need to leave, we swap numbers and they both say I can talk to them any time I want. They've given me so much to think about. My head's full of new ideas and a new way of looking at the whole issue.

"Do you want another drink, or go elsewhere?" I ask James.

The pub's very quiet and a bit dull, but it's been the perfect place for the four of us to sit around and talk, or rather for Rory, Jack and I to talk, because I'm suddenly acutely aware that James has said very little. If he has opinions on what's been discussed tonight, he's keeping them close to his chest.

"No, to both suggestions. But don't let me stop you if you want to go on somewhere."

His voice is clipped, almost brusque, and to be honest I'm a little taken aback.

"There's nowhere I want to go." Other than home, with James, but I keep that to myself.

"Then let's go." He throws back the last of his drink before he's on his feet and heading for the door, leaving me to rush after him.

The short walk takes us to the tube station. I want to talk about what Rory and Jack have said, I want James' view, and I want more than anything his enthusiasm, but he seems preoccupied, distant and kind of annoyed. The fizz of the evening's discussion turns flat.

The northbound platform of the Northern line is busy and when the train pulls in it's packed. We get separated, but he's in my line of sight. I want to know why he's suddenly cold, why the muscles around his jaw have tightened, why his eyes are unreadable.

And then it comes to me, it hits me right between the eyes.

He can't be thinking that I'm *thinking...*

The suggestion that James' home was the perfect place for me to set up had been a joke. Rory and Jack knew it, I knew it, and I'd assumed James knew it too. But what if he thinks it's what I'm angling for?

Working from home, even though at the moment I don't technically have one... Jame's huge kitchen in an affluent area...

He can't be thinking I'd seriously consider asking him if ...?

No, I'd never do that. I'd never put him in the position to refuse, or me to be refused. I need to shove that idea right out of his head, even though there's a little bit of me thinking it *would* be perfect and not just for reasons connected with elaborate tiered cakes, buttercream, and vanilla pods.

As soon as we're out of the underground station, I launch in.

"What they were saying, about your kitchen being perfect for me to start up, it was only a joke so don't worry that you'll find me refusing to leave when the time comes." I'm laughing as I say it, because I want to keep this lighthearted. "But they've got a good point, though, looking first and foremost for somewhere to live and making it my base. I need a decent kitchen, it goes without saying that's the key, but the more I think of it the more it makes sense, and that means the location won't be such an issue. I could find somewhere a little bit out of town, maybe further inland. It'd certainly be cheaper, which would make my parents happy."

The idea's taken hold and I'm running with it so it takes me a while before I realise James hasn't said anything as we stride towards his house, with me having to almost run to keep up with him.

"James?" I say, as we get inside and close the door, "are you okay? Honestly I don't want you to think I was taking what they said seriously, about setting up here I mean. It really was just a joke."

"I realise that, Perry. I'm not stupid." James hangs up his overcoat in the hall cupboard, banging the door closed with more force than it warrants. I have no idea why he's suddenly so distant — it was his idea to introduce me to his friends, after all.

"I'm sorry if you were embarrassed by it, or if it made

you uncomfortable." I honestly don't know what else to say.

"I was neither embarrassed nor uncomfortable." He sighs, and as he does so the ice that's marked his face thaws a little. He gives me a vague smile, which is something, but I can't pretend to read it. "In fact, what they said made a lot of sense. This area is perfect for you, and my very large, very underused kitchen is also perfect, and would give you everything you'd need to set up from home."

"But this isn't my home."

"No. Do you want a drink?"

"What? Erm, yes. Yes, please."

His abrupt change of subject has left me off balance. This wonderful house that deep inside does feel like home, isn't, and his stark *no* is a blatant reminder of that.

I follow him into the kitchen, and even though it's the last thing I should be doing, that doing it is so, so stupid, it's impossible for me to *not* look at it in a new light because it *is* perfect, just as James said. But it isn't mine, because this isn't my home…

"What's that?" I say, blinking at James. He's standing by the counter where he's holding the kettle up, and watching me.

"I said, what do you want?"

I can feel heat flood my face, because his slightly narrowed eyes tell me he knows exactly what it is I'm thinking, and that makes me feel, I don't know, a little cheap, a little shabby, because maybe he does think I'm looking at him and his home as something I can get something from. There's no way on earth I'll let him believe that of me. I clear my throat.

"A cup of tea, please. James," I say again because I really do want to clear the air between us. "They weren't being serious. I want my own place, somewhere I can reset my life and strike out on my own."

"Somewhere by the sea."

"Well, yes, that's the idea,"

"Why? Why go somewhere where you have no connections of any kind?"

He's leaning back against the counter, his arms crossed over his chest, the drinks forgotten. I feel like there's a big spotlight on me and I hesitate to answer. But I'm also annoyed by his reaction because I've done everything I can to make it clear that his home, his sodding but perfect kitchen, plays no role in any of my plans.

"Because I want and need a new start. You've seen why. I've always been drawn to the coast so why not try and make it a reality now my life's become a kind of blank slate that I can draw and write on any way I want? Working for myself, working from home — my own home — excites me. Now I've got no ties, nobody telling me what I should or shouldn't be doing, nobody telling me I'm — I'm useless—" I cough the word out, like it's a gob of phlegm that's been stuck in my throat. Useless, weak, a waste of space, it's what Grant called me so many times. He wasn't the first man to do so, but I'm determined he'll be the last.

"You're not those things." James, in a sudden burst of hot energy, springs away from the counter. The muscles in his face are tight, and an angry frown tugs down his brows. A few strides, and he's in front of me, his hands clamped to my shoulders. "Don't ever let me hear you say that about yourself again. Do you understand?"

His eyes drive into me. They seem even greener than normal, more intense, and emerald hard, and I look away.

"Perry?" There's command in his voice, forcing me to raise my gaze. His face is softer now, all hard edges gone. "Never believe that. Don't let others say it of you, and don't let yourself say it, either. A man who's determined to take control of his life and forge his own way through it is not those things."

His hands on my shoulders are solid and sure; they're not pushing me down but holding me up. His fingers move, a light kneading motion, round and round, tiny circles, easing out the tension that's made every muscle in my body tight and taut as piano wire. I sigh beneath his touch as my muscles begin to soften.

"Better?" James asks, his voice little more than a purr. "Good. Sit down and I'll make the tea."

His touch loosens and falls away and it's everything I can do not to grab him, not to pull him back to me, but he's out of reach and I sink into a chair at the table.

"For what it's worth," he says, as he places a steaming hot mug of tea in front of me a minute or so later, "I think the idea of basing yourself at home's a good one. Less of a risk. Even if it is on the dark side of the moon."

"The dark side of the moon? Brighton?" I can't help laughing. "It's not much more than an hour from Victoria station."

"Like I said, the dark side of the moon." His lips curve up in a languid smile, as he gazes at me through the tendrils of steam floating their twisted way upwards from the mug he's holding. "But if you really are determined to bury yourself miles away, don't rush into anything. Take your time."

"You said that to me before, when you insisted on coming to look at those rooms with me." I can't contain the shudder that runs through me.

"And I'll be by your side again. But wasn't I right about those places? Anyway, steering you away from those dreadful rat infested flea pits kept you here, didn't it?"

"And is that what you're trying to do this time? Keep me here with you?" I say it as a joke, I swear I do, but something stops me from laughing as my heart beats out a jerky, hard rhythm.

The hesitation's there, tiny, so tiny I could tell myself I'm imagining it. But why tell myself a lie?

"We've no need to rush anything, Perry, no need at all." His voice is a low rumble, the idling engine of a sleek, shiny car.

"We?" It's no more than a croak, and he's not heard it because he's already up at the sink, throwing out the tea he's barely touched, before he puts the mug in the dish washer, the jangle of crockery and knives and forks discordant and jarring.

"Goodnight, Perry. I need an early night." His touch on my shoulder is fleeting and light, but it doesn't stop the nervy tingle that runs down my spine, taking my breath away with it.

He's gone before I can answer. Alone in the kitchen, the aftershock of not only his touch but that one little word, *we*, shudders through me.

In some indefinable way, my world has tilted.

CHAPTER NINETEEN

JAMES

"You realise you owe me for this, Hendricks? Big time."

I glare at Elliot, who's standing on my doorstep hugging an old moth eaten brown and grey fuzzy blanket that's seen far better days. Closer inspection, however, reveals it to be Jasper, Elliot's arthritic mutt of which he's inexplicably fond. It doesn't even look like a real dog, but more like a Brillo pad pan scourer, on four very stumpy legs.

"I'm sure you'll extract your revenge in some way, and take great delight in so doing. We've got to rush because we need to get to the airport."

He turns to the car, idling on the curb side. Freddie's in the driver's seat and he gives me a little wave.

"And there are these." At his feet is a large bag. "His food, and some treats. We've written out a list of how much to give him and when. There's also his blanket, his cushion, and his favourite chew toys. He particularly likes the squeaky bone."

"Don't we all," I say, which is met with an eye roll from Elliot. "I still don't know why you couldn't put him in kennels. Or found somebody else," I grumble, as I eye Elliot's ugly little dog.

I'm not a dog person, and I'm particularly not a Jasper person. He seems to sense my antipathy, which means every time I'm forced into his company he insists on snuffling up to me and, dear God, even tries to crawl into my lap. His stiff back legs make it hard for him to scramble up so inevitably I'm forced to pick the thing up and do it for him.

"I explained over the phone. We tried. You were the last resort, and I mean the last resort."

"How kind of you to say." I understand what he's saying but I still can't help being a little peeved at being considered a *last resort*.

"We tried Freddie's parents but they're at a wedding all this weekend, Cosmo's away for work," he says, referring to my cousin and Freddie's best friend, "and my neighbour's broken her leg so obviously she can't help. Kennels don't suit him. He tends to get bullied by the other dogs so he gets very stressed, and that results in toilet issues for a few days."

"Toilet issues? You don't mean to say he shits everywhere? If he starts that here—"

"No, he won't. He is house trained, you know."

I peer at Elliot. My friend's looking shifty when he never looks shifty.

"But don't be surprised if he tries to pee in the corner.

It's because this is a new environment for him, but just give him lots of attention and lay out all his familiar things and he'll be fine."

I groan. Soggy puddles on the carpet stinking of dog wee. Is my friendship with Elliot really worth this?

"It's only until Sunday, and we'll pick him up straight from the airport. And anyway I'm sure Perry will be doing most of the looking after, especially as I've given him the day off to help get Jasper settled. Jasper knows Perry, he's very easy with him. Now, we really do have to go."

Elliot gives Jasper a big cuddle, rubbing his cheek over the dog's head, and is rewarded with a whine and a strangled yelp.

"Now you be a good boy, Jas. I don't want you to be too much trouble but if James is horrible to you, you have my permission to piss anywhere you want." With a grin that's got a touch of evil in it, Elliot thrusts Jasper into my arms.

The dog's small but stocky and surprisingly heavy as he wriggles in my arms. I meet his eye. The next few days are going to be war and to be honest I'm not sure who's going to come out the victor.

"I'll ring you when we get back just to let you know what time we'll pick him up. Must go." He swings around on his heel and rushes to the car, making his escape.

I don't know how, not yet, but Elliot's going to pay a heavy price for this.

I hold Jasper out at arm's length. "Do not give me a hard time, mutt. If you even attempt to cock your leg in this house, you're toast. Got that?"

Jasper doesn't shift his evil little eyes from mine but he tells me exactly what he thinks of my threat.

"Oh, fucking hell." I shift my head and try to veer back from the noxious stink that fills the air around me. I've forgotten, and Elliot has handily not reminded me, how much this dog farts.

"He's here!" Perry cries, as he walks up the garden path towards me. He's carrying a bag filled with a few bits of shopping but he immediately dumps it and takes Jasper from my arms, thank God.

"Hello Jasper, it's so lovely to see you again. Have you got a kiss for Perry?" Jasper wriggles in Perry's arms with what I swear is excitement, as his stubby tail wags from side to side. A strangled sound, which can barely be called a bark, pushes its way out of Jasper before a long, pink tongue emerges and catches the tip of Perry's nose.

"Errrgh, how can you let him do that?" My stomach's still rolling from the foul fart Perry doesn't seem to have noticed.

"Jasper's such a lovely little thing, he's so sweet and loving," Perry says, as he cuddles the dog close. He's got a big smile on his face and he looks thrilled with Jasper, and my antipathy towards the dog melts. Just a little.

"Come on, boy, let's get you settled. We can set all his things up in the corner of the kitchen if you like?" Perry throws over his shoulder as he strides into the house leaving me to pick up the shopping and the bag of Jasper's belongings Elliot's left.

"The kitchen? You must be joking." Jasper smells. He just does. He's a living, breathing stench bomb, and there's no way I want that floating around in the kitchen. "I thought he could go into the utility room." Or the shed, at the bottom of the garden, but from the way Perry's glaring at me perhaps it's best if I don't put forward those particular suggestions.

"You can't do that." Perry's eyes are huge with shock. "He'll think he's done something wrong. It'd be like banishing him."

Perry's still glaring at me, but so too is Jasper, and I'm sure there's a glint of evil in his round, button eyes. I've lost this round and the dog knows it. But I'm not giving up.

"He stinks, and he's very farty. I don't think it's too much for me not to want that poisoning the kitchen."

"He just gets nervous so if he picks up that you don't like him very much," Perry says, his scowl deepening, "that'll just make him fart all the more. Try and be relaxed around him, be nice. He's a lovely little thing and he'll be no trouble, and besides I'm happy to do the work. I've looked after him before, you know. But for now maybe Jasper would like to get to know the garden. You'd like that wouldn't you, you little cutie?"

I follow Perry through the doors that lead onto the patio, and the garden beyond. Jasper's leaning his snout on Perry's shoulder and I swear to God that dog's giving me a malevolent grin.

The garden's completely secure but Perry attaches his leash and tethers it to the branch of a large tree halfway down. It's one of those extendable things and Jasper spends his time sniffing and rooting around and cocking his leg. No doubt there'll be brown patches and dead areas but at least the dog's out the house and I pretend the smell is fading.

Summer's slipped into autumn, and it's come in with a vengeance with plunging temperatures and blustery storms. The kitchen, though, is warm and cosy, but it'd be a hell of a lot more cosy if Perry were sitting with me at the table, instead of on his knees in the corner, where he's telling Jasper he's such a good boy as he tickles the dog's belly. On his back with his legs spread wide, Jasper's such a little tart.

Perry's thrilled to have Jasper here, and that in itself is enough for the dog to earn his keep.

"And another tickle, and another," Perry says in a sing-song voice as he scrubs his fingers through the short hair on Jasper's pink stomach.

I have, I know, been completely forgotten, but I don't mind as it gives me the uninterrupted opportunity to drink in every inch of Perry. He's smiling, relaxed and happy, and I'm glad of that.

We haven't talked much about the evening we spent with Rory and Jack, and the shift in his idea to set up a home-based business. It's happening, I know full well he's been busy looking at places. I've advised him not to rush into anything, to wait until the New Year when properties flood the market, to take his time to find the right place and not let enthusiasm get in the way of clear sightedness. Not that I think anywhere will be the right place, not in bloody Brighton.

As I watch Perry play with the dog, my mind's turning over and over. Perry's desire for his own home and a thriving business are everything to him. I understand, I always have, and admire his quiet determination. But I have desires of my own and they're getting harder and harder to ignore.

I want him, and that's bad news for a man like Perry.

It sounds so basic, crude almost. But I do want him, I want *all* of him, and if I'm honest with myself I think I always have. I want his smile, his warmth, his goodness, but they're not all I want.

I could kiss him, and I honestly don't think he'd resist. I know the way he looks at me. He's easy to read, an open book in so many ways. And young — the age difference isn't an issue, but it can't be ignored. Life's not always treated him well, but he still retains a kind of innocence. Yet, if he has much to do with me beyond what we have now, all that'll be chipped away. Piece by piece by piece. Yes, I could kiss him and so much more, until I grow bored and restless, using him the way I've used all the men in my life. It's what I did to Alex, the only other man I've cared for, and I couldn't bear for that to happen to Perry.

That was in a different lifetime… I was younger, always searching for the next thrill… Surely I've changed since then? Learned there's more to life than the next easy lay, the next casual, emotionless fuck, before moving on to the next, and the next…?

But I don't know, I can't answer the questions and that shakes me. Yet there's one thing I *do* know, and that is I won't run the risk of finding the answers out on Perry, using him like he's some bloody lab rat to be experimented with.

"James?"

My name on Perry's lips pulls me back into the present. He's looking up at me from where he's still on his knees in the corner, his head tilted, his lips very slightly parted. He's waiting for the answer to a question I've not heard him ask.

"I said, I think we should take Jasper out for some proper exercise." He pushes himself to standing.

"We?"

"Yes. We could all do with walking off our lunch."

A walk. It's a distraction, and I grasp it with both hands, but the clouds are grey and heavy, promising rain at some point.

I shift my attention to Jasper. I'm sure exercise is the last thing he's thinking about as he wriggles up to sitting. Snorting and grunting, he lifts a back leg and takes great delight in licking his balls. For a dog with two arthritic back legs he's very agile when it comes to spreading them.

"I'm not at all sure I want to be seen in public with that thing."

Perry's face wreaths with smiles, but there's mischief in his glinting eyes.

"He says the same about you."

"Oh, he does, does he?" I look back at Jasper, still licking, snorting and grunting. "There are clear rules attached to our public appearance."

"Rules?" Perry drops down into the chair next to me.

"Yes, and ones you're going to abide by." I count them off on my fingers. "You're going to be responsible for him. You're the one who's going to hold on to his lead, and you're the one who's going to pick up his poo. There's no way I'm scooping up dog shit into a carrier bag. And if he gets wet and muddy, you're the one who'll be cleaning him off. Understand?" I try my best to glare at Perry, to look hard-faced and serious, but it's near impossible where he's concerned.

Perry tilts his chin up, a determined look on his face.

"You're on. We could jump in the car and head up to Hampstead?"

He must see the horror in my face, because he splutters out an explanation.

"Jasper's familiar with the Heath. It's only a short drive away. It'll be wonderful up there, all wild and windy."

"Wild and windy? That's very Kate Bush."

"Who?"

"Never mind." I groan and shake my head. Another reason for lines not to be crossed, if I need one.

Perry's looking hopeful and I know this is yet another round I've lost, but I'm not giving up without a fight.

"You do realise that having him anywhere near my car means it'll need fumigating?"

"He's not that bad."

A long and rasping fart blasts from the corner of the kitchen.

"You were saying?"

"Erm, all the more reason to take him out so he can walk off his, erm, indigestion?" Perry holds a hand up to his face, conveniently covering his nose.

"We could put him in the boot, I suppose."

"If I didn't know any better I'd think you were being serious." He gets up and goes to find Jasper's leash. I snort, because Perry obviously doesn't know me as well as he thinks he does.

A few minutes later we're in the car, heading towards the Heath. Despite my argument that the boot's the best place for him, Jasper's good as gold, curled up on a blanket on the back seat.

By some miracle, it doesn't take long to find a parking

space and soon we're heading over the rough ground and climbing high. Perry's holding onto the leash and Jasper's snuffling around stopping every so often to cock his leg. Now we're out on the blustery Heath, the little dog seems surprisingly sprightly. At least out here, in the chilly wind, I can't smell him.

"We had dogs when I was a kid," Perry says, suddenly. "Much like Jasper, we always got them from the rescue centres. It was my job to look after them and I didn't mind at all. In fact I loved it."

Perry's smiling wide as he recalls happy childhood memories. Jasper's bringing them all back and for that reason alone I'm glad I agreed to take him, even though I made Elliot listen to all my bitching.

"You didn't have dogs as a child?" Perry looks at me, even though I think he's already guessed the answer to that. "I thought it was in the job description, for all posh people to be surrounded by dogs and horses."

"It's not a requirement. Although I admit, my parents did have dogs. Setters and Labradors mostly, but I was away at boarding school from the age of four. In the school holidays I did as much as possible to avoid both my parents and their menagerie. When I went to university I rarely returned home, so was able to carry on avoiding the lot of them."

I can feel Perry's eyes on me but I keep my focus in front. I don't talk about my late parents much, or about my childhood. I had little interest in either my mother or father, and they in turn had little in me. They're gone, so there's no way of changing that. I'm a grown man and I've been around the block more than a few times, so I should be inured to the thought of them, but I'm always caught out and, I suspect, always will be.

Perry doesn't say anything sensing, no doubt, that it's not something I want to talk about. He's a sensitive boy; he picks up on atmospheres and he's picked up on this.

The clouds are thickening, and scudding across the sky as the wind rises. There's a biting edge to it, which is probably why there are so few people out on the Heath.

I slip Perry a glance. Wrapped up in an overcoat, a bright red scarf and a matching woolly hat, he looks happy and content, and warmth winds its way through me as we make our way to the top, high up on the Heath, our bodies bent into the wind, our shoulders and arms nudging each other's as we go.

Ahead of us and still on his leash, Jasper's making good progress but I can't help noticing he's slowed down. We get to the top and look at London spread out below under the leaden sky. Next to me Perry's breathing hard, his mouth slightly open.

"That was hard going. I didn't realise I was so unfit."

"Then you ought to join me on my morning runs."

Perry answers with a snort. "No, I'll leave all the pounding to you."

"Always better to pound with somebody else, I find."

His face turns from pink to cherry red and it's everything I can do not to laugh, or ratchet up the innuendo. I'm more than happy to be the one who does the pounding but it's not the streets I'm thinking of. My cock agrees as it thickens and twitches.

"I'll just let him off his leash for a little while," Perry mumbles, as he bends over to unclip the lead attached to Jasper's collar.

"If he runs away, you're the one who'll be running after him. Remember our deal?"

Perry shakes his head. "He won't run away. I've taken him out quite a few times, looking after him when Elliot's been stuck. He's not a very adventurous dog and he likes to keep close."

As though to underline his words, Jasper doesn't stray more than a few feet, sniffing around and not showing any sign of wanting to dart away, although I don't think with his stiff back legs he'd get very far. There's a bench up ahead and I jerk my head towards it, and Perry and I take a seat leaving Jasper to his own devices just steps away.

The wind's buffeting hard and there's a smell of rain on the air. Despite my earlier grumbling, I like being outside in all weathers and the wide-open view of the city, from this high up, makes it worth it.

We're sitting close, neither of us talking, almost but not quite touching. He's looking out over the city, transfixed.

"It's such an amazing view. Every time I see it, it takes my breath away."

I've seen it so many times from up here I'm used to it, but it's the first time I've been up on the Heath with Perry and I gaze out with fresh eyes. It is breathtaking, but not nearly as much as the man sitting next to me in the big coat and the woolly hat.

"It's funny, although I've lived in London all my life, I've never been to most of the landmarks. I've passed them on buses, but that's not what I mean. Sometimes I think I should just take a few days off and be a tourist in my own city, take advantage of what's on the doorstep before I move away."

Before he leaves.

A blast of wind, hard, cold and biting, whips its way around us. I say nothing because there's nothing to say. The clouds are darker than just seconds ago, and the first distant, angry rumble of thunder rolls in on the gusty wind. The already weak light is fading, and the first spots of rain begin to fall.

~

"Let's head back," I say to Perry, who nods his agreement.

We push ourselves up from the bench and look around. There are few trees up here but there are large patches of thick gorse and some bushes. What there isn't, is any sign of a small brown dog that looks more like a Brillo pad.

"Jasper! Jasper!" Worry fills Perry's face. "He can't be far, he never goes far. He's not that kind of dog," he says, but a thread of concern's running through his words.

He shouts some more for the dog and I join in but Jasper doesn't stumble out from under a bush, or emerge from a patch of gorse. There's nothing except our voices being whipped away by the wind and the rain that's starting to come down hard and heavy.

"Where the hell is he?" Perry darts this way and that, calling the dog. "I shouldn't have taken him off his leash, it's my fault. If we don't find him… Oh God, what will I tell Elliot?" Worry and upset crease his face.

"We'll find him, he can't have gone far."

This isn't Perry's fault, whatever he might think. Elliot entrusted Jasper to me, so if there's any comeback it's mine.

We make our way across the Heath, all the time calling, trudging through the torrential rain. The light's fading fast. I pull out my phone and flick the torch on. Up ahead, there's a dip in the top of the hill, the edge lined with over-grown, tangled bushes beyond which is—

"Behind those bushes, there's a pond."

God alone knows how I've forgotten. It's large, but shallow and muddy for much of the time, but it's been raining heavily on and off for the last few days, so it would have filled up.

I look at Perry at the same time he swings his head to look at me. Our eyes meet with the same thought connecting between us.

"Oh no, you don't think…?"

As one we run over the rough ground, stumbling and sliding on the already sodden earth that's turning to sticky mud. We stumble to a halt on the edge of the pond, our breath ragged with panic.

"I can't see—"

"No, look. There." My torch picks up a small shape in the water, bobbing up and down, disappearing only to reappear a second later before the water claims it one more time. A yelp, thin, frightened, and pathetic, is torn away by the howling wind.

"Oh my God, Jasper," Perry cries, as he lunges forward. I grab his arm and pull him back.

"No. You take the phone, aim the light on him. I'll get Jasper."

I don't give Perry time to argue as I thrust the phone at him, and slip down the slope to the edge of the pond. As I wade in, icy water fills my boots, soaking my jeans first to the calves then the knees. It's fucking freezing and I start to shiver, but I trudge forward, towards Jasper, whose frightened whining and pathetic attempts to bark spur me on. God alone knows why but Elliot loves the little sod, and I refuse to be the bearer of bad news.

Jasper's not far out, less than ten feet I estimate, but it's lethal underfoot. The pond's filled with thick, strong weeds which wind around my legs, and heavy mud sucks hard on my feet, making progress slow and heavy.

"Okay, boy," I breathe out as I edge towards the dog, keeping my voice low so as not to panic him even more than he is already. "Let's get hold of you."

Jasper's splashing about, but he's moving in an ever decreasing circle, and I know that can only be because he's caught up in the weeds.

The light from the phone barely reaches us, its beam weak and trembling in Perry's agitated hand. I edge myself closer towards the frightened dog. If I'm going to get him and me out, I need to free him from the knot he's got tied up in.

I'm within a couple of feet of him, and make a grab to stop him from dipping below the water's surface, but his fur's soaked and mud-covered and, smooth and slippery as an eel, he slides out of my grasp. Fumbling to keep hold, my balance goes and I lurch forward into the freezing, reed-choked pond, going under into solid blackness.

Bitter, acrid, muddy water fills my mouth and for a second I can't breathe. My feet scrabble to find a foothold on the muddy bottom and I push myself upright, spitting and gagging out the liquid mud that tastes of the earth, leaves, the dead and decayed.

The torch beam doesn't reach this far. Everything is shades of grey and I can't see Jasper anywhere.

"Oh fuck, oh fucking hell." I yell, angry not at the dog

but at myself for my failure both to save him, and to Elliot, who's placed his trust in me.

My heart's hammering hard, my breath's rough and ragged, and my blood's a harsh *whoosh* as it rips through my veins, all of it against a background of the wail of the wind and the beat of the rain hard on the pond.

I tread water, settling my breathing as I strain my ears to pick up any clue as to where Jasper might be. And I hear it, a tiny whimper that trembles on the edge of extinction. It comes from behind me, and slowly I turn. Jasper's given up the fight, as he bobs in the water just a foot or so from me.

And I grab him. One hand on a leg, the other gripping a floppy ear, I drag him to me and wrap my arms around him, hauling him into me and hugging him tight to my chest.

"Okay boy, okay, I've got you."

He doesn't struggle or put up any kind of panic induced resistance and for a moment I fear he's gone, but the beat of my heart is joined by another, and a tiny excuse of a bark.

"You stupid bloody mutt," I grumble, as I tighten my grip and begin the slow, cold, wade back.

"Oh God," Perry cries out as I get to the edge, "the beam, it didn't reach that far out. I lost sight of you and, and I thought…" He swallows hard, the phone wavering in his hand. "I was going to call the police, I was so scared you might have slipped and—"

"I'm fine, we're both fine," I say, cutting off Perry's panicked words.

"But—"

"We're both soaked through, freezing, and covered in slime, but that's all. We all just need to get home."

Perry's nodding hard and with a shaking hand he pulls Jasper's leash from his pocket ready to clip it to the collar. There's no way on earth Jasper, exhausted and trembling in my arms, is in any fit state to walk.

"No." My fingers are stiff with cold but I manage to undo some of the buttons on my sodden coat, and bundle him beneath it. "Come on, let's get back to the car as fast as we can, get this one cleaned up and warm. From now on, he's confined to the garden. No more adventures on Hampstead Heath, okay?"

Perry nods, and gives me a weak, quivery smile. Jasper's not the only one who needs to be wrapped up warm. Without thinking, I throw my arm around Perry's shoulders, hugging him close, as with the other I support Jasper as we pick our way down the hill towards the car.

CHAPTER TWENTY

PERRY

The wood burner's throwing out the heat as the storm rages outside. With the curtains pulled closed and the lamps set low, the living room's painted in a soft, buttery light.

Pulling my legs up onto the sofa, I sink deeper into the soft leather, and close my eyes.

As soon as we got home, we'd rushed as one through to the utility room with no thought of sorting out ourselves first. Jasper, cold and soaking wet and maybe even traumatised, he was our first thought. I'd been all set to call the vet. I've got the number on my phone because I still organise Jasper's regular health checks for Elliot, but the little dog's resilient if nothing else. A drink, a treat and a warm, soapy wash in the big, deep Butler sink, he was soon wagging his tail.

A snuffly sound prompts me to open my eyes, and I can't help smiling as I look down at Jasper, now nice and clean, warm and dry, curled up on his cushion near the burner. His wiry fur even looks fluffy. None of it's my doing.

It was James, the man who professes to loath dogs and with a special place in Hell for Jasper, who insisted on feeding Jasper a treat. He also insisted on washing him clean with gentle, careful hands, although as he soaped up the little scrap, he couldn't seem to decide whether Jasper was a good and brave boy or an evil little git who deserved to be muzzled and tied to a post for the rest of his stay.

"I think we deserve this."

I look up to see James come in, carrying a tray. I can already smell it, the aroma of rich hot chocolate. There's also the remains of the Victoria sandwich cake I made just yesterday, oozing strawberry jam and buttercream.

"I thought we should finish it off because it'd be a shame for it to go stale." James gives me a big grin. We both know that's not going to happen because as soon as I make a cake it's gone not within days but hours. "He looks like he's recovered from his ordeal," James nods over at Jasper, who's sleeping, snuffling and snorting, lost in his doggy dreams. Jasper twitches and yelps, and it jerks him awake. His head shoots up and he looks around and I can't help but smile as he gives himself a little shake and settles once more — and farts.

"Jesus," James rasps, his face scrunching up. "That bloody dog may have recovered, but I'm not sure my sense of smell ever will. I think the inside of my nose has been burnt."

It's all noise and fuss, because he doesn't banish Jasper

to the utility room, or even the kitchen, and I smile into my mug of steaming, sweet chocolate.

"No, you have it," I say, when James goes to place a slice of cake on a plate for me. He doesn't argue as he bites into the sponge and gives a deep and satisfying groan.

"You really should make these when you set yourself up," he says between mouthfuls.

"Victoria sponge? It's not really a celebration cake."

"I'll celebrate it. It's bloody fantastic." He attacks what's left.

I know I should be pleased he likes it, but it's a stark reminder I'm making plans to leave. A gust of wind, heavier and harder than before, rattles the windows, and the hot chocolate that a moment ago tasted so rich and creamy is now thin and bitter.

"I think we deserve to get a takeaway for dinner." James puts his crumb covered plate down next to his mug on the coffee table.

"You've just had cake."

"I needed something quickly to revive my strength after our ordeal, courtesy of the animal."

"I'm happy to cook." I go to stand up but his hand wraps around my wrist. Gently but firmly, he pulls me back. He doesn't let me go and I don't try to pull away.

"I know that part of our arrangement is that you look after the food, but not today."

We're sitting close enough for me to feel the warmth of his breath, laced with chocolate and vanilla. He's smiling, and his eyes, moss green and flecked with gold, are locked on mine. His grip around my wrist slackens, but just a little, and he must be able to feel my speeding, out of control pulse, because it's booming all the way through me.

"And I'm glad you do because I've not eaten so well for — well I don't know for how long. But I don't expect you to do it every night, and I certainly don't expect you to do it now, not after the last few hours we've had."

He's still holding my wrist as he holds my gaze.

"But I like doing it."

He smiles. "And I like that you like it, more than you know, but you're not my cook and housekeeper, although there's definitely an opening if you ever decide to revise your plans." He smirks, making sure I know it's the joke he means it to be. "And this is on me. No arguments."

He lets go of my wrist and jumps up from the sofa, and without thinking I trail my fingers over the place where his have been.

"But—"

"I said no."

He's looking down at me and although he's smiling there's hard resolution in his direct gaze, telling me that any arguments from me will be brushed away. But it doesn't stop me from trying.

"And I say yes. You let me stay here for not much more than a few quid, and you insist on buying virtually all the groceries—"

"I have a weekly delivery set up from Waitrose. I see no reason to change it."

"That's not the point."

I stand up and placing my hands on my hips, I look him in the eye.

"So what *is* your point?"

I huff. I think my point is very clear, but it's obviously not.

"Look, you're only charging me chicken feed to be here—"

"I don't want you to pay me a damn penny for anything, but you insist, you stubborn little bugger."

My jaw drops open. Stubborn? I've never been that. Too pliable, too willing to agree and say yes, too eager to please to ever be called stubborn.

"I want to buy you dinner." James' voice drops, his tone almost caressing and I shiver as his words curl around me. "It might only be a takeaway, but it's still dinner. So why not indulge me and let me do that for you, eh?"

Because every little thing you do for me weakens my resolve to reset my life, making it harder to leave...

"Thank you." He's giving me no choice.

"Then that's settled. We are, as they say, on the same page."

I've never felt more unsettled in my life, and the pages are turning too fast for me to read.

"Thai Me Up?"

"What?" I jump. My legs almost buckle, and my face heats... *No. Yes. Maybe...*

"Thai Me Up. It's new, not too far from here, and Elliot says it's very good." He's grinning at me, reading my mind, and my face throbs out another blast of heat. Just like my dick. Thank fuck I'm wearing loose trackie bottoms, and an oversized and long sweatshirt.

"Yes, that'd be great. Yeah I like Thai, it's really nice."

"It is. And so much better than being *tied* up. All that chaffing, it's not good."

He gives me a wink and a lopsided smile, and goes to

171

find his phone, leaving me to collapse back down on the sofa.

When he comes back he sits next to me and opens up the menu. My face isn't quite so hot and my dick's calming down as James and I weigh up the choices, but I make sure my sweatshirt's pulled down as far as I can. James places the orders and I have no idea what's going to turn up.

Mumbling that I need to go to the loo, I rush off. Ramming the lock home I fall back against the door, breathing hard. I stare down at my crotch. My dick, at last, is behaving itself, so at least that's one thing sorted as I don't want to be handling a red curry or whatever it is we've ordered when I have something else that's demanding a handling of its own.

I take a look at my reflection in the mirror over the sink, and groan. My cheeks would make a pickled beetroot look anaemic. Turning on the tap, I let the water run until it's really cold before I scoop up handfuls and splash it over my face until some of the heat starts to fade.

The food arrives soon after, and we eat in the kitchen, the heart of the house. Piled up in front of us on the blond wood table, this isn't just a takeaway, it's a feast, and my stomach rumbles. I'm more hungry than I thought and James laughs.

We're about to dig in when his phone pings with a text message.

"It's Elliot, asking about Jasper. The man's in Paris with his gorgeous fiancé for three days. You think he'd have more on his mind than his farty little dog." His eyes snap up at me. "Do you think I should tell him I almost lost my life, scrabbling around in a filthy muddy pond because his daft dog decided to run off?" There's a mischievous tilt to his smile and challenge in his eyes.

"Oh God, no, don't do that. Just tell him that he's been a good boy."

James snorts. "He'd instantly be suspicious and will probably end up telephoning me even though he's supposed to be getting down and dir— enjoying the cultural activities of one of the world's great cities. No. I'll tell him exactly what he expects to hear from me."

"What have you told him?" I say as I dish the food up for both of us.

"Oh, that we locked Jasper in the cellar to tenderise for a couple of hours, before cooking him with fresh seasonal vegetables. And roast potatoes. And with a good rich gravy." He says the words casually with a straight face.

"No, you can't say — that's—"

"Incredibly evil of me? Cruel and unfeeling? Especially as I know how fond both Elliot and Freddie are of that farting little bugger?"

"He's not *that* farty." But he is. James grins as his phone pings a reply.

"'I would expect nothing less from you, James,'" he reads out. "'I hope you enjoy a good burgundy with him, and don't forget to use toothpicks to remove the fur from between your teeth. It's very wiry.'" James barks out a laugh, shaking his head as he turns off his phone. "Lucky sod's getting a few days away," he says, as he digs into his food. "I can't remember the last time I had a break from work. It feels like forever."

"I know what you mean, I'd love to take a bit of time out." I fork up some noodles and stare at them. "Have you been to the cottage in Love's Harbour?" I ask, referring to

Elliot and Freddie's Devonshire hideaway. James is Elliot's best friend, so of course he has, making my question redundant, I suppose — which is why it's a shock when he shakes his head. "You really haven't? It's a lovely place, it feels like such a haven."

"He says I can go down there whenever I want but I never seem to have the time, but to be honest a cramped cottage in a Devonshire seaside village isn't really my idea of a good time. Although it's very beautiful in that part of the world," he concedes. "It's where Jack comes from," he adds.

Jack, James' baking friend.

"Really? He doesn't have a West Country accent."

James huffs out a short laugh. "Of course he doesn't. Expensive private schooling tends to see to that. His family's been in a twee little village called Polton Lacy for centuries, but none of them have a hint of Devonian. I got to know his brother George, first, and then the rest of the family. You've been down to the cottage, haven't you?"

I nod. "Yes, and it isn't cramped. It's actually bigger than it looks and also they've had the loft extended so there's plenty of room. You should take up his offer and go down there, especially if you need a short break. All that sea air's very rejuvenating."

"Hmm. I get a rash if I move too far from London. Besides, it'd be like staying in self-catering accommodation when full on, five-star luxury is more my thing. And anyway I'd just be going on my own which wouldn't be much fun."

His last words surprise me, and I'm sure I see his shoulders sag a little. A man like James could easily find somebody to spend a weekend with him.

Me. I'd spend a weekend with you there…

Some hope of that happening. Whatever my relationship is with James, I'm pretty sure it doesn't include weekend mini-breaks in cosy cottages.

Aiden, suddenly and vividly, fills my head. Tall, handsome Aiden, who knows way more about James than I ever will. I bite down hard on my noodles as I bite down on my jealousy, harder and way more indigestible.

"I'd jump at the chance to go down there again." Which is unlikely to happen, as there's no reason for it now the cottage is all set up.

"Why did you go down?"

"To take deliveries. For furniture, and things like that. I've been there three times, all in the first months after they bought the place. I was more than happy to go. I even had Jasper with me on one visit." I grin at James across the table.

"No drama? No Brillo pad dog getting lost at sea or into fights with the gulls and other locals?" His smile's broad and his eyes are glittering.

"Nothing so daring. We went out for local walks. I don't think Jasper likes the sea very much, but he certainly liked the little morsels of fish and chips I gave him."

"And these working trips to the cottage, they're the only breaks you've had in recent months?"

I nod. "Me and Grant, we were meant to be going away earlier in the year, but it never happened." I shrug. James is looking at me and waiting for me to finish. "Out of nowhere, he decided he was going to go away with his footballing friends instead. He was away for two weeks, on a football tour. Or that's what he told me. I didn't

175

believe a word of it but by that time it was easier than arguing."

Since I've been living in James' house I've barely thought of Grant. He seems like ancient history and I find I can talk about him and feel nothing. Not even humiliation for the way he treated me. I guess that's some kind of progress.

"Well, you look like you could do with a few days away if you don't mind me saying. You certainly look better now than when you first arrived here, but after everything you've been through recently some sort of break is in order I would have thought, even if you do like the sound of a clapped out English seaside town."

"Then it's clear you really haven't been to Love's Harbour. It's beautiful, and if Elliot offers me the chance to go there again, I'll grab it with both hands."

"What, you'd rush down there and leave me to do what? Cook my own dinner?" He says, his lips twitching.

Or you can come with me. We could take walks along the beach and afterward sit in one of many cosy little pubs... But of course I don't say that. It's a stupid thought because I have no doubt at all that James is what he says he is, a five-star luxury man.

He's right, though, about getting away, even if it's only for a weekend... Maybe I could go and visit my parents and soak up some Spanish sun? Much as I love them, it's not my idea of a quiet and relaxing getaway, and I put the idea aside.

We finish eating and James makes coffee and we take it through to the living room. Jasper's snoring quietly on his cushion. The flame in the wood burner has grown smaller but the room is still deliciously warm and the air's tinged with the slight tang of applewood. We both flop onto the sofa, full to the brim with Thai food.

"I could put the TV on, stream a film, or put some music —"

"Let's see what's on. If there's nothing much — *oh fuck*."

Jerking forward, I grab my leg. Out of nowhere, cramp tears down my calf and into my foot, clenching up my toes. The fiery pain's excruciating and I hiss through my clenched teeth as I try to massage the rock hard muscles. This is a rare but bad attack and I can feel the tears prickling the back of my eyes.

I gasp as James manoeuvres me so my leg's straight out. He shoves up the loose leg of my track suit bottoms, to my midthigh.

"Cramp, it's bloody painful. One of the ways of keeping it at bay is to drink plenty of water."

He digs his thumbs into my calf, and I scream. It's a high pitched, undignified sound, but I don't care. In some dim piece of my brain, I'm vaguely aware of Jasper jumping up and joining in with a howl.

"Arrrhhgg, oh fuck, no." I screw my eyes closed as I try to pull my leg away, but James' grip is like iron.

"Pain before pleasure. I'm going to massage out the knot. And stop howling. Between you and that bloody animal, it sounds like a badly made werewolf film in here."

He runs his thumbs hard along the muscle. It's agony and I can't even begin to answer him back. I screw my eyes closed even tighter. The pain eases a touch, and my calf muscle begins to soften. I prise my eyes open.

James is on his knees in front of me. His salt and

pepper hair, a little longer on the top, has flopped forward over his brow. His lips are set in a grim line as he pushes, squeezes, and kneads into my flesh. He's resolute and determined, all his concentration on me. I swallow, and he looks up.

The dark green of his eyes is eaten up by the black, dilated pupils. They laser into mine. My breath jerks and I can't look away. His hands, hot on my leg, have become a soft caress.

"Better?" His voice is rough and ragged.

"Getting there," I rasp.

"The arch of your foot's still hard. Needs some attention." He drifts a finger across the knotted muscle.

I jump as pain flares through the arch.

James tilts his head to the side. "Give me a chance to make everything better for you, Perry." His voice is deep and seductive, little more than a purr.

Make everything better... Oh, God, yes please...

James smiles and shifts up to the sofa, easing my leg across his lap. The cramp has drained from my calf, and settled into my foot.

"Pressure points," he says, as he works his thumbs over the hard ridge of my arch.

I hiss, but almost immediately the burn begins to ease. James' hands are skilled and talented, but I never ever thought it would be otherwise.

Pressure points. I've certainly got a pressure point in one particular muscle that's got nothing to do with cramp. James' touch is sure and deft and he clearly knows what he's doing. The pain's morphed into something intensely relaxing and I groan, this time from pleasure rather than pain.

"Where did you—?"

"Just lay back and close your eyes."

It's an order but a gentle one, and I'm more than happy to obey. And that's exactly what I do as I settle into the cushions and let my eyes drift close, as I give myself up to James' touch.

There's not the faintest echo of the pain that'd almost brought tears to my eyes. Instead, it's been replaced by a calm and loose relaxation that's been missing for so long I'd forgotten how that could feel. And it feels good, but what feels even better is a soft brush of something warm against my cheek. Instinct and a need for more has me pushing my face into the touch.

"Perry?" James' voice. It sounds distant yet close. "Time to wake up." I don't want to wake up, and be dragged out of this warm, fuzzy place I'm in. I mutter, and his laughter trickles over me. "Time to surface. Come on."

My eyes, acting to a will of their own, drag themselves open. James is looking down at me, his smile soft and indulgent.

"You went into a deep sleep, but I knew you would. Pressure points, you see."

Pressure points. My own pressure point is now not so… pressured. At least it means I can stand without embarrassing myself. I go to push myself up and, unsteady on my legs, I wobble, but I'm caught in James' strong arms.

"Careful," he murmurs. "It's quite normal to feel a bit shaky." He's holding me tight and close, and makes no move to let me go, just like I don't make a move to step back. Because I don't want to step back from this man. I try to move in closer, but his arms hold me still.

"Let's get you to bed."

I giggle. I know that's exactly what I'm doing but I can't stop. I feel drunk when I haven't touched a drop of alcohol, and the words are out of my mouth before I can stop them.

"Yes please."

I see something in his face, something that pierces my fogged-up brain, but as nebulous as smoke it's gone before I can catch it. My head's heavy, slow and foggy and it's hard to think or at least to think straight. Maybe I should feel mortified, maybe I should apologise. I seem to have a habit of drunk flirting with him, even though this time I'm not drunk.

"Sorry, only joking. Not that it was a very funny joke," I mutter. He doesn't answer, only gives me another of his guarded, unreadable smiles. "Yeah, best I go to bed. What a day. I feel kind of drunk, must be all those pressure points you… pressured."

James' hold on me has slackened, and I turn to go but I'm still unsteady on my feet, and once again he catches me.

His low, chuckling laugh is electricity sparking through my nerves.

"I don't think you're in any fit state to get yourself upstairs on your own, do you?"

"No, I'm okay. I think. If I take my time, I can—" The wind's knocked out of me as James sweeps me up in his arms — and throws me over his shoulder like a sack of spuds. "What? What are you doing?" I wriggle in an attempt to get him to put me down but a sharp smack on my bum makes me gasp.

"You can barely stand up unaided, let alone climb the stairs. For Christ's sake, stop fidgeting otherwise I'll drop you. This is the quickest and easiest way to get you upstairs to bed."

"Stop being a twat and put me down. The caveman approach is so yesterday." Although if the caveman's James, I'm sure it's one I could get used to.

He snorts, taking no notice of me.

The fog swirling around in my brain has mostly cleared, thanks to the stinging slap. He could put me down, and this time I'd be steady as a rock. I'm not going to tell him that, not when my face is almost bobbing against his arse as he makes his way up. For a moment I wonder which bedroom he's going to take me to, and I don't want to examine too closely if the little lurch deep in my chest is disappointment or a kind of dull relief when he turns in the direction of my room when we reach the landing.

He toes the door open and puts me down on the bed. I stare up at him, not quite believing what's just happened as he stares down at me through hungry looking eyes. My heart rate picks up and the muscles in my stomach tighten. I open my mouth to say something, anything, but all there is is a strangled noise that sounds worryingly like Jasper.

"Good night, Perry. Sleep tight."

"James…?"

But he's gone. I'm not sure what I was going to say. *Stay here with me? Let me come with you?* The words are best unsaid, of course they are, but as I stare up at the ceiling I'm not sure if I believe that.

CHAPTER TWENTY-ONE

JAMES

"I've had to have my house fumigated. I'm sure I've got fleas. And a rash somewhere I shouldn't have a rash."

"My dog doesn't stink and he doesn't have fleas. If you have a rash somewhere you shouldn't, then the least said about that the better."

Elliot's voice on the other end of the phone is as calm and measured as always, and I grin.

"I won't charge you for the men in hazmat suits, nor for the industrial sized pot of flea powder. We won't mention the ointment I've been forced to apply three times a day. As I've already told you, you owe me for the trauma of having your dog in my house."

"His name's Jasper." Elliot's sigh is exaggerated, bordering dramatic, and my grin stretches wider. "And here was me thinking you were happy to do a good friend a favour in his hour of need."

"And I was, which now means you can do me a favour in return. Well, technically it's two favours. I want to take you up on your offer of using the cottage, for a long weekend—"

"That's no problem at all, I've always said we're more than happy for you to use it. I have to be honest and say I'm a little disappointed you've not already been down."

A tinge of hurt colours Elliot's words. The truth is, it's not that I've not wanted to go, but I've always had the invite to go with him and Freddie, and I wasn't sure I had the strength to witness their lovefest. Being a gooseberry's never been my style.

"Whenever you suggested it, it's never been the right time. But the right time is the weekend after next — if you and Freddie aren't using it of course."

"I don't know why you wouldn't want to come down with Freddie and me... Hold on..."

I've already taken the time from work. Official time, with lines through diaries. No appointments, no interruptions. I'm not sure when the last time was I did that. It sends a ripple of excitement through my belly, but it's not the only reason.

"That's absolutely fine. In fact, due to various commitments we have, we won't be going down for the next month. But you said you had two favours to ask?"

Ah, this is potentially the trickier bit. I lick my lips, finding them drier than they should be.

"I want you to give Perry a couple of days off, either side of the weekend."

The silence stretches out like chewing gum. Telling

him I want to take Perry is provoking all sorts of questions. I can almost hear the wheels turning.

"Are you sure that's wise?"

"It's a long weekend, Elliot. I can do with the break, and so can he. Perry's waxed lyrical about your little love nest—" I wince, relieved my friend can't see me. It's a bitchy bite back to his question because going away for the weekend with Perry is, indeed, anything but wise. "He said it's lovely, and like you say, I've not been down yet." My words sound as limp as wet lettuce.

"Has he started looking for a place yet? I keep meaning to ask him, because I'd want to have a good handover with the new person."

Elliot's words both rattle and rile me.

"Yes, but he's not having much luck." If Elliot can hear the *thank God for that* in my voice, he doesn't say anything. "I've suggested concentrating his efforts after Christmas would likely yield better results. There'll be more on the market."

"Maybe there will, but it's good he's already got moving, seeing as he's made his decision. There's no point in him dragging his feet. Best for him, but for you too."

"Why best for me?"

Another silence, followed by a small breath. I clutch my mobile tighter to my ear, as I wait for Elliot to speak.

"James, you know why. He's fond of you, that's easy enough to see. And you are of him. Don't even attempt to deny it."

"Fond. Such a quaint word. I like him, he's become my friend and I've become his." I'm being evasive, my response flippant.

Fond? More than fond, so much more…

My lips are so arid they could crack, and I sweep them with a tongue that's as dry as old leather.

"Then just make sure you keep it at friends, because anything else would be dangerous." Elliot's words are as steady and level as the man himself.

"There's nothing to be concerned about, because we're—"

"I'm not talking about Perry. It's you who's in the most danger."

Elliot's words all but floor me. My grip on my phone almost breaks my fingers and I force myself to relax.

"I'm not in any danger, I can assure you. Or not the sort of danger you're alluding to."

My throat closes up, making it hard to speak. Elliot's words have pierced me to the bone, and drawn blood.

"You've no need to be concerned about me. I've been there and I've got the T-shirt, as they say. You've known me long enough to know that beneath my soft and fluffy exterior, I have a heart of stone and a severe allergic reaction to emotional attachments. Anyway," I say, desperate to navigate my way out of the perilous waters I've found myself in, "if you now have second thoughts about the cottage, I understand."

"Of course you can stay there, you little runt."

Runt. James' less than complimentary nickname for me, he's called me that since we were at school together. I let out a soft breath. Elliot's still my friend.

"He's not said anything to me about time off. Is he aware you're doing this?"

"No, but I know how much he enjoyed staying at the cottage and in Love's Harbour. I want to surprise him."

Whatever Elliot thinks of that he keeps to himself, and I'm grateful for it.

"If you want to keep the surprise you can tell him yourself he's got the time off. I'll text you arrangements, how to get the key we keep down there, and so on…"

We talk for a little while longer before we ring off.

A few days away, just Perry and me, I can't help but feel the thrill of anticipation. I'm excited by the thought of it and only hope he will be too. The niggles and doubts about whether or not I've done the right thing are shoved aside, because in all honesty I don't know. But there's one thing I do, and that's that I can't wait to tell him when he gets home this evening.

"I spoke to Elliot earlier."

I pour us both another glass of wine. We're in the garden under bright but chilly early evening sunshine, the bad weather of the last few days behind us.

"There were no concerns over Jasper, were there?" A shadow of worry crosses over Perry's face. I'm determined to wipe it away.

"Not at all, but I did tell him that as we did him a big favour he needs to do one for us in return. Next weekend, the cottage is free and it's ours if we want it. Well, actually Friday to Monday, so a long weekend."

Perry's looking at me with wide, surprised eyes and my breath catches in my throat because I hope he wants it, I really do hope. His smile's the answer I'm looking for. Slowly and quietly I let go of the breath I'm holding, and the tension in my shoulders I didn't even know was there relaxes.

"Really? You and me? Is he okay with that? I mean, he's my boss... But I have to check I can take the time off."

"Elliot's fine with the both of us going down there." It's not totally true, but that's for me to keep to myself. "I've already cleared it with him, so next Friday and the following Monday you're not at work. Nor is it coming out of your leave, because—" I hold up my hand to stop the protest I can see forming on his lips. "Because you did him a big favour at the last minute and Elliot understands that. I didn't have to persuade him into granting free leave if that's what you're worried about."

"It's never a problem looking after Jasper, he's adorable, so Elliot didn't need to—"

"Yes, he did. And he has. He owes you for looking after the poo end of things, and me for saving the ugly little mutt's life even though he doesn't, and won't, know about that. So, do you want to go or not?"

I'm going to look an idiot if he says no, but that fear's blown away by Perry's sunshine-filled smile.

"God, yes. Of course I want to go. And thank you, for thinking of it," he says, his smile now tinged with a hint of self-consciousness, but it lasts only seconds as his smile turns mischievous. "But how will you cope, in a cramped cottage in a clapped-out English seaside town? Will we have to engage the services of a butler to attend your every need, wish and desire? Somebody to lay a choccie on your pillow? And what about the five-star luxury spa treatments? Perhaps we can arrange for the technician from the nail bar to come and give you a mani-pedi? She's a lovely lady who also doubles up as chief fryer in the chippie."

"It will be utter hell. The smelly countryside and the grey English sea are to be endured, not enjoyed. God alone knows where I'll find a decent Americano. I doubt if they've even heard of such a thing. But I'm willing to suffer the privations for your sake. If I keep my head down and don't make eye contact with the locals I should be safe."

It won't be hell, of course it won't, because I'll be with Perry. As for all my needs, wishes, and wants being attended to…

Perry laughs and shakes his head. It warms me more than the fleece jacket I'm wearing, or the alcohol from the rich red wine and I know without any doubt I've made the right decision.

CHAPTER TWENTY-TWO

JAMES

It's barely past midday by the time we reach Love's Harbour on the South Devon coast and to my surprise, even though I don't admit it to Perry, I'm instantly charmed by both the place and the cottage.

The whitewashed former fisherman's cottage, at the end of a pretty and quiet lane, is simply and tastefully decorated. It's bright and airy and there are lots of warm personal touches, including framed photographs of Elliot and Freddie looking happy and content and sickeningly in love.

I get everything in from the car leaving Perry to get the boiler going and more importantly the kettle on. Once everything's inside I push the door closed on a bright but cold day.

"I can't believe I'm back here." Perry hands me a cup

of tea. "But more than that, I can't believe you've not been down before now. I'll give you the tour in a moment, but in the meantime we can have some of these."

Perry gives me an impish grin as he rips open a packet of chocolate biscuits.

"Did your mother never tell you that snacks would spoil your lunch?"

"Frequently, but I never listened to much she said." He laughs before he chomps on a biscuit and raises his brow as I take one too.

The plan is to get ourselves sorted out before we hotfoot it to the local pub. This is a short holiday and holidays mean eating out. I'm not allowing Perry to cook a thing, even though I know he'll try.

Outside the wind's picked up and the squawk of gulls fill the air. When I told Perry I'm all for five-star luxury I wasn't exaggerating, but I'm excited about being here. All my holidays for as long as I can remember have been somewhere hot and exotic except of course for skiing. I always go alone, but I'm never alone for long and certainly never alone in my bed. But this, this is so different, and I know it's all because of the young man sitting next to me on the sofa.

It's you who's in the most danger... Elliot's words, from the other day, slam into me as I gaze at Perry.

Of course I'm in danger. I'm in more danger than I've ever been, and I don't want to do a thing about it—

"There are some really nice cafés down on the harbour and some great old pubs as well—"

"What?" I say, jolted out of my daydream. "Yes, you said."

"Don't worry, I'll do the ordering so you don't have to

make any kind of contact with the locals. I'll keep you safe." He smirks before he bites on another biscuit, his fourth or fifth.

A crumb clings to his lower lip and I look away quickly when it's swept up on the tip of his pink tongue. I clear my throat, and take a swig of tea.

"Shit!" It's scalding and my eyes water. "I've taken the skin off the roof of my mouth. I need emergency surgery, there's only bare bone left," I splutter. If I'm hoping for sympathy, I'm soon disappointed.

"A pint of the local beer will soon anaesthetise you. Rat's Arse is a well known cure-all. Legend has it it's what saved the locals during the Great Plague, so I'm sure it'll sooth your internal burns."

"You're not in the least bit sympathetic, are you?" I poke my tongue at the tender flesh on the roof of my mouth; it's stinging slightly, but that's all.

No need for emergency surgery, then. Maybe a kiss would sooth it... Christ, how am I expected to get through the next couple or so days intact?

Perry cocks his head to the side and makes a show of thinking.

"No."

"Then I may as well take solace in another biscuit." I nab the rapidly dwindling packet out of his hand. "Why's it called Rat's Arse?" Although I can guess.

"Because it's strong and just a couple of pints will make you as pissed as a rodent's behind. The villagers probably couldn't have given two hoots about death and disease once they'd got a bellyful of the stuff. It's also revolting, and I fully intend to stick with wine."

He grabs the packet back, riffles for another biscuit, and holds what's left of them out of arm's reach.

A minute or two later we're collecting our luggage and making our way up the narrow flight of stairs.

"There are two bedrooms on this floor." Perry looks at me over his shoulder just as we reach the landing. "There's the original master bedroom and one that's only slightly smaller directly opposite, but they've had the loft conversion done making it into a big bedroom with an en-suite. That's now Elliot and Freddie's room."

We stop short of the new set of stairs heading up towards the loft and instead stand in the narrow hallway between the open doors of the two bedrooms. Two double bedrooms, one opposite the other. At home, our rooms are either side of the house, but here, in the much smaller cottage, the rooms are so close I'll be able to hear Perry's every breath, every sigh, every movement that comes from the bed taking up pride of place.

It's going to be agony.

"Take your pick, I really don't mind which one I have." My voice is loud in the narrow hallway and somehow overly hearty. *Jesus Christ. Am I nervous?* When was the last time a man made me jangle with nerves?

"Oh I don't mind, this one will do. This is where I've always slept when I've been down before."

He twists around me and heads into the room that's decorated in exactly the same pale shades as the room I'll be taking, and which looks out over the small but pretty back garden and up towards the hills that rise above the village.

"Shall we get sorted out and then head off to lunch

somewhere?" Perry's face is bright pink, and he's looking everywhere but at me. His nervousness settles mine.

"Are you sure, after all those biscuits you've just pigged out on?"

I smile and quirk my brow, wanting to put him at his ease.

"They were my starter, and anyway, you made us leave before breakfast." He pouts but it doesn't stop the smile twitching the corners of this lips.

The little moment of awkwardness is gone, but with the two of us in such close quarters, I can't be certain it'll be the last.

CHAPTER TWENTY-THREE

PERRY

"The views are amazing." James stands on the crown of the hill we've just climbed up. Or, maybe I should say the hill he all but sprinted up as I staggered and huffed and puffed behind him.

Our long and leisurely pub lunch ended up turning into a quick sandwich because the bright sunshine and the buffeting wind were irresistible and we were both eager to get out and make the most of them.

James plants his fists on his hips. Looking out over the majestic scenery, he's like a king surveying his kingdom. He's as fresh as a daisy but all I'm interested in is laying on my back to stare up at the sky whilst I try to recover.

As James breathes in the natural beauty, I surreptitiously remove the chocolate bar I've hidden away in the deep pocket of my fleece jacket. He won't hear the crinkle of the wrapper over the wind, and I might be able to eat it all before he's had his fill of natural beauty. Maybe it's a mean thought, but it's chocolate so I don't care.

I push myself to sitting and join James in looking out over the landscape. He's right, it is amazing, but it's not the only thing that is.

With his back to me, I suck on the chocolate so that it melts in my mouth. I know it's a disgusting habit, but I still do it anyway, as I ogle James. I can't help it. In his lycra running gear, clinging to every hard muscle, he's even more mouthwatering than the chocolate melting on my tongue.

In a smooth move he slings his arms upwards and reaches high into the sky, but it's the bend that follows, his arse sticking out and canting upwards as he stretches first one leg out in front of him, bending with smooth ease towards his foot, then swapping to the other. There's a strangled whine I could try and tell myself is coming from a nearby upland animal, but I know it's really from me. Strong but lithe, his muscles hard and defined but not bulky. He's fit, in all senses of the word.

Fit, fabulous, and fuckable.

No—*ooo*... I can't think like that, or there's no way I'm going to get through the weekend without my strength being sapped as all my blood heads straight for my groin, and stubbornly refuses to go elsewhere. As quick as I can, I adjust the growing bulge under my tracksuit bottoms, pulling my hand free just in time as he turns around, the smile on his face broadening when he spots the chocolate bar I'm gripping onto for dear life.

"Tasty?" he says, peeling off his light runner's jacket and dropping it to the ground.

"Ehhggg?" It's all I'm capable of saying. I've long since stopped chewing — or sucking — on it, and it's kind of broken in two under the pressure of my death grip. "Yes," I rasp.

"Good, because it's time to share."

He flops down next to me and without a word plucks the chocolate from my hand and chomps down hard on it before giving me back what's left with a broad wink.

Settling onto his back, James stretches his arms up above his head, holds the pose rigid for a few seconds before he relaxes and releases his muscles on a long, deep sigh.

"I'd forgotten what it sounded like. The countryside, I mean. Up here, you can't hear anything other than the wind and the call of the odd bird. I'm loath to admit it, but it's wonderful."

He's staring up into the bright blue sky, and I think he's more relaxed than I've ever seen him. Warmth spreads through me, and my heart leaps because he's feeling this here, with me. This is a time and a memory that will always be ours, shared with nobody else. He must feel me looking at him because he turns his head and his deep green eyes lock onto mine.

"Wonderful. So, so wonderful."

I can't say a word, I can't move. I can do nothing but stare into his glittering, bewitching eyes. He pushes himself up and edges in closer, placing his palms on my cheeks. Holding me with a gentle steadiness, his gaze roams over my face, drinking me in as though he's seeing me for the first time.

I should ease his hands away. I should move back. I

should shake my head, and say no. James is dangerous because if he takes a kiss, he'll take my heart.

I should ease his hands away, I should move back, I should...

He tilts his head, eyes never leaving my face. They're intent and serious, taking me in as though he's committing me to memory.

"I want to kiss you. I've wanted to kiss you from the first time I set eyes on you," he murmurs, his voice low and gravelly, his eyes still searching my face. "Will you let me? Will you let me kiss you, Perry Buckland?"

He must see the answer in my eyes, as his lips lift into a gentle smile. All thoughts of easing his hands away and moving back scatter to the wind. My eyes drop to a close as my mouth softens and parts, my heart leaping and tumbling as his lips brush mine.

James' kiss is gentle, almost shy and hesitant. It's not what I expect from this confident and assured man, and somehow that gives me the courage to press for more. He reads me, just as he always seems to, and as one we deepen the kiss, the tangle of our tongues sending a shivery tingle dancing down my spine.

Whether I pull him, or he eases me down, we're lying together on the rough grass, our bodies crushing against each other. His arousal's a hard ridge against my hip and I rock into him, the tug on my cock deliciously painful. I scrub my fingers through his hair, cupping the back of his head in my hands, dragging him in closer, wanting to absorb him into me.

Wanting him in me.

The heat I feel for this man, the lust, desire and want, mixed with something softer, is a heady, intoxicating and irresistible brew. I rut hard against him, making it clear what I need.

We break the kiss, desperate for air. I gaze up into his face, the thrill of the kiss rushing through me. James is so close, the waft of his ragged breath rushing across my heated skin.

His pupils are dark, deep depths with only the suggestion of green at their outer edge. His hair's messed and roughed up, his lips puffy and spit smeared, his face flushed. He's so removed from the controlled, sleek man I know and a heady mix of excitement and pride surges through me, because it's *me* who's brought him to this.

Me.

He trails the backs of his fingers across my cheek.

"Chocolate," he murmurs, his lips tilting into a lopsided smile. "Creamy, sweet, rich chocolate kisses, and totally irresistible." He's still smiling, still trailing his fingers across my cheek, still looking at me through dark, dazed eyes.

"Chocolate? It sounds like you've just snogged a Flake."

His answering laugh is low, deep and rough, making my skin goosebump and my cock beg.

"But it's not the chocolate that's irresistible." He shifts in closer, making my heart thunder. "It's you, Perry. You, who could make a sinner of a saint, and a saint of a sinner."

"Which are you?" I edge forward, so close we share the same breath.

James' hand coils around the back of my neck, warm, strong, and sure. He doesn't answer, but I don't care because I don't care about anything other than the dark and desperate kiss that—

Doesn't come.

"Matilda. Blasted, silly animal."

James lurches backwards, leaving the wide open sky above me, before it's filled with the red-gold furry face of an Irish Setter, all lolling tongue and dog breath.

"Sorry about that. The silly thing's just being friendly."

The gruff voice belongs to a ruddy, wrinkled faced old man, just emerging from the brow of the hill.

"Oh, that's okay."

I don't mean a word of it, because it's *not* okay, not in any shape or form or in my wildest dreams. I push myself up to sitting, self-conscious and awkward as I tug my fleece down, wondering what the man, who I really want to shove back down the hill, might have seen.

I shoot a quick glance at James, who's loose and relaxed as he leans back on his elbows, legs crossed at the ankles, his jacket laying across his groin. His hair's been tamed and although there's still a hint of red in his cheeks, it could be put down to the steady breeze. He gives me a quick wink before he focuses on the old man, who's fussing over the dog.

"That's a tough walk, all the way up here from the village," James says, his voice friendly yet at the same time clipped and authoritative. The old man almost stands to attention.

"It certainly is. I come up here as much as I can, which isn't that much anymore — the old legs aren't what they were — but the view makes it worthwhile. Are you visiting the area for the potato festival next week?" He looks from James, to me, and back to James.

"Sorry…" I say, trying not to gawp.

Has he really just said there's a potato festival…?

"It draws the crowds from all four corners of the county. It's a celebration of all the traditional varieties. There's a guess the weight of the potato competition, potato carving demonstrations, and stalls selling potato based products. The local radio station's even going to be sending down a reporter." I swear the old man stands straighter as his chest puffs out with potato filled pride.

"Sadly, no," James says. "Had we known about it we'd have timed our visit better. We're here for a short break, staying at a cottage owned by some friends in Rock Lane."

The old man answers with an approving nod. "Rock Lane, yes, very quiet and away from the hubbub and bustle of the harbour area."

I meet James' eye, the slight raise of his brow forcing me to look away to hide the grin tugging at my lips. Hubbub and bustle are not words that can be used of Love's Harbour.

Except, perhaps, for when the renowned potato festival is in full swing.

James and the old man start chatting, leaving me to gaze out over the village below.

It looks tiny, scattered like pieces of Lego on a green baize cloth. The village is protected by the harbour walls, but out to sea, the wind's whipping up the waves, and I lose myself in the view and my thoughts.

I imagine I can still feel the press of James' lips on mine, and the hard steel of his erection. He wanted me as much as I wanted him, and if the old man hadn't appeared, then maybe, probably… I bring my knees to my chest and bury my face in my arms.

Maybe, probably, and all the complications that would bring. Complications for me, that is, because James likes to lead a very *un*complicated life.

I'm going to have to keep reminding myself that I've a new life to set up, down on the South coast. A new home, a new business, a new start. I can't let *complications* get in the way. But with my face tucked into my arms, my eyes closed, and the heat of my breath a visceral reminder of the heat of James' kiss and the lingering tingle dancing over my lips, that new life doesn't seem quite so sharp and clear anymore.

"Perry? Ready to go?"

James' voice drags my head up. He's standing over me and looking down, a silhouette against the bright blue of the sky. The only sound is the wind, the gulls, and the beat of my heart. The man and his dog have gone.

He says nothing more, just holds out his hand for me to take. It's warm and firm and he pulls me to my feet with ease. James doesn't let go, and I make no attempt to slip free. Instead, I tighten my grip, holding fast as I let him lead me away, leaving the hilltop and all thoughts of complications behind.

CHAPTER TWENTY-FOUR

PERRY

By the time we get back to the cottage the light's beginning to fade, the blue of earlier giving way to pinks and
purples.

We've not said much on the way back. On the hill we
needed to concentrate on our footing, steering clear of
rabbit holes, roots and lumps of hard granite pushing
through the soil, yet even through Love's Harbour's quaint
little streets, we'd still been silent. I'd glanced at James a
few times, my gaze not settling, but nothing about him
gave a clue as to his thoughts over what had happened.

We leave our jackets and boots in the tiny utility room
and make our way to the kitchen. My first reaction is to
put on the kettle, because maybe I need a cup of British
rocket fuel, otherwise known as tea, to pluck up the nerve
to say something, anything, to break the quiet.

"Come here."

James leans against the counter running down one side of the kitchen, feet crossed at the ankles, arms crossed over his chest, head tilted to the side. He's looking at me, smiling his invitation. Putting down the kettle, I go to him, obeying the quiet command, because I can't not.

"I shouldn't have kissed you," he says, unwrapping his arms and trailing his finger over my cheek. I push into him, my response as instinctive as breathing.

"I'm glad you did."

He doesn't say anything as he gazes at me, his eyes unreadable. All I can hear is the steady tick of the wall clock and the unsteady beat of my heart.

"Are you? Honestly?"

His smile softens, becomes almost shy, another side to this man which he keeps hidden away. It gives me the courage to step forward, so close I can feel the heat of his body, breathe in his scent of citrus cologne, blended with the tang of clean sweat and the irresistible aroma of our combined arousal. I wrap my arms around his neck, easing his head down, pressing my body into his.

"Yes, and I want you to do it again."

The kiss is long and deep, edged with a hungry desperation. Wet, hot, sloppy, noisy, our sighs and groans fill the space around us. James slips his hands beneath the waistband of the heavy tracksuit bottoms I'm wearing and I gasp as he clasps me tight, fingers clamped hard to my hips.

I thrust into him, both of us rubbing and rutting, our steel-hard cocks dragging against each other's, all our sighs and groans turning to desperate moans. We're racing towards an edge it's impossible to veer away from, but I know with a clarity that's blinding that I want to plunge in headfirst. All those complications, they've faded and disappeared because this, here and now, is what I crave more than anything in the world.

"Is this what you want? Truly and honestly, is it?"

He's letting me decide what will happen next. He's giving me the power to say yes or no when so many others have taken what they want from me without a second thought. If I step back, he'll accept my decision.

I don't want to step back.

"It is. It's what I've always wanted. I think you're who I've always wanted."

"Even when I teased you?"

"*Especially* when you teased me."

His laugher gathers strength and pace, exploding from him as he throws back his head, filling the kitchen, the whole cottage, with its richness.

"Oh, Perry, Perry, Perry," he says, the laughter dying on his lips and from his eyes, as his smile turns wicked and his eyes darken. "I'm going to show you what it's really like to be teased."

James grabs my hand, pulling me through the kitchen, and up the stairs towards the bedroom.

In the bedroom, his room and the one that is now ours, James smiles into my eyes as he pushes away my fringe that's flopped over my brow.

"You're nervous, and you've no need to be. Not of me."

I am, he's right about that, and I don't want to be, but—

"Of course I am," I blurt. "Because this only happens in films and books, where you end up with the person you've always, erm, always had a…" I groan, and let my head fall forward from the weight of my embarrassment.

James tilts my head up. His face is split in two by a wide grin, but his eyes are soft.

"You mean a crush? You've had a crush? On *me?*"

"Maybe," I mumble. "All that teasing…" I sigh as he kisses me, as soft as silk.

His hands slip to my hips, where they come to rest, his touch light but anchoring as he trails a line of kisses down my neck. My sigh turns to a whimper, and I arch into him.

With one hand, he tugs at the drawstring of my track-suit bottoms.

"Think these might need to come off. What do you think?"

His voice is low with a hint of gravel, and my cock which in its nervousness at this turn of events has softened to half-mast, fills and thickens and twitches its agreement. I nod, hard and fast, like this is my first time. My shaky fingers tussle with the tie, all it should be is a quick tug for them to fall to the floor, but I'm making a hash of it. I can't even get undressed, and my cheeks burn because he must think I'm a young and clueless fool.

James eases my fingers away, and a second later, my tracksuit bottoms lay in a heap at my feet. He unbuttons the shirt I'm wearing, slowly, until it falls open. Pushing it from my shoulders, it too slides to the floor.

He steps away from me, and it's impossible to see the expression on his face as the room's in shadow. My heart hitches, and the fear along with the crushing, suffocating disappointment grabs hold of me that he's changed his mind, that this isn't a good idea, that I'm too jittery, too clumsy, too—

"Perry, there's no need to be nervous. Not with me. But, if this suddenly feels like too much, or you're unsure—"

"No. I mean, I am sure, but yeah, I am nervous." *Nervous I'll disappoint you, that I'll fall short of the kind of men a man like you would be used to.*

"I'll settle them for you. Let me take care of you." *Take care of me…*

No man has ever done that before, and the thought is intoxicating. My cock, which has had another attack of nerves of its own, has again found its courage as it presses hard against the restraints of my boxer briefs. I strip off the rest of my clothes and with James' promise ringing in my ears, I stand naked before him.

"Christ, you're beautiful." James' voice is little more than a croak.

He's trying to put me at my ease, I know that's what it is, because I'm not the word he's just called me. I know I'm not. Nobody has ever called me that, but for now, here, in this room that is stripes of hard shadow and soft fading light shining through the partially closed wooden blinds, I'm ready to believe.

"Get into bed," he says, his voice rough and edged with need.

He strips off quickly, discarding the layers of body hugging Lycra that leave me all but drooling everytime I see him in them, and he climbs in with me. I can feel his heat, hear his breath, smell the tang of not just his but my arousal too. Again, my nerves take over because the two of us like this, in bed together, me and *James*... I've dreamed about it, wanted it, even stroked myself into sweaty climaxes over it, but never, ever thought... All I can do is lie here, as jittery and clueless as I was when it was my first time.

The room's warm, or maybe it's me, and the light as air duvet slips to the floor as James pushes it away.

"I'm sorry," I croak.

"Sorry for what?"

"For being so—so awkward and stiff—"

He laughs. "I like you being stiff. Stiff is good." He looks at my cock, lying against my belly, which does a little twitch under his gaze.

"You're not awkward, just a little nervy, but believe me when I say you've no need to be. Like I said, I want to take care of you, but I want to do that how you want it. Which means we can just kiss, touch, explore each other. We can do whatever you want Perry, no more, no less."

The kiss he places on my lips is affirmation of his words. I sigh and chase his kiss with my own, as his fingers, so soft, deft, and sure, trail from my face, to my neck, and over my chest, brushing across my nipples, which fizz with electricity. He's read me right, the way he so often seems to. This is what I want, the sensuality of touch, of caress after caress. I want him, us, to take time.

James' kisses follow the meander of his fingers over my heated, tingling skin. His kisses and tiny licks and nips tremble on the edge of pain.

"Oh God," I gasp, as his mouth covers one of my nipples.

He chuckles, the sound low, deep, and dark, shooting

vibrations through my body, making my cock dance and my back arch upwards. Every part of me shudders and shakes as he sucks hard, teasing one nub and then the next into a long stretch before sucking it back into the wet heat of his mouth.

The bedroom's hot, the air filled with the sound of sucking and desperate breathy groans, my groans, as I scrub my fingers through his hair and gasp for more.

The whimpering sound that can only come from me fills the room as James' lips leave behind my throbbing nipples as they wander, taking their time to move towards the pulsing heat between my legs.

I spread myself wide, demanding, wanton, craving his mouth on me.

"Beautiful Perry. So fucking beautiful," James whispers, the heat of his breath washing over my throbbing, heavy, aching cock.

Beautiful. That word again, filling my cock as it fills my heart.

I groan as he takes me in his hand, his palm encircling my shaft, and I push up into his fist, not a leisurely push and slide, but jerky and impatient. Slow and leisurely, taking our time, has morphed into a desperate hunger that's demanding to be fed.

But James doesn't want to feed me yet as once more he gives me that dark chuckle.

"We'll get there, but not on the motorway. We're taking the scenic route."

"You bast—*ahhh!*"

His tongue laves across my engorged and straining cockhead, knocking all words and sense from me.

Kisses, sucks, long wide licks from the base to the tip,

again and again and again. With his other hand, he rolls and massages my balls and I jerk and cry out as he swipes a finger across my perineum, hurtling me towards the edge, pulling me back with a firm grip on the base of my cock.

"Not yet, baby, not yet. Scenic route, remember," he says, his voice muffled as he pushes his face into my groin, and breathes in deep.

I thrust my hips forward.

"Don't want any more side roads, so get on the fucking motorway now. And no stopping at services stations."

Between my legs, his shoulders shake as laughter bubbles out of him, and in the moonlight and shadows, I join in.

"Greedy, demanding boy."

He knocks the laughter from me as he buries my cock deep in his mouth.

"Jesus fucking Christ." The words explode out of me.

He's taken me not just onto the motorway, but into the fast lane.

Sucking hard and fast, his tongue dances over the head of my cock and around the rim. The wet slap of his mouth on me mixes with my cries, gasps and garbled words demanding *more, harder, faster*. The head of my cock nudges against the soft covered hardness of the back of his throat, and his answering hum is an electrical overload shooting through every nerve and lighting a fire in my blood. My hands find his fast-bobbing head, urging him on, as my hips jerk and judder upwards to meet him. A sweep of a fingertip on the rim of my hole, and my breath hitches hard as heat explodes deep in my belly. I squeeze my eyes shut as my orgasm rockets through me.

"James, I'm…" I cry out. My hands are weak and uncoordinated as I push at his head, trying to warn him, but it's too late as I hurtle over the precipice James has brought me to, shooting my release into his hot mouth.

My hands fall away as every bone in my body dissolves to mush.

I can hear nothing other than the thunder of my heart and see nothing other than the dying lights dancing in the blackness behind my clenched shut eyes. The bed shifts, knocking some semblance of sense into my numb brain. I drag my eyes open, and blink up into James' smiling face. He's switched on the lamp, bathing the room in a soft amber glow.

With gentle fingers he sweeps away my hair, sticky with sweat, away from my brow, and traces his fingers down my face with a gentleness that causes my heart to clench. I can't speak because of the hard lump filling my throat. He shouldn't be doing this, touching me with a soft tenderness that makes my heart flutter. He should be moving away because we've finished, we've got over the line, so there's no more reason or need for touch. It's what every other man I've been to bed with has done.

But James isn't every other man.

"Oh, Perry," he says on a sigh. He kisses me long, slow, and tender, and I melt into him because I just can't not, as I taste both him and me, warm and wet on my tongue. He breaks the kiss and rolls onto his back and sighs again as he crosses his arms behind his back and stares up at the ceiling.

I'm wracked with indecision. This is the bedroom he chose. I don't know whether I'm to stay here with him or go to my room. I steal a glance at him, still lying still and staring up at the ceiling and giving no clue, and I begin to shift off the bed.

"What are you doing?" His head whips around, and his eyes blaze into mine.

"I, erm, thought that maybe now we've… well, you know… that you might want your space and—"

"You think I want you to go? Is that what you think?"

Yes, because that's how it's always been… But I don't say that, because there's anger like a storm on the horizon in his eyes and in his tight, taut words.

He looks away from me, as though he needs a second to gather himself. He says something, low and under his breath, but I know it's to himself and not to me. When he looks at me again, he's reined that anger in, but it's still straining at the leash. When he speaks, his words are careful and measured.

"No Perry, I don't want you to creep off next door. What I want is for you to get back into bed and for you to be here when I wake up in the morning. If that's what you want too. Is it?"

He looks at me, a shadow of apprehension on his face as he waits for me to give the only answer I can give.

"Yes, it is."

The words feel huge, monumental in a way I'm too dazed to examine right now. As James holds me tight, and runs his fingers through my hair, I settle into him, feeling the steady rise and fall of his chest against mine.

Closing my eyes, and hardly able to comprehend what has happened, I drift into the dark depths of sleep.

CHAPTER TWENTY-FIVE

JAMES

Perry's lying on his back, his lips gently puffing in and out on each soft breath. He looks so peaceful, so relaxed, his auburn hair messy and tumbled. I itch to push it away from his brow, to run my fingers through the soft strands. The first signs of dark scruff are marking his fair skin. I take all this in under the soft lamplight, which we'd not switched off before both of us had tumbled into sleep.

I reach out, just to lay a soft touch on him, just to know that he really is here, with me, in bed, after a night of sleeping in each other's arms, but I let my hand drop, fearing that I'll wake him.

He mutters in his sleep, and shifts to his side, moving closer as though seeking me out, as he snuggles into my side.

"Perry?" I whisper, but his only answer is his deep and steady breathing.

It's been years since I properly spent a night with a man. I go or they do, leaving me to wake up every morning alone.

Some may think that's a cold and soulless way to live — Elliot certainly thinks so — but he and I are cut from very different cloth.

No sleepy, morning cuddles; no sharing a shower; no first coffee together. They're the acts of those in relationships, and I've worked hard to keep clear of those for more years than I want to remember.

There's no reason for me to change my outlook and my ways, not when they've served me so well. Keep it simple, keep it clear, keep it casual and no strings. Nobody gets involved, so nobody gets hurt. It's pretty much the rule I've lived by since I walked out on Alex — hell, it's what I lived by when we were together, to my eternal shame — but now, and for what I know is truly the first time in my hedonistic, self-centred life, that rule is not only bending, it's breaking.

Perry shifts again, and I slip out of bed. My naked skin goosebumps in the chilly early morning air, tempting me to climb back into the warmth, bundle Perry up in my arms, and breathe in the salty aroma of what we'd shared together.

I climaxed last night, the evidence crusted on my stomach, but what had happened between us hadn't been about me and my physical needs. Everything had been about Perry, giving him what he wanted and needed. Touch, caress… His response had been pure instinct, utterly and completely beautiful.

I run a finger across the dried cum on my stomach, feeling it flake under my touch. That's another chip of my defences falling away. I always wash the men off me, cleaning every inch of my body, scrubbing my teeth and mouth-washing. Literally and figuratively removing all trace. But not last night, not with Perry. I run my tongue over my teeth, over the insides of my cheeks, seeking out the lingering taste of him.

As I gaze down, he shifts again, and my lips curl up into a smile. The boy's a fidget, and a bed hogger, with his arms and legs spread wide beneath the duvet, like some kind of human star fish.

The urge to touch him, to have that connection that I never, ever seek, is too strong to resist this time, and before I can think to stop myself, I run my fingers through his hair. My heart leaps when he sighs, and murmurs something that, if I let myself, I can believe is my name on his lips. I withdraw my slightly shaking hand, and swallow down the lump that's lodged in my throat.

As quietly as possible, I collect some clean clothes and tiptoe out of the bedroom, leaving Perry to sleep and for me to head to the shower and try to work out how I'm going to navigate a landscape for which I have neither a map nor a compass.

The sun's just coming up, and I make myself another coffee and gaze out at the little back garden and beyond, to the hill above the village where Perry and I had shared a kiss so warm and tender just the memory of it makes my heart soar.

I hadn't meant to seduce him, or that's what I tell myself, but who seduced who is open to debate. A noise, a thump, that could be from the cottage next door, but I know isn't, has me looking up at the ceiling. My heart thumps hard in response. Perry's awake and up, and soon he'll be coming downstairs. My hold on the mug tightens. I'm nervous, and that's quite the confession, coming from a man in his fifties who's been around the block so many times I've all but worn a groove in the ground. I take a deep breath in an attempt to calm the nerves I've never had before, and only just in time as the kitchen door swings open.

"Morning. Did you have a good night's sleep?"

Oh, Christ... My shoulders hunch as I cringe at my question. I sound like the proprietor of a B&B enquiring after a guest. Perry smiles, but it's small and tight, and there's confusion in his dark eyes.

"Yes, thank you." He looks away, his grip on the door handle so tight I can see the whites of his knuckles. I take a deep breath, because we have to start again.

"Perry, come and sit down." I nod to the table. No matter how nervy I'm feeling, he's a thousand times worse.

He hesitates, and for a moment I have the horrifying thought he's going to shake his head and turn away, but he doesn't. I join him at the table, with no idea what to say but knowing I have to say something.

"Perry—"

"James—"

We speak at once, before we both fall silent. He's staring at me, and I'm staring back, both of us blinking like we've been dragged from the dark into the light.

"Last night—"

"About yesterday—"

We've done it again, and it's what we need to break free of the weird tension that's roped itself around us. A small smile breaks across Perry's face, little more than a twitch of lips.

"You first," he says. The smile's still there. It's a little unsure, a little hesitant, but it's there, and it's all I need for the butterflies in my stomach to land and be still.

"I never planned what happened. Coming away like this, it was never meant to be some kind of seduction. I want you to understand that."

Seduction. Perry seduced me long ago, but it had nothing to do with sex.

"No," he says slowly, as though he's thinking his next words through. "I don't believe for a moment it was planned, because that would be calculated, I suppose. Fundamentally dishonest."

"What?" His words are a punch in the chest, knocking the air from my lungs. That makes me sound like a — no, I really don't want to think how that makes me sound, because it's not true.

"And you're not those things, I know that. We should put down what happened to circumstances. The time and the place, or the sea air."

"The time and the place? The sea air?" I'm gawping at him, as I parrot his words back to him. This isn't going how I expected, not that I knew what to expect. This boy has pushed me so far out of my depths, I'm in danger of drowning. I need to get back to shore, and quickly.

"It had nothing to do with the sea air, Perry. I'm not sorry about what happened, not sorry at all. I don't regret a thing. I don't regret what we did last night. I don't regret us falling asleep in each other's arms, just like I don't regret watching you as you slept and—"

"You were watching me?" He tilts his head, and peers at me, like I'm a bug under a microscope. I'm so used to being in control, but this is all running away from me, too fast for me to catch.

"Yes. No. Oh, bloody hell." I throw my head back, squeezing my eyes closed as I push my fingers through my hair. It's all coming out wrong. I've made myself sound like some kind of obsessive, and if he decides to pack his bag and jump on the first train back to London, I've nobody but myself to blame.

"You do realise that makes you sound like a perv, don't you?"

I open my eyes and let my hands drop to the table. There's laughter in his voice and in his eyes. "But then I said you were a kinky fucker, didn't I, when you found me in the café?"

He's trying not to laugh, he's trying so hard. The little sod is playing with me and enjoying every moment.

I shrug. "I can neither confirm nor deny my level of kinky fuckery."

He shakes his head and laughs, the sound light, and I join in. It's everything we need to put us at ease and sweep away any lingering awkwardness. But there's more I need, and want, to say, and I'm determined to do it. I take his hand, and he lets it rest in mine.

"There's no way in this world I would ever take back what happened last night, but I need to know whether or not you feel the same way?"

In the clear light of morning, without the fog of lust. If he says no, I don't have a clue what I'll do.

I study him as his gaze drops to our entwined hands. My heart beat's ramped up and is in danger of smashing through my ribs. Despite the moment of playfulness, I've no idea what he's going to say.

He's been through a bad time with a man.

He wants to reset his life.

He wants to make a new start, miles and miles away.

It was a one-off, all about the time, the place, and the sea air.

He could say all of those things, and I'd accept them because I'd have no other option.

"No, I could never regret what happened. Ever." His eyes, bright and clear and beautiful, so beautiful they take my breath away, meet mine. "I—I've never felt so cared for. You made me feel that, James. You."

A soft pink washes over his face, but he holds my gaze.

I lean across, closing the small gap between us. I let go of his hands, and cup his face in between my palms, tilting his head up. His steady gaze never falters.

"Then let's never regret any of it." I whisper the words against his lips, which are softening, opening.

We kiss long and deep, slow and tender. It's dizzying, breathtaking, intoxicating. It's frightening and exhilarating. It's like nothing I've known, and everything I want to know.

Just like I know without knowing that something inside of me has clicked into place, that the world I know has tilted on its axis, and that nothing, ever, can be the same again.

CHAPTER TWENTY-SIX

PERRY

"Bloody nightmare of a journey. So glad we're home." James pushes the door closed with a hard thud. "Come on, let's get something to eat," he says, as he picks up the post scattered on the mat before heading to the kitchen, with me in his wake.

It's taken an extra couple of hours to get back from Devon, and we're hungry and tired. Well, I am. I'm hungry for James, and exhausted, even though we've spent most of our stay in Love's Harbour not exploring the beautiful countryside or the stunning coastline but in bed, where we've been exploring each other.

In the kitchen James leans against the sink, legs crossed at the ankles, as he scrolls through his phone.

He's wearing old and faded jeans, and a moss green shirt, the same colour as his eyes. Like the jeans, it's loose and well worn, the cuffs a little frayed, the antithesis of the sharp suited, urbane man he shows to the world. It's yet another layer of who he is. It's not just what he's wearing that's so different, but him. His hair, always groomed and immaculate, is messy and mussed. My stomach floods with warmth, as my dick begins to stir. I've spent the weekend running my hands through it, sometimes slowly and gently but mostly I've grabbed at it, scrunching it in my fists as he's—

"Perry? What one do you want?"

"Sorry? What do I…?

He's staring at me, one brow arched, a knowing smile on his face.

"Do you want it hot and meaty?"

"Ehhrr…?"

"The pizza? The Hot and Meaty?" The smile's turned into a shit eating grin.

"Oh, yes. Of course. Please."

James throws me a wink, and finishes off the food order, and I sink down into a chair, my legs weak and wobbly all of a sudden.

"You open up a couple of beers, and I'll take the luggage up." He pushes his mobile into his pocket, and disappears out of the kitchen.

I do as he asks. The kitchen, the heart of the house, is silent, except for the gurgle of the fridge. Pizza and beer. We've sat here in the kitchen many times sharing both, but this time is different. In the course of a couple of days everything has changed between us. I scrape my nail down the label on the bottle, soggy with condensation, leaving a little shredded pile of paper on the table.

But, has anything really, truly, and fundamentally

changed? It's a question I need to ask myself and answer with honesty.

James' kisses, his touch, the feel of his body, warm and naked and entwined with mine, it thrilled every part of me, but most of all it thrilled my heart. But now we're back, to our day-to-day lives, and the bubble of the weekend has burst.

Hands fall to my shoulders and I jump, before my body does exactly what it wants, which is to lean back into James' touch.

"You'll wear a groove in that bottle if you dig away at it any harder."

James' voice is deep and soothing, as his fingers begin to knead and massage, smoothing out all those knots that have tied up my muscles in just a couple of minutes. A soft kiss lands on top of my head, but James lingers and I sigh as he nuzzles into my hair.

"What's the matter, Perry, because something is. You going to tell me, hmm?"

Another nuzzle before he pulls back, but his hands are still working their magic on me.

"We're back, to our normal lives. To how it was before."

His hands still, just for a beat, before they resume their firm work.

"Not quite as it was before, wouldn't you say?" His hands slip from my shoulders and he sits down opposite me. Leaning back in his seat, his eyes narrow as he studies me before he sighs, long and deep. "What's wrong?" His eyes, always so clear and confident, cloud with uncertainty. "You regret it."

It's not a question but a statement.

"No, but…" My nervous fingers gather up the paper I've shredded from the beer bottle, rolling and rolling and rolling it into a smaller and smaller ball. "I know you can't offer me any kind of… anything long term. I know it's not what you want. I realise that, and accept your life is how you want it…"

No commitment, no strings, no entanglement, all the things I want and he runs from. My words have dried up on my tongue. I swallow hard, because I owe it to myself to say them.

"I don't want to just be a notch on a bedpost. I've been that, too many times. Somebody to fuck and forget."

James' brow scrunches into a hard frown, so hard it's as though he's fighting a real and physical pain.

"I'd never treat you like that. Ever." His tone's quiet yet hard, and brimming with vehemence. He drags his hands down his face, and when they drop away, his expression's softer, and his wry smile's back in place. "So many have been notches. I won't deny it because I can't lie to you. But not you, Perry. You could never be that. But what you say, about long term…"

He shakes his head slowly, and his gaze shifts, but not before I see something in his eyes that if I let myself I could call regret, or sadness. But he's told me the kind of man he is, he's never lied to me, just as he says.

"Can't we just enjoy each other, for now?" he says, bringing his focus back to me. "And I'm not just talking about sex. It's you I enjoy, Perry. *You*. Your company. Spending time here, or meeting up after work, I've loved every moment of it. And I think you have, too."

If I say no, he'll accept it, the same as if I'd said no when he first took me to bed… and just like then, I can't shake my head and walk away. I know exactly what it is he's offering me, which isn't any kind of forever. It's the here and now, it's for the next few days, weeks, maybe a month or two. It's until I go and never look back. It's everything I don't want, everything I've become determined to avoid because it's everything that will break my heart when it's been broken too many times before.

But this isn't any man. This is James. The man who rescued me, the man who's cared for me, the man's who's treated me with more respect than I've ever been treated with before. If I can have that, if only for a short time more, I'll take it.

"I think we can be those things. For now, until I go."

He nods and smiles, though his jaw tightens. Just a tiny, minuscule fraction.

"As you say," he says quietly, "until you move away to fulfil your dream."

All those complications I've told myself I have to avoid, they've wound themselves around me and tightened their hold.

I don't know if I've made the best decision in the world, or the worst; all I know is that I've made the only one I can.

On the surface, life carries on much as before. I go to work. I meet James for a drink or a meal, or I cook when I get home. We watch the TV together, or stream films or box sets. He goes running, I — don't. None of that has changed, but unlike before I'm woken up each morning not by the cheery chat of the radio show presenter, but by a long and leisurely blow job.

"Oh God, James, *o-hhhh*..."

My post-release slump back into the mattress is accompanied by a salacious smack of a pair of wet lips and a throaty laugh.

"So much more satisfying than a cup of tea first thing, don't you think?"

James inches up my body, his face hovering over mine so close our noses brush against each other's.

"Get off me. You've got cum breath." I do my best to look fierce, but as I'm still in an early morning post-climax fog, I very much doubt I'm succeeding.

"Hmm." James doesn't attempt to move as he runs his tongue around his mouth. "I've also got a few pubes caught between my teeth."

"Well, I'll book in for a wax, shall I? In the meantime, you can take your teeth out so you can properly unpick them. And give a better BJ."

I give him a hard shove and he topples off the edge, saved from totally crumpling onto the rug by one leg clinging to the bed — which I push off so the errant limb can join the rest of him. I peek over the side and look down at a very naked James, partially tangled in the duvet which went overboard with him.

"I do not have false teeth." He sticks his bottom lip out in a sulky pout. "I can't believe this is the thanks I get for lovingly relieving you of—"

"An extra few minutes of blissful sleep?" I'm grinning now because there's no way I can't. I'd give up minutes, hours, days and nights for James' mouth on me. The horizontal workout he's given me has left me both more relaxed and refreshed than the best night's sleep ever could — but it's also put me off my guard as James' sudden, out of the blue move has me tumbling out of bed. My breath's knocked from me as I land on top of him.

His arms tighten around me, their grip steel hard. I've no way out of his embrace even if I wanted it. James wraps his legs around my waist, his solid shaft pressing hard against my belly, and I suck in a sharp breath as he rolls his hips up into me and, even though I've just emptied myself down his throat, my cock's already thickening.

James kisses me hard, the taste of my release on his tongue thrilling through me as he rocks harder. The drag on my cock, trapped between our sweat-slicked bodies, is exquisite, mouth-watering agony. Messy kisses, spit smearing our lips, our breaths heavy and ragged, and hitching as our cocks slide across each other, slippery from our combined juice. But I need more.

I pull back, and James' arms around me loosen. Spitting into my palm I lock my gaze onto the dark and inky depths that have become James' eyes. He's breathing hard, and his lips curve up into a wicked grin as I wrap my hand around our—

James' mobile rings, slicing through the heated, lust-fogged air.

"Fuck. Fuck, fuck, *fuck.*" James' roar of anger and frustration fills every corner of the bedroom. I let us go, and climb off him, leaving him to leap to his feet, grab the phone from the bedside cabinet, and stomp off to his office.

I want to scream at him to leave it, to flush it down the toilet or throw it out the window, but I recognise the ring tone and it's one he can ignore. Work, but not just work.

It's his boss, although James having a boss is almost an anathema, but a call at 6.30am can't be ignored. I pick myself and the duvet up from the floor and sigh as I look down at my now flagging cock.

James comes back into the bedroom. "I have to go in. Now. Christ, but they demand their pound of flesh." He's scowling and grumpy, his dick as deflated as mine. He doesn't say who exactly *they* are and I don't ask.

He throws the phone on the bed and mutters about a shower.

"Good job it wasn't a video call." I lie back on the bed and prop my head in my hand and watch him.

James snorts, but his eyes narrow and there it is again, that dark smile that sends a shiver across my skin and blood to my dick.

"Maybe she can wait five minutes."

"Five minutes?" I do my best to sound outraged. "Although it's probably all you can manage at your age."

James' eyes narrow some more, and wicked turns to pure evil.

"When did you get so lippy?" He takes slow steps towards me, making me think of a cat stalking a mouse. I edge further into the bed, as I watch every step that brings him closer. My dick's on high alert, too, as it bobs against my stomach. "I can do more to you in five minutes than—"

His phone rings again. It's next to me on the bed, and I toss it over to him. He listens, barely even grunts a response, his brow puckered into a hard frown. Whatever's happening, he's needed. We'll just have to bank those five minutes.

"Get ready and go. Something's obviously up, even if

226

it's not us." I nod to our dicks, flagging for the second time in a handful of minutes. "I'll see you later."

"Sorry, but, yes I really do have to get a move on." With an apologetic smile, he leans down and presses a quick kiss to my lips.

Less than twenty minutes later the door slams closed leaving me alone in the bed where I breathe in deep, catching the fading aroma of his citrus cologne as I drift back to sleep.

I put aside the book I've been reading and stretch out on the comfy sofa in the living room. On the coffee table next to me is a cup of tea and a small slice of chocolate cake. It's only the second piece I've had, as James has snaffled most of it. It was definitely his favourite, he'd said. I can't help smiling, because he'd said exactly the same thing about the carrot cake, the lemon drizzle and the Victoria sponge.

Snuggling deeper into the cushions, I'm feeling lazy. I've a day off work and it'd be easy to lounge about doing nothing in this beautiful house where I feel so comfortable. And that's a problem.

I'm too comfortable, here in this house and with James, when I can't afford to be. I'm not staying here, and I have to keep reminding myself of that but it's getting harder. Whatever I might want to believe, this isn't my home. My stomach twinges hard, and I try to tell myself it's just indigestion.

"Come on, get moving," I say to nobody but myself. Yes, that's exactly what I need to do in all sorts of ways.

We haven't talked about my proposed move to Brighton since we got back from the cottage, almost a month ago, when we agreed to be whatever it is we are. It's the elephant in the room. We both know it's there but when we're together we ignore it. But I can't afford to, and I've been quietly looking, every single day.

I've lost count of how many places I've viewed online, along with the countless conversations with estate agents, who assure me they have just the right property on their books — and then email details of tiny studio flats. To be honest, it's all getting a bit depressing. Nothing new seems to be coming up, just the same old places. If they're not selling it's for a reason. Perhaps I really should leave it all until after Christmas, just a couple of months away. But I have to keep looking, just in case that perfect gem turns up. Thing is, it already has. It's called James' house.

My phone pings. Stuffed deep into my pocket, I fish it out, in the hope it'll be James. It isn't.

"No thank you." I delete the recorded message offering me the opportunity to make sexy times with beautiful Russian ladies.

I finish off the cake, slug back the rest of my drink and take the stuff out to the kitchen. My laptop's on the table, and I wake it up.

I've set up email alerts with a number of estate agents in and around Brighton. Not that it's really been worth it. There's a new one come through, and I open it up, always hopeful. Yes, the brightly painted beach hut looks lovely and it's only—

"Fucking hell." How can a glorified garden shed cost as much as I earn in a whole year?

I type in my requirements again: house, potential to

extend, fifteen miles from Brighton city centre, preferably close to the seafront — no, close to the sea front, I'm not going to compromise on that. At least not yet.

And… lift off.

The screen fills up with dozens of properties, showing nothing I've not seen before. I scroll through fast, and then scroll back. Something new, something that looks kind of okay, something that could be in my price range, with the promised help from my parents. I click on for the virtual tour.

A bungalow, in need of some updating. That's something of an understatement as it looks like the place was all the business — in the late '70s. I'm surprised the estate agent hasn't called it retro. A coat of paint and some new wallpaper would work wonders. Or that's what I think until I take a closer look at the bathroom.

"Awww…"

An avocado suite and baby pink tiling. If I look at it for too long, I'll get a headache.

Landing on the photo of the kitchen, I lean in closer, peering at the screen. "'Large kitchen, extended by a previous owner,'" I read aloud. It looks big, but so would a shoe cupboard, if a fish eye lens were used to take the shot, but the dimensions sound interesting. There's an old wooden twelve inch ruler, a relic of James' school days, in what he calls The Man Drawer. I root around for it, and start to measure, using mugs to mark each corner.

A tremor of excitement dances through me. Not as big as James' and full of ugly dark pine instead of beautiful sage green and blond wood, but still… It's the first, and only place, I've seen that's shown any kind of real promise. Taking a deep breath, I type a message to the estate agent to book a proper viewing, and I get a response within seconds of hitting send.

Today... one o'clock... agent will meet at the property... new on the market...

Slumping back in the chair, I have to make a decision. I've got the day off with nothing particular to do. I can't dither, I can't take my time. I bash out a quick reply and minutes later I'm out the door, and heading to Victoria station to catch the train to Brighton.

CHAPTER TWENTY-SEVEN

JAMES

As soon as I hear the key in the door I rush out to the hallway.

"Where the hell have you been?" I regret the words as soon as they're out of my mouth. I don't own Perry, he's not answerable to me, he can come and go as he wants. I need to remind myself of that, and I'm lucky his response is only wide eyes and a silent *O*.

"It's only six-thirty. I thought you'd still be at work."

It doesn't answer my question, but I need to take a figurative if not a literal breath. He peels off his coat and it's only now that I take in that he's soaking wet. A sudden thunderclap seems to shake the whole house.

"You're drenched." A couple of steps and I'm so close I can see the raindrops glittering on his lashes. His dripping hair's plastered to his brow; I push it back, and plant a kiss.

"That's a better greeting." He gives me a hard stare that really isn't very hard at all, but it's enough to wrench the apology I know he's due from me.

"I'm sorry. It's just that I expected you to be here." *Wanted you to be here, waiting for me...* "I tried to phone you, but it kept going through to voicemail."

"I'm really sorry, but I've been out for the day. It was all very last minute and although I had my mobile, when I tried to phone you from the train the battery was as flat as a pancake."

"Train? Where were you going?" He hadn't mentioned going on a jaunt, and if he had I'd have gone with him — although our plans would've ended up on the scrap heap because of my early morning call. But, I'm still miffed he's been out for the day without me, even though I don't own him, even though he's not answerable to me, even though he can do as he wants...

"I've been to Brighton. Well, not quite Brighton, but near enough. I went to see a property. It all happened so quickly. It looks, erm, promising."

His gaze slides away from me. His words sound almost apologetic, even though he's got nothing to be apologetic about. This was always his plan, to move away, start a new life, miles and fucking miles and miles away. I force myself to smile when it's the last thing I want to do. It feels distorted, as though I've become a gargoyle.

"Promising, eh? That's good."

The tinge of worry in his eyes dissolves. I must be a better actor than I thought. Or a better liar.

"Yeah, but early days. There's a lot to think about,

which includes talking to my parents. I'll tell you all about it, but I'd like a shower first — and to put on some dry clothes."

We're still in the hallway, still standing so close I can smell the vanilla scent in the shampoo he uses. Despite the warmth of the house, he must be freezing.

"Sorry. Yes, you get yourself sorted out then come and tell me all about it." I inject as much cheer as I can into my words.

With a wide smile he dashes upstairs, leaving me alone in the hallway with the fading scent of vanilla in the air.

Tell me about it is exactly what he does, over the remains of last night's casserole and the crusty herb bread he made to go with it. I know it's delicious, but I can't taste a thing.

Perry's enthusiastic, and I can't blame him for that. He wants to put everything that's gone before behind him. All the bad choices that caused him to make a basement a temporary home and to end up drunk and slumped over a table in the shadows of a Soho café. He's moving on and the plain truth is, I don't want him to. Not now, not next week, not next month. Not ever.

He shows me the photos on the internet again. It's the right size, it has potential, it has the large kitchen he needs. It ticks so many boxes, but it's ugly and dull and sort of dead looking. It's the decor, it's the fact that it's a bungalow, for God's sake, in a dreary Brighton suburb. He shows me more photos of "the village". There's nothing there, other than street after street of post-War bungalows. It's a vision of hell, and I know as much as I've known anything in my life, that Perry will wither and fade in such a place.

I want to tell him all this, I want to tell him to stop, but he's smiling and his eyes are aglow with visions of a future that's bright and full of sunshine but where I can only see perpetual grey.

"I need to go back down and take another look, maybe stay somewhere overnight so I can see what it's like at all times — I mean, I wouldn't want to find out that the local teenagers use the road it's on as a place to practise wheelies and donuts at ten o'clock at night."

He's looking at me, and there's expectation shining in his eyes. He wants me to go down there with him, but I can't say yes, I can't make myself say it.

"I suppose you will."

Perry doesn't say anything as he closes the laptop, and without a word we continue with dinner.

I glance up at him, across the table from me. His head's bowed and even though I can't see his eyes, I know that if I could I'd see disappointment in them. The tension around us feels like it's sucking all the air from the room. I've caused this, and that means I need to try to put it right, but what comes out of my mouth doesn't help at all.

"I thought we agreed you weren't going to start looking again until after Christmas."

"I know, and with all the same old places showing up, it made sense because I know a lot of properties come onto the market in the New Year. But I can't stop looking completely."

He hunches his shoulders, all tight and defensive. The playfulness of this morning, before the call that dragged me away, seems like a lifetime ago.

"It's stupid not to keep an eye out, even at this time of year. Wherever I end up going, it won't be a quick move. There's finance to sort, because even though I've got the inheritance from my granddad, and my parents have said they'll help me, I'll still need a mortgage. Getting all the permissions from the local council allowing me to produce edible goods to sell direct to the public, as well as making sure the kitchen's properly equipped and up and running. None of it's a five minute job."

Everything he says is right, and I have nothing with which to counter a single word.

I pile up our empty plates, the crash of china on china loud in the otherwise silent kitchen.

"Yes, lots of hoops to jump through. Let's just hope it turns out to be everything you want."

Perry opens his mouth to speak, but whatever it is he's about to say is severed by the shrill ring of my mobile. Unlike this morning, when I raged against its intrusion, now I'm thankful for whatever problem the call heralds.

"Minister," I say, as I head out of the kitchen, but it's not the measured, deep tones of the woman on the other end of the line I can hear, but words spoken so quietly I can almost believe I'm imagining them.

"It's not."

CHAPTER TWENTY-EIGHT

PERRY

James has been quiet over the last couple of days, since I told him about the bungalow. He's been kind of flat, and closed off — at least when I've seen him. Whatever's up with his work, it's keeping him there until well into the evening.

Yesterday and the day before, I left a note to say his dinner was on the hob, ready to be dished up, and I guess tonight will be the same. Maybe I should stay up, wait for him to get home, pour him a glass of wine and sit with him whilst he eats. It's a nice thought, until I realise it sounds too housewifey, or husbandy, if there are such words. It's still a nice thought, though, or at least for me, but I'm not sure how comfortable James would be with it.

I'm working from home today. In fact, everybody is. Elliot's having the office repainted, and as it's Friday the place should be sparkling and pristine and completely stink free come Monday. It also gives me the opportunity, and privacy, to phone my parents to update them — and to call in the promise they've always made to me.

"Mum, it's me."

"Darling, how lovely to hear from you. Just a moment, let me find a quiet spot. One of our regulars is celebrating a birthday."

Laughter and music travel down the phone line, from the bar my parents own in southern Spain.

"That's better," she says, her voice taking on the sing-song tone it always does when she's had a couple or so drinks. "So, tell me all your exciting news. Still lodging with your friend?"

"Yes." She knows about my split with Grant, but only the barest bones, and that I'm now staying with *a friend*. "But I really need to get myself sorted out with my own place, and now's the time to make moves on starting up my own business. It's why I want to talk to you."

"So, you've not phoned to chat and catch up? Or to say you're coming out to see us?" I can hear the pout.

"Mum…"

"Only kidding, darling. But it would be lovely to see you. What about Christmas or for New Year? We could do with some extra help at those times." She laughs, but I know my mum well enough to know she's not joking.

"I need to check with work." Which isn't a lie. "Mum, I need to—"

A sudden burst of drunken laughter, and my mum's muffled voice as she calls out something stops me in my tracks, and I'm starting to think now isn't the best of times to bring up the subject of the financial help she and my dad have always promised.

"Sorry about that. Now, where were we?"

I take a deep breath. Asking for a big injection of cash is harder than I thought it'd be. I clear my throat and leap in, rattling on about the bungalow, about Brighton, about making the move out of London, about the cake making business. I'm so wrapped up in telling her all my plans, I don't notice she's not said a word until I run out of steam and come to a stop. The silence on the other end of the line is almost deafening.

"Darling, do you really think there's a living to be made in making cakes? It could be a nice sideline, a paid hobby if you like—"

"Yes, Mum, I do." I hope she hasn't heard the snap in my voice, because I sure as hell have. But I've spoken to her about my ambitions in the past. They may well have been vague and not detailed enough — okay, they were very vague — but not now. "I know exactly what I want to do. I'm focused. I've been over the figures. I know the detail." I smile because I know I'm pushing the buzz words, the ones she'll want to hear, but the truth is I am. At least as far as the business is concerned.

"I'm sure you've done all your homework," she says, but she doesn't sound convinced. "Because you always were a good boy and still are."

I swallow the sigh, and decide not to remind her I'm a man in his mid-twenties.

"Mum, you and Dad have always said you'd help me out financially. Combined with the inheritance from Granddad—"

"Ah, yes."

Silence fills the airways, so hard and heavy it's all but crushing my lungs. It's like I'm trying to breathe though a pin hole.

"What do you mean, *ah, yes*?"

My grip on my mobile tightens. A creeping, itchy tingle crawls over my skin about what exactly that *ah, yes* means.

"Your father and I, we've expanded the business. We had to act fast, no time to dither. Another two bars. And a restaurant, specialising in traditional British pub grub. Expats, they're big spenders and they're very keen on a taste of home. We've got the grand opening for one of the bars, and the restaurant, just before Christmas. The other bar's been delayed, until the spring. It's all go, go, go here, plus it's all taken a lot of money, one way or another…"

I stop listening. The promises they've always made have disappeared like smoke on the breeze.

"… five thousand at the very most, but it would need to be a loan rather than a gift, although there wouldn't be any interest payable, of course. You do understand, don't you darling? We've sunk everything we have into the businesses. I'm so sorry, I know it's not what you were expecting to hear. The bars, the restaurant, they represent our pension. I admire your ambition, it's something we've always tried to instil in you, but cake making—" I bristle at the way quotation marks seem to wrap themselves around the words.

"It made Granddad a good living. You know, your own dad. All the extra dosh he earned from it paid for your riding lessons and ski trips when you were a teenager. And your first car. Isn't that what you've always told me?"

"Perry…"

I close my eyes, willing myself to hold back my anger. "I'm sorry," I say through gritted teeth, although I'm honestly not sure I am.

"You're upset, of course you are. Why don't you come out here, work with me and Dad if you want a change? We'd obviously pay you something," she adds, but it's an afterthought.

"I'm not upset, I'm disappointed. But if you can't help me, then you can't. Thanks, Mum, thanks for... Well, nothing."

"Excuse me?"

Her voice is sharp, with no sign of the sing-song tone. She's affronted, but I don't care. I can't help but wonder if I'd gone to her with a plan for something else other than *cake making* whether her response would have been different. But I haven't and I won't be.

"You've always said you'd back me, with encouragement and practical help. But now you aren't."

"Perry, we're not a cash cow, you know. And haven't I explained, about the bars—"

"What?" I jump up from the table and stride around the room as anger burns through my blood. "Are you accusing me of trying to somehow ponce off you? I've never, ever, asked you for anything, and I wouldn't have asked you for this if you and Dad hadn't always made a big thing about wanting to help me out when the time was right, when I found something I really wanted to do—"

"Perry, just—"

"I'm sorry you can't help me, and accept that you can't, but do you know what I'm more sorry about? It's the broken promises."

Silence stretches out. I sag against the sink, and my

shoulders slump as the flare of my anger dies to nothing more than barely warm embers.

"I'll speak to your dad, see what we can—"

"No. Thank you, but no. I'll make alternative arrangements." More loans, more debt. "Good luck with the bars and restaurant. And no, before you ask, I won't be coming out to stay over Christmas and New Year, so you'll just have to pay for the extra help you need."

I've got no option but to jettison any idea of help from my parents. It stings, it really does. It's not just the help they always said they'd give me won't now be coming my way, but the lack of faith in what I want to do — which is pretty rich given they've gone into the hospitality business with no background whatsoever, although I suppose catering to a crowd of sunburnt expats who dream of egg and chips and a Sunday roast is a good money spinner.

I want to be angry, I think I have a right to be angry, but all I can feel is let down. But I won't be *knocked* down. I've got the money Granddad left me, and it's not insubstantial. It'll be a healthy deposit, but I'm going to have to see about increasing the mortgage... All this is going through my head, and I open up my Operation Perry file, and pull up the spreadsheet I've set up, making changes to my projected costs.

Tight, it's all going to be very tight, even with the wiggle room I've worked in. I go through the figures again. Yep, it's official. I'm going to be living on Pot Noodle for years to come.

Yawning, I rub my eyes before I push my fingers

ALI RYECART

through my hair, scratching my nails over my scalp. My frantic scratching slows, then stops.

The idea settles on my shoulder, and whispers in my ear.

Maybe I could ask…?

No. There's no way I can do that.

I am not asking James to help me out. Whether he would or not, I have no idea, but the thought that he might think, if only fleetingly, that I see him as some kind of cash cow, as my mother so succinctly put it, makes my stomach shrink.

No, I'm on my own with this. Whether I sink or swim, it's all down to me. I close down the spreadsheet and attempt to put aside this new turn along the road I've called Operation Perry, and get back to organising Elliot's diary.

CHAPTER TWENTY-NINE

JAMES

Perry always looks so serious when he's working, even though today his work's taking place at the kitchen table. He's even dressed in smart trousers and a shirt, although the tie and jacket he wears when he's in the office are missing. With a headset on, and a small frown wrinkling his brow, he's the picture of concentration. He looks up, his eyes widening and battening on to mine. I make a sign for tea, and he answers with a wan smile and nods.

"You're early," he says, a few moments later, removing the headset before standing and stretching. The movement tugs out his shirt from his waistband, revealing a strip of pale torso.

"Hmm. My meeting finished sooner than expected, so I called it a day." I hand over the tea which he takes, smiling his appreciation as he takes a sip before he sighs and stares down into the mug.

"What's the matter?" I ask. His smile's limp and there's an air of dejection about him.

He shrugs. "Oh, I phoned my mum earlier, to talk to her about the promise to help out — or so-called promise. They can't do it, because they've bought more bars and a restaurant."

"So no assistance from them at all?"

Does this mean he's going to give up on the idea of moving to Brighton? It's a spike of excitement in the pit of my stomach, but it's a shitty thought that his plans might be scuppered, and it's especially shitty when his mouth is turned down and he's staring at the floor.

I could help him... And I could, but I'd be helping him to go when it's the last thing I want... Yet the new home, the new business, the new start, it's what he wants so much. I put my tea down, and get ready to say what I don't want to.

"Pe—"

"It's a kick in the teeth, I can't deny it, but maybe I should be looking at it in a different way. A more challenging, but ultimately more positive way."

"What do you mean? I'm not with you."

He's sucking in his lower lip, a frown settling between his brows. It's a look I've come to recognise, of Perry thinking hard.

"I was doing some calculations earlier, after I picked myself up off the floor," he says with a huff. "I can increase my mortgage — I've not gone for the maximum amount, so there's room to do it — and although things will be tight, it's doable. I'll just have to live with an avocado bathroom suite, pink tiling, and the orange shag pile carpet."

Those horrible photos of that grim bungalow. I force a travesty of a smile onto my face.

"But doing it all myself, it means I won't be beholden to anybody, except the bank of course. Despite what they always said, about helping me, I know my parents. They would've wanted a big say in how I run the business, so at least with them out of the picture it means I can do what I want, in the way I want. Sorry," he says, shrugging. "I know I keep beating on about this but perhaps not getting my parents involved is a good thing in the long term. If I could get the bungalow for the right price…"

He's sucking on his lip again, and the frown's back, as he thinks about his second visit tomorrow. I set my tea aside because I think I'll be ill if I take another mouthful.

"I'm off for a shower," I say, but he doesn't answer as he sucks harder on his lip and his frown deepens, as he contemplates a future life for himself that has no place in it for me.

As soon as I come back downstairs I know something's not right, something more, something beyond the disappointment of his parents. The light's off in the kitchen and there's an absence of anything delicious cooking.

"Perry?"

There's no response. The house is deathly quiet and for a second I wonder if he's gone out, but the door to the living room's ajar, and just visible over the top of the sofa is a shock of dark hair — and it is only just visible as the room's in deep shadow. Something isn't just not right, it's very, very wrong.

"Perry?" I say again, switching one of the lamps on. He's staring at his phone.

"Just got this." He holds it out to me, and I take it, reading the email from an estate agent in Brighton.

Cash buyer… no chain… offered full asking price… cancel the second viewing… other properties which might be of interest…

The horrible, ugly bungalow where Perry would lose all colour and light, will now blight somebody else's life. He's not going, he's not going to Brighton tomorrow, or the next day, or the next. The selfish bastard in me wants to punch the air in triumph that his plans have fallen through and it's back to the drawing board, but it's the other man who wins through, the man who's Perry's friend, the man who's so much more even though Perry doesn't know it.

"I'm really sorry." I hand him back his phone. He takes a last look at it, before he stuffs it in his pocket.

"What a shit storm of a day."

He looks up at me and my heart threatens to break, he's so bleak. He's had his legs kicked out from under him twice today, and all I could do was feel glad that his plans are unravelling.

"Come here." I pull him into me, and he doesn't resist, and I hold him tight and kiss the top of his head. I could offer him platitudes and say I'm sorry, but I know he wouldn't want to hear them and I don't want to say them.

I'm not sure how long we've been sitting here, like this, as I card my fingers through his hair. He's so still and silent I suspect he's fallen asleep and I'm just about to untangle myself when he speaks.

"You must think I'm pathetic."

"What?" I jerk from the shock of his words. "What makes you—for goodness sake, Perry, look at me and tell me why you believe I would think of you like that?"

"Why wouldn't you?"

"No, the question is why would I. You've had two major setbacks in one day, you're entitled to feel like a mushroom."

"A — mushroom?"

"Had a load of shit dumped on top of you."

He stares at me before a smile lifts his lips. "You can say that again. Back to the drawing board, I suppose. I know I'm in the same position I was just a couple or so days ago, but I really felt like I'd taken a step closer."

No, he'd taken a step away. I bury the thought along with the words tingling on my tongue. He doesn't want to hear that, not now, not any time. He needs cheering up, to be given a good time to help him forget about today. There's one way to do that, but there's another.

"Go and get ready. I'm taking you out for the evening."

CHAPTER THIRTY

PERRY

James insisted on dragging me out when all I wanted to do was climb into bed, pull the duvet over my head and pretend the world didn't exist.

I knew the double whammy was a setback, that none of this was ever going to be plain sailing, and that I just had to accept it, pull on my big boy pants and get on with things. But, for a little while, all I wanted was to wallow in my misery. James, however, had very different ideas and right now, in the buzzy little bar, I'm very glad he did.

"Try this, it's really good."

James forks up a chunk of meat from a small bowl, one of many spread out on the table, all served tapas style, and holds it out to me. I go to take the fork, but he pulls it back and smiles, his feline eyes narrowing.

"Come on Perry, open up for me." His voice is low and

growly and meant only for me to hear. My heart gives a jolt and so does my cock. I open my mouth and James' eyes, intent on mine, seem to glitter.

Closing my mouth around the meat, I pull off. Very, very slowly.

"Good?" he asks, as I chew.

"Hmm." I swallow. "Juicy, succulent, oozing flavour, and with a very distinct salty tang."

James' smile turns dark and dirty and he shifts position, just a little, putting his eyes in shadow. He looks good, so fucking good, the way he always does. With a couple of cocktails already under my belt, the urge to grab his hand, drag him into the toilets, and drop to my knees is becoming an imperative.

He laughs, a low, deep chuckle. It fizzes in my blood, because he's read my thoughts again.

"James." My voice is thin and reedy, full of desperate need.

"All good things come to he who waits. Were you never taught that in Sunday School?" He sits back in his seat. His eyes once more visible, sparkle with amusement.

He's teasing me, the fucker.

"Never went to Sunday School. My parents are confirmed atheists."

"I, much to my regret, did. Delaying gratification was the only lesson I learned, and it's proved to be a very useful one. The wait, and the anticipation…"

"Bastard."

"Guilty as charged, but—"

"More drinks, guys?"

My head snaps up at the waiter who's made a sudden and unwelcome appearance. He's cross-eyed and his wide smile displays a set of very large, very crooked teeth. He's a drenching of cold water.

"Yes, thank you. Same again."

"I might have wanted something different," I grumble, when the waiter departs.

"Not a good idea to mix your drinks. Remember what happened last time?"

I groan. "Don't remind me." If my cock needs another reason to run and hide, then drunk off my head and slumped in a Soho café, is it. "It feels like ages ago, now."

"In a good way?"

"Of course."

I'm surprised by James' question, but I'm even more surprised by the tone. In those four words there's uncertainty and apprehension.

The flirting, teasing man of just moments ago vanishes, replaced by a man who's a little less sure. It's a side of him I've only rarely seen. When he smiles, there's almost a shyness about it. This isn't the teasing, wicked, so hot he makes my skin sizzle James, the one who makes me want to do things that'd make a rent boy blush. *This* James is softer, hesitant, and stripped clean of all his confidence and certainties. I reach for his hand, our fingers entwining.

The waiter returns with our drinks. I don't know what he's saying, his words are no more than gibberish, because all my attention is centred on the soft brush of James' thumb running over my wrist. My heart's thumping hard in my chest and I wonder if he can feel its erratic rhythm in my pulse. His hand slips from mine, and a broken sigh falls from my lips.

"Cheers," he says, holding his glass up. I clink mine to his. "Feeling better?"

"Yes, I am. I don't feel crushed, the way I did earlier. The whole thing's going to be one step forward, two back. I just have to accept it."

He's looking hard at me, his gaze intense but not with the heat of minutes ago. James puts his drink down and leans forward, eyes still searing into mine. My skin's prickling, my spine's tingling. There's something he wants to say to me... My stomach fills with nervy apprehension...

"If you're still set on moving, to Brighton," he says, the words measured and even, "I can help you out. Financially, I mean."

"What?" I drag my jaw up from the table, and snap it closed.

"I don't expect an answer now, but just think it about for a day or two. I know how much of a blow it was, about your parents."

"It—it was, but why would you want to help me?"

"Why? Because it's your dream and you're willing to work hard to make it a reality. Even if that dream does include taking you down to bloody Brighton. I still don't understand why you want to go to the ends of the earth. If you want to be by the water, what's wrong with the Thames?"

His words are grumpy, but he's smiling even if I'm not sure it reaches his eyes.

"It's only Brighton, and I'm not there yet."

"But it's not here, is it?" His voice is quiet, almost a whisper, and whether his words are for him or for me, I have to know, I have to ask, but before I can take a breath he's become crisp and clipped. "Give it some thought and let me know, then we can look at the details."

Picking up his drink, he takes a sip, leans back in his seat and looks out over the busy bar, sure, confident and composed. I say nothing, as I lose the nerve to ask him *why?*

We stumble out of the bar. I've had another cocktail, making it three or maybe four. I should be drunk but James' offer of help has sobered me. I'll do as he says, and think it over. I already know what my answer will be, but my heart's full of warmth that he's willing to be there to catch me. To rescue me again, I suppose. But I need to stand on my own two feet, even if sometimes those feet are a bit wobbly.

"The night's still young. We could go to a club," he says.

"What, you want to get shirtless and bump and grind?" The idea's hot, but I'm not the only one who'd want some of that with James, and that's a thought that leaves me stone cold. No, I definitely *don't* want to go to a club.

He laughs. "I was actually thinking of a jazz club I know. Don't worry, it's not bearded blokes in Arran sweaters. It's more mellow and bluesy. More sultry. It's not far. Do you fancy it?"

He's doing that one brow arched thing, his lips curved up in a smile that borders on being a smirk. And I do fancy it, very much, but it's not all I fancy.

"Yes," I croak.

Taking my hand in his, he leads the way. We duck down side streets, left and right and what feels like going full circle until I've no idea where we are. We emerge into a narrow alleyway, somewhere in Hampstead, in front of a plain door that'd be easy to walk past without noticing.

James waves my hand away when I attempt to pay for our admission. He's already treated me in the bar, and his offer of help...

"You can get the first drink," he says, giving me a wink.

I follow him down a flight of steps. The basement club's dark, much darker than the lights leading down the steps from street level. My eyes have yet to adjust, and I stumble.

"Careful." James' breath wafts against my cheek as his hand grasps my wrist. Both his skin and breath are warm, but they send a shiver through my blood.

Now my eyes are adjusting, I can see the place is busy. It's also bigger than I expect, given that the entrance isn't much more than a hole in the wall. Small round tables fill the space, most of them taken up, but we find one tucked towards the back, and deep in shadow. Up at the front is a stage, set up with microphones and instruments, waiting for the band to come on.

A waitress comes to take our order; a whisky for James, but mindful of the last time I mixed my drinks, I go for a fruit juice.

"Oh, you're going to like this," James says, leaning forward as the band walks on to rapturous applause, cheers and whistles. "These guys are incredible musicians, but the singer's out of this world. Mabel. She works for Rory and Jack, and she pretty much manages the bakery day-to-day."

"What?"

I stare at the female singer, striking a pose but in a self-deprecating way as she laughs and nods her thanks to the audience. Cakes by day, clubs by night, the ultimate in a double life. She's tall, but that's more down to the killer heels and the gravity defying cherry-red beehive hairdo. In her oranges and lemons decorated fifties-style dress, she's an explosion of colour and heat and I'm already a fan.

The audience settles as trombone and double bass, deep and rich, fills the space. There's still a murmur of voices, but they fall silent when Mabel starts to sing.

Deep, rich, sultry, smoky, her voice is all of that and more.

"Oh my God, she's incredible."

In the shadows, James chuckles and picks up one of the drinks I never saw arrive.

I know nothing about jazz, absolutely nothing, but I'm mesmerised, hooked and completely sucked in as the band move from one number to the next.

"We're just going to take a short break," Mabel says, after yet another round of frantic applause, this time accompanied not just by cheers and whistles, but by the fast stomp of feet, too. "But when we're back, we want you guys on the dance floor."

"That was amazing. How come I never knew music like this existed?"

"Because you're far too young, and in need of a proper education."

"Yeah? You offering to teach me?"

"Oh, I could teach you all kinds of things."

I swallow hard. He could, of that I've no doubt, but I don't reckon much of it would be to do with jazz. I go to open my mouth, but I'm saved from whatever answer I'm about to give by the arrival of a couple of guys, a little older than me, stopping by our table. They greet James with enthusiasm.

One of them is big and muscular, his hair bright blond and spiky. The other's shorter and slighter in build, with dark curls. Both of them are hot enough to boil water. James introduces them and the blond, Archie, gives me a wide, open smile. Zack's smile is darker, more guarded, and I can feel his assessment of me.

The three chat for a minute or two, before hugging goodbye. Zack hugs a little too long, and a little too hard, and I want to rip him away from James. A laughing Archie gets there first, though not before Zack whispers something to James, who smiles as he throws me a quick, unreadable glance.

"I've not seen those two for ages," James says, beckoning one of the roving waitresses to replenish our drinks.

"How do you know them?"

"Oh, just from around. We've been to some of the same parties. They got married not so long ago and now they only have eyes for each other." His words seem to hang in the air, and I've a feeling I'm meant to fill in the gaps.

And I do.

"Oh. Oh, I see."

The three of them.

I swig back what's left of my orange juice just as another appears. It's a shame it doesn't contain a slug of vodka. Jealousy, as sharp as a razor, cuts me. It's the drink, it's the day's events, it's that James is being so damn good to me.

"Oh, Perry," he says, laughter bubbling behind his words. "That was all a while ago, now, and I've not the slightest interest in rekindling the past. The present is much more to my liking."

And there it is, that purr in his voice, that classic car purr that sends a tremor through me.

I twist around to look at him. In the low lights I can't see his eyes but I don't need to, to know his gaze is fixed on me. I feel their laser intensity like a flame held too close to skin. He's still, everything about him is still and watchful. I want to ask what he means, I want him to tell me, to spell it out, but the burst of applause explodes the strange little bubble we've found ourselves in.

"Ladies and gentlemen, girls and boys. We've got some super sultry numbers coming up, and that means audience participation."

The band starts to play, and Mabel's rich voice fills the air, as all around us people are getting up and making their way to the dance floor

"Ready?"

"Oh, you want to go?"

"No, I don't want to go. I'm asking you to dance, you wally."

Before I can answer, James tugs at my hand and leads me towards the dance floor which is already heaving, every single body swaying in time to Mabel's honey-rich voice. We find a space, to the far side, where the shadows are.

James slides his arms around me, and pulls me close, our bodies fitting together like two pieces of a jigsaw puzzle. My heart's beating thirteen to the dozen. I'm sharing this man's bed, I've discovered his body as he's discovered mine but this, encased in his arms as we sway in time to the music together, feels more intimate than anything we've shared so far. I close my eyes, giving myself up to the here and now, because that's all there is.

James sighs as he pulls me in closer. Holdng me tight, it's as though we've fused together. I'm hard, but so is he, and with every sway, each and every tiny movement, the friction on my cock is the sweetest agony.

"Hmm, this is nice. I think we should dance together more often, don't you?" James whispers into my ear, his lips brushing my lobe, sending a shiver all the way down into the pit of my belly.

He nuzzles into my neck, laying down feather light kisses, and licks and nips. It's not enough to mark my skin but more than enough for my breath to hitch and for me to groan as I push and rub my hips into his, feeling his rock hard erection against my own.

Tightening his grip on me, his lips never leaving my neck, he locks our hips together as his arms snake up my back. His fingers scrape their way up the back of my neck, his nails pushing through the short hair at my nape and I shiver even though there's an inferno burning up my skin. My scalp, so nervy the smallest touch burns, all but explodes when he scrunches my hair into his fist, pulls my head back and claims my mouth.

Our tongues tangle and slide, our teeth crash. The kiss is deep and desperate, hot and slippery and full of insatiable hunger. The music, everybody around us, have long since faded to nothing. There's only us, and I want him here and now. My hands fly to his belt, unstoppable, shaking with need, desperate to free his cock, to fall to my knees and take him deep into my mouth.

"Easy, baby. Don't want us to be arrested." The words

are breathed against my lips. They're shaky, barely in control, but he's got enough to still my hand.

I drag my eyes open. His are black, bottomless pools and his lip red, puffy and spit-coated. A light sheen of sweat covers his face and his chest rises and falls fast with his ragged breath. He looks wrecked, undone, disorientated.

Applause ruptures the air around us, and I jump. For a second I think it's us the crowds are applauding, for the show James and I have put on and I step back, not out of James' arms, but enough to swing my head around to meet the stares I know must be pinned on us. But they aren't. Nobody's taking any notice, all attention's focused on the band. Somewhere along the wild ride we've just taken, we've become detached from the crowd and we're in deep, deep shadow. A wave of relief floods me, not because of embarrassment but because what we've just shared is for us alone.

With hands I swear are trembling, James cups my cheeks between his palms and eases my face closer, tilting my neck slightly, and I part my lips for the kiss I know is coming. It's soft and tender, almost sweet, all the raging heat of moments before nowhere to be found. It's the perfect calming cool down and I give myself up into his care.

When he lets me go, he smiles as he pushes my hair from my sticky brow.

"Home?"

It's the sweetest of words and before I can answer he takes not just my hand but my heart, too.

CHAPTER THIRTY-ONE

JAMES

"I want you to put this on." Perry holds up a dark blue soft, silky scarf.

Standing up from the table, just cleared from the fabulous meal he's cooked me, I slowly begin to unbuckle, keeping my focus fixed on him.

"What? No! Cover your eyes, not your…" he gestures to my tenting trousers.

"It'd be far more fun if I wrap it around my…" I point to the bulge. "A nice little bow, which you can then untie."

Perry snorts. "It's you who's the birthday boy, not me. You're the one who's supposed to be unwrapping presents."

I pick up the scarf and run it slowly between my fingers. Perry's following the movement, pupils blown, a light flush colouring his cheeks.

We've not played games, or used toys or props, but from his rapt attention as I drag the scarf between my fingers, maybe now's the time for a little exploration. The moan escapes me before I stop it.

Perry, naked and spread out on my bed, silk restraints holding him down at the wrists and ankles. What little blood is left in my brain rushes to my dick. It leaves me lightheaded, a little wobbly on my legs, and I drop back down into my seat. My sudden change of position snaps Perry out of his trance and he blinks at me for a second or two, pink-cheeked and glazed-eyed.

"I've got something for you, something special, but I want it to be a surprise. That's why I want you to put the scarf on."

Perry's special, and he's a constant and delightful surprise. The words dance on my tongue, but he's taking the scarf from me and tying it around my head, plunging me into darkness.

"No peeking, okay? I really, really need you to do as your told," he whispers into my ear, his warm breath drifting over me.

"I've never been very good at doing what I'm told." My cock, so thick and heavy, pulses and pushes against the fly, teetering on the edge of pain, but it's the leap of my heart that truly takes my breath away, as his soft laughter ripples over my skin.

"Try your best, just for a minute." A quick and light kiss on my cheek, and he's gone, leaving me gasping for breath.

Fifty-four today. The subject of my birthday cropped up just a couple of days ago. Perry hadn't reacted and I'd forgotten about it.

I've never made a big fuss of my birthday, and any celebrations I've had have taken place in bars and clubs, my presents taking the form of men dropping to their knees, or treating myself to a highly-paid, highly-skilled, cold-eyed escort. But not this time. As soon as I'd got home, I'd been assaulted by aromas that had made my mouth water and my stomach dance. I'm used to Perry's amazing cooking, but I knew this was something more, something extra special.

A click of a switch and the darkness covering my eyes deepens.

"Still no peeking, I don't want you spoiling the surprise." Something's placed on the table, but I've no idea what.

"I'm rather hoping the surprise includes a lot of naked-ness." I smile as he laughs.

A rasp and the hiss of flames. Ah, it's a birthday cake. Of course it would be, and he's lighting some candles. My mouth twists as my throat thickens.

I can't remember when, or if, I was ever presented with a special cake for my birthday. My parents barely remem-bered I existed, let alone my date of birth. Is this really the only time somebody's gone to all this effort for me? No. Alex did, I shouldn't forget that, not that I appreciated any of it.

"You can take the scarf off now."

I pull it away, and it slips unheeded to the floor.

I'm literally speechless, as I can only stare at the cake that stands in the centre of the table, bathed in the soft glow not of candles decorating the top, but from two heavy church candles at either side. I've seen photos, the portfolio he showed me soon after he came here, but the real creation…

"Jesus, Perry, that's amazing."

It's a poor word to describe the work of art. The tall single layer cake is encased in glass smooth pale butterscotch-coloured icing, but it's what's on top that's truly inspired. Golden leaves, glossy blackberries, red-skinned tiny apples, acorns and sheaves of wheat, all of them made from sugarpaste. It's the only time I've truly witnessed his skill for the incredible artist he is and it's every reason why he has to make his dream into reality.

"It's an autumn theme, which I guess is kind of obvious."

"It's incredible, Perry. Absolutely incredible. When did you make this?" I drag my eyes away and look up at him.

"A couple of days ago, and I iced it yesterday, when you were working late. Everybody deserves birthday cake, even you."

I'm not so sure I do, but I'm so very, very glad Perry believes that, and I blink away the prickling behind my eyes that I won't pretend aren't tears.

"Happy birthday, James."

He leans down to give me what I know is going to be a chaste kiss, but I clasp his wrist and drag him down onto my lap.

I kiss him hard and long, not holding him but clutching him to me, locking my arms around him as though he's the most precious thing in the world. And that is exactly what he is. Perry Buckland, the man I teased and flirted with just to get a rare smile, the man who has found a place in my home, has found a place in my heart. I can't bear for him to leave, because I can't pretend that this is a temporary state of affairs, that what we have is transitory.

"Thank you so much," I murmur into his hair, thanking him for so much more than the cake, nuzzling into him, still holding him tight because I never, ever want to let him go.

"Don't you want to taste it?"

"Only if I can tie the scarf around it first. It is my birthday after all."

"Why do you want to—? Oh!"

He tuts and I can't help laughing. He's so easy to tease, and it lightens the weight pressing down on my heart. He slips from my lap.

"They may not be on the cake, but you still need to blow out the candles and make a wish."

I have only one wish, as I blow the candles out, plunging the kitchen into darkness save for the glow of moonlight streaming through the French windows.

Seconds later, Perry switches on the main light. The soft glow of the candles is gone, replaced by clean, bright light. Like my thinking, it's clear and sharp, nothing undefined and in shadow. I have to talk to him, about his business plans, about Brighton, about us. Who we are and what we've become. But not now, not at this moment, not when there are distractions, not when he sets out the plates and hands me the knife to destroy the masterpiece he's created.

The middle is a dark delight, rich chocolate sponge with layers of caramel buttercream. I pile some up on a dainty little fork I didn't know I owned, but suspect Perry's bought especially, and hold it out to him.

"You're supposed to take the first taste, it's your birthday cake."

"I want to taste it on your lips."

He flushes hard. I love that I can make him react like that, and it sends a thrill not just deep in my balls but deep in my heart, too. His lips part, and he leans in and nibbles at the soft icing, at the buttercream, the tip of his pink tongue licking across his lips, leaving a soft smear of damp sweetness, before he nibbles again.

It's too much, I can't wait. The need to taste the sweetness on his lips overwhelms me, and I jump up with such force the chair topples back and falls to the floor.

The cake, a thing of beauty, a work of art, is forgotten as I grip his hand in mine. I'm not the only one who's forgotten. Perry's eyes are dark with a need that's a match for my own. Like me he's breathing hard, his rock solid shaft outlined through his jeans. I cup him in my palm with my free hand and am rewarded with the shiver that races through him.

"Upstairs. Now. It's my birthday and I want to unwrap my present."

CHAPTER THIRTY-TWO

JAMES

In the bedroom I drag the curtains closed and switch on the lamp because I want to see Perry, I want to see every glorious inch of him as he unravels under my touch. He's dragging his clothes off, throwing aside his shirt, his jeans, chucking them to the corner. He hooks his thumbs under the waistband of his boxer briefs, ready to them pull down.

"No."

He goes still at my command. Just inches from me, he's close enough that I can see the questions in his eyes even though he does as I tell him.

I run my gaze over him, letting it come to rest at his cock. The hard ridge strains against the cotton of his underwear, outlining every inch, and I cup my palm over him, rubbing, kneading, stroking, running my thumb over his cockhead through the wet, arousal drenched cotton.

Perry pushes into my touch, like a cat seeking its master's touch. He closes his eyes, and moans my name. My heart thuds deep in my chest as my own straining, aching, agonising cock demands attention of its own.

I squeeze down on Perry, his heat filling my palm as he thrusts into me, his hips pushing forward. He opens his eyes, so dark and glazed, and stares into mine. His breaths come fast and uneven, ragged and tattered.

"Want you to fuck me," he rasps.

My mouth dries to sand as my heart swells, ready to burst.

"Want to feel you inside me, James. Want you to fill me up."

"Whatever you want, baby, whatever you need."

We've not done this. We've touched and teased, my mouth has tasted every inch of his body, I've made him come so hard I've reduced him to a quivering mess, but we've not done this.

He smiles, a slow lift of his lips, and even though he's full of need and lust, there's a sweetness to his smile that I can't resist and I pull him in to claim that gorgeous mouth.

The kiss is wet, sloppy, and juicy, as my tongue finds every corner of his mouth, tasting caramel, chocolate, icing and the sweetness that is Perry himself. I could lose myself in this kiss for an eternity but the impatient, insistent thrust of his hips and the hard dig of his cock against my own is a desperate reminder of what he wants from me.

"On the bed, and take these off," I whisper against his ear, snapping the elastic of his underwear and smiling as his body answers with a spasm.

I strip off, leaving my clothes in a heap on the floor. My cock, long and hard, bounces against my belly.

Tunnelling my hand, I stroke myself, shuddering at the drag of my foreskin, back and forward, and back again over the engorged head, glistening with precum. A strangled moan comes from the bed, and I lift my eyes to Perry. I swallow hard and have to press down at the root, because if I don't I'm going to spill.

Beautiful. He's so fucking beautiful.

Perry's bent his legs at the knees and, spread wide, they hide nothing. His entrance taunts and teases, his hips thrusting upwards as he jacks himself with one hand, the other massaging his balls, and all the time his eyes are on me, never wavering, challenging me to give him what he needs so badly. And I could, I could do exactly that, now, this moment. I could give him everything he wants and everything he doesn't know he wants. I could have him begging, unravelling, coming harder than he ever has before as he yells my name. But he's going to have to wait.

He follows me with his eyes as I go to the beside cabinet, and retrieve a condom and a small bottle of lube. We don't need them yet.

I climb on the bed, spreading his legs wider, covering his hand still working his cock, with my own. He rolls his hips high, the head of his perfect, beautiful shaft, pushing through our joined and fisted hands, dark, swollen and wet. My mouth waters at the sight, the need to taste him overwhelming.

Easing his hand away from himself, his shaft bobs against his belly, a thin strand of precum stretching out from the slit, and I push my face into the warmth of the short dark hair between his legs. He lets out a long, low moan, animalistic and primitive. I breathe him in deep, drenching my senses in his scent. His fingers find me, pushing through my hair, scraping at my scalp, and I smile into his musky heat, as I remember the blue silk scarf abandoned down in the kitchen.

"Where, what…?" he says, as I slip off the bed and cross the room to the wardrobe. "James? Oh." His eyes widen as I find and hold up a silk tie.

Perry's Adam's apple bobs up and down as he swallows. His hand finds his cock again, his strokes long and steady as all the time his eyes flit between me and the tie, as nerves, apprehension and excitement fight for dominance.

I trail the fine silk across his chest, over his belly, his muscles twitching and quivering as it brushes his skin. In the warm silence of the bedroom the only sound to be heard is Perry's breath, shallow, rapid and ripped to shreds.

"Only if you want, baby. I'd never push you into anything you're not happy with."

I lift the tie up so it swings just above him; he follows it with his eyes, mesmerised by what it could mean. Licking his lips, he drags his gaze away to me, and smiles.

"Good boy," I murmur, and his breath hitches. "But you're going to have to let go of that gorgeous cock of yours."

"You're going to tie my wrists?"

"Hm-mm. Nothing heavy, and only if you're sure?" I give him a steady stare, giving him another chance to know that every decision is his. I'm not into heavy play. Ropes, handcuffs, paddles, none of that's my thing, but the feel of silk, loosely tied, is more a winding caress than it is a restraint. "More of a bow than a knot. You can release yourself at any time, I promise."

He smiles, sweetness replacing hard edged lust.

"I believe you."

My heart jumps.

Trust.

He's placing all his trust in me, giving himself over completely to my protection, trusting me to be honest with him, trusting me not to hurt him and to keep him safe.

I'll keep you safe, I'll never, ever betray your trust…

His face swims out of focus and I blink hard to bring him back in.

Straddling him, I lean forward to kiss him. I take my time, letting him taste my promise. I could kiss him into forever and beyond. Perry's nervous, I feel it in the light tremor running through his body, but he's not the only one because my heart's thundering, its erratic beat booming in my ears.

I guide his arms, taking them above his head. Crossing them at the wrists, I slip the tie around the heavy struts of the wooden headboard, threading it through and circling it around his wrists a couple of times in a loose restraint, before tying the ends in a bow.

"O…oh, *oh yes*," he breathes, as I nuzzle into his neck, his back arching upwards. I shift lower, scraping my front teeth over the skin just above his collar bone. He squirms and hisses, as his body writhes.

"You bastard." His moan is laced with laughter as he wriggles beneath my onslaught.

"But I'm being so nice to you. Very nice, like this." I suck at the fine, thin skin along the edge of the bone, teasing it out, pulling it hard.

"No…" he cries, but it turns into a shuddering breath and a throaty groan as he rocks into me, dragging his needy cock over my own, sending a lightning strike to my balls and turning up the heat on my own need.

I take a breath, a tiny break to bring myself under some kind of control. I'm on the edge and all it would take is the smallest nudge to send me hurtling over with nothing but my own pleasure in mind. But this isn't about me, this is all about Perry and the trust he's placed in my hands.

My head's clearer but only just, as I make my way down his body, meandering across his chest. It's smooth, the skin creamy with a scattering of freckles linking the dark pink circles of his areolae surrounding the hard nub of his nipples.

They're too good to resist, and I mouth one, and then the other, switching between the two, sucking hard and long as under me Perry gasps and whimpers and ruts into me, his cock iron-hard and hot, the head wet and slippery.

"Christ, James, you're a fucking sadist," he says, through gritted teeth, bucking with rising desperation into me.

I cast a look up at him, and Jesus, but it's all I can do not to come here and now. Puffy, pillowy lips, damp and bruised looking; his face flushed and sweaty; hair glued to his brow; eyes brimming with dark storms. He looks wrecked, broken almost, and he takes every one of my breaths away.

Working my way down, across his lightly muscled stomach, nosing my way through the dark treasure trail leading down from his belly button all the way to the light covering of hair between his legs.

"James, please…" His name on my lips is little more than a plaintive whine as he rolls his hips, canting himself up in a frantic demand for me to give him release.

"Not yet, baby, not yet."

He answers with a moan that's almost a growl, and mutters words questioning the legitimacy of my birth, and I smile as I lick a long, wide stripe from the base of his cock to its weeping head.

Licks and kisses, sucking and tasting, nuzzling his length, breathing in the hot musk of his need. His cock could tempt an angel, but I've never been that. I shift and position myself between his knees. Grabbing a pillow, I push it beneath him, raising him up. Perry opens his legs, his entrance exposed and waiting. I look up and our gazes fix and lock. He smiles, full of faith and once again my breath catches knowing that he trusts me with every ounce of his being.

Running the tip of my tongue around the rim of his hole, the muscle responds with a nervy, fluttering pulse. I lick and lave, drenching him with my spit. With the tip of my tongue I press, advancing, retreating, advancing again, pushing forward a little more until I breach him.

Groans and broken sighs fill the air, and whether it's me or Perry or both, I don't know, as I push deeper and fuck him with my tongue.

Clenching my eyes closed, the darkness speckles with white pinpricks as I savour his bitter, musky heat. With-drawing, I push his legs wider, opening him more, his taint and the tender skin of his hole wet and glistening. I breathe in deep as I push my face into him, licking, kissing, suck-ing, running my hands across his thighs, his hips, caressing his heated skin, wrapping a hand around his cock, riding him with my fist as he rides my demanding tongue.

I tear myself away. The need, overwhelming and irre-sistible, to be inside him, to feel his heat and the hard pulse of his muscles around my cock can no longer be held back, as unstoppable as a storm wave crashing onto the shore. My heart's all but pounding through my ribs and my breathing's out of control. Scrambling for the condom, I rip the foil off with clumsy fingers.

"We don't need that." His voice is rough and stops me in my tracks. He's glaring at the condom between my fingers.

I hate the fucking things, but I'm scrupulous about my health. I should say no, that there's no debate, that I never—

"Don't we?"

He shakes his head.

"No. I'm on PrEP, but I got checked out too, a few weeks ago. I've got the all clear." A flush further reddens his face.

"Are you sure?"

"Yes." He says the word so quietly it's little more than a breath.

I let the condom fall from my fingers. With any other man I'd shake my head, but the man gazing into my eyes isn't and never could be *any other man* as trust wraps itself around my heart and squeezes so tight it leaves me breathless.

"You're sure?" I need him to be sure, and I hope to God he is. "Do you have that much trust in me?"

He nods, his eyes on mine serious and steady.

"I do. I trust you to be honest with me and not to hurt me. I'm surer than I've ever been."

My heart jolts and I fumble for the lube, my hand shaking. Nerves, out of nowhere, are shredding me, and I make a mess slathering it over myself. It's not just my heart that's nervous. My cock has retreated a little, but some not so gentle persuasion gets him back on track. I glance up at Perry. His eyes are narrowed, and there's wry amusement sitting on his lips.

"You poor old boy. Having a bit of difficulty?"

"This old boy can show you a thing or two." I thrust into the tunnel of my fist with long, slow, teasing strokes, pushing soft groans out from between my lips.

Perry's gone quiet. Lips slack, he's breathing hard, all his concentration on the steady slip-slide of my hand.

Not so cocky now…

I trail my fingers, soaked with lube and precum, against his fluttering hole, ready to push in and—

"No," he barks. "Not your fingers."

It's the only green light I need.

Lining myself up against him I push forward and Perry gasps as I breach the muscle. I stop. There's no way I want to hurt him, and start to pull out.

"Fuck's sake. I said—" He huffs as he glares up at me. "James, I'm not made of glass. I won't break, no matter how hard you go." His lips curve up into a dark smile as challenge gleams in his eyes.

Two can play at this game.

"You've got no idea how hard I can go. No idea *at all*." I surge into him, thrusting deep, a primeval thrill shuddering through me as Perry's cry fills the bedroom.

I thrust deeper, pushing into him, my cock pistoning. There's no finesse, only basic and desperate need.

Our bodies ram into each other. His hips snap up, meeting every single one of my thrusts with an urgency and want that has him gasping for breath.

"Oh, Jesus," I pant. "So good, so fucking good, so…" My words dissolve to gibberish mutterings.

Perry's *everything*. His muscles clench my cock, so hot and tight it makes my head swim. I clamp and squeeze my hands to his bound wrists, with such force that in some tiny, and growing smaller by the second, clear and logical corner of my brain, I know he'll be bruised in the morning. Possessive pride surges through me. The marks will be mine, because Perry's mine.

Mine. Only mine.

I force my hips, harder and deeper, but it's not deep enough and I hook his legs up and over my shoulders, damn near breaking in two this shy, sweet boy who can moan and gasp and fuck like a whore.

I'm deep, but still not deep enough. He's crying out for me, demanding more, demanding harder. I shove his legs up some more, changing the angle and ramming his—

"Oh fuck. Fucking, oh, fuck, yes, yes, fucking *yes*!"

Laughing, crying, his head's twisting from side to side. He's pumping his hips up hard as I nail him over and over and over. And he's still laughing and crying, and I laugh and cry too for the sheer fucking, amazing, out of this world joy of this, here and now, with this incredible man who I—

"I can't hold on, I can't—oh, God…" he cries.

Underneath me, Perry spasms as his frantic and hard rhythm falters, as he falls apart shooting his release, splattering our stomachs in hot creamy cum. Still laughing, still crying, he's saying something but I can't understand because all I know is that my own orgasm is crashing through me.

"Jesus." I squeeze my eyes closed as fireworks explode

in the darkness and I release, filling him up with my cum, emptying myself into him in wave after hot wave.

The bones in my body dissolve and I collapse, gasping for air as my lungs burn. Beneath me, Perry's breathing is as out of control as my own, but there's more, I can feel it even though I'm dazed and wrung out. I push myself up onto my forearms, but God alone knows where I find the strength, and open my eyes. My heart rate, already at danger level, skips a beat, as Perry gazes up at me with tears running down is face.

Panic surges through me.

"Perry? I'm so sorry, I didn't mean to hurt you—"

"No," he shakes his head. The tears roll down his face but he's smiling, smiling harder than I've ever seen before. He's alight with happiness. "You didn't, you couldn't hurt me, not ever. I'm just… Oh, I don't know. God, you must think I'm an utter twat, crying when I've got nothing to be crying about. It's never been like this, I've never felt…" He squeezes his eyes closed and turns away as though embarrassed by his outpourings.

I've never felt like this… about anybody. Except for you… Deep in my chest, my heart twists and tumbles, spins and somersaults as silently I finish his words for him, words that have become mine.

His arms are still stretched above his head. He's not tried to pull himself free, even though he so easily could have done. It's a sign of his trust in me. A light tug is all it takes for the bonds to slip from his wrists, and I gather him up, holding him close as his arms loop around me, floppy and loose.

"I've got you, baby, I've got you." I whisper the words, in between scattering soft kisses over his silky hair.

His heart's beating fast and hard against my own, but wrapped in my arms his pulse calms and steadies, and I rub my cheek over the top of his head, telling him over and over that I have him. But it's only half the story, because the other half is that Perry has *me*. He has my heart, every little piece of it. He's always had it.

Our cooling bodies are sticky with sweat and more. He's filled with my release, and I can't help the flame of possessiveness that flares within me, the instinct basic and primitive knowing I've claimed him and made him mine. My lips twitch a smile. Take off the suit and shed the tie, and the caveman is revealed.

We should shower, and wash it all away, but there's not the slightest chance I'll let Perry escape my arms, not tonight. He's fallen asleep, I can feel it in the steady rhythm of his breathing as soft warmth wafts against my neck where he's nuzzled into me.

Slowly, carefully, I settle us both, and pull the duvet over us. He doesn't move a muscle, and I close my eyes, more content than I've ever been as I let sleep claim me.

CHAPTER THIRTY-THREE

PERRY

"Time to wake up head, sleepy head."

James' words come to me through a fog. I don't want to wake up and let go of those soft and gentle kisses filling my dream. I groan and turn over, but his laughter and the fingers trailing over my back slowly return me to life. But it's not just my head coming back to life, as I push my hips into the mattress in response to the pulse between my legs.

"Come on baby, rise and shine."

I open an eye, and peer at James. He's lying next to me, as fresh and awake as I'm not. He's smiling and he looks so happy it makes my heart dance. His face is only inches from mine and I know all those delicious kisses were no dream, and my heart does a full-on jig.

"Morning," I croak.

"It's a beautiful day." A soft smile plays on his lips, and his eyes are warm. It's not just the weather he's talking about.

He runs his palm down my cheek and over the scruff that's prickling through my skin and I can't help but push into his touch. My dick's fully awake and even though James is as fresh as a daisy, I want to make him dirty again. I tilt my head to lay a kiss on his arm and look up at him through my lashes.

He laughs before he places a quick kiss on top of my head and rolls off the bed. My seduction technique obviously needs fine tuning. Then again, I am covered in dried cum, and stink of sweat and sex.

"Jump in the shower and then get dressed. We're going out for breakfast."

"Can't we make it lunch?" I pat the bed, still warm from where he was lying on it.

"Greedy boy." The words have nothing to do with food, not if his sultry smile's anything to go by.

Maybe all he needs is a bit of gentle persuasion… The growly rumble of my stomach puts paid to that. Maybe breakfast isn't such a bad idea after all.

He presses his lips to my ear and a shudder dances down my spine as his warm breath caresses my skin.

"You've got half an hour. If you are not ready by then I'll drag you out."

"Even if I'm still half-naked, for all the world to see?"

He narrows his eyes, dark and stormy, all playfulness gone. "I'm the only one you will ever be naked for, Perry Buckland." His voice is low and tight, almost a hiss.

My breath catches in my throat, and the last traces of fog clears.

"Half an hour," he says, as he whips the duvet away and dumps it on the floor.

I gasp as cold air hits my skin and I scramble to retrieve it, but he kicks it out of reach.

"You git."

"Half an hour."

A moment later he's gone.

~

By the time we get out it's closer to an hour and despite his growly threats, James doesn't drag my partially clothed form out onto the street.

The café we pitch up at is buzzing. It's just gone eleven o'clock and it's packed. Breakfast has turned into brunch.

"This is great." It's also very Highgate, affluent with a touch of bohemian.

We order from the specials board, a kind of Full English but with a twist. When it comes, so much is piled up on the plate I swear the table groans under its weight.

"Oh God, this is lovely." I crunch down on the thick slab of sourdough toast slathered in butter. I expect James to be equally enthusiastic but instead he answers with a hesitant smile.

The cocky and confident man of earlier is nowhere to be seen and I swallow the toast that now feels like a hard ball of concrete. My stomach bites down on itself and I wonder why there's this sudden change in him. Maybe it was last night, maybe he regrets what happened... But I can't believe that. It was perfect, absolutely perfect. For me. But maybe it was too much for him. Maybe my tears, my bloody stupid tears that came from I don't know where have made him want to retreat.

My hands find the salt cellar and I turn it around and around and around. James is a man who wants no commitment in his life. And I agreed. I agreed because I was pathetically grateful for whatever he could give me, for the little time he could. But now—

He wants to step back, he wants his life to be as it was before. He's brought me here to tell me that it's time for us to move on…

I'll smile and nod and agree and try to convince myself that this was always a deal.

"James?" I want him to say something, anything to relieve the heavy tension in my chest and allow me to breathe. I want this to be over.

"There's something I want to talk to you about and I thought that doing it here might be easier."

A crowded place where I'll be less inclined to break down, or cry, or have a fit of histrionics. But I wouldn't do any of those things and it pisses me off that he thinks I would. I sit up straight and pull my hands away from the salt cellar.

"I don't know what it is you feel that you can't talk to me about in the house, but if it's about asking me to leave and make new arrangements then I understand. Staying with you was only ever meant to be a few nights but it's turned into a lot more than that. You want your space. I get it. And anyway I need to put a rocket up myself to get somewhere in or close to Brighton." I try to smile to show him I'm okay with what he's on the brink of telling me, but my lips are refusing to obey.

"What?" His eyes open wide in a kind of horrified surprise, and the blood drains from his face as he stares at me.

"What do you mean, *what*?" I don't understand his reaction. I'm confused and disorientated and all I can do is meet James' stare across the weird kind of no man's land that is the breakfast-strewn table.

"You think I'm asking you to leave?"

"Well, aren't you?"

"No. Oh God Perry, no." He pushes his fingers through his hair as he starts to laugh. I'm still not catching up with what's going on and he must see it in my face. His laughter dies away and he takes my hands in his. "No, that's not what I'm doing." He looks down at our joined hands and brushes his thumbs across my knuckles. "What I'm trying to do, and very badly, is ask you to stay. To stay with me. To live with me, I suppose. Properly live with me."

I can't do anything other than gaze at him. I can't speak; I can hardly even breathe.

"Can you say something? Anything?"

"Erm."

"Erm. Is that it? *Erm*?"

"No. Yes. I don't know. This wasn't what I was expecting."

"No, of course it wasn't. Why would you? You've got all your plans. Moving to Brighton." His shoulders sag. "I'm sorry. I've thrown a spanner in the works, I should never have—" He sits back and takes his hands from mine.

"No." I pounce on his hands and drag them back. There's no way, no way at all, I'm going to let this moment go. I suck in a deep breath. "It's just a massive surprise, that's all. But you're right about something. I do have my plans, and I won't give up on them. So I need to know, James, I need to know exactly what it is you're asking me."

My heart's all but punching its way through my ribs. Me and James, and what we could be together… But he's right about my plans.

I've always put myself second to every man in my life, always put what I wanted and needed to the side and all I've got for my trouble is a kick in the teeth. I'm drawn to the coast and Brighton's a great place, but it's also a symbol of my independence, of setting up on my own and carving out a business on my terms. As much as I want to jump up on the table and fist pump the air I can't just roll over and say yes. God, as much as I want to do that, this time I can't.

"I'm asking you not to leave, but to stay as—as my partner." Two red patches appear on his cheeks. He laughs, but it's unsure and nervous, and he can't meet my eye. "I don't have much of a track record, if any. You know what I've been like, I've never tried to gloss over that, but I've changed and it surprises me more than you can ever know."

James looks up at me, at last, and when he does his eyes are somber and serious, another facet of this endlessly fascinating, captivating man.

"I've changed because of you, Perry. You. You've made me want to change. You've made me want to be a better man."

A better man… To me, he's the best man there is.

"I—I don't know what to say."

"I'm hoping you're going to say yes. But I'm not, and

never would, ask you to sacrifice your dreams and ambitions. I want to help you with them, Perry, I want to help you in any way I can to make them a reality. We can find you proper premises, a professionally set up kitchen with everything you need on a small business unit that's aimed at start-ups. Do that here in London because you'll have a better chance at making a success of it here rather than in some grim bungalow in Brighton. You can look at getting tangled up with me as a kind of business decision, if it helps." He gives me a wan, tentative smile.

No, James will never be a cold business decision, not to me. He's thought about it, he's thought about what I need to help me become the man I want to be. I don't have to think about it, I don't have to take time, because I already know what my answer's going to be.

"I rather liked the bungalow. It was the avocado bathroom suite and the pink tiling that sold it to me."

"I'm not averse to retiling the bathroom in pink if that's what you want." He smile's surer as hope lights up his eyes, but it flickers and dies. "I know you were enthusiastic about setting up on the coast—"

"Yes, but going down to Brighton was always about more than the place itself. It was about starting again, about doing what I wanted to do on my own terms. It was a symbol."

"I know there's a lot to consider. I'll never stand in the way of what you want to do, I promise. You've got a remarkable talent and you need to use it. I want to help you realise your ambition but I want to help you realise it here, with me. Do you think that's something you could want as well?"

It's like he's asking me if I want the sun to shine, or for

it to snow on Christmas Day. Of course I want it. I answer him the only way I know how. I ease my hands away from his and place my palms on either side of his face and kiss him.

"Is that a good enough answer for you?" I murmur against his lips, before I kiss him again.

CHAPTER THIRTY-FOUR

PERRY

We hardly finish our breakfast, both of us eager to get home.

Home. It really is home now.

As soon as we're through the door, we slam it closed and I all but leap on James. His eyes widen in surprise as I push him against the wall but surprise turns to dark heat as I grind myself into him. I need to mark this new beginning in the most basic and dirty way I know how.

"I hope this is how you mean to go on Mr. Buckland?" he says, as I drag his jacket from his shoulders and throw it to the floor.

"This is very much how I mean to go on."

I'm scrabbling at the buckle of his belt, my fingers clumsy in their need and eagerness. Somehow I manage to undo it, and drag the zip of his jeans down over the hard bulge between his legs, letting them pool at his feet.

I drop to my knees.

James' cock is a huge ridge in his pristine white briefs and I nuzzle into him, closing my eyes as I breathe in deep taking in a heady mix of shower gel and the tang of his arousal. I look up at him through my lashes and my heart trips and stumbles. His neck's arched backwards, his eyes closed, and his breath comes in hard, ragged gasps; a deep flush covers his face. How did he ever think I could say no to this?

Dragging the edge of my teeth over his erection, James' whole body shivers as a groan escapes his lips.

The tip of his cockhead's breached the waistband of his briefs. I swipe my tongue over the slick purple head and he mutters something deep in his throat as he thrusts his hips forward. I could take him in now, take in every inch. My mouth waters at the thought. But not yet, not now. Instead, I kiss and nip and suck my way along his shaft, through the straining cotton, and once again run the edge of my teeth over his length. He hisses but he's not in pain as he grinds forward and rubs himself over my face.

I want to tease, I want to draw the moment out, I want to make this slow, but who am I kidding? I need to taste him, feel the weight of him in my mouth, and drink down every single drop of him.

Pulling down his pants, I free his cock. Flushed and pulsing with a long fat vein running along the underside, James is fucking glorious. Precum beads from his slit, salty and juicy, and I lick my lips. I'm scant inches from him, and I suck in a deep, shuddering breath, saturating myself in his arousal. It's heady and overpowering and as I lean into him he snaps his hips suddenly, slapping his burning cock against my face. I gasp and look up.

He's staring down at me, his eyes darker, heavier, hotter than I've seen before. Without breaking the contact, I take him in my hand and drag his cock over my cheek, over the light scruff that's pushing through. He hisses and his legs tremble, his whole body trembles, as I drag his cock backwards and forwards across my stubble.

James is breathing fast and jagged as his hips roll forward and back. I spit on my palm and wrap my hand around him, making a tunnel of my fist. On a ragged groan, he fucks into my hand. I tighten my grip, just a little, as I match him thrust for thrust, mesmerised as his foreskin slides over his cockhead and drags back, over and over.

With my free hand I press against his hip, stilling his movements. Our eyes lock again, and I lave my tongue across his slit and rub his cock across my lips, smearing them with his tangy, salty juice. He shoves his hips forward, begging for my mouth, but I'm quicker. I back up and smile, all the time never breaking eye contact.

"Prick tease. Did you know that's what you are?" His words are rough and gravelly. I answer with another lick across his hot, flushed cockhead.

Thrusting his legs apart, widening his stance, I push my face up under him, taking his balls into my mouth, sucking and stretching and rolling them around my tongue. Above me he's groaning and grasping as I slide my hand up and down his heavy cock, swiping the pad of my thumb over the supersensitive head.

"Oh Christ," he grounds out, as he grips fistfuls of my hair.

I let his balls slip from my mouth. They're harder, tighter. He's getting close but I'm not going to let him release, not yet. Squeezing down on the base of his cock, I pull him back from the edge.

My own cock's demanding attention of its own as it presses so hard against the zip of my jeans it's in danger of breaking through. Tugging down my own zip I pull myself free, wrapping my palm around my length as I slide up and down in long, smooth strokes.

Above me, James' breathing has got harder, more frayed, more erratic. I glance up. He's staring down at me, eyes glazed and jaw slack, watching as I pump my dick. With my eyes still welded to his, I take him deep.

Our groans fill the air. I close my eyes, tasting him as his weight pushes down on my tongue. He's big, and he stretches my lips wide. I suck him between flicking him with my tongue and sucking again, before I slip my lips all the way back along his length, up to the tip almost but not quite letting him go, milking his swollen cockhead of his salty precum before I glide my lips back down to his root, feeling him nudge against the back of my throat.

He fills me up and I breathe noisily through my nose. Saliva seeps from my mouth and drips down my chin. We're wet, the two of us so wet, as I slip and slide my lips, keeping rhythm with my hand on my own cock. His fists tighten in my hair, and my scalp tingles as he yanks my head forward. I gasp but don't gag as he thrusts his hips forward.

"Ah, shit. So fucking good." The gravel in his voice goes straight to my dick.

I'm harder than I've ever been. The frantic rhythm I've

set for myself is savage. I suck James with everything I've got, my head bobbing hard as I take him deep.

Our groans grow louder. Neither of us is going to last, but I don't want us to last because I want this here and I want it now. He explodes into my mouth coating my tongue and throat with his thick, salty semen. I drink him down, I drink every last drop of him down, sucking, slurping, milking him of everything.

"Greedy boy, so fucking greedy," he growls above me.

His gravel-laced words explode in my head... *greedy boy, so fucking greedy...* They're all I need to send my own climax racing through me, as I jerk and moan and spill over my hand, coating my fingers as I empty myself.

I collapse into a heap on the floor as all the tension drains from my body. It takes all my effort to gaze up at James. His chest's heaving fast as his cock, flushed dark and soaking wet, begins to soften.

His legs give way as he slides down the wall and settles into a crumpled heap next to me.

Taking my hand, he licks me clean of my release before he kisses me with a ferocity that makes me see stars. I taste us both, our arousal combined and mixed on the heat of our tongues as we kiss into eternity. He pulls back, breathing fast, his hands clamped to my cheeks.

"If I knew that taking you out for brunch was going to get me that reaction, I'd have been doing it every day," he says on a trembling laugh.

"Not just the brunch, although I think that was a deciding factor."

We try to stare each other out, but neither of us has the strength and we both laugh. He kisses me again, this time softer, sweeter, slower, as I run my hands through his hair.

"We've got a lot to talk about, a lot to discuss," he says, peppering my face with kisses before he gets up and extends his hand to me.

I clasp it in mine and let him pull me to my feet and take some of my weight, just like he's been doing since the night he found me and changed my life completely.

CHAPTER THIRTY-FIVE

JAMES

The next few days are a whirlwind because I don't want anything to stop the forward momentum that is me and Perry. I long ago vowed to never again commit myself, but not committing to Perry is an impossibility. The shy boy from whom I made it my mission to coax a smile or a laugh has burrowed under my skin and into my heart. This is everything I've told myself I've never wanted, but it's everything I now do.

I've been in touch with Jack and explained about the change to Perry's plans. I handed the phone over to Perry and left him to talk to my friend in private, but I couldn't help standing outside the closed office door as the phone went on to speaker as Rory joined in the conversation. It made my heart warm, hearing my friends talk with enthusiasm about the plan to find premises. It's right to say in

London, they said, so much more chance of success. They've got contacts, they'd give Perry as much help as they could…

We've already looked at a couple or so units, but none have been quite right for different reasons, but the search is well and truly on and we'll find somewhere Perry can set himself up and start the business I know he has his heart set on. I'm here by his side and I'm determined to help make his dream turn into a glittering reality.

Perry's father's been in touch and he's persuaded Perry to go out to see him and Perry's mum in Spain to try to heal the breach that's grown up between them. He hadn't wanted to go, not at first, but the last thing I want is for there to be a serious rift between him and his parents, so a week after we became official, Perry headed off for a long weekend. Already the house feels empty and unlived in without him. I hadn't suggested I go with him and he hadn't suggested it either, because it's way too early to meet the parents — and maybe a little awkward too, considering I'm more their age than I am their son's.

For now, I'm on my own. And I really am. The hook up apps are long gone, along with my account with the upmarket escort agency. Aiden's number's gone, too, although I felt I owed him some kind of explanation. I sent a text, it's pretty much the only way we've ever communicated. I kept it brief, but he'd have read between the lines. James Campion, reinvented. I can only imagine his smirk when he opened the message.

With the working day drawing to a close, and no Perry to rush home to, I do what I've always done when I've felt restless and at a loose end. I call Elliot.

"Meet me for a drink at The Breaker's Yard."

"And hello to you, too."

I laugh. "You know you want to, just for a quick one. It's either that or I go home to an empty house and I don't much fancy that yet."

"What about me? I'm left without my Executive Assistant until Tuesday morning. Perry runs this office like clockwork and when he's not here it teeters on the edge of anarchy."

I take his comment as my cue.

"It's actually about Perry I want to talk to you."

There's a short silence on the other end of the line. Elliot's one of the smartest men I know and he's probably already worked it out.

"I'll call Freddie and tell him I'll be late home. Have a G&T waiting for me in half an hour."

I've barely got Elliot's drink before he arrives.

"You're looking very pleased with yourself. Or should I say more pleased than usual." Elliot shakes out the light drizzle that's settled on his raincoat and drapes it over the back of the chair before he sits down and looks at me, waiting for my answer.

I pick up my own drink and take a leisurely sip, drawing out the moment. Elliot scowls, impatience sparking off him.

"So you want to talk about Perry? Or is it that you want to talk about you and Perry?" He sits back in his seat and smiles.

Now who's looking pleased with himself?

"First of all, you'll be pleased to know he's not hot

footing it down to Brighton but," I say, immediately extin-guishing Elliot's hope that he'll keep hold of Perry for the foreseeable future, "that's because he's staying in London. He, or I should say we, are looking for premises so that he can really start to get going on his business."

I pick up my own drink, finding my hand's not as steady as it should be. I'm about to tell my oldest friend something that goes against everything I've always claimed. I don't doubt Elliot's already worked it out, and I know or at least I hope, he'll be happy for me because he's a complete believer in a settled and committed lifestyle. But I can't help but be nervous.

"I see. Not that I'm in the least bit surprised." He gives me a broad smile and leans forward, squeezing my hand briefly, and I feel a weight slide from my shoulders.

But I'm curious.

"You see what, exactly? Why aren't you surprised?"

Elliot takes time to answer, a small and thoughtful frown wrinkling his brow as he works out what to say.

"What do I see? I see somebody who appears to be happier and more settled in himself and that's good. More than good. You've lost that restless edge you've always had. Even when you were with Alex it was always there, but now?" He shrugs. "I don't believe you've been truly happy with your life, despite all your assertions to the contrary. There was something missing. I could see it, even if you refused to. But these last few months, it's as though you've found the missing piece, and it's Perry. He's brought something into your life you never had before. He's filled the gap you always denied existed. I get that, I understand it. That's what Freddie did for me. He made me whole, and Perry's doing the same for you."

"So, you're saying love's been your saviour, or some such." I want to dismiss what he's said with a smirk and a cynical arch of the brow. But I can't. It's what I'd have done just weeks ago, it's what the old James would have done, but now…?

"Love? I've not said anything about love. It's you who's done that. But, yes, it's true."

I feel the heat burning in my cheeks. He's right, it's me who's said the word I've not yet said to Perry and even hardly to myself. Elliot's laugh is low and soft, and he shakes his head.

"Okay, okay. I won't embarrass you any further though it is rather fun."

"You're a fucker, Hendricks. You know that, don't you?" I say without any force or ill-feeling. He just laughs and I join in.

I briefly tell him what's happened.

"So, he's properly moved in with you. All thoughts about relocation to the coast now shelved, then?"

I nod. "We're looking for a kitchen unit, like I said, proper business premises where he can operate from. We've already seen some places and I'm calling in a couple of contacts of mine for them to put their ear to the ground."

I beckon a waiter over for a couple more drinks and when I turn back to Elliot he's studying me with his cool blue eyes.

"You're scrutinising me. Why?"

"Because you've changed and it suits you. I only hope it stays this way."

"What do you mean?" Although I know exactly what he means. All my years of refusing to entertain any kind of commitment and even when I did, I treated it with little more than contempt.

"I'm not going to dice words with you, James, I've known you too long to do that."

He leans forward, his eyes grave and steady as they lock onto mine.

"Don't do anything stupid and risk screwing this up with him. Perry's good for you, that's easy to see. You feel like this now, and I hope to God that three months', or six, or in a year's time you still do, but if things change you have to do your level best to let him down gently and not break his heart."

"You have that little faith in me?" I should be angry for what he's said, but Elliot knows me as much as I know him, and if there's any man in this world who can be honest with me, it's the one sitting opposite me with the serious blue eyes.

"It's not about me having or not having faith in you, it's about you having faith in yourself. That'll be the real test. If you want, you can throw your drink in my face and tell me to back off."

"If anybody else had said that to me it wouldn't just be a drink they'd be getting in their face. I have got faith in myself, just like I've got faith in Perry. This can work, I know it can."

"Yes, it can, if you're committed to making it work." He smiles, his voice dropping a notch when he speaks. "Maybe, like me, you just had to wait for the right man to come along. Ah, just like our drinks."

Two more G&Ts arrive, breaking up the charged atmosphere that's spun itself around us.

"This is going to work, Elliot. I'm not going to screw this up. Surely you believe that?"

Elliot smiles, inclining his head before taking a drink.

We move to safer ground, talking of other things. It's only when he gets up to leave, a short while after, that I realise he never answered my question.

CHAPTER THIRTY-SIX

JAMES

"It's a contender, don't you think?" I say, raising my voice over the music in the pub.

"It's certainly the best place we've seen so far." Perry flicks through the photos he's taken of the kitchen unit we've just been to see. "A bit larger than I need, or at least for now, but it means there's room to expand."

I sit back in my chair and smile. He's thinking ahead and that's good. The unit's more than a contender. On a small business park just a couple of miles away from the house, it's perfect for a start-up. The costs are reasonable too, but they're going to be even better because I'll be negotiating on Perry's behalf.

"Shame it's not available until the end of January, though," he says, putting his phone away. "But then I suppose it gives me time to get everything else set up. God, there's going to be so much to do."

"Yes, but I'm here to help, don't forget."

"I know, and I'm kind of glad I'm not doing it all myself." A warm smile lifts his lips.

"*Kind* of glad?"

"*Very* glad." He leans in and lands a quick kiss on my cheek, his smile widening to a grin. "Thanks for... Well, for everything I guess."

"Why don't we finish these, go home, and then you can show me how glad you really are?"

Perry blushes, and it flips my heart that I can still make him do that. I hope I always will.

"Let me give it some thought." He cocks his head to the side and makes a show of considering my suggestion. "Hmm, I might be able to do that. After we pick up a take-away. Chinese, I think."

I huff and do my best to appear put out by the idea.

"How have we come to this, and after such a short period of time? You're putting a bowl of noodles and some sweet and sour sauce ahead of showing me your *appreciation?*"

"You really are losing your touch, old man. You don't think I actually want to eat the Chinese, do you? At least not off a plate. I'm thinking about getting inventive with pork balls."

He tilts his chin upwards and stares at me. There's a dare in the dark chocolate depths of his eyes, and I mean to take it up. I lean forward and lower my voice.

"Old man? You're going to regret those words, Buckland. The sky's the limit when it comes to what I can do with a couple of spring rolls, and as for crispy aromatic duck…"

We're locked in a stand-off, and I intend to win. Perry's Adam's apple dips and rises, and I smile.

"Well," he croaks, "if you want to put it like that, we—ohh, fuck." He all but leaps out of his seat as his phone, buried in the pocket of his jeans, leaps into life.

"It's Alfie," he says, a wide smile wrapping its way around his face. "It's been weeks and weeks… I've got to answer… Alfie!"

Sorry he mouths to me. His off-grid friend who's back on grid just at the wrong time.

So much for fun with pork balls…

I sit back and take a sip of my G&T.

"Sorry? What's that?" Perry frowns as he covers the ear not clamped to his phone with his free hand. The music's loud but the customers are louder. "Hold on, I'll go outside." Perry throws me an apologetic smile as he gets up and pushes his way to the exit.

Left on my own, I let my gaze roam. I've been here before, but not for some time. It's a gay pub, but not exclusively so, and the whole vibe is pretty laid back. Friday evening, and couples and groups of friends are marking the start of the weekend.

My attention fixes on a small group of guys up at the bar. Early thirties, I guess. All toned and fit. Very toned and fit, in slim fitting track suit bottoms, and striped sweatshirts.

Of course… There's a rugby club not far from here. I'm about to look away when one of the guys, on the fringes of the group, looks across. He catches my eye and smiles. It's light, friendly, and casual, not an obvious come-on. So I smile back, before I let my gaze continue on its meandering way.

Who'd have thought it? Passing up an opportunity to flirt, and more.

Not me, and not in a million years. But here I am, and I'm happier than I've ever been and it's all down to Perry. I wouldn't want it any other way… The thought that he might have disappeared down to Brighton, that I could so easily have lost him sends a shiver across my skin.

Yet, there's no denying it's a huge change, after years and years of playing the field, having who I wanted when I wanted, and steering clear of entanglements.

My gaze drifts back to the guy standing at the bar. He's talking to somebody, laughing and nodding his head, and doesn't notice me looking. Which is all I'm doing. I'm realistic enough to know that a lifetime's habits can't be overturned in a matter or weeks. No doubt I'll always look. Looking's harmless, it's what comes after that isn't.

Don't do anything stupid and risk screwing this up with him… You feel like this now and I hope to God that three months' or six or in a year's time you still do…

Elliot's words, out of nowhere, rock me, and I jerk back in my seat, almost dropping my glass.

What the hell…?

There's no way on this earth I'm going to do anything to risk what I've got with Perry.

Everything Elliot said to me that evening when we met up had been out of friendship and concern, but it'd also been said out of knowledge of the kind of man I am. Or the kind of man I was.

Was, not *am*.

Still, irritation prickles my skin that my oldest friend's faith in me might be built on shaky foundations.

"Fuck off, Elliot," I mumble, picking up my drink and chugging it back.

A burst of laughter, loud and raucous with a dirty edge, as though somebody's just told a particularly filthy joke, jolts me out of my ill-tempered thoughts, and I look over at the knot of rugby players.

They're all laughing hard, and one or two are wiping their eyes. The guy's still there, the one who smiled at me. He's tall with dirty blond hair and there's no denying he's easy on the eye. In another lifetime… Which is not *this* lifetime. Yet, my gaze lingers.

He must sense my scrutiny, because he turns and catches my eye. Like before he smiles, but the lightness has gone. It's more intense, more focused. He says something to the guy standing next to him and hands him his pint. I know what's coming next, and it's everything I don't want. I swing my head around so fast I hear the crunch of bones in my neck — and just in time to see Perry pushing his way towards me.

"He's coming home next week."

"What?" I can feel my cheeks throbbing and as Perry throws himself into his chair and stares at me, I feel like I've been caught out.

"Alfie. Who do you think? He's finished his shepherding job. As soon as he's back we're going to meet up. That's brilliant. Another drink?" He points to my empty glass.

"No, let's go." All I want is to get out of here.

"Oh, okay. Perhaps we can get that Chinese then?" Perry laughs. It's a light and happy sound but all I can do is answer with a nod as I bundle him out of the pub, and refuse to look back.

CHAPTER THIRTY-SEVEN

PERRY

As soon as Alfie opens the door he envelops me in a big, hard hug. It feels like both yesterday and a million years ago since I was last with him.

Like me, he's on the shorter side, but that's where the comparison ends.

Alfie holds me out at arm's-length, his face wreathed with smiles. His skin's tanned although I suppose weather-beaten might be a better way of describing it and his blond hair's cropped close to his head. As ever, his style is... eclectic.

Patchwork harem pants and a T-shirt that's got to be older than the two of us, if the *Maggie Maggie Maggie, Out Out Out* slogan's anything to go by, are baggy and out of shape, but they don't conceal his muscular frame. He looks every inch of what he is: sometime shepherd and urban poet, and always my best friend.

"You're looking good, mate, you're looking really good. Come here." He pulls me into another strong Alfie hug, before he clamps both his meaty hands to my cheeks and gives me a smacker of a kiss on the lips. I roll my eyes, and Alfie answers with a cackle. It's him, it's what he does, but I'm kind of glad James isn't here to see.

He disappears into the kitchen for a moment, and returns with a couple of bottled beers, thrusting one into my hand.

I follow him through the living room and throw a quick glance at the sofa, and I'm happy to see it's covered with a multicoloured throw, hiding the stains of God knows what.

The flat's empty apart from us. No trapeze artists, no yogis, no knife throwers, none of the weird, wonderful, and sometimes slightly scary people Alfie attracts like a magnet. For now it's just the two of us and time to catch up.

Alfie's itchy feet mean he could take off again at a moment's notice. I hope he doesn't, because I've missed him, especially when things went south with Grant. He knows all about that particular shit storm, as I sent him a long message about my change in circumstances. I wasn't sure he'd got it, what with him exercising his shepherding skills deep in the Scottish wilds, but the short, blunt and very Alfie response of *thank fuck for that* had dropped into my inbox and made me smile.

"How long are you back for?"

"Indefinitely. I need to dust off the suit and join the rat race again for a while, because the coffers are pretty bare."

He knocks back his beer but he still doesn't meet my eye, and that's not Alfie. There's more to this and I want to know what it is.

"What aren't you telling me?"

"Don't know what you're talking about."

"Yes, you do. I know you too well and you're looking furtive."

He laughs, and gently shakes his head. "You could always read me and you're one of the few who can." His smile's warm and full of the friendship and closeness we've always shared despite being so different from each other. "I've met somebody, up in Scotland, but he actually lives in London. He was there for the emotional transcendence course at the place where I was working, and staying in one of the yurts."

"Oh. That's nice." I try my best to keep my face straight. "So what was he doing? Trying to get his wonky aura straightened out, or his dreams defined, or—"

"Don't be a cheeky fucker," he says, but he's laughing. "He wasn't actually attending the course. He'd come with his sister who's going through some sort of crisis. Whilst she was being, erm, transcended, he went walking in the hills and helped me with tending the sheep. We'll see how things go. Another beer?"

He jumps up and dashes to the kitchen. It's likely all I'll get out of him, at least for now, so I won't push.

"So no come back from that tosser Grant?" he asks, before he takes a glug from his bottle.

I shake my head. "No, nothing. He's long gone." *And he won't be coming back, not after the pasting James gave him.* "It's all in the past. I'm with James now."

He's peering at me over the rim, his eyes narrowed.

For a moment he reminds me of James, which is kind of weird because the North and South Poles couldn't be further apart.

Alfie's blue eyes blaze out from his weatherbeaten face. "The guy who always flirted with you? The one you've always had the hots for? I thought you were just renting a room in his gaff, and the next minute you've properly moved in with him? You sure that's wise?"

He's sounding almost censorious, and I shift on the lumpy sofa. For such a free spirit, unfettered by the bonds of societal norms — his words, not mine — he can be surprisingly traditional in his outlook. I'm feeling judged, for making the best and probably sanest decision in my entire life.

I tamp down my annoyance. He's being a friend, that's all. He'd warned me what a twat Grant was, and said I was crazy to get involved. I wished I'd listened, but there's no comparison with James, not in a million years.

"It's the wisest thing I've done. I like him. A lot."

"Should hope so, seeing as you're shacked up. Which kind of raises the question, what's happening with your plan to move down to Brighton?"

The question he couldn't not ask, and the one I can't not answer.

"Obviously I'm staying in London now. We're looking for small kitchen premises I can work from." I do my best not to squirm. I should have expected the question, but it still makes me feel a little defensive, like he's questioning my judgement — which of course he is.

"So, you've turned all your plans upside down?" Again, for another man, he may as well add.

"No, I've adjusted them, that's all."

His impassive expression tells me he's not convinced. I'd hoped for more enthusiasm from my oldest friend, but I have to remind myself that he's often had a front row seat to watch the farce that's been my relationships. But James, and what I have with him, is different and I need to make him understand that.

"Alfie, I know what I'm doing. Believe me when I say he's different — when you meet him you'll realise that."

James in his handmade suits, and Alfie dressed like he's raided the fancy dress shop. Despite their surface differences, I think they'd not only take the other in their stride, but even like each other.

Alfie releases a long breath, and nods. "Okay. Tell me about him."

I take a sip from my beer, as I think how to begin.

"Well, he's older and by quite a bit. No, he's not some kind of Daddy," I say, when Alfie cocks a brow. "That's not my thing at all, and I definitely don't have an older guy, silver fox fantasy thing going on."

Or not really… Or maybe just a bit…

"I don't really think about the age difference. James is just — well, he's James. I guess being older gives him confidence and self-assurance, and that's attractive in itself, and that makes me feel more confident, I suppose."

I look down at my hands fiddling with the damp label on the beer bottle. I'm silent for a moment and when my words come, they come slowly.

"He listens to me and values my opinions. And he respects me, too. Let's face it, most of the guys I've been with couldn't have cared less about what I thought of anything. I feel safe with him. It's not that I'm looking for some sort of safe harbour because I'm not, but I feel that with him I can truly relax and be who I am. I'm not on edge, I don't feel I'm having to run around trying please him all the time, like I've always done in the past."

"And the sex is fucking hot?"

I burst out laughing. Alfie being Alfie, direct but never cruel. It's one of the reasons I love him.

"Yes, it is. It just sort of happened and it's gone from there. There was never any expectation on his part, when I started renting a room," I say quickly, meeting Alfie's eye. "Sex was never, ever part of the deal. Don't think that because it's not true."

Alfie doesn't say anything for a moment. He's thinking, wondering what to say or how to say it. I know because I recognise the sign, the rapid tap, tap, tap of his right heel on the floor.

"Being older means he'll have a history—"

"Of course he has, and he's told me some of it. What's your point?" I snap when I don't mean to, but Alfie's words have put me on the defensive. I'm living in my James bubble and I don't want it burst.

"My point is, if he's a lot older and he's not attached that might be because that's not what he really wants, not deep down and long term."

"So what are you saying, Alfie? That I'm some kind of novelty for a few months? I've told you, it's not like that."

I'm angry, but I'm also upset, but I need to keep a lid on it, and tell myself that in being devil's advocate, Alfie's being the friend he's always been. Yet I can't help the ice that settles low in my stomach.

"No, I'm not saying that, but what *I am* saying is be careful. You meet someone and five minutes later you're getting all serious and settled down."

"There's nothing wrong with wanting a long term relationship." Heat throbs in my cheeks. I can protest all I like and although he's exaggerating there's some truth in what he says and we both know it.

"Perry, most blokes our age aren't looking for that."

"That's the point. You've said it. James isn't our age. And anyway, we're just starting out."

He keeps his steady gaze on me before he nods, leans forward, and rests a hand on my thigh.

"Okay. But just be aware that after the honeymoon period there might be a mismatch. He's rescued you, and I don't think that's an overly dramatic way of putting it. He rescued you from living in a fucking basement for God's sake, and he rescued you from trying to talk Grant around so he'd let you crawl back under his boot again. Because it's what you would've done. You got somewhere nice to live with somebody you like and the breathing space you need. And you've added sex into the equation. You're both getting a lot out of the current situation but what you ultimately want might not be the same thing he does. Look, enjoy what you've got. For now. If it goes on to be more, then that's great but don't invest everything in this guy—"

"His name's James."

"James," he says gently. "Be careful, that's all, although I guess that's like telling the sun not to shine or the tide not to ebb and flow."

Don't invest everything... But Alfie's words have come too late, because invested is exactly what I am.

CHAPTER THIRTY-EIGHT

JAMES

Another bottle of champagne arrives. I'm not sure how many that makes because I stopped counting long ago.

A smart, expensive Soho bar, with drinks including the never ending flow of champagne, courtesy of the host. I've had more to drink than I normally would. I'm not drunk, exactly, but it's fair to say the edges have been blunted.

The evening started out sober and restrained, in one of the council chambers at work. Worthy speeches and polite chitchat all served up with warm cheap wine and under-seasoned canapés. A long-standing colleague's overseas posting has been officially marked and as soon as it was over, a small group of us made a discrete departure to here, to the chic, sleek bar for a private party that's a lot less sober, in all senses. I hadn't really wanted to go, but it would have been churlish to say no. I'd intended on staying for a couple of drinks, before heading home to Perry. But that was hours ago, and the champagne keeps on coming.

"Anything take your fancy?" Sam, my soon to be departing colleague, slumps into the seat next to me.

I follow his gaze beyond the roped-off area that's for our party alone. There's plenty to take my fancy, or there would have been not so very long ago. Now, I'm only looking. That's all. The way I was in the pub not so long ago, when Perry dashed off to talk to Alfie. No harm in looking. Just as I thought then, it's all about whether you let looking turn into more. And that's not going to happen.

"No, not tonight."

"Really?" Sam tops up my glass. "That's not the James I know and love. What's happened to the man who can fuck his way through half the population of London without putting a hair out of place?" He half snorts and half burps and I shrug. There's a lot of truth in what he says, but I can't say I'm thrilled with the description. "Not seen you around the clubs and bars much in recent weeks. It's been noted, you know."

I don't for a moment believe my absence has been deemed noteworthy.

"I've been busy with other things." I don't say anything more but Sam's drunken, beady eye is on me.

"Don't say you've met somebody? You? James Campion, who pounces on anything with a pulse?" His eyes widen in almost comic incredulity, but I don't rise to it.

What and who Perry and I are to each other is for us

alone. Other than Elliot, nobody knows about him. I've not introduced him to any of my other friends yet, but I will do soon. For now I want Perry all to myself, and if that makes me selfish then so be it. Perry's not a topic up for discussion and certainly not with Sam, not when he's pissed and not when he has a loose mouth.

"So, you're off to the fleshpots of…"

Sam's plum posting overseas is enough to knock him off the scent, and we spend the next few minutes talking all about that before one of his friends, somebody I don't know, comes to drag him away.

I'm left alone for barely a minute or two, before I'm joined by a couple of guys, one of whom I know slightly. The other's a stranger.

The one I don't know wants to get to know me a lot more, if the press of his thigh against mine and the overt and frankly laughable come-on in the way he licks his lips and runs his gaze up and down my body is anything to go by. Sam's little barb is wrong. I don't go after anything with a pulse. I have my standards, and can more than afford to be fussy. And this guy doesn't meet them, even if I were on the lookout. Which I'm not.

I get up to get away from his clumsy and drunken attempts at seduction. I could tell him straight out I'm not interested, but I don't want to embarrass him by telling him he doesn't have a hope in hell's chance, and decide instead to be kind.

"I'm just heading outside."

His eyes light up.

Oh, Christ… Of all the things to say. He thinks it's an invite.

"I'll join you." In his haste to get up and follow me out for something he definitely won't be getting, he stumbles and knocks over his chair.

"No, that's okay. I've got a phone call to make. To my boyfriend," I add.

A least that got through.... The guy's face drops just as he slumps back into the chair he's just uprighted.

I shove my way through the crowd. It might be new and sleek, but it's a typical Soho gay bar and it's full. Hips, arses and cocks nudge, and arms snake round waists. Men in twos or threes or even more, slip off to the toilets, sometimes surreptitiously but mostly brazen. It's hot and sweaty, and excitement and anticipation pulse in the steamy air.

I've been to a million and one places like this and I've done it all and taken everything that's been on offer. It's exciting, the thrill of what the night might bring, it's impossible to deny and it's exciting still, even though I'm going to refuse anybody or anything that puts itself in my way. I haven't been to a place like this for ages, and I'd be lying if I said I'm immune to the thrill that's running through the air. The issue is whether or not to give into the thrill, and there's only one answer to that.

I push my way out, not through the main door, but a smaller one that takes me outside and into a side alley.

The air outside is cold and crisp, and I take a deep breath and lean back against the wall. The alley's long but narrow, and although Soho's teeming streets are only footsteps away, the sound of the crowd's muted.

Plunging my hand into my trouser pocket, I pull out the squashed packet of cigarettes. I rarely smoke anymore, but just sometimes I crave the hit of nicotine. It's a filthy habit and at odds with keeping fit, but still, here and now it's what I want. I light up and take a lungful of smoke before letting it go on a long, steady exhale. God, but it tastes good. It's another thing I haven't done much of recently.

My phone, which is the whole excuse for me being out here, presses against my chest from my jacket inside pocket. Perhaps I can give Perry a call, just to see how he's doing… But I decide not to. He's with his Alfie, who's now back in London from wherever he's been shepherding, or reciting poems, or what not. It's hard to imagine Perry having a friend like that. No, I won't phone, I won't disturb him, but just as I decide not to my mobile pings as a text drops in.

Long journey back to Highgate… had a few beers… staying the night…. The message ends with a row of kisses and I can't help but smile. I plug in a quick response telling him I hope he's having a good time and I'll see him tomorrow, adding a row of kisses of my own. Putting my mobile away, I take another drag on my cigarette and close my eyes.

I really need to give this up properly, and for good. But not yet.

"Hello stranger."

My eyes snap open. In front of me just a step away is the last person I expect to see.

Aiden.

He smiles and looks at me through hooded eyes.

Despite the cold, he's only wearing a T-shirt which hugs itself to his muscled torso. Intricate inked patterns

315

snake their way down both arms. His jeans sit low on his hips revealing a flash of firm abdominal muscles. He looks good, but he's always looked good. And I smile, returning the one he's giving me, because I like him. We've never been anything to each other beyond filthily glorious sex, but I've always liked him.

"You never returned my text messages. I'm hurt James, I thought I meant more to you than that." He pouts but his eyes glitter in amusement. He's not hurt, and we both know it, but maybe he's a little disappointed and it feeds my ego to think that.

"I sent you a text. I told you things have changed." *And then deleted your number...*

"Didn't get it." He shrugs. "So what's changed?" His eyes bore into me, as sudden realisation widens them. "*Changed.* You mean with that friend of yours, the one who was with you in the café?"

"Maybe."

I don't offer any more information and he doesn't ask. I take another draw on my cigarette and blow the smoke to the side.

"Got a spare?" Aiden asks, and I fish out the packet from my pocket.

He takes the cigarette but before I can offer him the disposable lighter, he plucks mine from my mouth and uses it to light his own. Aiden draws hard to light up, his generous lips tight around the tip. Something tightens deep in my stomach. He keeps my cigarette and gives me back the new one. Raising his eyes to mine, he smiles, as dark and dirty as ever, before he flops against the wall next to me. He's close although not touching but I can feel his heat and I detect a tang of salt and sweat and cum on him. It's a heady aroma and almost without realising, I breathe in deep.

"It's good to see you again, James. Seriously." There's a sincerity running through his quietly spoken words, cutting through the heat of his flirting.

"It's good to see you, too."

He snorts. "But you're only saying that because we've run into each other by chance." He stares at me and even under the weak lamplight I see all his cocky artifice stripped away. There's real hurt this time, in his voice and in his eyes, something I've never seen or heard before, and for a moment I have no idea what to say.

"Don't tell me you're actually properly with that young guy?" He laughs, and shakes his head. "I thought hell had more chance of freezing over."

"Like I say, things have changed." It's all he needs to know.

"Changed. That word again." Aiden pushes himself off the wall and steps in front of me. His body brushes mine, enveloping me in the sharp tangy aroma which is now illicit and out of bounds. "Changed? Really?" His lips lift in a lazy smile as he moves in closer.

He's hard. I clamp my hands to his waist ready to push him off. Through the thin cotton of his T-shirt his skin's warm and damp, and before I'm even aware of it, I'm breathing him in and digging my fingers into his flesh.

"You've not changed, James." He's hardly a breath away. His drink and cigarette roughened voice is low and gravelly, and he chuckles as he presses his erection against my hip. Tilting his head back, he moves in to kiss me and I slide my hand around the back of his neck.

"Oh no," Aiden murmurs, "men like you, men like me,

we never change. If you're telling yourself that, you're lying to yourself and that sweet thing—"

I whip my hand from him. It's as if I've been burnt, and shove him away with all the force I can muster. He stumbles back, keeping his footing but only just.

"Fuck, no," I rasp. "I'm sorry Aiden, I shouldn't…" I squeeze my eyes shut and rub my hands down my face. I feel off centre, disorientated and sick to my stomach.

Jesus, but I'd nearly…

I pull my hands away from my face and open my eyes. Aiden's staring at me, studying me, assessing me under the weak lamplight. His mouth lifts into a slow smile, but like the shine in his eyes it's hard and cold.

"No, James, you've not changed. Haven't you just proved that? It really didn't take very much to tempt you from your newfound straight and narrow, did it? Men like you don't change; they never do. Don't fool yourself you're any different."

A moment later he's gone. I scratch at my skin, feeling dirtier, filthier than I ever have before, wanting to scrub it all away until I bleed.

The champagne, the cigarette, and what I almost did, burn a hole in my stomach. I double up and vomit it all out on the pavement, emptying myself of everything except his words which clamour in my head with a dark and undeniable truth.

I don't go back into the bar, but I don't go straight home either. I walk around the busy, winding, twisting Soho streets, my footsteps getting faster as Aiden's words seem to chase me down.

Clearer headed, but not by much, I tell myself I should bat what he said aside, that he's wrong, that I have changed, but it doesn't stop his words burrowing under my skin like a stinking parasite.

I can't go home, not yet, because I'm ashamed. Ashamed of what I nearly let happen. It would have been easy, so, so bloody easy. A filthy kiss, a fumble for the belt and the zip, and then…

The sickness rises up in me again, but there's nothing left to leave splattered on the pavement. Temptation, easy temptation I could never resist, grabbing it and gorging like a greedy child. This time I did resist, but what about the next time, or the time after that? I should go home, shower, clean my teeth and wash it all away, all the grubbiness I know is more than skin deep.

Lifting my hands to my face I sniff. I can smell Aiden on me, I'm sure of it. Cigarettes, sweat, and cum, the stench of clubs and bars and temptation. It makes me gag, and I stop for a moment, in a shop doorway, taking deep breaths to steady myself.

I've been walking the streets blindly with no idea where I've been going, but up ahead is a comforting neon sign, known and familiar. Café Alberto, where I found a drunk and dejected Perry all those weeks ago. His clumsy flirting, almost boyish, it made me laugh but even then it struck a match inside me lighting up a dark little corner of my heart. A chance encounter. I took him not just into my home, but into my heart, and everything changed.

But men like me don't change. *I* don't change.

I barge in and seek out the table in the shadows where I

319

found Perry. It's occupied, by lovers smiling and kissing half hidden in the gloom, and instead I stumble into a seat up against the large plate glass window overlooking the busy street. I order a coffee but barely taste it as I stare out at the life tumbling around outside.

A couple of young guys come in, laughing aloud in between whispering and giggling all over each other. Mid-twenties, Perry's age or thereabouts. They flop down at one of the tables, kissing and whispering and kissing again, totally wrapped up in one another.

This is what Perry should be doing, with a guy his own age. He shouldn't be with me, he shouldn't be having anything to do with a man like me.

Don't screw this up, is what Elliot said to me. My friend knows me so, so well. It's exactly what I'm doing. The guy in the pub, the men in the bar tonight. And Aiden, let's not forget Aiden, but there's another man I should never forget.

Alex, the man I betrayed over and over, to my ever-lasting shame. The man I didn't love enough. I ditched my slutty ways for him, that's what I told myself, all those years ago. And I did, for a little while, until temptation crooked its finger and I didn't think twice about following. I broke his heart and I vowed I'd never do that to another man.

I won't do that to Perry.

As one, the two guys turn and look at me because I've been staring. One of them throws the other a questioning glance before he smiles at me. I stagger up, almost knocking over my seat, wanting to get out to escape their sudden sharp scrutiny, and the light in their eyes that tells me they know the kind of man I am.

I've made choices tonight, and they've been the right ones, but will I be able to make the right choices next week, or next month, or next year? Will I be able to shake my head and turn away from future temptation when I've never done so in the past? I don't know, and that's what frightens me. But there's one thing I do know, and that it's men like me don't change.

CHAPTER THIRTY-NINE

PERRY

"James? I'm home."

The weather's turned very cold overnight, but the house is lovely and warm and I shrug off my coat and hang it up in the hallway cupboard.

I call out for James again but there's no answer and as I walk through to the kitchen I instinctively know the house is empty.

Nothing's out of place in the kitchen, except for a mug that contains the last dregs of coffee. I can do with a hot drink. The journey across London, south to north, from Greenwich to Highgate, has been long and difficult, but I'm home now and that's what matters. I glance up at the clock; it's lunchtime and I wondering where James is, on a cold and blustery Saturday.

Work, I guess. He must have been called in. He seems

to be on call pretty much 24/7, and late evening or weekend calls or meetings aren't that uncommon. I check my phone to see if there's a text, but there's nothing.

I can't be bothered to fire up the coffee machine. Flipping the kettle on, I hear the slam of the front door. He's back and that fills me with a warmth that's hotter than the central heating pumping out. Seconds later he's standing on the threshold of the kitchen, his running gear soaking wet and splashed with mud. He normally runs early in the morning but it's getting on for one o'clock. And then I remember. Of course, he'd have been out late last night. He looks tired, with dark shadows under his eyes, the telltale sign of too little sleep and too much booze.

"Hey." I stride over to him.

He's not smiling and I can only assume his hangover's really, really bad, so bad it hurts to even smile. I've got a cure that doesn't include raw egg yolks or paracetamol. I sling my arms around his neck, not caring about the dampness seeping into my clothing. I kiss him on the lips but his own barely respond.

Boy, but this is one monster of a hangover.

"How was your evening last night? Or maybe I shouldn't ask," I say, going back to making coffee.

"It was okay." He doesn't offer more, and I look over at him.

"It was okay? Is that all? Didn't you go on somewhere, after the official do? You must have had a good time." I laugh as I fill two mugs with boiling water.

"Why do you say that?"

There's something in his words, in the tone, which makes me jerk and I spill some of the water on the counter. I put the kettle down carefully.

It's his monster hangover, that's all. He's not up for lots of questions.

"Well, it was a party you went to afterwards, wasn't it? The temptation of lots of free booze, which you took full advantage of, from the look of you." I laugh and shake my head when James grimaces.

There, I'm right. All he needs is a gallon of water, painkillers, and to spend the rest of the day in bed — I'd suggest with me, but somehow I don't think he's quite up to that.

"Have you eaten?" I ask, when he slumps down at the table. He shakes his head, and mumbles that he doesn't want anything.

"It looks like I had a much more sedate evening." I sit down opposite him. "We had a few beers and ate pizza and then worked our way through a whole box of fudge that's been sitting in the back of one of his cupboards for God knows how long, and then we bunked down together. Oh."

I glance at James, expecting to see a frown or an arched brow, but his face is sort of blank.

"I can promise you it was all very innocent." The words rush from me. "The bed in his spare room's broken and I wouldn't sleep on his sofa because I'd probably catch something from it. It was like having a sleepover with an old mate, which I guess is what it was. I suppose. We were talking until well into the small hours. It was really nice, catching up and putting the world to rights. Scouts honour there was no impropriety on either part."

I start to laugh and expect James to join in even if he is hung over. He doesn't, and I take a closer look at him.

His skin's pasty and his mouth's slightly twisted and stiff, but it's not just his face. His whole body's stiff, except where it's fun to be stiff. Oh God, I really hope he doesn't think... I lean forward across the table.

"James, I don't want you to get the wrong idea, about me and Alfie. We've never been involved in any way. We've shared a bed millions of times and there's never been any suggestion of—"

"I'm going to have a shower, and then I've got some work to do."

"Work? Are you sure you're up to it? You look more like you should get your head down for the rest of the day. Is there anything I can do, anything I can get you?" He doesn't just look washed out, he looks ill and concern grips at my stomach. "James, are you okay? You don't seem yourself in all kinds of ways."

He smiles, but there's no humour or lightness to it. It's all effort, and he doesn't meet my gaze.

"I'm... Fine. Really."

I don't miss the tiny hesitation and as for him being *fine*, I certainly don't believe him, but I'm not going to push. If he's feeling like shit because he got plastered and he doesn't want to admit it, that's okay.

"You do what you need to do. Although I reckon sleeping it off rather than working is what'll really do you good. I'll cook later, something easy on the stomach."

I want to go to him and wrap him in my arms and give him lots of kisses before he goes for his shower and starts his journey back towards the James I know, leaving behind this man who feels strange and unknown. But something stops me, something keeps me riveted to my seat.

James gets up and looks down at me, his eyes flat and blank in a way I've not seen before. I coil my arms around myself as a shiver runs through me.

A couple of steps brings him around to me. He reaches out, almost hesitantly, and lightly touches my cheek before his hand falls away.

"I'm glad you had a good time last night."

I don't know what to say and so I say nothing. Instead, I watch as he turns and walks out the kitchen, quietly closing the door behind him.

CHAPTER FORTY

PERRY

"Jimbo!"

The stocky young guy almost throws himself at James, who laughs and gives him a big hug.

I hang back a little and watch the two cousins.

Cosmo's around my age, maybe a little older, and the family resemblance isn't striking. Or not until Cosmo unwinds himself from James and lets his attention fall on me. It's the eyes. The same moss green, feline and assessing. His smile, when it comes which probably only takes a second or two but feels like hours, is bright and friendly.

"And you must be Jerry?" He sticks out his hand for me to shake.

"Nearly. It's Perry." It's a common mistake people make and I'm used to it, and Cosmo's wince followed by a sheepish smile is enough for me to know it's a genuine oversight.

"I've already had a couple of cocktails," he says, by way of an explanation.

"A couple?" James quirks his brow, at the same time he shrugs off his coat.

Cosmo pouts and tries to look put out. "I'm allowed because it's Christmas."

It isn't, it's a few weeks off yet, but I'm getting the impression Cosmo doesn't need excuses for a party.

"Drinks and food are in the kitchen." He takes my and James' coats and stashes them in a wall cupboard already overflowing, before disappearing into what looks like the fairy light lit living room, where dance music's playing.

"Jimbo?" I say to James.

He rolls his eyes, but his smile's fond. "He's always called me that, ever since he was a young kid. I've never broken him of the habit and never will. Come on, let's get a drink."

We dodge our way through the press of bodies. It's noisy and everybody seems to be well on the way to being drunk, but that's not surprising as we're late by a couple or more hours as James got caught up on a work call he couldn't get out of.

"There's enough stuff here to open up his own cocktail bar." I look at the array of bottles, some containing neon hued liquid, many of which I've not heard of.

"I think I'll settle for a glass of wine. You too?" He opens the fridge and pulls out a bottle of white.

"A bit too early to say Happy Christmas, whatever Cosmo says. Cheers." James chinks his glass to mine.

I give him a cheery smile, but to be honest it doesn't

feel very cheery. He could have said *to us* but he didn't. He hasn't said that for a little while, certainly not since he returned from the leaving party he went to a week ago. In fact, it feels like he's not said very much to me at all since then, but I guess that's hardly surprising since I've barely seen him.

He's spent long hours at work, and we've reverted to how it was when I first moved in, with me leaving a note about dinner before I've made my way to the bed we're sharing. I'm asleep before he comes home, and he's gone before I wake up. At times, I've even wondered whether he's come to bed with me at all.

Tonight, at this party where I know nobody, is the most I've seen of him in the last few days. He's insisted on coming, but I've the creeping feeling it's been as much to do with us not spending the time together, just the two of us, as it is about wanting to come for his cousin. We're out of kilter suddenly, and he's not giving me the chance to find out why.

"Do you know anybody here?" I ask, looking out over the throng in the kitchen. Cosmo must have a varied group of friends. Men and women of all ages, and all of them shouting over the noise, which has got louder.

"There are a few I recognise."

I turn to look at James. He sounds distracted, and he's not looking at me, but at the other guests. His gaze is intense as though he's looking out for someone in particular and I look, too, to see if I can pick out whoever it is. Somebody he knows well, perhaps, an old friend, an old—

I look away, not wanting to know.

The table's within reach, and it looks like the remains of a battle. A few cocktail sausages are scattered on a plate and I reach out for one, but the thought of it makes my stomach turn over, and I let my hand fall to my side.

"Perry?"

James' voice is warmer than before, and I instinctively turn to face him. He's smiling and he's studying me, not in his cool and inscrutable way, but in a way I've not seen before, something I can't put my finger on, something indecipherable.

"What?" I croak.

"Just this."

He plucks my glass from my hand and places it along with his own on the table. Cupping my face between his palms, like he's done so many times before, and as though I'm something precious and worthy of reverence, he tilts my face up and lays a soft kiss on my lips.

The sounds of the party fade to nothing. Here and now, it's just us.

I close my eyes as the heat of his hands warms me and the brush of his lips over mine flips my heart and sends a wave of flutters through my belly. I want to fall into him, I want to feel his arms encircle me and hold me tight, so tight I can feel our hearts beat as one. The words rise up in me and tingle on my tongue. I want to go, I want to leave this house where I don't know anybody, I want us to go home where it's just us, and where we can turn the lights low and kiss and touch, entwine our bodies and make love and try to bridge the gap that's broken the ground beneath our feet and is pulling us further and further apart.

"James, can—"

His hands slip from my face and I open my eyes. He's looking not at me, but over my head, his eyes dark and intent. My heart plunges and for a second I feel dizzy and faint, but I turn and search the crowd for what — or who — he's looking at but—

James' face lights up, and he grins.

"I thought it was you," he says, as Freddie pushes his way through, a bottled beer in his hand. He's grinning and red-faced.

"Not interrupting anything, I hope?" Freddie's swaying a little, and he bumps into me. "You looked pretty..." he frowns as though searching for the right word. "Intense," he says with a decisive nod, before he takes a glug from the bottle.

"Is Elliot here?" James asks, and Freddie shakes his head and snorts.

"No, he said he had a stomach ache and didn't feel well, but I know he wants to snuggle up with Jasper and OD on a Line of Duty boxset. Or maybe Drag Race. He thinks he can fool me, but I see through him every single time, 'cause he's pretty easy to suss out, isn't he, Perry?" Freddie grins at me, blinking his bloodshot, drink-fogged eyes.

"Well, I suppose it's my job to work him out so —whoops." I catch hold of Freddie.

He's gone to put his empty bottle down and almost tripped over. He slings an arm around me and leans down. Like Elliot, he's tall. When he speaks I have to stop myself from veering backwards from his beery breath.

"You're so sweet. Has anybody ever told you that before? He is, isn't he?" Freddie shifts his very out of focus gaze to James.

"Very sweet indeed." James unfolds Freddie from me.

"Unlike you." Freddie staggers into James, who has no option but to wrap his arms around Freddie to stop him falling. "You were always trying to talk me into bed, whenever you came round here to see Cos, but I didn't fancy being just another nutch... nitch..." Freddie's face scrunches up in a frown. He's pissed as a fart, and everything he says is down to that, but his words make my blood run cold.

"Notch." Even above the noise of the party, my voice is clear, the word cutting through like a rapier.

Notch on James' bedpost.

"Yeah, that's it, Perry. Got it in one. Never did give up the goods though. Didn't want to be a... notch."

He takes his time with the word. I can hear the grin of triumph in his voice, whether for saying the word correctly or because he'd resisted James' seduction, I don't know. Because I'm not looking at Freddie, I'm looking at James, who's staring back at me.

"It was a game, that's all. Flirting. The more he resisted, the more I pushed."

Like me? Except in the end I did give up the goods... My stomach rolls over, the few sips of wine I've had burning my gut like acid.

Still clinging onto James, Freddie mutters something. Neither of us take any notice.

"You were a free agent; you both were." I shrug my shoulders in an attempt to look unconcerned. James flirts, he always flirts. It's built into his DNA.

Then why does a winter chill wrap itself around my heart?

James' eyes bore into mine, but Freddie shifts suddenly and James has to steady him, dragging James' gaze from me.

"I think you need to sit down and have a coffee," James says.

There's a chair in the corner of the kitchen, near the door leading to the back garden, but Freddie refuses to budge.

"Don't you dare let him make you a n—n—nudge… oh fuck it, you know what I mean," Freddie says, ignoring James, swinging around to me and almost stumbling. He locks his gaze to mine. His hazel eyes may be drink glazed but they're steady. "Fucks anything with a pulse. That's what Cosmo says. James and his slutty ways. Elliot says so too. Fucks 'em and leaves 'em. James—"

"That's enough Freddie. You're drunk and you need to sit down and get some coffee in you."

James barks out the words, as tight as his face, and he tries to steer Freddie to a chair in the corner, but Freddie shakes him off.

"Cosmo said you were going to get married, ages ago, but you couldn't keep it in—"

"Married?" The word feels like glue in my mouth.

James pushes Freddie down into the chair, his hand planted on Freddie's shoulder stopping his attempts to get up.

"That's not true. I don't know where Cosmo got that idea from."

James' attention is all on me, Freddie forgotten. His gaze is fierce, and I look away fearing I'll be burnt.

"Don't bother with the coffee," I mumble, looking at Freddie. He's fallen asleep.

James doesn't even spare him a glance.

"I can only think he's talking about Alex, but civil partnerships and same sex marriage weren't even thought of, let alone legal, when we were together. But you know we were serious, until I screwed up."

He winces as though realising how apt the use of the word *screw* is. Because that was the problem by his own admission. James had loved Alex, but hadn't loved him enough to not screw around, adding notches to his bedpost.

"You know all about him, and why it finished."

"It's not my business, what you did or didn't do before we got together."

James sucks in a deep breath, his jaw clenching, eyes narrowing. He looks away as though he's trying to steady himself. As though he's trying to tamp down on a rising anger, but when he turns back to me his words are measured and though quiet, are sharp and crystal clear.

"Everything he said… Look, I've got a history, Perry. You know the kind of man I am."

I force myself to meet his hard and unflinching gaze, looking out at me from a face that's as still and unreadable as granite.

I am.

Not, *I was*, but *I am*.

"I know."

And I do know, because he's never tried to deny who and what he is.

It's not James who's deceived me, it's myself.

CHAPTER FORTY-ONE

JAMES

It's almost three in the morning as we stumble out of the cab and into the house, slamming the door hard behind us. We're drunk, or at least we should be.

We'd both hit the booze hard with an almost frenetic desperation to get rid of the tension, not only because of Freddie's clumsy words but of the last few days, too. It'd been the same on the makeshift dance floor in the living room.

Under the pulsing multicoloured light ball hanging from the ceiling, we'd writhed and rutted against each other, lips locked on lips in wet and dirty kisses. We'd been like starving men, frenzied in our gorging, yet never sated.

My gaze falls to Perry. His black jeans are so tight they could be painted on, and his shirt's ridden up to reveal a strip of tantalising pale skin. Desire, need and want, over-laid with more complex emotions I don't want to examine, combine to heat low in my belly.

Perry edges round me, or tries to, but I grab him by the wrist. He doesn't pull out of my grip as his gaze meets mine. His dark eyes are made darker by his distended pupils. There's a kind of defiance in them, just as there is in the slow upwards curve of his lips and the tilt of his chin.

I step in close, crowding him, never breaking eye contact as I force him back against the wall. Force? No, I don't force him. He doesn't push me away but just stares, full of provocation and dare. I crush my body to his and claim his mouth.

Perry doesn't resist and kisses me back with a heated fervour I've not felt from him before. It's sloppy, soaking, a fevered, starving clash of teeth and tongues. He groans low in his throat and ruts up against my leg, the hard length of his erection igniting further the inferno raging inside me.

Without breaking the kiss, refusing to lose the wet heat of Perry's mouth, I fumble at his buckle, at the zip on his jeans, forcing them open, hooking my fingers beneath the waistband of his underwear and shoving them down over his hips. I stagger back a step, ripping our lips apart.

Perry kicks off his shoes, his jeans and boxers follow-ing, as I tear my own away. I'm panting hard but so is Perry. For the briefest moment the dense haze of lust that's overtaken me lifts, and all I can do is drink him in.

Messy dark hair, wet lips bruised and puffy, his skin warm and flushed. His sweet beauty, just as it always does, catches at my heart. He moans, guttural and deep, as he wraps his palm around his dick and begins to fuck into his hand.

The haze descends, and thickens.

I'm on him in a second, just as he's on me. Our kisses are hard and frantic as we feed on each other. The hallway echoes with our groans and gasps, our panting, ragged breath. He humps hard against me, the drag of our cocks wrenching a tattered moan from deep in my chest. But it's not enough. I need to be inside him, I need to fill him up, I need to hear him gasp my name as I empty myself into him. I have to slake the thirst that's burning through me.

My eyes lock with his. There's an urgency about him I've never seen before, but every inch of it's a match for my own. His eyes narrow and his lips turn upwards and it's there again, that challenge daring me to make the next move.

I do.

Grabbing him away from the wall, I see a moment's surprise spark in his eyes as I shove him down to his hands and knees, knocking a loud *ommphf* from him. He turns his head and looks up at me, grinning as he begins to rock backwards and forwards. His high, tight arse is a provocation, a taunt, and a low rumbling growl, primitive and brutal, rises in the back of my throat as I drop to my knees.

Clamping my hands to his arse cheeks, I force them apart, exposing his pink hole. Flicking the tip of my tongue over his entrance, I'm rewarded by Perry's low groan. His muscle flutters, his moans grow thin and needy as I kiss and suck and lave my tongue all along his crease, from the base of his balls back to his hole, my tongue circling and probing, pushing through his resistance. I breathe him in deep, drenching and saturating my senses in his intoxicating, musky scent. With one hand, I find my dick. Swiping my thumb over my cockhead, I hiss as every one of my nerves explode into life.

Below me, Perry's panting hard. He's saying something, too, but it's slurred and incomprehensible. He's drunk, just as I am, not only on alcohol but with the insatiable need to fuck and rut and screw, as mindless as animals.

I spit into my hand, slathering my dick, saliva and precum mixing in a wet sticky mess. Clutching his arse, I spread him wide. His head's fallen forward and he's breathing so hard it's almost a grunt. He turns and stares at me, feral and wild, his grin not a smile but a snarl. I line up and in one savage thrust I push into him, squeezing my eyes closed.

Perry's shuddering cry fills the hallway, the whole house, and stripping away the dense fog of lust that's possessing me. I freeze.

This is wrong... I'm using him like I've used every other man... He's not every other man... I can't...

I won't use him like he's nothing, not when he's everything.

Everything I don't deserve.

Inside him, I begin to soften.

"No." One word, hard and angry, pushed out through Perry's gritted teeth.

My eyes snap open. His face is unreadable and masklike. I shudder, I can't help it. I've never seen him like this. Something slithers and turns in my stomach, because I don't like it, it's wrong, it's not who he—

He shoves his arse back with force, riding my cock,

and against the friction, I harden. Every rational thought deserts me as I respond, thrusting into his tight heat.

I hammer into him, every surge tinged with violence. Our panting, shredded breaths, our moans and cries, ricochet from wall to wall. I pound him hard, the slap of flesh on flesh deliciously obscene. Perry's cry, high and keening, shivers through me as I find and pummel his prostate. I'm laughing, or crying or maybe it's a mix of the two as a tiny voice breaks through the fog that this is *too much, too much, too much*, before it fades as though it never was.

He's close, I feel it in his broken, erratic rhythm. My hands are welded to his hips, but I snake one between his legs, my palm wrapping around his hand, frantically jacking his own dick.

It's the touch that pushes him over the edge and with a shudder and a broken breath he releases, coating our hands with hot, slick cum. His release is the starting pistol for my own climax as my balls tighten and tingle and my dick swells, buried deep in Perry's arse. I screw my eyes closed as I grunt out my orgasm, pumping wave after wave of semen deep inside him.

My dick, softening and wet, slips from Perry, and I collapse onto my back. I'm breathing hard, my chest rising and falling as I chase lungfuls of air. The fog's beginning to thin and break.

I turn my head to say something, anything, but Perry's already on his feet, grabbing his jeans and shoes, his gaze averted, his face wet with more than sweat. My tongue cleaves to the roof of my mouth, rendering me dumb, and all I can do is stare as he rushes away and up the stairs, as the house all but shakes from the hard bang of a door that I somehow know doesn't belong to the bedroom we share.

On the hard wooden floor, I'm as limp and lifeless as a rag doll. My skin's burning but an icy hand plunges into my chest and clutches at my heart as I squeeze my eyes closed as I try, and fail, to block out the shame of who and what I am.

CHAPTER FORTY-TWO

JAMES

Climbing out of the bed I've slept in alone, I stumble into the shower. My head's hammering and I feel sick, but it's got nothing to do with the booze from last night's party. I have to speak to Perry and try to explain, although how in God's name I'm going to do that I have no idea.

It's not you, it's me... Bitter laughter bubbles on my tongue, that clichéd line that's never been more true. Because this is me, this is who I am and always will be. As I think of the man who's sleeping away from my arms, all I want to do is weep for what I believed I could have. I lied to myself, but I won't lie to Perry.

Sunday morning, and I have to go into work. A shit storm's hovering on the horizon. Angry headlines and a public baying for blood, if the storm dumps its load. My role, along with a small group of others, is damage limitation. Heads will roll, but fewer of them. I don't want to go, but I've no choice.

On the landing, I listen hard, but there's no sign of Perry stirring, and I'm glad because in this moment I don't think I have the courage to face him. For now, I have to manage an angry, frightened, and cornered government minister, loathed and loved in equal measure by the public. It's nothing to what I'll face later, when I get home.

I creep downstairs, and let myself out, clicking the door closed quietly behind me as I slip away into the grey drizzle of a London winter's day.

I've sent Perry a text to say I'll see him at home, and will be coming back with a takeaway. I don't want him to cook, not tonight.

"Perry?" I call out as I let myself in and make my way to the kitchen. It's always been his favourite room in the house and nine times out of ten it's where I'm likely to find him, and I do so again.

On the threshold of the kitchen, I watch him at the table. He's wearing a pair of jeans, loose and comfortable looking, and an oversized sweatshirt, but they can't disguise the fact that he's lost some weight. He doesn't exactly look skinny but he's starting to head that way. The bitter taste of bile coats the back of my throat and I know it for what it is. Guilt. He's like this because of me.

Perry's not heard me call out, he doesn't even know I'm standing here, he's so intent on whatever it is he's looking at on his laptop. Headphones are clamped to his head, further cutting him off.

I study him the way I've studied him so many times and there's that guilt again, burning in the back of my throat.

He looks tired and strained and his pale skin's even paler than usual and even from this distance it makes the freckles scattered over his nose darker. All this, in just a few days, since I froze on him, since I closed down. Pain explodes behind my eyes, and I suck in a breath and hiss as I clamp my eyes closed for a second. When I open them, with the echo of the pain beating the inside of my skull, he's still not seen me.

Whatever it is he's looking at, he's not happy. A deep frown crinkles his brow as he scrolls. He stops and leans forward, taking a closer look at whatever's caught his attention before he shakes his head and moves on. I take a couple of steps into the kitchen and he must spot the movement from the corner of his eye because his head snaps up and he looks at me wide-eyed and blank, before he takes off the headphones and closes the lid of the laptop with what sounds like a hard thud.

"Thai. From the place down the road. Your favourite." I hold up the white plastic bag before I deposit it on the counter. He pushes himself up from the table.

"Lovely, thanks. I'll just get some plates."

This is what it's come to. There's no kiss, no cuddle. There's no idle chitchat about our days. There's no touch or smile or any of those things we did just days ago. There's no — anything, other than two people in a room.

"Don't you want to go and have a shower before we eat?" Perry asks me. It's what I always do but this time I shake my head.

"No, it can wait."

He doesn't comment further as he sets out all the little tubs and trays in the middle of the table for us to dig into.

We sit opposite each other, the laid out food a barrier between us. Sampling pieces of this and that I'm wondering if, like me, he can't taste a thing.

"What's happened, James? What's gone wrong all of a sudden?"

My fork drops from my hand, clattering against the plate.

"Perry, I'm so sorry. Christ, I am so, so sorry." The voice I can barely believe is mine, is weak and rasping. This isn't how it's supposed to go, although I'll be damned if I know how it should.

"What is it you're sorry about, James? What is it, precisely, you've got to be sorry about?"

There's an edge to his voice, hard and uncompromising and his eyes, always so warm and soft, are cold and stony. It's a side of him I've not seen before, but it's the only one I deserve. Not a muscle moves, as he stares and waits for me to answer.

"I—I can't do it," I whisper. Pain once more explodes in my skull, and I press my fingers to my temples.

"What is it you can't do?"

He's not giving me any quarter, but why the hell should he?

"Us. A settled life. A—a proper relationship. I thought I could, Perry. Honestly, I thought I could. I thought I'd changed, that something had shifted and clicked into place. Because I wanted that, I—I wanted that so much…" My words stumble to a halt as Perry continues to stare at me, still stony-eyed, still cold, over the plates heaped with the food we've hardly touched.

He jumps to his feet, the movement sudden and jerky, and I rear back. He's piling the plates and tubs on top of each other, squashing them down hard. Food oozes out and slops over the sides. Slamming his foot hard on the peddle of the bin, the top swings open and he dumps it all, everything, into the bin. Spinning around, he glares at me.

"So what's happened to change your mind? Or can I guess?"

I get up. My legs are heavy and slow, and all I can do is stand and clutch the back of the chair as we stare at each other across the chasm that's cracked open between us.

"I promised you something I had no right to, because I'm not the kind of man who should make promises like that."

"And what kind of man is that, James?"

I wince as my name falls hard from his tongue.

"A man who promises fidelity. A man who promises not to break your heart. A man who promises to—"

To love you.

Words I can't say.

"Who was it?"

It's as though he's fired a gun, as his words blast into me. I catch my breath, but his eyes widen as dark knowledge lights up inside him.

"Him. That guy. Aiden. The one you had some kind of fuck buddy arrangement with. Has this been happening all along?" His voice wavers, but the muscles in his face harden.

"No, I've not—" I take a step towards him, but he lurches back.

"Keep the fuck away from me." He's shaking, every part of him trembling as his icy demeanour cracks.

"I've not... but I was tempted. I came so close to—to—"

"Fucking another man."

I drop my head and say nothing.

The fridge gurgles, the wall clock ticks out the seconds and in the distance a car roars past before fading to nothing.

"I'm sorry, Perry. I'm so, so sorry. I'd do anything for this not to have happened."

"But it has, hasn't it? Yet, in some warped way I guess I should thank you."

"What?" My head snaps up. "I don't understand."

All the stoniness in his face and voice has crumbled to dust. He looks tired, worn out and Christ, but it makes the jagged line breaking my heart in two break a little more. I want to go to him, hold him as I whisper *sorry, sorry, sorry* into his hair. He wouldn't believe me, he has no reason to believe anything I say ever again.

He hugs himself around his middle, the *keep away* message as loud as if it were screamed through a megaphone.

He shrugs.

"You rescued me when I needed it. You gave me a home when I had none and for that I'll always be thankful. You even made me happy when for a long time I'd not had very much of that in my life. And yes, you made me believe in something that was really just an illusion. But you can't be who you aren't. I realise that now. Just like I realise the only one I can truly rely on is myself. I have to stand on my own two feet, I mustn't let myself get side-tracked and you sidetracked me, James, but then I suppose I wanted to be, so it's my fault too."

"It's not—"

"I'm going to rely on myself," he says, raising his voice as he tilts his chin up, sweeping away my words. His arms drop to his side. "I'll rely on myself because I can't rely on anybody else. And you've taught me that, James, you've taught me that lesson very well. I'm going to talk to Alfie about moving in with him, as soon as possible, just like I'm going to make sure I get the new start I've promised myself. But this time it's going to be down to me, and me alone."

A moment later he's gone. I slump down into my chair as my legs begin to buckle.

It's for the best, it's for the best, it's for the best... I tell myself that over and over, tying the words around me like rope because if I don't, I'll unravel and fall apart.

CHAPTER FORTY-THREE

PERRY

"Of course you can come here, and for as long as you need to you dipstick. I'm sorry, mate, I really am."

I close my eyes and all I can think is, *thank God for Alfie.* It'd taken all my courage to send Alfie the text, telling him things haven't worked out with James, and could I come and stay? Alfie's call had come less than a minute later.

"You think he might be going with other blokes?" At least there's no *I told you so* tone to his voice, and for that I'm grateful.

"No. He said he hasn't and I believe him. But…" I swallow hard, before I tell Alfie what's happened.

"Jesus Fucking Christ." Alfie explodes on the other end of the line, and I jerk the mobile back. "So it's, *sorry Perry, but I've decided that, going forward, I don't think*

I'm going to like keeping my dick safely tucked away, so bye bye. What a wanker."

"No, it wasn't quite like that." Wasn't it? I'm not so sure, when it comes down to it.

"Want me to come around and kick the shit out of him?"

Alfie would, and I can't help the smile that lifts my lips. I don't tell him James would have him stunned and knocked to the floor within seconds.

"Easy tiger. No, I think I just want to leave with some of my rapidly dwindling dignity."

A brief silence before Alfie speaks, softer this time, all his belligerence gone.

"You liked him a lot, didn't you? More than any of the others."

I close my eyes to stop the fall of tears.

"Yeah," I rasp. I still do, but none of that matters, not anymore. "Thing is, he never lied to me. Not really. He told me exactly what he was like."

"How d'ya mean?"

I suck in a deep, long breath. "Years ago he had somebody in his life he cared for — loved — very much."

Loved. The word catches in my throat.

"But James couldn't be faithful. He told me that, he never tried to hide it. He never lied." *No, I've just done that to myself.* "He realised he was in too deep, I suppose, that he'd committed more than he could deliver. The life he really wants doesn't preclude all that *temptation*." I spit the word out, like something rank.

"Shit, Perry mate, I'm sorry. Really, I am. Then I guess it's better you realise all this now before you got any deeper. I don't just mean between you and him, but with the practical side of stuff as well. Like the cooking premises for the cakes. You don't want to get yourself tangled up into a contractual agreement if the basis you're building it on has collapsed. You've been talking about moving down to the coast for years, on and off, but you never have. But now's your chance, and you should take it and not tie yourself to what somebody else wants."

It's a gentle reiteration of what he said to me before. Always putting the man in my life first, always taking second place, shoving my wants, and needs, and dreams aside.

But it's what I wanted, to be here with James more than I wanted to go to the coast...

"Perry, you've got to put yourself first. You never do it and somehow it always seems to land you in the shit."

Ah, so not such a gentle reminder.

"Thanks for your belief in me."

"You silly wanker, of course I believe in you, but sometimes you just have to be selfish. That doesn't make you a bad person — you're the best person I know — but falling in with other people's plans all the time even when they derail your own doesn't win you any friends in the long run."

He's right. I've spend my life being a people pleaser and in the end I don't please anybody.

"Walk away with your head held high, because you've no reason not to. Much as I'd like to beat him up for you, just draw a line under it. At least this time you won't be getting locked out, or living in a basement."

"No, I'm over basement living. It's so yesterday."

We both laugh and I'm glad of the light relief it brings. But Alfie's right that I need to draw a line under this. I have to move on and regain control, even if it does feel like I'm freewheeling downhill.

"Perry? Perry, you still there?"

"Yes. Yes I am. Sorry."

"Come at the weekend. Just a couple of days away. Is that all right? It'll give me a chance to get the place sorted out."

It's more than all right.

"You mean cleaned up and not disease ridden?" I smile when he huffs down the line.

"Yeah something like that, but I'll be around then to help you get settled." He hesitates for a second before he speaks again. "I'm sorry this has happened, but better to find out now before you get in too deep."

Too deep? I'm already in too deep, but this time I have to swim to shore and save myself, because nobody else will do it for me.

CHAPTER FORTY-FOUR

PERRY

"I said I can take you. There's no need for a cab."

"I'm not getting a cab. Alfie's borrowed a car. He's coming to collect me, and he'll be here in a minute."

With a large suitcase and a bin bag at my feet, my life with James is packed up and ready to go. I scoured the house to make sure I'd got everything. If there's anything left it won't be important and he can throw it away.

I look at my watch, willing Alfie to get here so I can leave this phase of my life behind. James is hovering, still and awkward like he's a stranger in his own house.

"Perry…" His voice sounds so small, pathetic even, it's not the voice of the man I know. Or knew. Thought I knew.

Fuck it. I rub my eyes, dry and gritty from a sleepless night.

"Perry?"

"What?" I snap, glaring at him. I have to snap, I have to glare because if I don't I'll cry.

"Please, if there's anything I can do, any time, you've got to let me know."

I can't believe what I'm hearing. He's done plenty, he's done more than enough. I keep my gaze locked on to his and a red tide washes up over his face. There's a part of me that wants him to squirm, but a bigger part only wants this to be over.

"If it's easier for you," he says quietly, "I'll go out and—"

He's interrupted by a long ring on the bell. It's Alfie, I know it is, keeping his finger pressed to the button. I almost smile. Thank God for friends who act like twats.

I drag on my coat which has been lying on top of my suitcase, as I make for the door.

"Thanks Alfie," I say quietly. "I'll just get my stuff." I jerk my head towards the sad little pile of belongings that represent my life in this house.

"I'll get it." Alfie pushes past me and I follow him back down the hallway, where James is still hovering.

Alfie doesn't even acknowledge him as he picks up my things before striding back down the hallway and out of the house. I'm on his heels, and he hefts it all into the back of a large estate car, idling at the curb. For a moment I wonder who it belongs to because Alfie doesn't have a motor.

"It's Leo's," he says, answering my unspoken thought.

I wrack my dull and heavy brain, trying to remember who Leo is. Of course. Leo, the new man. The one Alfie's decided to stay in London for. I make a mental note to pass on my thanks.

"You ready? Got everything?"

"Yes. Oh no, wait. Just a minute." I may have everything, but there's something I have to return because there's no way I'll be using it again.

The front door's still wide open and James is standing in the hallway, exactly where I left him.

"Here." Delving into my pocket, I pull out a set of keys.

I hold them out to him, but he only looks at them as though deciding whether or not he should take them. My heart, my fucking treacherous heart, picks up the beat in the sudden hope that he doesn't.

He does, of course, because this is real life and not some crappy romance.

There's no last minute change of heart, no last minute declaration of love, no last minute begging me to stay, there's only quiet acceptance as he takes the keys I hold out to him. But it's not quite that simple, as he wraps his palm around my hand and brings it to his lips to place a gentle kiss on my knuckles. I should drag my hand away, but I can't. He looks up at me, his eyes sadder and duller than I've ever seen.

"I'm sorry."

My throat's frozen. I can't talk. But what would I say if I could?

Turning, I walk away and James doesn't follow. I close the door quietly, on the man I love and on the life that could have been.

It doesn't take me long to get sorted out at Alfie's. He's my best friend, and he knows me well enough to leave me alone. I'm not in any great mood to dissect what's happened with me and James and I don't want to pick over the bones. What I need now is to look forward, not backward, but at the same time I don't feel like doing much more than huddling in the corner and just losing myself in the TV or a book. Alfie gets it and, the good friend that he is, he lets me do just that.

For the first couple of nights he stays at the flat, keeping me quiet company, but he's also been on the phone a lot to Leo and when I tell him to piss off and go and stay with him he gives me a sheepish grin. My own life might be a pile of steaming shit at the moment, but I don't want that for anybody else. Even James. I don't think I have the energy to hate him, even though it's what I'm supposed to do.

I throw myself into my job even more so than normal, but after a few days of wallowing as soon as I get home, I tell myself it's time to get Operation Perry up and running again.

It's just gone three o'clock and my stomach rumbles, reminding me I've not yet taken a lunch break. I'm hungry yet I don't feel much like eating, but I suppose I should pick at the sandwich I've brought in with me. Closing down the spreadsheet I've been working on, I pull up a list of Brighton estate agents, but there's nothing new on the market, just the same grotty old places. With barely three weeks until Christmas, it's probably not worth even looking until the New Year.

My heart lurches.

Christmas.

James had told me he always has a tree delivered, and I'd imagined we'd decorate it together. The wood burning stove crackling, mince pies and mulled wine…

The thought of Christmas and all its forced cheer and jollity turns my stomach, and I shove the sandwich away. I've always loved Christmas, always embraced it, but this year I want to bundle it into a box and drop it in the Thames. But it's unavoidable, it's a monster devouring everything in its path, even here at work.

The first of the corporate Christmas cards are starting to arrive and some of my workmates have even decorated their computers with various bits of Christmas tat. The office decorations and the tree will go up on Friday afternoon and then, in the evening, everybody will decamp for the office party to a smart nearby bar with a private function room. Everything's been organised to within an inch of its life. I know, because I'm responsible for sorting it out. Elliot's employees and their partners, although not many partners come, and a small handful of invited guests of Elliot's, which has always included James.

This year I shan't be going. I'll go along ahead of time just to make sure there aren't any last minute issues, and then I'm going to make myself scarce. I think it's fair to say I'm not in the party mood.

"Perry? Can I have a quick word, please?"

I jump, and swing around. Elliot's poking his head around his office door. Normally he would just ring through, and my heart drops because I already know what this is about.

In his office I sit down in the chair on the other side of the desk to him.

"I'm not going to beat about the bush. I know you and James have split up."

Of course he does. The two of them are best friends. I haven't missed the slightly awkward glances Elliot's thrown my way over the last couple of days. He's a good man and he was probably wondering whether or not he should say anything as, technically, my personal life doesn't have anything to do with him. But, he's also Elliot's oldest friend and I was James' partner even though you could have blinked and missed it.

"Yes, we have. It's probably for the best. I don't think we were very well matched."

Elliot huffs and shakes his head. He's scowling and he looks annoyed.

"He's an idiot. I don't know the details, he just told me you've parted. Nothing more. He's done some stupid things in the past but this beats everything. I'm sorry Perry, I truly am."

I don't know what to do or say other than stare at him. Elliot's a great boss but he's always coolly professional. We never cross the line into talking about anything remotely personal and I've always been happy with that, so to hear him berate his oldest friend like this... I look down and smile.

"Thank you, for thinking he's an idiot, but the truth is we're just too different. What I want from life isn't what he wants. I just hope he finds what it is he's looking for."

Which isn't me.

"He had found it, if he'd just had the sense to see it."

I start at Elliot's words, as a little flair lights up in my heart. But no. Elliot's talking from his own perspective, that of a man who's happy and in love and looking forward to a life with the man of his dreams.

"So what's happening now? Are you still looking for a place so you can start your own business?"

We're back to the purely practical, and that's fair enough because what I choose to do next affects my position here. Elliot certainly looks more at ease talking about this and, to be honest, so am I.

"Yes, I'm still determined to give it a go. If I don't, I know I'll always regret it. All those *what ifs*. And now seems the opportune time."

Whilst I've got no ties, whilst I'm not involved with anybody…

Elliot nods, reading between the lines.

"I'm still looking in the vicinity of Brighton, because it's not all about the business and striking out on my own. It never has been. It's about starting completely afresh. Brighton's the ideal, but I'm widening the net and there are one or two other places I'm happy to consider if Brighton doesn't work out." Which are also cheaper. Now that everything's on my back, that's no small consideration. "I'll keep you informed of everything, so we can plan for my replacement."

And you can maybe tell James…

Elliot nods but he doesn't look happy. "I'm all for people starting up their own businesses. More should take the plunge and I completely support you and what you're doing. If I can be of any help, in any way," he says, his gaze steady on mine, making me understand he's not just talking about my potential new venture, "don't hesitate to let me know."

We talk business for a little while, taking us back onto

safe ground, before I retreat back to my own desk and bury myself in work so that I don't have to think.

~

"I thought we could get in pizza, have a few beers and watch some porn."

Alfie walks in from work seconds after I do. Despite how crap everything feels, I can't not laugh. I look him up and down. My favourite shepherd and urban poet has turned into Mr. Corporate Accountant.

He knows why I'm laughing, and he glares at me.

"Thought it might cheer you up a bit," he grumbles.

"It's a nice thought and I do appreciate it, but you seem to forget I've seen some of your porn collection. Very hairy men dressed in thongs, stockings and tutus doesn't really do it for me."

"I was going through a phase." Alfie tries to look affronted but it's not very successful. "We can go for whatever you want. What makes you get hot and sweaty?"

Men with moss green eyes who wear fuck off three piece suits... but I guess that's not the answer he's looking for.

"I'm all for the pizza and the beer but can we shelve the porn? I'm really not in the mood."

"You should be. Kind of get you back on track, you know?"

Alfie, my good friend. He may be way *off* track with the porn idea but his heart's in the right place just as it's always been, and I can't help but wrap my arms around him.

"Hey, what's this all about?"

"Oh, for being a twat. You know."

Alfie chuckles before he disentangles himself from my death hold and phones up the order as I head off to get showered and changed.

"Here, have one of these," he says, handing me a beer when I re-emerge. Flopping onto the sofa, I knock it back and close my eyes.

It's Thursday evening, five days since I walked away from James. I tuck away the thought, refusing to keep count.

"... from him?"

"Hmm? What? Sorry, what was that?

"I said, have you heard anything? From James?"

So much for not thinking about James Campion.

"No, but then I don't expect to. It's not like we were together for long so there's nothing much to unpack. You know, emotionally speaking."

Lies, lies, and more lies.

"The man's a fool to let you go."

I shrug, and swallow the sudden very hard lump lodging in my throat.

"Maybe, but now we'll never know."

Alfie wraps a muscly arm around me and pulls me in, and I rest my head on his shoulder.

He doesn't say anything, he just holds me. I'm grateful for his touch, almost as much as I am for his silence.

A few minutes later the pizza delivery guy arrives. We set up the boxes on the little coffee table in front of the telly. It reminds me of when we were students together, living in one crappy flat after another, eating pizza straight out the box and licking greasy fingers. It's a nice, warming memory from a life that seems like it wasn't as complicated as the one I'm living now.

Deep in my pocket my mobile pings, and so does my bloody heart. Every time it does, I think… What I know I shouldn't think. I fish it out, and try to ignore my hammering heart.

"What's that?" Alfie shifts over to look at the message. "Fuck me. Talk about silver lining."

"Yeah." I re-read the message, once, twice, three times.

The cash buyer on the bungalow has pulled out. The owners are desperate to sell and have slashed the price. It's not just a bargain, they're virtually giving it away, and I'm being given first refusal.

"Well, that's a turn up. You better get your signature down on the dotted line, because I reckon you're going to Brighton."

CHAPTER FORTY-FIVE

JAMES

I beckon to the barman to bring me another G&T. He's young, fair-haired, and flirty and in another lifetime I would have flirted back. Now, it's the last thing I feel like doing and I wonder if I ever will again. I don't return his smile and he moves off to the other end of the bar.

It's Thursday, and five days since Perry left. I shake my head. I shouldn't be counting, because his leaving is best for both of us, long term, but I can't not count. I simply can't not.

I haven't been here before. The pub doesn't know me, and I don't know it. Here, I'm anonymous, and I'm more than fine with that.

From my place at the end of the bar, I look out at the life going on around me. Groups of friends all laughing and chatting, and couples who have eyes only for one another. Sometimes the couples lean into each other and kiss. I turn away, the heat of other people's happiness too searing. I should go home but I don't want to, because all I'll find is an empty shell. No life, no warmth.

No love.

Thrusting my hand deep into my trouser pocket, I pull out my mobile. The hook up apps, and the account with the upmarket escort agency are all gone but it wouldn't take long to reinstate them. My hand tightens around my phone, as the oily, aromatic gin gurgles in my stomach, making me feel vaguely sick. I shove the mobile back into my pocket.

I have to go home sometime, and it may as well be now. I'm about to get up and leave when a shoulder bumps mine.

The place is getting busier, and it could just be an accident but I know it's not. I turn my head to look at the guy who's set himself on the seat next to me.

He's handsome. The lights from the bar pick out the deep copper strands in his hair, and his eyes are dark brown. My stomach knots, and I can't help but stare. He takes it as an invitation and, smiling, opens his mouth to speak but he clamps it closed when I shake my head hard. His smile disappears and he turns away.

I leave, making my way back to a house that for a brief time was a home. There's nothing there, now, nothing waiting for me other than silence, a cold and empty bed, and all those promises I can't keep.

"Oh, Christ."

Peeling my eyes open I stare up at the ceiling. My head's hammering with the power of a hundred pneumatic drills, and something from a sewer has crawled into my mouth and died. I'm not even in bed, but sprawled out on the sofa and still dressed. The reason's on the coffee table next to me. A bottle of forty-year-old brandy, half of it gone and the top sitting next to the empty glass.

Peering at my watch, I groan. Five-thirty in the morning. My body, despite the alcoholic beating I've given it, is conditioned to wake up at this time.

I fumble for me phone, but I'm clumsy and drop it to the floor. My head spins as I lean down to pick it up, and at the same time sickness bubbles in my guts. I take a deep breath, then another, before I sit up and tap out a quick text to my PA, telling her I won't be in today. I'm just about to add that I'll be working from home. Screw that. Instead, I tell her to cancel all my appointments, that I'm uncontactable and I'll see her on Monday. Wishing her a good weekend, I hit send and switch my mobile off before I can change my mind. Slumping back on the sofa, I close my eyes as I think about taking a shower and cleaning my teeth.

I wake up two hours later, still feeling like crap, but a couple of pints of water, a large mug of black coffee, some aspirin, and a hot shower later, I convince myself I can pass for a functioning human being. Now, all I have to do is wonder what the hell I'm going to do with myself.

The day stretching out in front of me is long, blank and featureless, and for a moment I regret my earlier text. I could go into work, say my plans have changed…

The doorbell rings, making me jump.

A couple of burly guys stand on the doorstep with a very large green object balanced between them.

"Mr Campion? Mr James Campion?" one of them asks as he looks at his phone. "Your Christmas tree, delivered as ordered. Where do you want it?"

I hadn't told Perry when it was coming, because I'd wanted to surprise him. I'd imagined us decorating it together, eating warm mince pies and drinking too much eggnog before getting very dirty together on the rug.

"Sir? We've got a lot of deliveries to make today," the same guy says. I can virtually hear his eye roll.

"Yes, of course. Take it round the back, will you? I'll open the gate."

The two guys carry the tree down the side of the house and set it up against the wall in the garden, taking a photo to show it's been delivered, before they rush off. It's a dull, gloomy day, and heavy, freezing rain, edged with ice, starts to fall, but all I can do is stare at the tree.

I don't want it. I don't want the fucking thing in the house. There must be some local charity who'd welcome the festive donation. A thunder clap and a blinding flash of lightning send me scurrying indoors.

Soaked to the skin, I head up to get changed. In the en-suite I breathe in deep and imagine I can smell the lingering aroma of Perry's vanilla scented shampoo, but there's nothing other than my own, citrus and sharp.

Dried off for the second time, I wander back downstairs. The kitchen feels like a wasteland. No delicious, savoury aroma from something bubbling away on the hob. No buttery sweetness from a just-baked cake, or a batch of biscuits cooling on the rack. There's nothing. It's as empty, cold and lifeless as it was before Perry arrived and turned my house into a home.

I make more coffee because it's something to do, and think about maybe eating something, anything. About to dig through the fridge, I spot the blue and white spotted cake tin. Perry brought it home one evening, something he'd seen in one of those retro shops close to the office … He's forgotten it, and for a wild moment I wonder if I should return it to him… take it around to Alfie's, if I knew where he lived… bump into him at Elliot's… call him, arrange to meet him for a drink to hand it over…

"What the fuck," I mutter, as I rub my hands over my face. There's no way on God's earth Perry would want to see or hear from me ever again, and to think anything else is nothing more than a delusion caused by too much brandy and self-pity.

Maybe I should get rid of it, knowing full well I could never do that. Instead I prise it open, and am enveloped with sugar sweetness as I peek inside, blinking hard to clear my fogged vision. The scant remains of a cake, not just any cake but a Victoria sandwich. Sponge, jam, buttercream, that's all it is, but it was — is — my favourite.

I tip it out onto a plate. It's stale, and seen better days. But none of that matters. I slice it up and work my way through it, tasting not the dryness of the sponge or the sour turn of the buttercream, but the delicious sweetness of a time when I was truly happy.

CHAPTER FORTY-SIX

JAMES

I jerk upright so fast I almost topple my chair backwards. My heart's racing as snippets from confused and disturbing dreams run from me. I grab my mobile, in front of me on the kitchen table, almost sending the cake tin crashing to the floor.

"Good, I was hoping you'd pick up," Elliot says.

My attempt to answer is nothing more than a strangled, dry-mouthed groan.

"Are you okay?"

"Yes." I clear my throat and swallow down the lie.

"You don't sound it, which is hardly surprising I suppose." Elliot huffs. "No, not now…" The words are muffled and I'm about to ask what all this is about when I realise it's not me he's speaking to. The thud of a door closing comes down the line. "That's better. No interruptions. I've got news, which I think you need to know about. And deal with."

I scrunch my brows. "What do you mean, deal with?" Tension turns my muscles to iron.

"Perry tendered his resignation earlier today. He's leaving. He's given me longer than he actually needs to, but he's still leaving. There's a suitable property near Brighton—"

"The bungalow? That fucking horrible bungalow?" The words explode from me. Perry, in a grim, nondescript suburb... All his brightness will fade away to nothing.

"I don't know if it's a bungalow, but he said he was interested in the property before and it's come back on the market. He's made a provisional offer, which has been accepted. Vacant possession apparently, so he can move fast on it."

I close my eyes and pinch the bridge of my nose in a futile attempt to stem the headache that's blossoming.

Perry, in that place...

"Then he's got what he wanted," I croak.

"Oh, for God's sake." Elliot's voice is an angry bark on the other end of the line. "It's not what he wants. It's not what he wants at all."

"It is. He wants to set up his own business." *Miles and miles away from me.*

"But not like this, James. You've got to do something about this."

"And get in his way again? I got in his way before and screwed up his plans because it suited me. Moving away, it's what he always wanted. He should do it, and not let men like me stand in his way."

I pinch harder between my eyes, my nails digging deep into the thin skin.

Silence, for long, long seconds. I almost think Elliot's cut the call. When he speaks his voice is low and lethal, his anger held back by strength of will alone. Ice shivers down my spine and over my skin.

"You're a fool, James. Why are you putting yourself and him through this? When the two of you were together there was a brightness about you I'd never seen before. Not even when you were with Alex. It was because you were happy, probably for the first time in your life. But I saw it in Perry, too. Why are you so afraid of owning up to what you feel for him? Why can't you admit it?"

More silence, more long seconds.

"Admit what Elliot? What should I admit?"

"That you love him."

And I do. God knows it, but I do. Elliot knows too, because he knows me. But there's something he doesn't know, because I was too ashamed to tell him.

"I do love him. You're right. And I'll never stop loving him, but it's not enough."

"What do you mean?"

I close my eyes for a second, summoning up my nerve, before opening them.

"I thought I could do it. Being settled with someone — with Perry. I really thought I could. But I fell at the first hurdle. Christ, if I were a horse I'd be shot."

"I don't understand."

"Don't you? You know what I'm like, Elliot. Can't you guess? An opportunity came my way, and I was tempted. I was a beat away from—" I stumble to a stop, unable to drag the dirty confession into the light.

Aiden's face rears up in my mind. His smile, the press of his body hard against mine. My hand cupping the back of his neck… And the whispered words that chilled me to the bone.

"Tempted? Is that what you're saying? What matters is whether you resisted. Did you?"

"Yes," I rasp. "I did, but who's to say next time I'll do the same thing? Or the time after that?"

"For the love of God, James, you're to say. *You*. If you truly love him you'll turn your back on every scrap that's thrown in your path. Please, don't let your fear stand in the way of you finding real happiness."

I jolt. "Fear? What are you talking about?" I press the phone harder against my ear, as though to get closer to James' words.

"Fear of breaking out of the cycle you've set for yourself. I don't know if it is even the right word." His huff's loud and impatient. "This isn't the time or place to examine it, but over the years you seem to have convinced yourself that you're incapable of love and fidelity or loyalty. But that's not true. You're my oldest and closest friend, and I know you as well as I know myself. More so, I sometimes think. You're telling yourself lies. Maybe it goes back to how it was with Alex, I don't know. All I know is that you've been beating yourself up over what happened for too many years, and you have to stop.

"You're a good man, under all your don't give a damn crap. You're a loyal friend. You stick up for those you love. You fight for them to the death. You did that with me, remember? You made me face what it was I felt about Freddie, when all I wanted to do was push him away because I was scared. The way you're now scared. Listen to me, and let me be to you the friend you were to me."

My heart clenches hard as I hear the catch in his voice.

"Face your own fear, James," he says, his voice barely steadier. "And conquer it. Fight for Perry, fight for yourself and for him. Everything that's gone before, it's in the past. You need to think about your future and if you let him walk away I don't think you'll have one that'll be worth having." He sucks in a deep and shaky breath. "He's going down to Brighton this afternoon, to meet the estate agent to sign on the dotted line. He's catching the two-thirty from Victoria. Whatever else you do, don't let him get on that train."

CHAPTER FORTY-SEVEN

JAMES

Friday afternoon, and Victoria station's heaving. As many people are escaping the capital as pouring into it. The cacophony all around me is deafening: laughter, shouts, gleeful screams, a bunch of angry commuters arguing with a station official, and the bass muffled tones of a tannoy announcement. None of it, though, is as loud as the hard thump of my heart.

I jab speed dial again, just like I've been doing since Elliot's call. Nothing, other than Perry asking me to leave a message. And that's what I've done, over and over. *Call me, we have to talk, call me, please call me...* Nothing but a piece of useless plastic, I shove it back into my coat pocket.

I'm scouring the departures board, frantically looking

for the Brighton train. I can't see a Brighton-bound train. Why the fuck can't I see it?

Have I got the right station?

Did Elliot get the time wrong?

Did I mishear?

Panicky sweat drenches my clothes.

I need to calm down, I need to think.

Taking a shuddering deep breath, I look again. And there it is, the two-thirty to Brighton.

It's a fast train, making only a couple of stops before its final destination, and it's leaving in fifteen minutes.

I scan the crowd heading for the platform, but I can't see any sign of Perry. He's got to be onboard already, waiting for the train to leave and take him away from me. The thought makes me feel sick, but it puts a rocket up me.

Running for the ticket barrier, I shoulder my way through the press of bodies, ignoring the angry shouts and expletives thrown my way. Passengers are pouring through the barrier, and I tailgate.

I'm on the platform.

It's a short train, only four carriages, and it's filling up fast.

Bundling my way on, my head swings from left to right and back again as I search for him. He's not here, Perry's not on the bloody train, and I stumble off.

Scrubbing my fingers through my hair, and bending low at the waist, I try not to scream. Nobody comes near me, because right now I'm just another crazed, burnt-out Londoner on the edge of collapse. I straighten up — and I see him.

He's coming through the barrier, clutching a takeaway coffee, his face serious, not a hint of the shy smile that sits so readily on his lips. For all my frantic searching, I'm frozen to the spot.

He's just a couple of steps away, but so wrapped up in his thoughts he's not noticed me.

"Perry," I croak.

He stops dead, and stares at me as though I'm a stranger. My heart shudders, but it's nothing more than I deserve.

"What are you doing here?"

"To stop you making the biggest mistake of your life." I take a step towards him, but he stumbles back, a sickening reminder of him growling at me not to touch him when we stood in the kitchen and everything crumbled around us. Days ago, only days, it's been the longest, bleakest, loneliest time of my life.

"No. I already made that, when I believed your lies."

He twists around me, ready to walk away but I'm not going to let him, not this time. I grab his arm.

"Let me go. Please." He tries to pull away, but I tighten my grip. "What the hell do you think you're doing? It's over. I don't know why you're here or what you're trying do, but it's useless."

His voice is low and trembling, and his face is so, so pale the freckles scattered across his nose are like dark flecks from a paintbrush. Deep shadows stain the thin skin beneath his eyes, and I feel sick that this is because of me. It's all because of me.

"Let you go? No, Perry, I'm not going to let you go. Not this time. I'm not going to make that mistake again."

"No." He shakes his head hard and wrenches his arm from my grip. "What right do you have to do this?"

Red patches colour his cheekbones, stark against the

rest of his face. Anger's surging through him, righteous and justified, and I deserve everything he throws at me.

"I don't have any right, and if you walk away and get on that train and don't look back, it's everything I deserve. But please don't do it, Perry, don't walk away from me."

"Why shouldn't I? You betrayed me, James. You made promises that crumbled to dust as soon as they were put to the test. Why wouldn't I want to walk away from a man like you?"

His voice is shaky as anger and upset do battle.

"Because I have to break the cycle."

"What?" Confusion shadows his eyes. "Cycle? What are you talking about? I don't understand."

"Neither did I, not until Elliot read me the riot act earlier."

A tannoy blasts above us... *the Brighton train will be departing platform seven in five minutes... will passengers please board the train...*

The noise of the station, the rush of last minute travellers erupts all around us, a stark and frightening reminder that, one way or another, in five minutes my life will be changed forever.

I step in closer and my heart flips when he doesn't step back, but we're teetering on the edge and I can't afford to make a wrong move.

"I want to break the cycle. I don't want to be just another sad example of how the men in my family are. I don't want to be like my grandfather, my father, or my brother. Do you remember I told you about them? They all betrayed those they professed to love, causing havoc and heartbreak. That's not who I want to be."

The Brighton train will be departing platform seven in four minutes....

"But it is who you are, James. You broke my heart."

His voice falters and the tears break through the dam. Christ, but I want to kiss them away, but he's closed in on himself and if I touch him now I fear he'll shatter.

"Like you broke Alex's heart. You told me about him, too. I won't be another Alex. The train's about to go, and I have to be on it. For both our sakes. Goodbye, James."

No. There's no way on this earth I'm going to let this happen. He's turning away from me and I grab him by the shoulders, swinging him around.

"Leave me alone. I can't go through this again, I can't."

He shoves at me, with more force than I expect, and the coffee he's kept a death grip on drops from his hand, forming a spreading lake at our feet.

From the corner of my eye, I see two guards watching, ready to step in.

"Perry, please. Please listen to me. Just give me one more minute."

"You don't deserve it—"

"I know, but—"

The Brighton train will depart in three minutes. Doors will close one minute before departure...

"I did break Alex's heart, and I'll always be ashamed of that. Yes, I loved him once, but I never loved him enough. I've gone through my whole life convincing myself I'm incapable of wholehearted, complete love, believing that in some way I was defective. So I held back, and kept my heart under lock and key. But then you happened, Perry. You."

"How can I trust you? Why should I believe you? Give me one good reason?"

I lift my hands to his face, cupping his cheeks in my palms, feeling the faint rasp of stubble.

"Why should you trust and believe me? I've not done much to earn those things from you. As for the reason, it's this."

I move in closer, my heart thundering in my chest when he doesn't step back, when he doesn't resist. Tilting his head, I brush my lips to his.

"I love you Perry. I love you more than enough for us both. I love you with every piece of my heart. With you, I can never hold back. Please, let me spend the rest of our lives proving it to you."

A whistle screams, but we take no notice.

The two-thirty for Brighton has just departed platform seven...

CHAPTER FORTY-EIGHT

PERRY

As I step through the door, I know I'm home. Truly home. For a moment I close my eyes as the truth of that hits me.

James takes my hand, leading me through to the kitchen, always the warm beating heart of the house. He holds on tight, as though he's expecting me to make a run for it and jump on the next Brighton-bound train. I'm not going to do that. I'm never going to do that. I knew it from the moment he brushed his lips to mine and told me he loved me.

I watch as he makes tea. He's clumsy, slopping the milk over the counter, squeezing the teabags out and dropping them on the floor before scooping them up and chucking them in the bin. The uncoordinated man stumbling around the kitchen is so far removed from the James

I know that, despite the earthquake that's rocked our worlds, I can't help but smile.

He sits down opposite me at the blond wood table, just as he's done so many times before. My heart lurches with the familiarity of it.

"I was such a fool for letting you go."

He turns his mug around and around, spilling the tea he's not attempting to drink. His eyes are downcast, as though he's ashamed to meet mine. I place my hands on his, halting his frantic, nervous movements.

"You were, but I was a fool for not fighting enough to stay."

He looks up, and there's the ghost of a smile in his green eyes. We hold each other's gaze. In the quiet of the kitchen, the fridge rumbles and gurgles as the clock ticks away the seconds.

"Elliot told me about the bungalow, that you'd made an offer, and I think it was then that it hit me. That place..." He looks away, his brow creasing as he shakes his head. "It's not right for you, it was never right. All I saw was you fading, all your bright lights going out one by one. And I couldn't let it happen." His eyes flicker back to mine. They look tired, so, so tired. "I want you here with me, Perry. I want you to make this your home, I want us to make it *our* home, because without you here it's nothing but an empty shell. Do—do you think you could want that too?"

His voice trembles, the muscles in his face are strained; he's like a rubber band, stretched so tight the tiniest nudge will snap him. This isn't the James I know, and it isn't the James I love. I want that man back. I want the self-assured and confident man. I want the man who has that edge of arrogance. I want the man who can so often read me better than I can read myself.

I want the man who made me feel alive and loved, valued and cherished, the man who made me whole and complete.

That man, James Campion, he broke my heart so thoroughly I wasn't sure it would ever be put back together. But here, now, as James gazes at me, his moss green eyes fixed on mine, he's gathering all those broken pieces and making my heart whole once more. Only he can do that because without him I know, more than anything I've ever known before, my heart will never heal and never, ever be whole.

I get to my feet and James jerks back, his eyes wide, his face stricken and deathly pale, but I put out my hand.

"What do they say about home, James? It's where the heart is."

I yawn but don't open my eyes. I'm warm and cosy, my limbs loose and relaxed as I snuggle into the strong arms wrapped around me, smiling as James nuzzles into my hair.

If either of us were expecting torrid make up sex, we were grossly disappointed. Instead we'd closed the bedroom door and the curtains, shutting out the world, and crawled into bed. Holding each other tight, within moments we'd fallen into the oblivion of sleep.

"I know you're awake, sleepy head," James murmurs into my hair.

Peeling my eyes open, I blink at the soft lamp light bathing the room, and I shift out of James' embrace.

Propping himself up onto one elbow, James stares down at me. He still looks wrecked. His hair's a mess, stubble's shadowing his jawline, and he looks drawn and tired but his eyes, his beautiful green, feline eyes, are shining. My heart flips, because it can never not, not when this man looks at me like this. I reach up, and trail my hand over his cheek, along his jawline, and he presses into me as though seeking warmth and reassurance.

"We've got a lot to work out," I say.

"I know, but we can. We can work everything out. I know that more than I've ever known anything."

"Even more than loving me?"

He laughs, low and deep, that classic car purr that winds its way up my spine.

"Nothing could ever be more than loving you."

He leans down and lays his lips on mine. The kiss is soft and gentle, almost reverent, but it's also a promise of what we can and will be together.

From somewhere in the pile of my clothes at the bottom of the bed, my phone pings as a text drops in. I groan, knowing already what it is.

"I never got in touch with the estate agent…" I roll out of bed and rummage for my mobile.

Lots of texts, even a couple of missed calls, and I tap out a quick message: *my situation's changed… I'm withdrawing my offer… I won't be relocating…* I tap *send* and switch it off. Brighton, the bungalow, it's like scraps of paper all scattering to the wind and I have no desire to chase them and gather them up.

Peeking through the curtains, I gasp.

"It's snowing." Fat flakes drift down, adding a layer to what's already settled. All the houses in the small street are ablaze with festive decorations, bright and colourful beacons in the night sky. Christmas trees light up windows, festooned with softly glowing fairy lights. It's a magical site, and I press my forehead to the cold glass.

"It's beautiful," James says as he joins me, coiling his arms around my waist. I lean back into his nakedness and he tightens his hold. "The tree arrived, it's in the garden. I thought of giving it away…" I feel him shrug against me, as I hear the catch in his voice. I let my hand drop from the curtain, and twist around in his arms.

"I'm glad you didn't. Tomorrow, we can bring it in and decorate it, just like we promised ourselves."

"We can do all the things we promised ourselves. All of them."

And we can, but the tree and all those promises, they can wait until the morning. For now, it's nothing and nobody but us, locked away from the world.

Us, only us.

I crush my lips to James' and kiss him hard. Tomorrow, when Operation Perry becomes Opearation Perry and James, can wait.

Taking James by the hand, I lead him back to the warmth of our bed.

EPILOGUE

SIX MONTHS LATER

JAMES

"You do realise the newlyweds are about to commit murder?" I whisper into Perry's ear, snaking my arm around his shoulders to pull him in closer.

The wedding guests, including us, begin cheering, whistling and applauding as a very smiley Elliot and Freddie plunge a long and lethal looking silver knife into the elaborate tiered cake, festooned with delicate pale pink flowers and glossy stems and leaves — all made from sugarpaste.

Perry snorts. "It's a cake. It's meant to be sliced up and eaten."

True enough, but Perry's almost cavalier acceptance that his amazing creations will end up as nothing more than crumbs and scraps of spare icing never fails to surprise me.

It *is* an amazing creation. It's also incredible, fantastic, brilliant and so many other superlatives, all of them too limp and insipid to describe Perry's artistry and talent.

"It's a triumph. Every time you finish a commission, I think you can't possibly do any better. But you do. Every time." I place a soft kiss on his cheek, which has gone the same colour as the roses festooning the wedding cake he's made for Elliot and Freddie, and a thrill of pride races through me.

Perry did this, Perry. My Perry, I want to stand up and crow because I want the world to know what a talented and amazing, incredible man he is. Ah, those weak words, again, that don't do justice to who he is.

The cake's soon whipped away out of sight, for the hotel's kitchen staff to slice it up into dainty portions. Even though I've just eaten to bursting, my mouth waters knowing how good it'll taste.

The wedding planner invites us all to move into the courtyard garden, where more champagne will be waiting for us, and I guide Perry out, my hand resting on the small of his back.

Snagging a couple of flutes from a roving waitress, I hand one to him.

"To us." We chink glasses. "It's been a rollercoaster." I smile into his eyes, as warm as molten chocolate.

"Yes, it has been." Neither of us are talking about Elliot and Freddie's wonderful wedding day. "How can so much have happened in just six months?"

My stomach clenches. Six months since I raced to Victoria station, my only thought to stop him from boarding the Brighton-bound train. I'd succeeded, but it'd been a near thing. My eyes start to well up, and a heavy weight presses against my chest. I'm on the point of crying, for what might have been and for what is, and I don't give a damn who sees.

Perry rests his palm against my cheek, and I press into his warmth. "You have a habit of rescuing me," he says, stroking his thumb backwards and forwards.

"Somebody has to, because you're no bloody good on your own." My pathetic attempt at flippancy is belied by the catch in my voice.

"My Knight in Shining Armour. But you're only half right. I'm okay on my own, but why would I want to be just okay when I can be the best version of myself? That's all down to you, James. You've made me the best version of me."

He leans in and brushes his lips over mine. It's barely even a kiss, but I swear it's both the sweetest and most intimate moment we've shared.

"Perry, I—"

"Oh! I'm sorry." The pretty young woman who's bumped into me is looking suitably embarrassed. "Too many of these," she's says, holding up her almost empty champagne flute. "I'm more used to Sainsbury's cava."

Her laugh's bright and cheery, and I can't help but smile. I don't really mind that my words have been knocked away, because what I have to say is for Perry and me alone.

"Can I get you another?" I ask.

She nods her head, cheeks dimpling as she smiles.

"Yes, please. Do you mind me asking," she says, turning to Perry, "but I understand you made the wedding cake. Is that true?"

"Yes, I did." Perry, already pink cheeked, is now going red.

I produce a business card — I just happen to have one or two on me — from the inside pocket of my suit and hand it over to the woman. Perry's climbing the scale to crimson.

"Thank you," she says, taking it. "Do you think I can have a quick word? Just a couple of minutes? Ah, sorry." A flush of embarrassment colours her face. "Maybe this isn't—"

"Not at all." I hand her a fresh glass of champagne.

"No, that's okay." Perry's eyes flicker from the woman to me. *You sure it's okay?* they seem to say.

"I'd best find Elliot, as I don't want to be accused of falling down on best man duties." I wink as I give him a smile, and I've barely turned away before the two of them begin talking.

Over the other side of the courtyard, Elliot and Freddie are laughing with Cosmo, who's Freddie's best man. Taking Freddie by the arm, Cosmo leads him off, as Elliot, still laughing, shakes his head.

"What was all that about?" I ask, as I join Elliot.

"Cosmo was telling us about his latest exploits, with somebody he met on one of his apps. It was very entertaining, extremely filthy, and I'd say improbable, but then he is your cousin so as outlandish as it was, I suspect it's true. *Whoops.* That's probably an inappropriate thing to say."

"You mean my slutty ways are genetic?" I stare at my

best friend and try my hardest not to laugh when he begins to fluster.

"James, I didn't—"

"I'm joking." I can't help smirking, because teasing Elliot can be such good fun. Even on his wedding day. "But you would've been right, not so long ago."

"And now?"

I shake my head. "No. Never."

Elliot plucks a couple of flutes from a waitress. "Let's go and sit down," he says, nodding to a small table in a sunny corner of the courtyard.

It takes us a few minutes to get there because Elliot's stopped every couple of seconds by well wishers. We sit down and Elliot releases a long, satisfied sigh. I smile across at the man I love like a brother. He's got a lot to be satisfied about and for that I'm so very glad.

"No regrets?" Elliot says, his steady blue eyes meeting mine. I've no need to ask him what he means.

"None at all, and there never will be. My life's better than it's ever been and it's all down to Perry. And don't look so smug, Hendricks."

He snorts. "I told you it would be. With the right man by your side, everything's better."

"You did tell me, although it pains me greatly to admit you were right. There, I've said it, so you can put your self-congratulatory face away now."

Elliot chuckles. "To you and Perry," he says raising his flute.

"Shouldn't you be toasting yourself and Freddie? It's your big day after all, and as you know I'm never one to steal the limelight."

Elliot snorts at the blatant untruth as his clear blue eyes lock with mine.

"To all of us."

We chink glasses, and for a few moments we sit in companionable silence.

"How's Perry's business going?" Elliot asks. "I saw the article in the *Ham & High* last month. Lots of satisfied customers from the sound of it, and rightly so."

I can't help grinning as pride in Perry wells up inside me.

"Yes, the local rag did a good job, and they even got his name right. He's going from strength to strength. I have to admit, I'm so glad the kitchen unit on the business park we looked at fell through and that he's ended up working from home."

Our home, not in some grim bungalow in Brighton…

"It's about time that big showroom kitchen of yours is finally being put to good use. Perry's certainly shown that with our wedding cake. It's a masterpiece. I always knew he was good, but both Freddie and I were speechless when we first saw it. Thank goodness he could fit us in at such short notice, after the original guy's shop burnt down."

"Oh, I set it alight. Didn't you realise? It was all part of my marketing campaign for *Perry Buckland Cakes*. We're expecting a glowing review on the website and for you to sing Perry's praises to all your business contacts."

"Why do I think you committing arson isn't totally outside the realm of possibility? But you're right about a review and recommendations."

Laughing, I close my eyes and tilt my face to catch the warm, late afternoon sun.

When the kitchen unit on the start-up site fell through,

I'd been secretly thrilled. The truth is, I wanted Perry working from *our* kitchen in *our* home. I was even more thrilled that he jumped at my suggestion. It made a lot of business sense too, not that either of us had to push that point very hard.

We had to make some changes to the kitchen, which included putting in an additional large double oven so Perry could bake several things at once. The utility room also got a complete refit, providing all the storage and refrigeration he needs — and to comply with food safety regs — not just for now but for the growing business it's already proving to be. There was, however, one bone of contention.

Perry insisted on paying for the adaptations with the money he'd inherited from his grandfather. We had some lively arguments over that, but they'd all resulted in lots of make up sex, so... But I really didn't want him to touch a penny of his inheritance. For somebody so sweet and soft natured, he's got an iron hard core. And a hell of a lot of pride.

"Life's good," Elliot says, his voice soft and warm, like the sun on my face. The words are for him and Freddie, but they're for Perry and me, too.

I drag open my eyes, and look across at my best friend. He's smiling at me, and I return it with interest.

"It is. It's more than good."

Once again, I close my eyes and tilt my head to the sun.

More than good... It's the plain and simple truth, and they're the only words I need.

≈

PERRY

"Hmm, this is nice."

I nuzzle in closer to James and he tightens his arms around me as we sway to the sultry jazz number the band's playing. Mabel's voice is as sweet as sugar, butterscotch smooth, and underscored with a smoky tang.

Along with James, I've become a diehard fan of Mabel and her band. We're almost groupies, and both Elliot and Freddie had been hooked when we'd dragged them out one evening to one of her gigs. They'd booked her for the reception on the spot.

It's the last dance. It's been a glorious though long day, yet most of the guests have stayed the course. But it's nearly over and now I'll be more than happy for James and me to go home.

Home.

The word still has the power to send a delicious shiver down my spine, because that's what the lovely Highgate house really and truly is.

But it so nearly wasn't. Before I can stop it, a hard shudder rushes through me.

James pulls away, just enough to fix me with his moss green eyes. He arches a brow, and it's so James I can't stop the little laugh that bubbles up on my lips, but it dies away a second later.

"Perry?" he says, a frown creasing his brow.

"I—I was just thinking that us here today, the business, all of it, how close it was to not—"

James presses a finger to my lips, stilling my words.

"Don't. You never got on that train, and that's all that matters. No *ifs*, no *buts*, none of it."

He's right, of course, although it still doesn't stop me from thinking about it. Yet in a perverse way I like to think about it.

It's a heart thumping reminder not just of how much I have with this man, but of how much I love him. I never, ever want to forget or take that for granted, because I know — we both know — how close we were to letting it all slip away.

The music's stopped. This beautiful day filled with warmth and love has come to an end, and I yawn as the long day catches up with me.

It's time to go home.

~

"Lovely," James says as he wipes his fingers clean of the last of the little almond tarts. "You know, I think I like these even more than your Victoria sponge."

"You say that about everything I bake." I laugh and shake my head, before taking a sip of the sweet, heavy almond liqueur.

It's almost two-thirty in the morning and I should have crawled into bed when we tumbled out of the cab, but James persuaded me into the garden. To look at the stars, he said, but in Highgate it's more about the glow of street lamps.

It's beautiful in the warm night air, the garden bathed in soft light from lanterns hanging from trees and bushes. And so quiet, in the early small hours. Somewhere in the garden there's a faint rustle as a night animal makes its way through the shadows.

"Happy?" James asks.

"How can you even ask?" His hands are resting on top of the little garden table and I take them in mine and squeeze hard.

My phone's lying next to our joined hands. We'd been flicking through the dozens of photos we'd taken throughout the day, and it pings as a text drops in.

"Who's sending messages at this time?" I untangle my hands from James. Then I realise who.

Of course... Life in Spain is lived late.

"It's Mum. Confirming the flight details for the beginning of next month."

I can't help smiling. The last time I saw them was soon after James and I reconciled. It feels like too long a time, but in just a couple of weeks that's going to be put right. I glance up at James.

"Are you sure about them staying here?"

It'll be the first time James and my parents will be meeting properly. Sure, there have been lots video calling — and calls from Mum to me afterwards telling me how much she and Dad like him. It's been a huge relief, and one I've kept to myself, because I thought they might have had something to say about the age gap. After all, as James points out, he and they are both old enough to remember the New Romantics the first time round. *Who...? What...?* I say to him, making sure I turn away before he sees my grin.

"This is your home as much as mine, so of course they should stay here." *What a stupid bloody question*, he may as well add.

"I'll get back to them tomorrow." I switch off the phone and put it aside, not wanting any other interruptions.

James pours us both another drink. After all the champagne I've had, I should be drunk but instead all I can feel is a bone-deep relaxation. Sagging back into the cushioned garden chair, I let go of a long, deep sigh.

Happy? It doesn't even come close.

"I've got something for you," James says, as he stands up. "I wanted to give it to you at the right time, not when we were busy getting ready for the wedding. Wait here."

Where exactly he thinks I'm going to go, I'm not sure, as he strides into the house. Maybe it's a new palette knife. He bought me one a couple of weeks back, the handle shaped like a very big, and scarily lifelike, dick.

Phallic kitchen utensils… That could be an interesting side business…

James returns, and places something down on the table. It's oblong, wrapped in brown paper and bound up with string.

"This came the day before yesterday but, as I said, I wanted you to have it at the right time."

Whatever it is, it's not another dick themed baking accessory.

"James—?"

"Just open it. Please."

Nervous anticipation wraps me in its arms. I don't do as he says, not immediately. Instead I look from the plain little package to James. His eyes are in shadow, but I don't need to see them to know his gaze on me is intense. The air around us, warm and balmy just moments ago, is now charged with skin-prickling electricity.

The string's lightly tied, and it slips away easily. The

brown paper's crisp under my fingers. Unfolding it I gasp, as its hidden treasure's revealed.

"I don't believe it."

I can barely breathe as I stare down at the book. Shadows from the candlelight dance over its worn cover, the cloth frayed at the edges. With trembling fingers I turn to the title page, and there it is, in Granddad's spidery handwriting.

"'To Perry, my favourite grandson xxx.'"

The words blur as tears fill my eyes. *My favourite grandson...* It was his little joke; I wasn't just the only grandson, but the only grandchild.

"I've been keeping an eye out, on a few sites. I'm sorry I've only found the one, but I'll keep looking for the others."

"Oh, James, I don't know what to say. God, I thought they were gone for good. Even if we only ever find one of them..."

My tears stream down my cheeks, but I don't bother wiping them away. Putting the book aside, I jump up to hug this wonderful, thoughtful man who drags me into his lap and nuzzles into my hair.

"I've something else," he murmurs. "But I didn't find this online."

He reaches into his pocket. Opening his hand, a small dark box sits in the center of his palm.

All I can do is look at it, hardly daring to reach for it, or touch it. My heart's hammering hard, all the nighttime sounds of the garden drowned out by the *boom, boom, boom* filling my head.

"Don't you want to know what's in it?" James' voice,

low and seductive, the classic car purr that never fails to shoot a delicious shiver through me.

My eyes flicker from the box to James. He's watching me, his feline eyes dark and unfathomable.

With nervy, quivering fingers I take the box and lift the lid. I swallow hard.

The ring nestled on a pad of velvet is plain and unadorned. With an unsteady hand, I pick it up. It's cool to the touch, and heavy.

"It's… Are you…?" My words stumble from me as I clutch the ring, holding it tight and never, ever wanting to let it go.

"Yes, I am. I love you Perry, I love you so much. You rescued me, as I rescued you. I was a drowning man. I couldn't admit it to myself, too scared to, I suppose, but I was barely keeping my head above water. You saved me from going under."

James takes the ring from me, and slips it on the ring finger of my left hand. It slides on as smooth as fondant icing. It's a perfect fit, its weight solid and reassuring. Taking my face between his palms, he places a gentle kiss on my lips, so soft, so light it's like the thinnest, finest silk.

"It's my promise to you, an unbreakable promise I'll always keep that my heart is yours. Yes, I'm asking you to marry me. But there's no need to rush, because we've got all the time in the world."

"All the time, and all the love. Always all the love. I'll keep your heart safe, James. That's my promise to *you*."

I close my eyes and deepen the kiss, wrapping my arms around him as our promises, never ever to be broken, wrap tight around our hearts.

WANT MORE JAMES & PERRY?

Thank you for reading Take My Breath Away.

If you'd like to find out what happens next to James and Perry, why not sign up to my mailing list? You'll get a copy of **A Day at The Fair** short story, as a thank you.

To sign up to my list, use this link to access a copy of the bonus story:

https://BookHip.com/CTQWWXW

WANT MORE SILVER FOXES?

Commitment Issues, book one in the Silver Foxes series, follows Elliot and Freddie and is available on Amazon.

From fake date to friends with benefits, commitment's not an issue

Elliot

Freddie's way too young. I'm twice his age and old enough to be his father. He's an adorable mix of sexy, smart, sassy, shy and sweet. But that doesn't mean I'm going to be forced into taking him as my fake date to my oldest friend's wedding, just because my cheating ex will be there.

Freddie

Elliot's everything I want in a man, he's my ultimate silver fox fantasy. But I've had my heart ripped out by an older guy before, and I've vowed it'll never happen again. So why have I let myself be talked into posing as Elliot's arm candy at a posh wedding?

From fake date to friends with benefits, commitment's not part of the deal. So where does falling in love fit in?

◆ ◆ ◆*Commitment Issues is a May-December MM romance. Expect to find plenty of snark, a touch of angst, friends who think they know best, slow burn sexual tension leading to high heat. And a scruffy mutt of a dog. HEA guaranteed*◆ ◆ ◆

THANK YOU

Thank you for reading Take My Breath Away, the second in the Silver Foxes series. If you've enjoyed the book, a brief, honest review would be appreciated. I'm an indie author and reviews are so, so important.

STALK ME!

You can find all my books at:
www.ryecart.com

I also have a readers group on Facebook, which can find here:

Ryecart's Rebel Readers

MORE BOOKS FROM ALI RYECART

CONTEMPORARY GAY ROMANCE

SILVER FOXES

Commitment Issues

Take My Breath Away

BARISTA BOYS

Danny & Jude

Stevie & Mack

Connor & Ash

Bernie

DEVIANT HEARTS

Captive Hearts

Radical Hearts

Perilous Hearts*

also available as audiobooks and complete series available as an ebook box set

URBAN LOVE

Loose Connection

The Story of Love

Corporate Bodies

Complete series available as a box set

RENT BOYS

Release

Faking It

RORY & JACK

A Kiss Before Christmas*

An Easter Promise*

A Christmas Wedding*

also available as audiobooks

All series novels can be read as stand alones

Company for Christmas

(A stand alone, but can also be read as a prequel to the Rent Boys series)

The Boss of Christmas Present

Christmas Spirit

Imperfect

ABOUT ALI RYECART

I used to tell my stories to myself, now I tell them to the world...

The stories I only ever told to myself took place in a world where it was boy meets boy, where best friends became more, where the hero didn't save the damsel but the hot guy he'd been secretly crushing on.

I wanted to read those stories. I *craved* to read those stories. But those stories weren't out there. Or that's what I thought... Until one Christmas, when I unwrapped a shiny new e-reader. All it took was a few clicks, and my world changed forever.

I found my tribe.

But there is life outside of MM & gay romantic fiction in all its configurations. Allegedly.

When I'm forced to switch off the trusty, faithful word machine, there's a husband to feed and talk to, pubs to drink in, and cake to eat. I love to do all those things and more, before I rush back to write all the words.

I'm a Londoner, born and bred, but I now live just outside of the big bad city, but close enough to hop on a train so I can get my regular metropolitan fix.

Printed in Great Britain
by Amazon

25510577R00235